Lifting the mass of hair from her moist neck, Cathelen raised her face to the stars. Suddenly she knew she was not alone. Turning around, she was seized by terror. There stood a pirate!

"Aye, but you are a lovely morsel," the fierce-looking buccaneer chuckled. "You are like an enchanting white phantom—or perhaps a shimmery mermaid risen from the sea. Could I have your name? I want to remember you—forever."

"C-Cathelen."

"I will give you a warning, fair lady."

"A warning? As to what?"

"That I am going to kiss you."

He came to her then, and Cathelen thought it was like being thrust up against a rock. He muffled her cry with what was Cathelen's first kiss ever. Delicious shocks of pleasure seemed to be coming from his lips, setting her flesh afire. Unable to bear what he was doing to her inside and out, Cathelen wrenched her mouth away.

"Please—no more!"

Before she knew what he was doing, he was easily pressing her to the grass, his mouth returning at once to her tender pink lips.

"Do not do this to me," she begged. "I have never had a man before and—Please do not hurt me. . . ."

"I'll not hurt you, my lovely. I'll just teach you the meaning of love. . . ."

MORE RAPTUROUS READING

Windswept Passion

SONYA T. PELTON

ZEBRA BOOKS
KENSINGTON PUBLISHING CORP.

ZEBRA BOOKS

are published by

Kensington Publishing Corp.
475 Park Avenue South
New York, N.Y. 10016

First printing: December 1984

Printed in the United States of America

For two of my favorite readers,
my beautiful daughters:

Suzanne Mayer
and
Lisa LeBeau

Part I

Flaming Suns, Velvet Nights

Chapter One

Edinburgh, 1716

Cathelen O'Ruark half smiled while tittering laughs ran through the class. A soundless sigh escaped her soft lips as her classmates tossed long curls, stuck aristocratic chins in the air, and with pretty steps forward and rustles of pansy-colored dresses, reintroduced the dainty promenade. Light as a butterfly, Cathelen followed suit.

Even though the lesson that morning dealt with no more than the art of wearing a fashionable skirt with hoops, Miss Roberts's chin was hoisted into its usual authoritative position, her wattles having disappeared for the moment.

"You must learn to wear the hoop skirt with

restraint," she said imperiously, dominating her class of demure shining-haired maidens.

Discipline was rigid at Miss Roberts's Boarding School in Scotland, near the Firth of Forth. Like a mother duck, the Spartan mistress watched the girls once more attempt to glide around the room with dignified manner and carriage.

Cathelen wrinkled her fine retroussé nose. Indeed the enormous hoops were tricky devices and the least awkwardness could start her skirt jouncing up and down in a crazy motion. She could see Miss Roberts's satisfied smile, for Cathelen skillfully bore herself, conveying an enchanting lilt to the full skirt as she carefully paraded about the high-ceilinged Regency room.

Miss Roberts clapped her hands, and the parade of floral-skirted girls came to a giggling, self-conscious halt. All but Cathelen who slowed with womanly reserve, looking almost bored with her surroundings.

"Miss O'Ruark," the mistress said, "it may be that the good Lord has gifted you with a natural daintiness that some here would do well to envy, and to copy. . . ."

A flush tinged Cathelen's fresh young cheeks to a delightful pink that surged from her hairline down her alabaster neck and shoulders.

The sun streamed through the tall windows, catching Cathelen's platinum blond hair and her dreaming violet eyes. Again she sighed unobtrusively. Oh, for an adventure . . . to catch the flood of destiny that would carry her far, far away. Her young blood yearned for . . . what she did not yet comprehend.

Smiling almost too brightly, Miss Roberts went on. "Please, Miss O'Ruark show the others how a young lady might glide with a lilting step and yet keep from revealing her garter to every man—uh—I mean, every gentleman of the town."

Hell's blisters, Cathelen thought, but she picked her way forward, her soft violet eyes hooded from embarrassment. How dare the old crow single her out for display! Even so, her silvery blond head went high while she walked among her friends—and some who were not. She could well sense the envy of the latter girls.

"She's just like a fair-haired princess," one kindly, pimply-faced girl whispered to a smirking enemy of Cathelen's.

The heavy lavender brocade cloth of Cathelen's gown stirred and whispered, the only other sounds coming from her hard shoes as she clicked each measured step across the bare wood floor.

The watching eyes of some girls narrowed, their noses lifting with haughtiness. Cathelen's long thighs swished freely beneath hoops unhindered by any nearness of cloth. It was as if Cathelen's body walked in a private cage of gilded latticework.

Nodding her stern approval, Miss Roberts appraised the blond maid's charm and gracefulness, her dainty step, her proud carriage, as

11

Cathelen proceeded without instruction to lift one side of the large hoop in a most enviably ladylike manner, at the same time pressing the other side, while she walked through the portal with no trouble at all; then she reentered the room the same way.

"Again, Miss O'Ruark!" Miss Roberts ordered, watching as her class grew even more envious of the beautiful blond.

Old crow! Cathelen thought shrewishly and gritted her perfect pearl teeth in her mouth. Even so, Cathelen smiled sweetly at the mistress, all the while wishing to strangle the woman.

Just as Cathelen was approaching the door for the second, exasperating time, it was filled by an excited lad. As he dodged past Cathelen he flashed her a secretive smile. Cathelen was one of Walter's favorites because she was not petty or arrogant about her family's wealth.

Walter drew himself up before the mistress to deliver his urgent message. He did not falter before the haughty woman who stared down at the houseboy imperiously.

"Michal O'Ruark, ma'am," Walter announced. "It's an urgent matter, he says."

Her delicate features revealing her surprise, Cathelen stepped forward. "My brother is here? But why?" Why now, when she'd not seen Michal in over two months?

A worried gleam came into the impressive violet eyes that a moment before had held only softness, and noticing, Walter regretted the news he must reveal.

Miss Roberts waved for the curious class continue their practice. Not meaning to, she frowned at the unusually flustered Cathelen.

"Miss O'Ruark, you may come along to my study." She pursed her lips at the artless houseboy. "This had better not prove to be a frivolous visit of Michal O'Ruark's."

They rustled along the hall, Miss Roberts's manner and gait impeccable but stiff compared to the dainty stride of the lovely young woman who trailed behind, a worried frown upon her fine brow.

The young doctor was wearing a path across the colorful carpet in Miss Roberts's cluttered salon. He was of medium build, firmly muscled, a young man whose curly blond hair, peeking from beneath his peruke, marked his relationship to Cathelen.

Urgently, Michal swung around as they entered the salon, and Miss Roberts sniffed at the cravat that was awry, at his trousers splashed with mud. She was about to chide him for walking across the Turkey carpet, when Michal's mouth opened first to speak.

"Miss Roberts, I must apologize. But"—he spoke mostly to Cathelen—"I have bad news for my sister. Cathelen sweet, I am sorry to say that father has been arrested."

"A-arrested?" Cathelen stammered.

"They took him to prison just this afternoon. He will be facing trial today. . . ."

"Whatever for?" Cathelen wondered.

"It is—a charge for murder."

"Murder?" Miss Roberts exclaimed questioningly.

"Yes, murder. My father killed the town commissioner this morning."

"Mr. Webberly?" Miss Roberts, as she asked this, sat down heavily.

Michal nodded, while Cathelen stood numbly by although her eyes searched her brother's face.

"But," Miss Roberts began, "Mr. Webberly was elderly. H-his age should have protected him from dueling with anyone."

Michal laughed shortly, with bitterness. "Not even white hairs stopped Mr. Webberly from being a villain. Edinburgh well realizes by now that my father was not in the last rebellion. But Webberly chose to revert our estate by false witness. You see, he came today to serve his warrant."

And it was his own death warrant he collected, Cathelen thought morosely. She took in the miniature ship's wheel on the mistress' desk, stared, then shook herself. She faced her brother.

"You say father killed him." She studied Michal more closely then. "Michal, you are not drunk, are you?"

Without anger, Michal answered. "I am sober today, Cathelen."

With dainty hands pressed tightly against her waist, Cathelen stood. "Mistress Roberts, might I go now?"

"Of course, child," Miss Roberts's manner softened.

"Michal, take me to father, please. . . ."

Miss Roberts interrupted. "Oh, the prison is no place for the likes of you, dear child."

"But I must!" Cathelen displayed her streak of defiance for once in her life.

"I see that," Miss Roberts said gently. "You do have your carriage waiting, Dr. O'Ruark?"

Michal hesitated, looking to Cathelen. "No . . . I was in such haste. All I've come with is my horse, she must bear us both, I'm afraid."

Within moments Cathelen was mounting behind Michal. As best she could, she adjusted her purple velvet cloak, pulling its fur-trimmed hood low over her forehead, and clung to her brother while he urged the horse between the school gates.

"I've the carriage waiting up the road apiece, Cathy," Michal used his pet name for his sister, as the mare broke into a light gallop. "I did not wish Miss Roberts to see our luggage aboard."

"Michal, why our luggage? Are we going somewhere?"

"You see, it may very well be that you'll not return to school." He looked back at her a bit sadly.

Cathelen knew her brother and his motives well. "Have you a plan then to save father?" she asked, shivering but unaware of it.

"Just trust me, dear sister?"

"Yes, of course." She dearly wanted to ask him where he had gone to this last time away.

15

Cathelen knew now why she shivered. If all went amiss, that might result in a hanging for the both of them. Already she could feel the noose tightening around her own slim neck. I'm too young to die just yet, Cathelen thought.

"Good girl," Michal said, touching her small fingers which entwined his sword baldric. "Under the trees, see. Dany is there with the carriage. Dismount here, lassie, and get to Dany. She'll explain. If my plan is to succeed, I shall need every spare moment."

While Michal wheeled his horse and galloped away, Cathelen snatched up her hoop, this time in a most unladylike fashion, and ran with skirts high and awhirl. All dignity forsaken, she ran toward the carriage. If Miss Roberts could see her now! Dany, her old nurse, was waiting.

"Och, my darling," Dany said, enveloping Cathelen with a hug that revealed her sympathy for the lass; then she assisted Cathelen into the equipage and climbed in after her.

The carriage swayed and jogged uneasily as the horses began to churn up the road, but Cathelen minded this not a bit. Her uppermost thoughts, and her heart, went with Michal.

"Poor, dear child," Dany crooned. "Dreadful business this, and your poor father."

"Oh, Dany, how is Michal ever going to save father?"

Shivering from the stress of her grief and from the chill, Dany settled her worn tippet around her thin throat. She glanced at the worried girl, and then away.

"'Tis a mad scheme, lass, and you'd best not hear it."

"Dany, please, I'm a grown woman now . . . !"

Dany groaned, reluctant to tell the lass the scheme that could have them all on the gallows.

"Tell me what Michal is going to try to do. Please!"

"Ah . . . your dear brother has some wild notion that he can bribe the hangman. 'Tis been done before, Michal says, and can be again."

Cathelen thought she knew then. "A loose knot . . . a clumsy shove off the ladder . . ."

Dany winced, but the girl knew what she knew. "Och, someone to jostle and disturb the base of the scaffold supporting the good Master O'Ruark's poor . . . body. I've heard of such tricks being attempted—"

"It could succeed. . . ."

"Aye, Michal's a good lad to try, and dear God we must pray he succeeds."

Wetting her lips slowly, Cathelen said, "He must know what he's about, Dany."

"Uh, I'm not so sure, child. One thing, you must not be in Edinburgh on the morrow for the . . ." Dany did not say the fatal word.

Pray, that is what I shall do, Cathelen told herself. Anyway, what help could she, a mere maid, be to her father? Unconsciously she flexed her arm muscles, wishing she were as strong as a—she thought for a moment—a pirate, that's what!

"We'll go to the eastern seaport, lass, on the

17

Firth of Tay. You will be safe there, with my brother."

"Papa and Michal will join us there . . . after a time?" she said, hopefully.

"No, lass. Scotland will not be safe for them."

"It will be a year or two before they dare return. . . ."

"Aye, lass."

Cathelen straightened resolutely. "I shall go with them then!"

"No, the journey would be too much for the dainty likes of yourself."

"How will I know if Papa has been saved?"

"Somehow, lass, Michal will let us know."

Trundling on, the coach swayed along the four miles of broken track between Edinburgh and the harbor. Pressed back into the familiar leather cushions of her father's landau, Cathelen felt hot tears begin. Try though she might, she could not hold them back.

She had been so happy that morning, even though Miss Roberts had made a spectacle of her. Perhaps the old hag was not so bad after all, Cathelen thought, now that she realized the last moment of her childhood had vanished. If only you could call back moments and feel more kindly toward others. She sighed.

"Here we are," Dany said all too soon. "Tuck your curls inside your hood, lass. I know something of these docks, and we shall find villains among those here. Indeed, to find a man who is not one will be hard. We shall find a ship in this harbor, lawless or not. There's a Captain

18

Trask, a mild acquaintance of Colin's. Pray he is not one of the disguised pirates we've been hearing so much about lately!"

For tonight, Cathelen thought longingly, all she wanted was to go home and crawl into her nice, warm bed. Surely they would not leave so soon? Of course not.

Chapter Two

Two cloaked ladies sat tense and watchful at the tavern table, and it could be noted that one, if her face turned fully to the dim light, was a fresh young creature of marriageable age. But not many noticed, most being in their cups and too befuddled to glimpse the lovely face beneath the gray velvet hood.

"Will we be going home soon?" Cathelen asked, impatient and nervous, wanting only to get away from the reeking tavern.

Dany sniffed, her eyes gone bleak. "Dear child . . ." Dany seemed to be having trouble speaking.

"Dany, what is it?"

"Oh . . ."

"Why have we taken our luggage along, this

far? Michal did not say, Dany, but you know, don't you?"

Dany looked around, as if seeking aid from the smoke-darkened timbers and the blazing hearth fire which perhaps could speak too, to tell her the least painful words to say.

"Dany . . . please!" Cathelen hissed low, urgently.

"Yer Pa's house is shut to yer and yer brother. The estate has been . . ." She blinked painfully as Cathelen leaned closer, to hear her fate, finally. ". . . it has gone to the Bailiwick. Och, I had to tell ye sooner or later. The sooner's the better."

"But"—soft violet eyes sparkled with bewilderment—"what about Michal and—and Papa?" Even as she asked this, Cathelen took the news that she was to leave the only home she had ever known silently.

"I cannot tell ye, lass, what is to happen to yer poor pa just yet. We must be away from Edinburgh, though, before they catch up with ye. Ye could become a bonded servant, ye see, if yer Pa sees fit to sign such papers." She patted Cathelen's cold, white hand. "He would think it to be for the good, but, lass, ye could be in bondage to a nasty plantation lord, the likes of which would work ye to death, never mind that ye not be colored like the others who are shipped to the West Indies. Ye would toil from sun-up to sundown on one of those plantations, with yer skin burned brown by the sun, yer pretty nails cracked . . . Oh!" Dany covered her

21

mouth with her kerchief. "Good Lord . . . we must get ye to my brother's where ye will be safe, before—" at that moment Dany noticed the huge man.

"What is it, Dany?"

As Cathelen looked up an imposing presence loomed beside the table.

"Here he is now," Dany said low, then louder, "'Tis the captain of the *Windward*. I know these docks, and I believe ye are the good Captain Trask." She leaned to whisper in Cathelen's ear. "Shh now, and keep yer bright curls inside yer hood, lass."

Captain Eric Trask, of the *Windward Lady*, came to a halt before the table, grinned through yellowed teeth and hauled up a chair beside the bench. Before the lass could lower her face, though, the captain caught a glimpse of her and he thought to himself that this was not a harborside trull, but a sweet-faced thing, as clean and pretty as sea spray. Unnoticed by the ladies, his sea-bleached eyes crinkled with cunning as he observed the youngling's finely made cloak.

Cathelen stared down at the glistening black hairs on the captain's hands and his meaty wrists, her eyes swiftly following the ropelike veins that ran up under the sleeves of his bulky reefer pea jacket. Slowly, lifting her eyes, yet keeping her chin down, Cathelen became aware, as she had upon first entering the low-raftered tavern, of many sea-brown leathery faces. Now she tucked her face deeper into the sanctuary of her hood.

"Dany Muir," Captain Trask nodded over to her, politely enough, avoiding the younger woman for now while he set about his business. "I've spoken to your brother, aye . . ." he drawled out.

"Aye," was Dany's only response, but her eyes wore a waiting expression.

Cathelen caught something else besides, and she began to wonder why it was Dany appeared suspicious, as if she were having second thoughts about this captain that her brother knew. Just how well did Colin Muir know this burly salt?

"Ye'll be comfortable, you and the little lass here. She's a good craft," Trask was saying, a flicker of movement in his eyes as they roamed from the older to the younger woman, "my *Windward Lady*. She's made twenty or more voyages on the West Indies trade, she has, and her captain is well known and respected."

Dany seemed to make up her mind suddenly, although the matter actually had been settled much earlier in the day. "Not a soul will harm or provoke this lass here?" She nodded in the direction of the silent, contemplative girl.

Captain Trask growled as if offended that the older woman would even think such a thing of his crew. "Me oath an' vow upon it, Dany Muir. Now"—his voice lowered, becoming deep and unnaturally husky—"two hundred pounds?"

"Aye," Dany said, almost coldly Cathelen thought, surprised out of the near trance in which she'd been mulling over the day's disastrous events.

Dany reached inside her muff, deep into the hole in the lining, and passed—as if she couldn't give it away quickly enough—the two hundred sovereigns over to the eager-eyed captain.

Benignly, Captain Trask smiled. "Ye won't be sorry, for I've two fine staterooms on the *Lady*. It'll be an adventure for the lass and your good self, Dany Muir."

"What sort of ship is your *Lady*, Captain Trask?"

Dany's head came around and the captain's sea-water eyes blinked with surprise at hearing the lilting voice of youth. "She"—he coughed deeply once—"she's a true-blue, sea-bound, West Indies merchantman. . . ."

"Very well, Captain. Then I am sure we shall not be too uncomfortable on the *Windward Lady*."

"Aye," Captain Trask drawled, eyeing the poignant profile peeping from the deep cowl of her cloak. He sucked the dregs of his drink, banged the tankard down on the table and growled, "Come along then, ladies!"

Chapter Three

Outside, looking across the silence of the moonlit harbor, Cathelen studied the tossing masts, and the carved and painted prows of twelve or more deep-sea vessels that were bobbing and beginning to stir with the rising tide.

Sperm-oil lamps gleamed, their reflections shimmering orange tails on the black water. Swaggering, Captain Trask led the ladies among the misted, purplish shadows of the quayside. He tossed over his shoulder:

"Ladies, yer trunks will be carried aboard by a pair of my strongest lads to make sure your things arrive intact."

"Very good." Dany nodded, but the younger woman remained silent.

Cathelen's senses were alert to the raw odors of salt-encrusted timbers and of crude cookery—these smells wafted from the larger vessels—and to the deep mumbled curses and loud revelry of the sailors. This was, she realized, a whole new world of which she had been unaware and ignorant before this day.

How strange, Cathelen reflected, that although Leith harbor lay only a short distance from Edinburgh town, she had rarely, if ever, seen a seafaring man in the town where she lived. These men, unlike people who lived a land-based existence, dwelled in their own dangerous world. Sea gypsies, she thought.

Cathelen watched her footing as she walked along, for the heavy timbered boards were not placed very close together on the dock. She wondered what it should be like to live on the sea, or even on a small island for that matter. An island, in the West Indies, like one of those Dany had mentioned. Already the sea beckoned to Cathelen. It seemed to have a magical spell all its own. Of course, Cathelen knew, she would not be traveling all that far by ship for Dany had said as much.

Cathelen caught herself up in her musings. Here she was fretting about her own fate, but dear Papa, what would his be? And Michal's? Exactly when would she be seeing her brother again?

Sighing, Cathelen heard the spring night mourning like a lovely seashell in her ears.

"Watch yer step, ladies."

"Oh, indeed we will," Dany said, walking before her young charge.

Cathelen was surprised, after finally discarding her self-pity, at the new calmness that was settling over her. But this state was, she would learn very soon, not to last.

Standing outside the small chamber entirely fashioned from wood, Cathelen stared into the stateroom. They had boarded the ship, crossed the deck, and entered the long corridor.

Why, she thought, this is no larger than the dimensions of my largest closet at home!

"You mean us to sleep"—Cathelen pointed straight ahead—"in that?"

"Ye'll be snug as ladybugs in here," Captain Trask boasted even as the younger woman's eyes enlarged incredulously.

And so we shall, Cathelen kept the barb to herself. After a second glance around the tiny cabin, Cathelen took in the narrow bunk fitted to the bulkhead, and in the alcove beneath it a pallet laid in a wooden trough upon the rough deck planks.

"Captain," Cathelen began boldly, "you said 'two staterooms,' did you not?"

She waited for him to nod in affirmation of his earlier statement. "But—"—she swept a hand briefly—"this is only one. Can you show us where Dany will stay?"

Dany nodded, "Aye, Captain, you did say two?"

Trask cleared his throat, looking as if he might be embarrassed of a sudden. "This is two, ladies. A nice bed above, and one below." He shrugged at last.

Dany was about to put in an argument, but just then she noticed her young charge was drooping like a fresh-opened bud in the summer sun. Cathelen, the dear lass, was used to so much better. She had never known what it was like to go without, or to settle for second best. Dany glared icily at the captain who was looking Cathelen over more thoroughly, now that her hood had slipped to reveal the lass's snowy blond tresses. He stared at Cathelen as if hypnotized. Cathelen might be used to luxury and freedom to roam the hills of Scotland, but men she was innocent of, unaware of the strength and extent of their desires.

Dany bristled protectively. "Captain Trask!"

The seaman stared at Dany now as if he were seeing an ugly crone come to life. His eyes lost their leer for the lass. "Mistress Muir?"

"I'll have ye know, Captain, I am unmarried." Dany looked pointedly at Cathelen, to change the subject as she intended. "Now. Do ye give your word the young lady will be safe? As ye can see for yourself, Captain, Miss O'Ruark is not a child anymore. Even so, I mean her to stay innocent. If ye know what I mean?"

"Aye . . ."

"She knows nothing of men and their ways!" Dany hissed low, to make her point clear and to keep Cathelen from hearing what they discussed as she stepped into the cabin to get a closer look at the tight confines.

Blue watery eyes narrowed. "She'll have to be stayin' out of sight of the crew, now I've seen the lass better." His gaze came away fast from the gentle sway of young hips. "If she stays put, only takes her air at night, she'll be safe and not be tempting the crew with her innocent beauty. I've a ship to command, Dany Muir, and if I cannot be around every minute of the day to protect the lass, ye'll have to see to it yerself she don't get too restless. Otherwise my men are going to want to test her charms."

"Och!" Dany gasped, then hoped Cathelen had not overheard. She realized the captain might not have taken them aboard had he witnessed Cathelen's charms beforehand. But now the coin was in his pocket and he would not easily part with it.

Aye, Captain Trask thought lecherously to himself, I'd not mind sampling a bit of that virgin fluff meself. Many years had passed since the delightful task of making love to one so young and beautiful had been his. He had deflowered many a lass in his younger days.

Captain Trask growled, "We'll be leaving with the night's tide. Soon's we get clear of sight of land, we'll heave to in Forth Channel."

With that, he left Dany staring after his broad back and plagued with doubts as she listened to his heavy boot falls along the companionway.

Having seen her fill, Cathelen came to stand beside Dany once again. "What were you and the captain discussing so softly and urgently, Dany?"

"Eh, something ye'll learn about, lass, when the right man comes along. But not until then," she added determinedly.

"Why were you and the captain discussing my marriage?"

"Eh?" Dany blinked; then understood. "Because, lass, to make certain no man looks at ye until that time to wed."

"But, Dany," Cathelen began confusedly, "men have looked at me already—" she shrugged—"somewhat."

Dany stared moodily into the tiny, suffocating cabin, her concern for her ward growing considerably.

"Aye, so I've noticed," Dany confessed and looked at Cathelen with a worried expression. "But they must not touch ye, lass."

The smoky lantern tossed shadows against the low rafters as Cathelen readied herself for bed. Despite all her fears for the lass, Dany was already snoring in her pallet.

Blowing the light out in the little cabin, Cathelen stumbled against Dany's bed while climbing into her own bunk. She bumped her head and employed one of Michal's strong oaths.

In the night, Cathelen awoke to hear shouting and noises she could not name for what they were. It sounded as though there were more women aboard than just her and Dany. But no, she told herself, this could not be. The captain would have told them this. Once in a while she heard footsteps along the corridor, some heavy, some light. And was that crying she heard? Again she told herself no. How could there be crying?

Cathelen could not sleep now—alone in the dark with her thoughts. *They must not touch me.* Dany's warning still haunted Cathelen. She sighed softly. *I must be totally ignorant of what it means for a man to touch a woman.* Would it be pleasant? She shivered. Not if that man was Captain Trask!

She rolled over, bumping and cursing again. After a grimace of pain, her features regained their soft loveliness. But what would it feel like if one she loved deeply touched her intimately? Cathelen giggled softly. Of course she didn't know such a man just yet. When would she know what making love was all about? That men have stronger desires, she'd already been told. Oh, look at me! She had to surmount first things first—like to pray her Papa did not go to Tolbooth prison, or worse, that he was not hanged by the neck in Edinburgh town. She loved him, even though Papa had not wanted a daughter. He had had a son first, Michal, but he had wanted another son badly. In his way Cathelen believed Papa had loved her, though he'd never showered any affection on her as other fathers did with their daughters. She sighed. She might never know if, or to what extent Papa had resented her because she had not been the son he wanted. Now she wondered truly if that resentment had grown when Papa had discovered Michal's drinking problem, which made his first son, in his eyes, less than a man. Perhaps she would never know.

Cathelen rubbed her soft cheek on the rough surface of the musty-smelling sheet that covered the serviceable pillow. But she did not settle into a light sleep until just before the black horizon was gradually rent by a splash of daylight.

While falling asleep, Cathelen realized with a nice, warm glow that she would know just what making love with a man was like when she married. But at that moment the possibility seemed further away than the trade wind raking the West Indies.

Chapter Four

West Indies, 1716

Barbados, the most eastern of the West Indian islands, had been settled in the early seventeenth century. When John Powell had landed in 1624, he had taken possession in the name of "James, King of England and this Island," and had secured from his patron, Sir William Courteen, sufficient backing to begin settlement on a substantial scale three years later. . . .

Now, three quarters of a century later, Adam Sauvage strolled the shops of Bridgetown, Barbados. Many frilly heads turned to stare at the handsome plantation lord. Since returning home to Barbados after a three years' absence, Adam had discovered an entirely new life waiting for him.

Adam had never wanted to be a planter, to belong here, even though Barbados enjoyed the distinction of possessing the most compact and best organized society in the British West Indies. Adam was not like his brother, Jonathan, who had always been a dashing plantation lord favoring the attire of a dandy.

But Jonathan was dead. Killed. And as a result for the first time in ten years, Adam had cursed himself for being a buccaneer. He still blamed himself because his brother had been run through by a careless sword. A pirate had killed him, thinking Jonathan to be Adam. But Adam meant to find Jonathan's murderer, even if it took him the rest of his life. He had plenty of time.

Adam was indeed Jonathan now. He had had the overseer teach him all there was to know about how to run Sauvage Plantation. Only two men knew who Adam really was, Deke Jameson and Hondo, his trusted mate of ten years.

The Sea Wolf had never been caught. He had a price hanging over his head still, for he had plundered not only Spanish vessels but had also lifted ill-gotten goods from his fellow buccaneers, those other lean marauders who plied the Spanish Main.

Recently the Wolf had swung into action again, and there was evidence that some of the English pirates had made common cause with the French who pursued the same calling. But assisting the Spanish was one thing the Wolf's buccaneers would not do.

The Sea Wolf worried the north coast of Jamaica, robbing Spanish merchantmen and seizing eight or twelve trading sloops a month. Then he transferred his attentions to the pirates, from whom he took a much greater toll. Everyone was out for the Wolf's blood, while he was out for one man in particular. Adam, the Sea Wolf, was known to the world as Jonathan Sauvage. Not only was this identity a good disguise to slip into while running from his kind, but he also knew no one else would be seeking the Wolf in a plantation lord. Only time would tell if someone would connect him with his buccaneering activities. Until then, Adam meant to live dangerously and ruthlessly.

Besides, the Wolf was supposed to be dead. Those who were possessed of superstitions trembled when the *Legend*, the Sea Wolf's fleet ship, appeared on the horizon.

"Jonathan, eh, *Master* Jonathan . . ."

Today, with a mischievous grin, Hondo stepped up to the gentleman attired like a dandy, in black breeches that encased lanky thighs and a fashionable brocade walking jacket. Hondo's unusually bright blue eyes lit up in his leathery face as he glanced over the large, clean streets of Bridgetown; the strong, well-built houses with glass windows; the shops and stores. Children ran about the streets like myriad brown-hued ants. Hondo himself, though forty-five, was a child at heart.

"Cap'n," Hondo began, but swiftly a lean

brown hand clamped over his mouth. Hondo stared up into brown eyes flecked with yellow. He gulped.

"I'll slit your slimy throat," Adam warned with a touch of amusement at the small fellow's sudden alarm. Adam let go of the lean, freckled face slowly. "You should know me by now, Hondo. Would I do that to my friend?"

Hondo grinned, feeling more at ease now. "S-Sorry, *mastah.*" He aped the plantation folk.

"See that you're more careful from now on." Adam grinned as he stood in the Barbados sunshine. "Where in the hell did you ever get a name like Hondo?" Adam shook his burnished brown head. Hatless now, he dabbed at his forehead with a hanky. Then he placed the fashionable, wide-brimmed plantation hat back on his well-shaped head.

"Me mother give it to me, gov'ner," Hondo said jovially, looking over the shops and stores that contained goods from every quarter of the globe.

"Lookee there—goldsmiths, jewelers, clockmakers. I could go on living here forever, uh"— he faltered but a moment—"*mastah.*"

"Do you know why this general air of opulence, my good fool?" Adam asked with a dashing, devilish smile, tipping his hat meanwhile to a blushing shopper, a prim little young lady. "Good day—"

"Good day, Monsieur Sauvage."

Hondo grinned, showing a few teeth missing

36

top and bottom. The sweet-faced brunette looked Hondo over dubiously as the little sailor sketched her a gallant gesture, minus agility or grace.

Adam hissed deeply in his mate's ear. "Idiot, did you have to appear so damn clumsy? You're supposed to be my manservant, not a dolt!"

"Indeed . . ." Hondo sniffed, putting on the same airs his captain had assumed though Adam had done it quite naturally. Hondo scratched his head beneath his Irish-made cap and hurried to catch up with Adam's long strides.

Adam's brown eyes grew darker. He was doing something he would regret, he told himself, because it always made his temper build. He was remembering his grandfather, the old taskmaster who used to beat him black and blue, the old devil who had brought him and Jonathan up on the island. Adam dipped his well-shaped head to another passerby. A pretty one this Samantha Gable. Which brought Adam back to musing on Étienne Sauvage. His grandfather had told six-year-old Adam that the climate in the West Indies was unhealthy; still he'd brought his grandsons from New Orleans here to live. But Adam could detect no sign of ill health in the complexions of the Colonists—particularly in those of the women.

Hondo caught up. "Gov'ner, what was wrong with that one? Why didn't you ask her, huh? Whatsa matter with you?"

"Let's not go into that again. I've had women enough, Hondo man."

"Enough! You ain't even begun, you young pup! And you could have had a nice toss with that one, Samantha. She's willin'."

Adam shrugged lightly. "What if I do not want it?"

"You haven't had it for over a year now!"

Brown eyes glittered down on the smaller man. "How would you know that?"

Hondo grinned. "'Cause you got one thing on your mind—one!"

"What's that?"

"Murder!" Hondo whispered fiercely. "And you're gonna lose your manhood if you don't have some fun, gov'ner."

"You mean 'family jewels,' don't you?"

"Aye, your jewels," Hondo snorted.

"My friend, I do not intend to take up with a woman—family jewels or no. But my old friend, you seem to be the homey type. I would not have guessed it in a million years."

"Well. Mark me words, gov'ner, some pretty little lass is gonna get you one of these days. You're gonna groan then. Ahhh, I just want to see ya settle down. You're gonna get yourself killed, for sure!" His voice lowered as they stepped up to Adam's rich equipage, a fine plantation carriage. "Why don't you leave off looking for your dead brother's murderer? Jonathan's gone now, and you got your life to live."

"I've no room in my life for a woman. She

would distract me. There's only one thing in my heart."

"Aye. Hatred."

"I'll not rest until I find Jonathan's murderer and put an end to the man's miserable life."

Adam climbed into the driver's seat, soothing the team of dark chestnuts as the black boy handed him the ribbons. Then he frowned bemusedly at Hondo. "I believe you have grown soft." Adam stressed the words. "Come on, friend, smile. We are supposed to be the most splendid and gayest people of all his Majesty's Dominions, us Barbadians." He chuckled warmly.

"Fool! I ain't no blasted Barbadian."

Hondo climbed aboard just as the carriage began to roll away from the picturesque wharf. Soon they joined other carriages and carts on the road that led from Bridgetown to the scattered plantations. All roads were made to transport produce to Bridgetown, so all roads led through the town. Simple. Like the routine life followed on Barbados—even the social life.

"You going to any of those parties you been invited to, Cap'n?"

Adam peered at Hondo askance, then back at the dusty road, a brown ribbon between cane fields. "Don't think so, matey. I'll be pulling out again soon. Got a ship, namely the *Black Hawk*, to catch up with. Are you staying here this time?"

"Sure, I'll stay. Olivia, she, ah, she wants me

39

to go to church with her. . . ."

"Church!" Adam exploded. "I would have never believed it if I didn't hear you say it just now. Church . . ." Adam, shaking his head, pondered what had come over his wiry little friend. "So, you're going soft in the head over a little native gal!"

"She's only a few years younger'n me, Master Jonathan," he said now that they were approaching the broad avenue that led up to the stately mansion. "And Olivia's a quadroon, from a mulatto and a white."

"Her husband passed on recently I've been informed."

"Aye. Her daughter Sophie is a mustee. You should take a closer look?"

"Sophie's father is white? I take it not the deceased's offspring?"

Hondo dipped his head. "Sophie's the result of Olivia being taken by force. Her master couldn't see her worth to treat Olivia kindly."

"So he raped her?" Adam said, close to a growl.

"Don't you know him, the planter over at Sugartree?"

"Tell me now, so that I can avoid the bastard. I'll soon be acquainted with all the planters, anyway. I'd like to know who this animal is."

Hondo, forgetting to give the planter's name for now, said, "Some pirate you are!" he snorted. "Never even ravished a woman, for shame, tsk, tsk."

40

"Have you?"

"Once or twice."

"Why sack what's so easily given away?" Adam said arrogantly.

Hondo scratched beneath his cap, humming out loud as they halted before the wide, front steps. He watched Adam look up at the house as if willing the white walls to speak to him and foretell his future here.

"Master Jonathan, would you like me to take in the goods you purchased now?"

Adam grinned wolfishly as Hondo employed his new speech and airs, which he was becoming quite good at. In fact, Adam couldn't believe how much Hondo sounded like a real dignified manservant.

Hondo jumped down, forgetting for a minute to be more refined. And he leaned over the seat to taunt the younger man once more before entering the house. "One of these days, you arrogant sea pup, and sooner than you think, you're gonna find a gal whose going to be keeping what she's got. A smart lass. She'll cast her spell over you. And you, me lad, are gonna have to fight for what you be wanting so badly. So much so that you may be seeking the marriage bed!"

"Me? Bewitched by a mere fluff in skirts?"

Adam tossed back his dark curling hair, laughing aloud, and a rare, tempestuous wind snatched his hat up and knocked it into the dirt. He shook his head, but his chuckles soon died

41

when Hondo stood by grinning most confidently.

Then Adam shouted vehemently to that
troublesome wind, "Never!" He bent over,
picked up his hat and, before entering the
house, grinned back at his friend, saying softly
but firmly, *"Never!"*

Chapter Five

"Never!"

Dany heard the anguished cry coming from the bunk above, and she left her pallet quickly. Concerned, she stood on the balls of her toes and gently shook Cathelen awake.

Cathelen rose enough to lean on her elbows. "What is it, Dany? Are you ill again?"

"No, it is not me, lass." Dany coughed even as she said this. "You cried out in yer sleep, and woke me. Was it a nightmare?"

"Oh, Dany, I've had the dream before." She frowned, feeling frustrated in the dark cabin. "I do not know what the dream means."

"Och, now I be remembering—that dream," Dany said, another cough following.

"Dany, are you sure the fever has not returned?"

"Aye, it only lasted for an hour or so." Dany stared into the darkness at the foot of the bunk. "Now, lass. Tell me again about the dream."

"Is it better to talk about it, Dany?"

"Aye, lass."

"What did I say when I cried out?" Cathelen wondered, vaguely recalling a face in the dream.

"Ye said 'Never!'. Ye said it with such pain and sadness in your voice, lass."

"Oh, Dany, I wish I knew who all the faces belonged to!"

"Who are ye saying never to, lass?" Dany tried to see the small face, but all she could make out was its delicate outline.

"It—seems to be coming from a man, but I say it. I do not recognize this man because . . ."

"Aye? Why not, lass?"

"Because he is—He turns away when I walk toward him. Now I remember. I could not before." It was better talking it over, Cathelen discovered. This way she was not so frightened, she found.

Dany remained silent, for she was thinking the lass had been dreaming of her father. He had always turned away from her. Cathelen had never been able to capture Cathmor's attention. Cathmor O'Ruark had hated his own mother, a stern woman from the Netherlands. Dany believed he had never loved a woman in his entire life, not even the beautiful Scotswoman who had died after birthing Cathelen. Cathmor did not grieve overmuch, Dany had noticed. He even changed his name from Ross to O'Ruark. He hated the Scots, even though his own father had been of the proud Scotch clan Ross. Cathmor had always wanted to return to Ireland. Dany had a feeling he never would now. Possibly he had already hung from that noose and been cut down and buried.

"Go back to sleep now, lass."

"Thank you, Dany," Cathelen mumbled sleepily. "I love you. . . ."

"Yer such a good lass, Cathy."

Dany could not go back to sleep. Memories plagued her, those that usually came with midnight. Cathelen had been a cheerful youngster, always looking on the sunny side, despite the unhappy circumstances of her childhood and her worries about where her brother could be. For even as a lad, Michal had been a drifting young Scottish renegade.

Dany herself spoiled the poor lass terribly, lavishing on her love that should have come from doting parents instead of a governess. Cathelen had often been naughty, doing things she would not normally have done with her sweet nature. But when she could not gain Cathmor's attention, not even his anger when she misbehaved, her sweetness turned to temper tantrums. Unfortunately Cathelen barely existed for Cathmor!

Finally a striking change occurred in Cathelen. It was as if she had come to accept her fate overnight, to realize that her father hated everyone, including herself. She was even gracious when her Dutch cousins came to call, but they had snubbed her last time, remembering her antics from a previous visit when she had tied their little terrier in the wine cellar and sent them on a wild-goose chase into the woods, saying that their pet had run off. When Cathmor himself had found the dog tied to his favorite wine rack, he had only said to his confessing daughter, "Ha! What a little witch ye can be, Cathy. Just like your mother was." He had walked crisply out the door to hand over the pet to his sobbing nephew and niece.

Dany winced as her head began to throb, and the sweating began all over again. Merciful God—*don't be taking me now, Cathelen needs me.*

Chapter Six

Dany could see by the frightened pallor of Cathelen's face that she understood the Grim Reaper was drawing near.

"She be dying, lass," Trask said unnecessarily, his bulk framed in the door.

"How can she die of seasickness—how, Captain?" Cathelen tried to stave off the desperation hovering in her voice.

"'Tis not that, Cathy," Dany mumbled feebly, trying to stroke Cathelen's dainty white hand, but not strong enough to complete the caress. Her blue-veined hand fell back to her side on the pallet. "Fever—that's what it is. . . ."

"Aye," Trask confirmed. "She must've contracted it from one of the sailors back there, in from an island with a bout of plantation fever."

Cathelen had done all she could to keep the fever down, bathing Dany's sweat-curded face with sea water from the leathern bucket. Now the sweating had again ceased, a frightening sign with a very high fever. Dany had taken a bad turn. No thanks to the captain!

Cathelen stared over her shoulder at Trask irritably. "Is there no doctor on board this ship?" She could not bring herself to call him captain. For most of the journey so far, he had left them alone. And now it was as if he was just waiting for Dany to die.

Trask shook his huge head. "No doctor at the time, lass. At next port I'll be taking one on, hoping to, at least."

The captain was reliving the scene he had come upon at dawn. The lass had been standing by the fife rail, her white blond hair stirring against her pink cheeks. What an elegant treasure she is, he had thought with a hidden leer. The morning wind had thrust her gown against her long thighs and he had realized she had no unwieldy hoops under her skirts. Her soft violet eyes had been lovely in their alarm as she'd turned to see him standing so close behind her. He knew she would want to head for shore once the old woman drew her last, or even return to Leith harbor. But he had other plans now. There would be no putting the lass ashore.

Now Trask would be rid of the only person who could have reported what became of Cathelen O'Ruark. A sly grin lurked at the corners of

48

his greasy lips. Plans for profiting very nicely were crowding into his huge head like floatsam at bulkhead planks. Aye, it's Barbados for the girl. The idea formed in his mind then, and Trask was extremely pleased with himself.

One as outright gorgeous and gentle birthed as this lass would be worth something to one of the planters. She would be useful as a house servant, aye. This was too perfect, Trask thought. How much would Tandy, for instance, pay for her? Or Theodore Decatur? That's the man. Aye! A devil, sure, that man is. He might even put her in the house with that scent-stinking Barbados dandy, Vance Moore. He would use her well. Too bad Trask had no time to look for the Wolf. Ah, that unsavory buccaneer-turned-pirate would have made the highest bid for a beautiful young virgin. Not that the Wolf would keep her for himself. No. For he seemed to prefer slim lads—so Trask had heard. But he would turn around and make a handsome profit with a plantation lord. Ha! The Wolf could even sell her to his own brother if he was inclined that way. Rumor had it, though, that the Wolf was dead—but Trask could not believe it. The man was too mean to die. And if he was dead, then his lean dark ghost must be riding the waves and plundering whatever happened to become sorry enough to get in the Wolf's path. No, Trask did not relish running into that one, even if the pirate's ship was now captained by someone who had taken the Wolf's place.

Whoever would want that spot was *bad*.

Dany passed away that night, and Cathelen stood on deck, seemingly emotionless as the dear old body was lowered into the sea's shadows. Her shawl was draped over her velvet blond head, but Trask watched her closely. He would have expected the lass to be weeping at such a moment, but she was incredibly dry-eyed. He licked his thick lips. Maybe she was frightened. Somehow the idea intrigued Trask, gave him a perverse pleasure.

The captain read the funeral service at the short ceremony while many lustful eyes tried to see the little beauty's face. Word of her loveliness had been spread by a mate who had glimpsed it as she stood by the rail for a moment's air, the sea breeze having snatched her head protection. The mate had said her haunting beauty could move a heart made of stone. Now only a tiny sob could be heard from her as the shrouded bundle that was Dany Muir slid off its tilted plank into the sea.

No one said one kind word to Cathelen as she returned to her closet-sized chamber. But the room now seemed strangely larger and empty without her Dany. Cathelen sat on the pallet, unmindful that it was soiled, and she struggled not to weep.

A skinny little leathery brown sailor brought her food later that evening. It rested between two plates and was wrapped in a thick linen to retain its warmth. His rheumy gray eyes held a kind of dumb pity, like a sad old hound dog's.

"Oh—what?"

Cathelen became alarmed when the old salt leaned closer, his breath reeking foully of cheap rum and tobacco. "Shhh—I'll not be hurtin' ya. I tell ya lass, to warn ya." His voice grated and rasped. "'Tis better ya break ship at the next port. Aye, lass, don't be waitin' for Barbados. Get away to the old lass's relatives like ya planned ta do at the first—while ya still can. I overheard the captain, and he means to sell ya."

"S-Sell me?" Cathelen stammered, confused and shaken. "What do you mean, old man?"

"He means to make ya the indentured woman."

"But he cannot. I am free, and I've no record of crime!" Cathelen cried low.

"Aye. But ya be penniless now, I've heard tell. Ya must get away. The plantation is no place for the likes of ya. Ya would have no legal protection against the plantation owner. He can freely whip you, starve you, and make, uh, unspeakable use of ya. Get out while ya can, little lady."

"They do all that, these plantation owners?" Cathelen said, trembling just to hear of these abuses.

"Aye . . ."

Like a rat sniffing the air, the old sailor leaned out and cast an eye about the corridor. Then he nodded to her that all was safe. No one had heard him warn her what the captain was about. He closed the door on her unblinking stare.

Cathelen was pale. *Sell me?* But he cannot. I am not for sale, at any price! She tried to hold her temper in check. She wanted to go to the captain's cabin and confront him with the rumor she had just heard. But was it a rumor?

She set down the untouched food, trying desperately to control her shaking hand. Barbados? Was that where this ship was headed? What kind of ship was this, actually? Were there indentured servants aboard? Was Barbados where this ship was headed? Since when did the captain decide to go there? Then she knew. As soon as Dany became ill, that's when. But why? He couldn't just go ahead, take the liberty and sell her. She was free—not an indentured servant to be sold into seven years' hard labor in the sugar field. There were no papers stating this.

Cathelen gulped. What if Captain Trask had discovered her father had been arrested? Had Dany again talked in her sleep? Could Trask be so underhanded as to try and sell her without bond papers?

Cathelen stared down at the floor, more distraught than she had ever been. He could, she decided. Yes, it showed in the icy glint in Trask's eyes. That, and something else she had no knowledge of.

A knock sounded boldly at her door just then. "Who is it?" she called softly but firmly.

"Captain Trask."

Cathelen gasped softly.

52

He cleared his throat on the other side of the door. "I've some papers yer old nanny signed for me."

Cathelen's heart began to pound as she asked, "What—what papers?"

"Let me in, lass, and we'll discuss them. It's yer bond papers."

"Go away, Captain Trask. Those papers are not valid. You lie."

"Lass, a dinghy has just pulled alongside with a message, uh, yer father has been hung."

"Oh!"

Nausea rose in Cathelen's throat, along with a lump of fear. Her father had never loved her, yet she had always cared for him.

"Yer brother's friends, some Scottish renegades, tried to keep O'Ruark from his death. The executioner was even bribed. News travels fast, lass. It did not work. He might not have died if those fellows could've got to him before the life was squeezed out of—"

"Enough!"

"Nay, lass, you'll hear it all. Yer brother is wanted for treason, lass, for fooling around at a High Sheriff's hanging, ye know."

"Say no more, Captain!"

"Now, lass, open the door so—"

"No!"

He cleared his throat gruffly. "Prison is not a comfortable place, lass, especially not for the proper likes of ye, little lady, neither Tolbooth nor Canongate. At night they're all locked in together, men and women, some worse than criminals. The rooms are stone, cold as January's thumb, and have no windows. All in a room, humans crowded in together like fish in a net, and they, uh, cannot hold their bowels. . . ."

"I—I will go to Colin Muir's!" Cathelen cried, desperate and growing afraid.

"Ye cannot, lass. Yer father's a criminal." Trask paused for effect before going on. "They'll be hunting ye down at the Muir's. Ye cannot go there safely now. That is, unless ye be wanting to be took back to prison? . . ."

On trembling legs Cathelen went to unlatch the door. When had she locked it? She could not remember. The captain's eyes gleamed as if he were the devil himself, yet his smile was benign. Cathelen wondered how genuine his concern for her really was. He was holding out a brown bit of parchment, and she stared down as if the paper were aflame, envisioning her soul surrendered for seven whole years.

"The Sheriff's man dropped this off."

Cathelen's eyes darkened to amethyst. "How could Dany have signed it then, Captain"—she tossed her head—"tell me that?"

He dug into his reefer jacket and produced another parchment. "I've another paper." He waved this in front of her nose, but not close enough for her to read.

Cathelen shook her head, but she refused to hang it. A silvery curl bounded over her shoulder to rest there delicately. "Never mind, Captain. I understand now. What must I do to avoid

54

prison?" Although Cathelen already knew before she asked, she wanted to hear it, to make sure she was not having a nightmare. She knew about whole families of Scottish emigrants, debtors who had purchased their way out of Tolbooth and Canongate prisons. The desperate measure of signing indenture papers bound them to work for seven years in the West Indies. But she had not realized how cruel a planter could be. She shivered now. A whip was about the worst weapon she could think of for torture.

"Which island, Captain?"

She steeled herself again, for she already knew the answer.

"Barbados."

It was as if that planter's whip had already descended to flay open her white back. In reality, she would die first rather than be whipped!

"A lovely place," Trask went on, "lovely, for a poor little lady such as ye. Ah, ye'll love the flaming suns, the velvet nights. Here, I got a pen right over here on this table—if ye'll just come over here."

Cathelen, resigned to her fate, followed the captain meekly across the corridor, squaring her trim shoulders. Her hair was coming loose and fear flushed her cheeks, giving her the look of a young girl afraid to go out and play in the dark.

"Scrawl yer mark right there," Trask said eagerly, pointing to a line on the brown parchment.

Cathelen, affronted, tilted her chin at a proud

angle before bending to the task. "I will have you know, Captain, that I write my letters very well—without a scrawl!"

"Good, lass. All the better it'll go for ye." Trask nodded, satisfied as a wolf pinning a dove.

She straightened and placed the pen back into its well. After looking over the document and releasing a sigh, the captain spoke softly, as if she were a little bird he wished not to scare away.

"Ye've indentured yerself as a plantation slave. Seven years with yer body and soul and all human rights surrendered by legal document, to a master ye've never seen. But it is better, especially for a delicate lady like yerself, than being chained to a prison wall while ye turn to a skeleton."

Shuddering but not wanting to cry silly tears, Cathelen turned back toward her tiny, lonely cabin. The captain bid her good night, he would see her in the morning to discuss the next step.

Chapter Seven

Cathelen huddled between decks, willing herself not to cry. But she was not alone, for several families of Scottish emigrants were there with her in the dark, airless space.

Illegal cargo, human beings, debtors who had purchased their way out of prison.

She looked around as the families stored away their pitiful bundles of provisions, some foodstuffs already gray with mold. Cathelen was hungry too, but this inferior, near worthless fare turned her stomach.

Cathelen could not believe her fate. The captain was an animal, no, worse. Nobody had warned her, or these wretched folk, that this would happen. It was a calculated part of the captain's profit making, that he would sell provisions to the emigrants from their own private stores. Some had even gone so far as to sell their daughters for a night or two in order to feed their smaller children and their babes. The captain was a two-horned beast! Cathelen thought contemptuously.

Cathelen determined not to cry, not for herself, but sometimes she could not help but cry for the wretched voyagers she had gotten to know after signing the bond papers. Still, she must be strong. Yet it was almost her undoing when an old woman, weakly clutching an orphan wrapped in a worn plaid shawl—a wee bairn—began shuddering and crying. Cathelen left the corner where she had huddled beneath the low timbers, staving off self-pity.

"Here, let me help." Cathelen held out arms that had become slimmer but still retained the strength of youth. "Please. You can trust me. You are too weak to care for the child," Cathelen told the old woman. Having been handed the poor little bundle of flesh and rags, Cathelen looked up after cooing at the half-asleep, very ill infant. "Is she your grandchild?"

"She is," the woman said weakly. "There be no food for the bairn, no milk." The woman rocked back and forth. "She will die soon. She hardly breathes now, ye see."

Cathelen could not check the flow of tears then. And as she sat there, helpless and sick at heart, the tiny infant girl died in her arms. She never knew what happened to the babe's parents, nor did she want to anymore. Life had suddenly become a nightmare. Would the sun ever shine on these people or herself again? Did God even care about them? The prospect of a happy future, even a comfortable one, seemed very remote and bleak indeed.

Cathelen and the emigrants came blinking up onto the deck when Captain Trask ordered the hatches removed. Groups of broken men, women, and children stood with her in a disordered line while the captain strutted about like a royal peacock.

Still weak from her recent confinement, Cathelen's stomach churned. Beside her stood a woman that Cathelen guessed, despite the grime and hollows on her face, was a woman of no more than nineteen or twenty years, not much older than Cathelen herself.

Cathelen took deep breaths to calm her queasiness. On the other side of her was a mother cuddling her whining bairn. The woman lifted her eyes that were sad but otherwise expressionless.

"I wish"—she choked on a sob—"I wish to God I'd never had this bairn." The woman addressed Cathelen, remembering her as the girl who had held the dying babe below. "He's a burden to me."

Cathelen felt something explode inside of her then. "Don't say that!" But when she saw the alarm in the mother's face, she said quickly, "I am sorry . . . but the good Lord gave you that precious bairn. You are very lucky, for some young women such as yourself can never have children. Do not wish he had never been born.''

"You are right," the mother conceded, directing a tremulous smile at her babe. The infant boy reacted with a sweet smile, rounding his rosy mouth to coo at his mother. The woman began to cry, and Cathelen wrapped a slim arm about her waist, speaking words of encouragement and passing some strength from her own frail body to that of the mother.

"He is a fine boy—healthy too," Cathelen said cheerfully.

The mother nodded, saying, "I know. What is your name?"

"Cathelen O'Ruark."

"Miss?"

"Yes."

"Miss O'Ruark, God bless you."

Cathelen knew the young mother's name; she had heard the old woman say it. "And God bless you and the bairn, Margaret Rowan."

Tears blurred Cathelen's vision as Margaret lifted her haggard face to the sun that beamed down on the deck, and smiled more confidently. Everything was going to be fine for Margaret Rowan and her son.

It was a day of shimmering, golden heat. Cathelen's hair glowed as if fireflies flitted in her glossy tresses. The silken mass was curling up at the ends, while tendrils coiled at her temples and hugged her cheeks due to the tropical sultriness in the air.

"Get her back," Captain Trask roared to his mate. "Cover her head. Tandy is coming over to the dock and I want Miss O'Ruark out of his sight. She's to be for the overseer from Sugartree. He'll pay more for her, to hold her bond papers."

Cathelen did not mind that the fat mate hauled her into the shadows of some stacked crates, for it was cooler here, but when he shrouded her head with a bit of loosely woven wool, that she did mind. The wool was scratchy and made the heat even more unbearable. Still she could use this time to look over the island of Barbados. There hadn't been much of a chance to see it when she had had her first glimpse from the rail. After that she and the other women had been ordered to wash up below decks and had been given serviceable frocks to wear. Hers was faded Indigo. Blue was not her best color. However, who would see her but the island folk now?

As she gazed around at what she could see from her secluded spot, the sounds of the island stroked her ears. Cathelen found them not unpleasant. Cargo was being loaded into schooners headed for other islands in the Indies, and the captains of these ships shouted commands. She heard speech in a strange dialect mingled with these commands. Later she learned this was the Creole English of Barbados. She wished she could again see the gently undulating landscape, the white coral beaches, and the green fields she had glimpsed from the ship's rail.

The sun was now at a high angle overhead, almost directly above the harbor. Here were bright birds, butterflies, blue-green water, palm trees, and sunshine. And the sun seemed like a flaming ball. All this tropical beauty, so sultry and languorous—but would she find happiness here? That was the question.

"Sun hot," one black man said to another who, taking his cue, looked up, squinted into the glare, and nodded "yes." It was "high noon."

Cathelen watched them stop to rest, sliding glistening brown bodies against the crates and boxes, until their buttocks contacted the ground. Was this how she would labor in the fields, stopping to rest for a spell only when the sun was at its hottest? Could she withstand the backbreaking tasks without becoming an old stooped woman by the end of seven years? she wondered.

So engrossed in musing over her fate was she that she was not aware that someone was calling her name until she was aware of him standing before her. The person she disliked most in the world right now. Captain Trask pulled her from her cranny between the crates, and Cathelen realized too late that she could have escaped while the captain and his mates were otherwise occupied. But Cathelen wondered where she would have run. Probably they would have hunted her down. She was glad she would soon part company with the captain.

Cathelen had never detested a human being more.

When the captain pulled her toward a powerful- and nasty-looking man wielding a black whip, panic seized her. Did he actually use that thing on humans as the old mate had told her? This man, looking hard and cruel, could he be the plantation owner? She would find out soon enough.

Luckily for her, the captain was called aside by his mate. The man looked her over once and came to a decision. She was grateful for this because she did not wish to be haggled over. This man, if he was the planter, was in a hurry, it seemed, and looked tired. When the captain returned, he made his hasty offer.

"Did ye see her hair what's like moonbeams?" Captain Trask inquired of the man named Decatur. "Her skin?"

"Yes, yes," Decatur said irritably. "I have the coin here, and you'd better decide fast. I have some slaves back at Sugartree giving me some trouble. They need a taste of the lash to calm them down," he added cruelly.

Again the captain had to depart, for a fight had broken out aboard the *Windward Lady* and he was needed at once to break it up before his deck cargoes were swept overboard, his hatches smashed. Drunken seamen could do much damage, Trask knew by experience.

"The damned fools!" Trask swore as the clamor heightened. He stood undecided. It was

63

his ship or the girl. He could gain some, and then again lose some. He could see Decatur was in a hurry to return to Sugartree with the indentured servants. But the heavy scufflings and boisterous howls of his crew made up his mind. First he caught the bag of sovereigns tossed over by Decatur and weighed them in his palm. Then he dug into his jacket for bond papers and, with a sigh and a strong oath, handed the parchments over, after which he strode viciously to his ship, prepared to knock some brawling heads together.

Cathelen, the wool scarf securely over her bright head, kept her chin down as she was loaded into the plantation wagon. Here she could not carry herself like a lady of gentle birth, nor wear the proud look of the noblewoman she was. She would not place herself above those in the wagon with her.

As the wagon bumped along the road out of Bridgetown heading north, Cathelen looked neither to the left nor the right of her. She stared at the brown ribbon of road below, at the pale green cane fields in her peripheral vision. Shortly Margaret turned to Cathelen.

"It is good that you wear the scarf, Cathelen, to hide your pretty hair. Never in my day have I looked upon such fair blond locks—and so much of them too. How came you to be Irish?" she asked, wondering about the pale color.

"Our name was actually supposed to be Ross, but papa—"

"Oh," Margaret broke in, excited over this

news, "the proud Scots clan Ross. I have heard of them!"

"Yes." There was no need to add that her blond hair actually came from her mother's side—Dutch descendants. Although Cathelen did not know much about these ancestors. No one had ever told her about her family—except Dany. Her former governess could have answered all these questions. And Michal, he—She could not think of him now. He was so far away, and she doubted she would ever see him again.

"Do you think that the driver of the wagon is the plantation owner?" Cathelen asked, mainly to change the subject and direct the conversation away from herself.

"The man with the whip? Nay. He would be the overseer." Margaret shook her kerchiefed head. "Watch out for that one."

"He does appear to be very mean." Cathelen shuddered, having seen him caress his coiling snake of leather. She wondered if the man's name was Satan, for surely he looked as though he could sport a tail and horns easily enough.

Silence reigned for a time; then Margaret suddenly whirled to face Cathelen, a hint of excitement apparent in her face.

"We will grease your hair with some brown salve my husband keeps in his pocket for cuts and bruises!"

Baffled, Cathelen shook her head. *"What?* I do not understand, Margaret. Why would I put some awful grease on my hair?"

"Because—don't you see? That horrible man

is going to get a better look at you, and when he does, there's no telling what he'll do when he has glimpsed your golden looks."

Murmurs and nods of the head accompanied this remark, as one and all in the wagon agreed. They liked Cathelen very much, had witnessed her gentleness and her kindness on many occasions above and below decks. They had watched her hold a dying babe to her breast as if the child had been her own wee bairn.

"She's right," chimed in many of the women-folk. "Yer like a porcelain doll I seen once," said one gaunt Scotswoman in her thirties, "and that nasty devil will break ye until yer nothin' but a rag doll. I've seen what the likes of him could do to a pretty lass lak yerself!"

Cathelen was becoming increasingly alarmed. Apparently the worst was only about to begin— if she was not careful. She watched, mesmerized, as Margaret's husband Jack handed over the small canister of salve to the lady next to him. Crouched down, with the women surrounding her, Cathelen felt globs of the brown, sticky substance being rubbed into her hair. Ugh, she thought and shuddered. It would take more than a few washings to restore her locks to their natural pale beauty. Not that she was vain, she wasn't. But her hair was her pride and joy, and she had often imagined the man she would someday love stroking and caressing it, threading it through his lean fingers. But now she resigned herself to her luckless fate—that no man would ever stroke and admire her crowning glory. What a dream that had been!

"All out!"

The cry rang out harshly, even before the wagon had rolled to a complete halt. As she stepped down, Cathelen got her first real look at a West Indian plantation. Some distance away stood a white mansion, gleaming in the slanting sun. Green lawns stretched away and wrapped around the great house that was approached by a broad avenue lined with trees she would come to know as tamarinds and palmettos. She could imagine the lady of the house, pretty, in a belled-out dress, stepping out onto the wide veranda to gaze dreamily out over her green fields, the brilliant flowers of exotic hues, and the sweet-smelling fruit trees.

As she stood in the dusty lane that stretched between cabins arranged in regularly spaced rows, she felt the island's sultriness and experienced a yearning entirely foreign to her experience. If this overseer standing here with the whip was mean, how much more possessive and cruel could the plantation owner be, this man she was yet to come face to face with? Cathelen did not want to think about it, not at all.

Later that same day Cathelen discovered she was not to become a servant at Sugartree plantation after all. She was bound for another plantation, further north by several miles, where the shoreline was wild, and huge rocks stood in the surf.

But at the moment she was witnessing something that made her angry. The overseer was lifting his whip to flay open the back of a young black girl who had disobeyed his orders.

Outraged and shivering from head to foot, Cathelen left the well where she and the others had been washing up before their evening meal—some gray slop she had seen a plump girl dishing up outside one of the palm-thatched huts. Now Cathelen stepped right up to Decatur to stay his heavy hand.

"Don't you dare beat her!" she shouted angrily, spitting like a little she-cat and struggling with the overseer's wrist for possession of the black snake. "She is a human being!"

"Oh? Can't I?" Easily he overpowered her, though Cathelen fought him, and he tossed her to the dirt at his booted feet. "You little witch, think you're better than most here just because your skin is white? Your color makes no difference here at Sugartree. Look there, missy," he snarled, waving the hand holding the coiled whip in the direction of the bondservants. "They're much smarter than you, keeping their mouths shut." He glared down at her. "You ain't no better, missy. Fact is, you're skinnier than most"—he poked the butt of his whip into her ribs—"so I won't be punishing you as hard as the others, you think? Say, you do look a little scared now, missy, seeing as you know you're gonna get a taste of my whip here. Sorry to have to make an example out of one so frail and stupid as you!"

Cathelen jerked once in spontaneous reflex as the whip hissed and cracked in the air above her head. Her scalp crawled with the prickly sweat of instant fear. Mesmerized, she watched the black snake recoil to the man's side, as if indeed he commanded a living serpent.

The overseer threw an evil leer at the crouching girl, never realizing she was hiding a pair of long, shapely legs from him and a golden triangle that concealed an unawakened source of delight for some fortunate man. If Theodore Decatur had only known what he was about to give up, he would have moved heaven and hell to keep this treasure housed at Sugartree.

But as it turned out, fate was about to step in and Decatur would be damned for his mistake for the rest of his fool's life.

Cathelen steeled herself for the bite of the lash just before a deep resounding voice rang out. "Hold there!"

A high-sprung carriage halted nearby. Cathelen looked toward it just as a tall blond giant of a man swung down to his feet, leaving his buggy whip in its holder. She found herself hoping and praying he had come to stop the flogging she had been about to receive. He was dressed all in white, save for the tall black boots climbing all the way to his knees. Like an avenging spirit, Cathelen thought.

Theodore Decatur stood, resting one hand negligently on his hip; the other held the now-lax whip hanging at his side. He spoke to the blond giant.

"You are to tell me when I should beat my slaves, Jameson?"

69

Jameson, lean and with hair of darkest gold beneath his plantation hat, smiled laconically. "Not that, Decatur. What you do with your slaves is your business."

"Hmm, yes," Decatur said, as if he doubted the latter comment. "Just see that you keep your ideas to yourself. I know just how lenient you and your men are over at Sauvage Plantation."

As Deke Jameson looked down at the young white woman he had saved from a beating in the nick of time, he caught the shape of a well-turned ankle before she yanked her skirt down to cover her legs. But he had already seen quality in the lass, something Decatur had overlooked, an oversight he was going to regret.

"We're short at Sauvage Plantation. I came over to see if you could help me out, even though I almost did not make the trip."

"What is it, Jameson?" Decatur asked, though his lips curled up in a sneer.

"A bout of the fever," Jameson explained.

"As we've had here," Decatur said, then interjected, "Just picked these bondies up."

"Yes, but I see you have more than enough," Jameson said. He cast a learned eye about the line of clean, but bedraggled, women.

Decatur glowered. "Now I see what you're getting at. Why didn't you go into Bridgetown to get your own?"

"Missed the ship. Next one in is two weeks away. Master Sauvage is away, been gone for over a month."

"Again? Hell, he's just about as absent as

70

Moore, isn't he?" He shrugged indifferently. "So you're short and you want to do business?"

"Right. Need someone "clean" enough to work in the house." Deke Jameson casually eyed the girl whose finely tapered fingers were still splayed in the dust. She stayed like that, still as a statue. Jameson's eyes lifted, away from the girl. "Wanda contracted the fever too, so we're short a housekeeper. We have one new one in the house as kitchen maid, but she's an old Scotswoman. She's been forced to turn to mending and sewing, to take it easy. Don't know how long she'll last. She was sick about a week ago."

A light turned on in Cathelen's brain at the mention of the woman. How nice it would be if she could work in a great house with a Scotswoman, especially one the age Dany had been. She would not be so lonesome then.

Swiftly Cathelen performed the crudest gesture she could dream up. She spat upon the overseer's boots, first one and then the other. Shocked at her unbelievably daring behavior, Decatur peered down at the glistening twin smears on his tall boots and bristled with rage.

"What a little bitch you are!" he growled, lifting his whip to deal the girl the biting lash she had not yet received.

A hand shot out and grasped Decatur's wrist, staying him, this time not with words but physical strength. The better man won. Deke Jameson, overseer from Sauvage Plantation, received a dark glare from the only slightly weaker Deca-

71

tur, who relaxed his whip hand.

"I've got enough wayward and tardy slaves around here to handle!" Decatur glowered at the girl now slumping in the dirt in great weariness. "See there, there ain't one strong bone in her body. All she can do is spit fire!"

"I can use her, if you're willing to let her go?" Deke Jameson did not look at the pale girl. He already knew she would be quite lovely when washed up and freshly gowned, and he wanted to take Decatur's mind off her. "And how about her, the woman with the baby?"

"Her husband stays here, though."

Margaret let out a tiny sob, but her husband shushed her with a look she understood. Decatur seemed to be considering the deal.

"How much?" he asked, his eyes already gleaming with greed. He had come out short, having beaten a slave to death a few days ago. That death would come out of his own pocket. Vance Moore, the master of Sugartree, was one of those who thought that even on the best-managed plantations it was impossible to keep men for long. But Theodore Decatur counted himself a lucky man. So far, there had not been very many deaths despite the heavy punishments he served out to the slaves. Brutal and licentious punishments they were, but Decatur had no real personal interest in the slaves' welfare. Though a slave's health did not increase his capital, he did not gain if one died by his hand. At times he could conceal the death of a weak old slave, call it a natural death, but this last one had been the boss's prize, a healthy black stud. Now Decatur was more than a bit worried. He hated to be a loser.

Decatur took aside Sauvage Plantation's overseer, his odd-colored eyes running over the greasy-haired young woman who had already given him more trouble than he could handle at this time.

"How much?" Decatur repeated.

Chapter Eight

Cathelen gave a shocked gasp. Her eyes widened with excitement as she looked inside the closet in the room Deke Jameson had unlocked for her. Here was a treasure house of costly gowns. She tentatively fingered rolls of silk, fat bolts of rainbow-hued satins, heaps of ribbons and bows, gold- and silver-trimmed laces fit for a grand Spanish lady—all obviously of rich quality.

"Where did all this come from?" she said breathlessly.

"Supposed to be a secret, little lady. So you take what you need to change into after your bath. Someday maybe you can have more, that is if master Ad—I mean, master Jonathan—will let you. You just keep that to yourself, will you?"

"Yes, and thank you. You have been most kind," Cathelen said, strangely shy with this big man.

"I'll leave you now so you can take your time and choose." He held the key out to her. "I trust you with this, Miss O'Ruark, so give it to Mairi and she'll return it to me."

"Is Mairi the Scotswoman?"

"That's her. She's been ailing, so you might find her in her room belowstairs, off to the right and down at the end of the hall." He smiled. "I'll leave you now so you can dress for your job as housekeeper." He stopped to tip his hat and scratch the blond mop beneath with a long thick finger. "Hope you don't mind my asking, but you do know how to keep house?"

"Of course." She smiled, hoping she did not appear too unsightly with her greasy strands. "Could I ask you a question, if I may?"

"Sure." He grinned, showing large, even white teeth.

"Do you also oversee the house servants?"

"Nope. I'm just doing this because the woman in charge died not too long ago from the fever."

Cathelen cleared her throat delicately. "W-Will I be in charge now?"

A small laugh escaped the large man. "No. Mairi is in charge, that is when she can manage. Otherwise Mattissa will be in charge. She's got a drop of black blood, a musteefino, but you'd never know it, she's as white as you. But her hair

75

is as black as midnight. Don't let her spook you. Mattissa is a quiet one, and she never bothers a soul. She might stare at you, but don't let that get to you either. Well. I've got work to do now. Been away from my slaves too long."

Cathelen wanted to know if he beat them, but dared not ask. At least he did not carry a wicked whip like Theodore Decatur did. She looked up at Jameson again and smiled sweetly.

"Thank you, again."

"My pleasure."

After Deke Jameson had left her, Cathelen set about choosing a dress, one that would be serviceable. As there was not a pair of shoes to fit her, she picked a pair of women's riding boots of soft brown leather. They were expensive, the kind a grand lady would wear with a velvet riding habit.

"That should do it." Cathelen said to herself, adding a dark lilac ribbon to her bundle. She sighed, looking with longing at all the clothes she must leave behind. Oh, well. Maybe someday she would be rich enough to have a wardrobe of her own. Maybe some nice gentleman on this island would ask for her hand in marriage. That would break her indenture, would it not? She was certain it would. Positioning the key over the lock, Cathelen began to back out of the door.

Master Jonathan Sauvage was just alighting from his dusty carriage when he spotted the overseer striding up the lawn, eating up the distance in no time. Jonathan paid him no mind as he hauled a weighty bundle out from the back of the seat.

"Jonathan, could we talk for just a moment before you go inside?" Jameson asked quickly, seeing that Sauvage was in no mood for any sort of conversation. But he could not wait. He had to tell Sauvage about the girl before he went inside and found her bathing in his tub. Sauvage always took a bath first thing when he arrived home—at least he had done so the last three occasions. Damn, he should not have had the lads set the bath up in there. It had been easier than hauling the brass tub from behind its screen to another location. He had not expected Sauvage home this day. But then one never knew about Jonathan. Jameson was just hoping she had not slipped into the tub yet.

"Not now, Deke," Jonathan said, jerking on a cord that, dangling from his bundle, had gotten stuck in the carriage door.

"Just for a moment—" Deke persisted.

"Damn it!" Jonathan snarled, reopening the door and yanking the cord free. "Can't you hear? Not now!" He slammed the door hard and motioned for Hondo to take the carriage out back. Then whirled on the overseer who followed him. "No!" he shouted into the man's face.

"Jonathan, you had better listen—"

"*Merde!*" Jonathan swore in his father's French. His mother had been Irish, and had she

77

been alive she would never have tolerated such language.

Removing his wide-brimmed hat and striking it on the porch steps, field dust flying, Jameson took his turn at cussing. He was just about to sit when he saw a trail of dust. Horses coming up the lane. When the horses halted and the dust cloud lifted, a black carriage became visible. A carriage in poor repair, at that.

"Where the hell is he?"

The driver alit, swooping down like a bat from Hades. He was just about to enter the house, with a frowning Jameson at his heels when Jonathan Sauvage stepped to the door. He still wore the dandified plantation lord's outfit in which he had arrived. The package he had carried must have contained his change of clothes.

"What can I do for you?" Jonathan said arrogantly, flicking his wrist. "I was just on my way out to have dinner with a neighbor. I don't think I recognize you. Are you a resident planter?"

"No, I am not. I am from Jamaica, your neighbor in a sense." The man frowned, wondering what had gone amiss. He had been certain he was on the tail of the right man. Where had he gone wrong? "To make a long story short, my name is Buckley, ah, Raymond, and—my ship has been overtaken by a blasted pirate."

Sauvage lifted a hand to smooth an eyebrow. "So sorry to hear that, Raymond Buckley. My name is Jonathan Sauvage. If I can be of assistance, please let me know."

Buckley shook his head. "I cannot understand it. My ship was to be unloaded here and—and some sea robber overtook me," he repeated, as if in a daze.

"Why did you follow me here in such haste, sir?" Sauvage asked the man.

"Ah. Well, my mates told me to follow the carriage that the pirate captain slipped into." Buckley reddened with embarrassment. "My mistake, sir. I can't understand it."

"What is that?" Jonathan Sauvage asked.

"He could have taken my entire cargo. His ship was crawling with armed men, but all they took were a few meaningless trinkets. That's strange," Buckley remarked.

"What is strange?" Sauvage said, his brown eyes twinkling merrily.

"One of his mates was going around checking faces, as if looking for someone in particular. But the captain himself never appeared, at least not until—"

"Until?" Sauvage echoed, leaning a little closer to hear the answer.

Buckley saw the dangerous yellow flecks that were coming alive in the planter's eyes. "Ah— One of my boys said he saw a man that looked like the pirate captain being rowed ashore up a ways from the harbor."

"And you thought I was your man? A case of mistaken identity, Buckley." Jonathan said. "I forgive you," he added smoothly. "Just see that you do not follow me again?"

"No, I— It was a foolish thing to do anyway,"
Buckley confessed. He looked at his skinny,
stooped driver. "I really don't know what I
would have done if you were that pirate and I
caught up with you."

"Yes. If I were that pirate you might have
found yourself in much trouble, mate." Jonathan laughed then, but the humor never
touched his sparkling brown eyes. "As you can
see, I am not. Now, if you'll excuse me, I really
must get to that party."

"Oh, yes, yes. I'll be bidding you good day,
Jonathan Sauvage."

For all his girth, Buckley made a hasty retreat
to his carriage, and was off in a swiftly moving
dust cloud down the lane.

Eyes narrowing after the vanishing carriage,
Jonathan pivoted on his booted heel and
entered the house before Deke could open his
mouth to warn him that a surprise awaited him
upstairs. Actually, Deke thought, both Jonathan and the girl were in for a mild shock. Deke
Jameson just hoped it would be pleasant. But he
doubted this, having seen the dark mood Sauvage was in.

"I might as well let nature take its course,"
Jameson said to himself, moving across the
lawn to enter the wooded lane to the cabins.

Upstairs in Jonathan's bedroom, a willowy
leg, lathered with soap bubbles, jutted straight
up from the tub. The blonde in the bath had
given her hair several soapings, and her tresses

now floated in the water, looking like white-blond seaweed. Cathelen was humming a soft tune about a sailor and a mermaid; she had learned it from Michal. She did not hear the door open, so engrossed in her delightful soaking was she.

"Mon Dieu!"

Clutching the fat sponge to her small breasts, Cathelen whirled about, at the same time whispering, "What was that?" Her startled eyes lifted, up, up, until she was staring into the darkest pair of brown eyes she had ever seen. Even as she looked, without blinking once, the color in those eyes shifted and they were lit up by yellow flecks. His crisp lower lip moved to speak and Cathelen's stare dropped as his words emerged, ever so softly.

"So. There is a mermaid in my tub. I suddenly count myself very lucky today."

Cathelen swooned.

Sauvage bent one knee beside the tub, and his heart skipping a beat, his eyes swept the fascinating creature before him. He smiled, and his eyes danced. He wondered how she came to be in his room—taking a leisurely bath obviously—yet he didn't dwell too much on that for the time being.

It was hard for him to keep his eyes from studying her. Long flaxen lashes spiked over her lower lids, closed now, as she swooned against the back rim of the tub, and several tempting tendrils of hair curled like liquid silver at her temples.

81

Sauvage was stirred, his body aroused by this sylph in his tub. Just looking at her triangle of womanhood, submerged in such a splendid rippling golden way, made him push through the bubbles surrounding her pointed breasts and kneecaps to pull her gently up through the water.

Now that he stood with her, dripping like a slippery fish, in his arms—a mermaid no less—Sauvage laughed softly and could not help but ask himself what it was about this gently curved female that made his body react so strongly. Even before he had touched her he had become aroused.

The lights in his eyes danced faster and brighter. But he stared at her tender form for several unbearable seconds as if trying to decide exactly what to do with her. Finally, moments after he had pulled her from his tub, Sauvage blew the rainbowed bubbles off her breasts, wanting to see the rest of her. Shell pink nipples, taut and tempting, rose from the bursting bubbles of soap.

A dreamlike quality surrounded the heated man holding the water nymph, and if it had not been for the girl's tiny sigh, so weary and lost, he would have bent his head to sample one of those rosebuds between his lips.

God! She is just too damn vulnerable. His nostrils twitched. She had washed her hair, too. She smelled like a summer garden of roses and baby's breath. His blood thundered as if a wild stallion galloped inside him; and his man's body was growing very uncomfortable, his trousers nigh unto bursting with his great need for a woman. Not just any woman.

Why? Damn it! Why this woman—now? he asked himself.

Then he made his way over and placed her on his big bed, damning this lovely slip of a girl for making him aware he had feelings again. And God, such feelings they were!

He stood looking down at her. She lay in a sweet curve of femininity, a snow-white curl wrapped in one tiny finger. How could a woman be so small and sweet and pretty? he asked himself over and over.

Unable to halt his questing fingers, Sauvage reached out once more—just once—to feel the texture of this angelic mermaid. Unconsciously his hand splayed over the coolness of her chest, his fingers testing a small mound of white flesh. She shivered as if from chill, but the man at the bedside continued his search over the hillock of breast until two fingers topped the peak of pink flesh. Shivering himself, he didn't remain there but slid down the gentle slope to her rib cage. God, she is slim! She must eat like a bird.

Sliding over her midsection and on down to the concavity of her pelvis, Sauvage gulped and his head pounded as unbearable heat raced through his blood. Hypnotized and emboldened by intense desire, his fingers drew nearer her source of heat.

"Mmmm . . ."

Sobered, Sauvage snatched his hand away from the sweet place he would have loved to explore. He made his way over to the door and yanked it wide. The mermaid once again moaned, a sound evening-breeze soft and gentle. His own groan caught in his throat; then Jonathan bellowed down the hall, "Mattissa!" He ran his hands through his hair in a frustrated motion before slipping on his black gloves and staring down at them, a tick working in his cheek.

By the time he heard the woman coming along the hall he had his desire under control, but not his tormented emotions. "Never," he said with a deep-seated vow. "Never . . ."

Chapter Nine

The setting sun created shifting patterns that cut a red-gold swath across the floor. Her lashes beginning to flutter, Cathelen lay stretched out on the big bed, her nakedness covered with a towel, and a sheet pulled up over that. The sheet reached the upper hills of her small breasts, leaving her shoulders bare, her too-slim arms lying stretched out at her sides.

"Looks like she's dead," Sauvage said to Mattissa.

Mattissa frowned at the very still girl whose eyes would be soon opening. So this is the new housekeeper? Mattissa thought. She will not even be able to hold a rug sweeper. Either she was awfully young, or she has been starved half to death. Then her black eyes shifted to Jonathan Sauvage. He looked frozen to the spot, staring at the girl. He was a mysterious man. His moods—even his looks—often changed with lightning speed. Just when Mattissa thought she was getting to know Jonathan, that he might take her as his mistress so she could have the baby she wanted, she had returned from visiting her sister on St. Martin to find that he had had a change of heart. That had happened six months ago, but Mattissa was still very disappointed that he had not made love to her. Now this sickly girl was here, another interruption in her plans.

Cathelen slowly opened her eyes. Her body tingled as the man continued to stare at her. What had he called her before she had swooned? A mermaid? How appropriate, for she had been humming a tune having to do with a mermaid. But she did not much care for the way he was studying her now. What could he be thinking? Why did those odd-colored brown eyes twinkle one second and then darken the next? He was incredibly handsome, she concluded. His face and throat were completely bronzed by the sun. He must be the plantation owner. She could not see his hands.

"I am Jonathan Sauvage," he said, then, "Can you cook? Mend clothes?" He continued brusquely after she had answered. Mattissa here has informed me that Deke Jameson appointed you housekeeper?"

"Yes, he did." She was suddenly so flustered she could not recall if the man had or not.

"I am sorry to say this but"—his eyes swept over her outline, so slim beneath the sheet—"you are much to frail, I'm afraid, for this monumental task. It will be enough for you to handle that which I have already mentioned."

With no more ado—Master Sauvage showed her the lean length of his back as he left the room. Over and done with her, just like that! How arrogant he is! Cathelen flushed from head to toe as Mattissa watched her.

"D—Did he carry me to this bed?" Cathelen asked with a shaky voice.

"*Oui*," came the clipped reply.

"What?" Cathelen could not make out this language at the moment, the patois was too strange.

"Yes." Mattissa flung back the sheet then, exposing Cathelen with only the skimpy towel covering her.

Cathelen bristled. Why the very nerve of this woman! No one had ever assumed she had no modesty. The only human being who had seen her exposed thus was her beloved Dany. Was this handsome black-haired woman trying to humiliate her for some reason? But why?

"Oh!" It hit Cathelen full force then. "He really *did* carry me to this bed?"

Dark eyes snapped as the woman looked pointedly at Cathelen's white willowy legs. "I already say yes. Master Jonathan would have let you drown if he did not take you out of the water."

The lofty-minded maid had said this in a

haughty and precise manner as she swept her dark eyes over Cathelen's too-slim shape, blind to the inevitable beauty the girl truly was.

Cathelen caught her breath. He had seen *all* of her? Dear God! Then Cathelen studied the maid. She seemed to be cruelly enjoying her discomfort over this. Amethyst eyes flashed at Mattissa's proudly held back as the woman moved about straightening the room. Cathelen swung her legs over the side of the high bed. What should she do next? Get dressed? Being a coward is not like you, Cathelen, she chided herself. But that woman; why did Mattissa seem to dislike her so much? She has not even given me a chance to be a friend, Cathelen thought dejectedly.

Cathelen! Dany would say, *Och! Now ye stop that feeling sorry for yerself!*

"Uhmm, Mattissa, do you suppose you could hand me the dress there and—and the boots?"

Mattissa halted her task, turning to flash even blacker eyes at Cathelen, and with an armful of dirty linen, she straightened, her fine nostrils flaring. "You do your own work, white woman," she hissed so low that Cathelen could barely hear her.

Cathelen blinked only once as the musteefino swept out the door like a regal Spanish duenna, her arm cocked over the bundle at her hip. Mattissa was very slim in the waist and hips, but her breasts were generous and pointed, and she owned a wavy gloss of abundant black hair. She was very beautiful and fiery, Cathelen concluded.

As she sat there, staring at the dress she would wear on this day—and most likely every day now that Mattissa had taken charge of her—Cathelen wondered how she was going to brave it with that beautiful tyrant in the house.

Chapter Ten

"She hasn't eaten in two days? Really, that's hard to believe. Yet, I've seen how skinny the wench is."

Master Sauvage tossed these words over his shoulder upon entering the tigerwood-paneled room where he would be doing most of his future business. Tossing the dusty white plantation hat onto a chair, he sat down at Jonathan's desk—he would have to stop thinking of it as his brother's desk—and picked up the brown parchment.

Deke Jameson followed the tall, bronzed man into the room. "All those indentured servants look as if they are starving, if you ask me. There's her papers, Adam—" The overseer clamped a hand over his mouth, glancing back over his shoulder to make double sure he had shut the door.

Jameson faced the glittering-eyed man leaning laconically back in the red leather chair. "Damn. Sorry, uh, Jonathan."

"Devil take it!" Sauvage's lips were drawn back from his white teeth, his eyes were glinting as if he stared into the sun's glare.

Sauvage rose to pace the highly polished oak floor, and Jameson watched him, his eyes going to and fro. Suddenly Sauvage spoke harshly. "Have I a pack of simple, jackassed fools working under me?" He stopped to stare out the tall windows at the grounds, neatly landscaped with exotic manicured gardens and lawn. He was forced to remind himself that he was master at Sauvage Plantation now, and he had great responsibility. But if those closest to him were going to blunder and betray his true identity, and if someone at the plantation was not loyal . . . He snorted. His game would be ended, and maybe a noose would grace his neck.

"Please, Deke, try to be more careful with your tongue in the future. I've already come down on Hondo for doing the same, but"—he sighed as if weary—"I suppose I'll grant you both one tiny mistake. Now, tell me, has it leaked out to anyone else here that I am not— *whoa!*" He grinned sheepishly then. "Damn, even I almost let the puss out of the bag. Satan's whiskers, someone could have been walking on the veranda, and me with my big mouth flapping!" he said in a husky tone.

So, Jameson thought, our handsome boss, Adam Sauvage is after all, a human being. But he was still not sure. Adam had always been the wild dark one of the family, and even after his demure little mother and his rakish grandfather had passed on, Adam had stayed away. Jameson had thought the sea-roving Adam would be around more after the old tyrant had died, but he had only come by about three times a year. In the event of Jonathan's death, the plantation would go to Adam Sauvage, the will read. Otherwise Étienne had left Adam nothing.

Deke Jameson had been a grown lad when Étienne Sauvage had brought the two tall boys to what was then called Wild Orchid Plantation. Old Étienne had hated that name with a passion, and had changed it at once, even going so far as to have all the lovely orchids ripped from their beds. Jameson had grown up with the Sauvages, been like an older brother to them. But willful, adventurous Adam had gone off to sea while proper, business-minded Jonathan had taken over the plantation. Adam had not wanted anything to do with what was not going to him, it seemed. He had found out from his mother beforehand that he would be left penniless. Adam had even spat on his grandfather's grave during his first visit home after the funeral.

Jameson looked over to where Adam Sauvage stood. The man had relaxed and become himself behind closed doors. But he would become Jonathan at once if someone entered the room, and he had given strict orders that from now on his privacy was not to be intruded upon.

Now Jameson was getting to know Adam all over again—not that he really had known the lad in the first place. The fact of the matter was, no one could know him. Jameson wholly believed this. Adam would forever hate the world and would swiftly destroy any impediment in his path. Jameson had to remind himself not to get too close to the young sea devil.

"Now," the impostor Jonathan was saying, "you said that the new girl hasn't eaten for two days?"

Jameson wondered about the man's preoccupation with the new girl. Ah, she would become a beauty someday soon; maybe Jonathan, too, had noticed.

"That's right," Jameson began, "but she—"

"She's had her fill, I hope? I will not have any of my slaves or servants starving to death." He turned to face Jameson now. "Lord, she's skinny!"

"But lovely."

"Yes," Jonathan confessed.

"I was about to say she has not eaten much, though. Mattissa said so. Jonathan, Master Sauvage, sir, damn this is not my job, seeing that servant girls get enough to eat. I'm an overseer, remember?"

"Sorry, Deke, I am just beginning to realize what a tough job you have. I know what it's like to have to beat a mate for disobeying orders or inciting a riot aboard ship. Still I can let no man get off easy. Too many accidents happen that way, causing deaths that could be avoided."

"You don't have to explain to me, Jonathan. I let no slave get off easy, black or white, but I never beat women like Decatur does over at Sugartree."

Jonathan's face hardened. "Sometimes it's a must, Deke. For women can get into a lot of trouble and be tardy often. You just don't beat them as hard or as many times."

Jameson said nothing.

"As for the running of the plantation, you'll just have to instruct me a little more, huh, friend?" Jonathan said carefully.

"Yes, sir. I was just about to say," Deke began in a conspiratorial tone, "the plantation's attorney has taken ill and died. You'll have to appoint a new one, seeing as you're absent so much of the time."

"What the hell do we need an attorney for?" Jonathan tersely asked.

"You see, the system gradually takes on a large burden of debts and liabilities—to merchant creditors, to trustees. Owners like yourself who are absent so much of the time leave the conduct of the plantation to an attorney."

"How are they paid?" Sauvage wondered as he sauntered over to a ledger left open on the littered desk. Jonathan may have left it this way, but Adam decided immediately that this litter had to be cleared away.

"They are usually paid a percentage of the gross output—"

"—and are therefore disinclined to exercise forethought in social or economic matters," Sauvage finished for Deke.

Jameson ambled over to the desk to whisper into the younger man's ear. "If you catch onto all this business so damn fast, what the hell you doing playing the pirate?"

Jonathan came eye to eye with the overseer. "You should know by now why, Jameson—to catch my brother's murderer, which I fully intend to do."

This new plantation owner shouldered Jameson aside, growling, "Now let's get to work and get this mess cleared out of here. I grow sick and tired of looking at it!"

Jameson nodded, having decided that Adam was doing very well as Jonathan. He was even beginning to sound like that one. "Yes, *sir*, Master *Jonathan*!"

A week later Jonathan Sauvage was going strong. The successful conduct of a plantation required much knowledge—knowledge that ranged from the best type of oak for rum casks to the best treatment for each slave, and for those of each race. Sauvage had put his nose to the grindstone and was learning fast.

Many changes, in fact, were taking place on Sauvage Plantation. As Jonathan stood looking out the window, he saw one of them outside, just returning from the garden with fresh vegetables cradled in her crisp white apron. When Cathelen O'Ruark looked up and saw the plantation owner watching her, she rushed into her kitchen through the back door.

Turning back to his desk, Jonathan breathed deeply, as if taking her sweet and delicate fragrance into his flaring nostrils. He said to himself, "Yes, the little mermaid is filling out quite nicely." Then he sat, daydreaming, his loins growing warm.

Jonathan tossed his dusty booted feet onto the corner of the desk, and leaned far back in his leather chair. Yes, indeed, Hondo was right. It was about time he sought some pleasure between a pair of lily white thighs. Why not? Cathelen O'Ruark was not some fancy lady he must woo to win for a night, but neither was she a waterfront trull. She was at a tender age, but she must have had plenty of opportunities to become deflowered on that long voyage aboard the slave ship.

He laughed. *"She is now my slave,"* Jonathan whispered to himself, knowing she would come to the master willingly—at one look of hot desire from him. For Jonathan knew she could not have been down in that ship's hold with all those bonded men and on that ship full of randy mates and come out a virgin. It was unheard of!

However, he would have to be careful with his own emotions, for he had no desire to be getting serious with any woman. All he needed was a little free sport. And the blonde appealed to him more than the dark-haired Mattissa.

Jonathan Sauvage smiled, amused. Look at me, the Sea Wolf, planning to seduce a silly little servant girl. His mates would roar to the skies!

Chapter Eleven

Clad in her simple calico dress and cradling a peck of vegetables in her apron, Cathelen made her way to the kitchen. Carefully positioning her lumpy apron on the work table, she slid the raw fare onto the cutting space.

"That is done."

She wearily drew an arm across her forehead, grateful that she was slowly getting accustomed to all her tasks. But the heat, that was sometimes unbearable.

Dirt from the garden covered her white apron and some also smudged the skirt of her new calico dress. This dress that she had been allowed to choose from the "secret room" had been nearly ruined due to her daily chores.

Today she wore a pink-and-orange calico that had been given to her by Mairi. Where the old woman had obtained it was a mystery Mairi did not intend to reveal. It was an old dress, but serviceable. Mairi had smiled almost apologetically, saying it was all she had in Cathelen's size. If the woman liked to hoard things in her room, let her. That was none of Cathelen's concern anyway. She only wished that her trunk had not been stolen—so Captain Trask had said.

Cathelen had no time for further musings, for Mattissa burst into the kitchen just then, her back up like an untamed cat's.

"You are late in making dinner for Master Jonathan!" Mattissa hissed each word. "Why have you been so slow?"

Cathelen squared her slim shoulders and faced the woman with the large, expressive eyes. She had seen Mattissa watch the master as he left the house. Tenderness had melted the severity of her eyes. But those fine, dark eyes could flash with animation and anger as they did now.

"I did not take my time, Mattissa, it just took longer than usual," Cathelen said firmly. "It was hot in the garden and the new okra was hard to find."

Mattissa exploded. "You should weed the garden!" Her white face took on unusual spots of deep crimson. "I have never seen someone slow like you, wh—"

Cathelen swished her skirts as she came to stand at the edge of the table, holding a hand up.

99

She had interrupted the raging woman by pursing her lips and surging forward. "Please. Do not call me 'white woman' again. I know what I am, you need not remind me. And, Mattissa, my name is Cathelen."

"I know your name. But you are white!" Mattissa spat.

Cathelen gritted her small teeth and exploded herself, "So are you!"

"I am musteefino—"

"—and you are jealous because you are not all white. That is, your blood is colored, Mattissa," Cathelen taunted, knowing she was right. She could not stand for much more of Mattissa's constant exercise of tyranny.

Mattissa appeared about to choke, and Cathelen knew she had discovered Mattissa's sore spot. She had heard the woman's slow, singsong voice as she spoke in the hall with Master Jonathan about household affairs.

Cathelen was putting two and two together finally. She guessed that Mattissa wanted Jonathan Sauvage. But surely the woman knew that the plantation lord could not marry her, for the very idea of marriage to a woman with black blood, even a little, was shocking. Mairi had filled her in on that much. Cathelen was going to bring the ailing Mairi a tray in her room later, and she decided now to learn about that situation. What else was there to do to keep from dying of weary boredom? Cathelen asked herself.

After tossing Cathelen a look of pure loathing, Mattissa swept regally out the kitchen door. A moment later Cathelen heard Mattissa complaining to Jonathan Sauvage. She could hear his low answers, but Cathelen shut her ears to the conversation in the hall and hurriedly bent to her task of preparing dinner so the master would not find cause to dismiss her to the fields. As she worked, Cathelen sighed, wondering if field work would be better than trying to endure Mattissa's constant hostility and harassment.

Every day, Cathelen gathered, prepared, and served the dinner to Master Sauvage and a man she had heard called Hondo. This small, wiry man was Jonathan's manservant and constant companion, she knew, and he always had a pleasant smile for her though he said very little when he was around. He made her feel at ease, but not so with Jonathan Sauvage. The plantation owner's infrequent looks gave her butterflies and gooseflesh. Though Cathelen could not fathom why.

She had prepared the typical West Indian fare of black crab pepper pot, along with okra, sweet herbs, and early summer vegetables. She had also made a mixed salad of cucumber, beetroot, and onion. Now, the meal at its end, Jonathan sat with Hondo and sipped sweet brown Madeira, the master's usual after-dinner drink.

101

"You are a very good cook, Cathelen O'-Ruark."

Jonathan said this to her as she was clearing some of the dishes away to make room for dessert. "Thank you, sir," Cathelen returned, quelling her urge to blush this time. He had been studying her more intensely this evening, and she wondered what was on his mind.

Jonathan leaned back in his chair, tossing Hondo a wink that Cathelen missed. "No dessert for me tonight, Miss O'Ruark. How about you, Hondo?"

"Hmm, ah, sure. What is it, missy?" Hondo asked politely.

A bullfrog gurgled from the pond out back. Hearing it Cathelen longed to be finished with her work so she could step outside before her bath. She enjoyed her nightly strolls in the garden, with no one to bother her.

"I am sorry," Cathelen said belatedly. "I was listening to the tree frogs and crickets make music and—"

Jonathan interrupted her as he snorted softly in low laughter and exchanged a mysterious smile with Hondo. "So, the little mermaid is also a nature lover. How interesting, wouldn't you say, Hondo?"

"I—"

Cathelen cut off what she had been about to say. Obviously he had been speaking to Hondo, but she had not realized this until he spoke the older man's name. She turned her back on the

102

table to hide her embarrassment, pretending to arrange dishes on the tray. The master had been making fun of her. He is a strange one, she thought all of a sudden. He dines with the odd scar-faced little man who is supposed to be a servant and they sit together speaking in low tones while watching me move in and out of the room. They look like two birds of the same feather—hawks. This master of Sauvage Plantation comports himself at times not like a dandy lord but an outright rogue! Cathelen wondered why the mask of propriety was lowered from Sauvage's face at night. Why was he such a different person when other planters came to call during the day? He puzzled her, and somehow this bothered her very much.

"Miss O'Ruark, you did not say what is for dessert? Is it soursop custard again?"

When Cathelen turned about to give her answer she caught his gaze just lifting from her skirts to her flushed face. Now her color turned from a delicate flush to a deep red. The two at the table watched the change and grinned as if they shared a private joke.

"Devil be damned!" Cathelen swore, too angry to realize her blunder, and she went on, "What do you men find so amusing that you both have to grin like monkeys swinging from a tree?"

"Heh, heh, you have seen our little backyard friends?" Hondo said, breaking some of the tension in the room.

But Cathelen, now gasping over what she had dared retort, clamped a hand over her mouth before more sound emerged. She had gone too far, she saw, for Jonathan was not smiling any longer. He sat there with a cold expression on his face. Indeed he looked almost shocked by her outburst.

"Uh, I think I'll be goin' back to my cabin now." Hondo stood up, excusing himself. "See you later, gov'ner, ah, Miss O'Ruark."

Slowly, Cathelen began to edge toward the door. "I will take these things to the kitchen now, if you do not mind," she said, surprised to find her voice steady.

The chair scraped loudly as Master Sauvage stood. Cathelen took in his ominous countenance and shuddered inwardly. What was he going to do? she wondered. Would he have her whipped for talking back to him and his friend? He looked like a man who was not used to being defied. He did not look happy now, either. Would he do the whipping himself?

"Blow me down," Sauvage breathed to himself, thinking, the girl has spunk. Out loud, he said, "Bring me my dessert upstairs in a little while, Miss O'Ruark."

"But you said you did not want dessert."

"I do now."

She had taken a few more steps backward and now saw that the black breeches he wore were awfully close fitting. Like the skin of a plum, Cathelen thought to herself. Oh Lord, those butterflies started again in her stomach. He was enjoying himself hugely, at her expense, for a lazy grin split his devastatingly handsome face.

Then her eyes flew to his hands, and she sucked in a short gasp. Why had she never noticed this before? All the while he had been dining he must have kept his hands on his lap when she served the meal. His hands were encased in slim black gloves. She dragged her eyes away from them in time to see his lips move again.

"The dessert, my dear. In my room."

Cathelen found that her legs were both shivering badly, her kneecaps dancing up and down in apprehension of what he planned to do to her. She gulped, still standing where she was holding the loaded tray. She had been unaware he had vacated the room, until now.

"He is gone." She breathed the words in relief.

But Cathelen had been deeply aware of the musky maleness of Jonathan Sauvage as she'd stood serving him at the long table. He took her breath away. Even so, she'd desired very much to swift-kick him in his plum-taut shins when he'd made sport of her. Tonight had been the worst occasion. She was beginning to think that the man was quite a rogue.

The weight of the tray in her arms was beginning to make her shake, and so Cathelen shook off the dust and hurried back to fetch the custard for Jonathan Sauvage. She prayed that the man was not going to punish her too severely. She had a feeling this was the reason he wanted her to serve him the dessert. But she would make him change his mind if he meant to beat her. She just had to.

Chapter Twelve

The nightlong piping of the tiny tree frogs enticed Cathelen outside, but she realized her walk would have to wait. She had finished clearing the table, and in the middle of straightening the kitchen, she sat down to have a bite to eat and a small glass of lemon and water.

Suddenly she shot up, going to fetch the soursop custard. She had tarried too long in the kitchen and that man, she knew, would brook no waiting.

Keeping her eyes on the tray she carried, Cathelen made her cautious way up the stairs to his room. She straightened slowly to settle the tray of lemon water and custard on her hip and then she knocked on the high, wide portal.

"The door is open." His deep reply came to her.

Hesitating, then very slowly pushing the door wider, Cathelen peered around to see where the master was. She saw him, seated at an oak desk, a smaller version of the one in his study, and he appeared busy with some papers. Even in the dim light of the two small lamps, one on the nightstand, the other on the desk, Cathelen could not mistake that male form.

"Shut the door, Cathelen."

About to balance the tray on her hip and close the door, Cathelen jumped and cried out when an ear-splitting shriek rent the silence of the room.

Squaaawk!

"Oh!"

Cathelen's tray went flying, and though Jonathan had turned at the same moment the parrot squawked, he did not reach her in time to rescue the tray. He stood before her now. What he had planned fled from his mind when he took in the shimmering, tremulous light in her eyes.

"You aren't going to cry, I hope?"

When she said nothing, Jonathan pulled her into his room and closed the door. He kept her hand in his, mainly because it felt so good to touch her. But his heart began to pound strangely when she peered up at him in apprehension.

"I am sorry," she mumbled softly, her frightened eyes falling to the mess on the colorful carpet. "I should have been more careful."

Gently, surprising her, he smoothed back a snowy tendril that had escaped the heavy bun at the nape of her neck. "I'll not hurt you, Cathy. What did you think I would do—whip you because Sinbad caused you to spill the tray?"

She stared up at him, breathless and fascinated, noting the tiny yellow flames in his dark eyes. "Sinbad?" she said, having forgotten the loud, nerve-shattering screech.

His hands went up to her shoulders to turn her gently around to face a scarlet macaw. Then he quietly informed her, "This is Sinbad."

"Why is he chained to the stand?" Cathelen asked Jonathan who stood immediately at her side. She held out her hand to the macaw just as he was answering her.

"Because he—" Jonathan never finished.

When her hand was snatched up by his, she gasped. "What is it? What did I do?"

Jonathan released a warm breath of relief. "I should have warned you, Cathy. Sinbad is not used to you. He can take off a finger, you see."

"He does not appear to be mean."

Sinbad's beady eyes rolled as he cocked his red head at the young woman and blurted in a scratchy voice, "Hell's blisters! Ho! Satan blister me—what a girl!" Then he pealed off into laughter.

Jonathan stepped up to the macaw to clamp a hand over the large head and powerful bill. "Perky little devil today aren't you," he stated casually, reaching over to a huge bowl of tropical fruits. "Here"—he sliced off a section of tangerine with a hastily secured knife—"a goody to silence your big mouth."

"Where did Sinbad learn such language?" She shivered for a moment before she continued. "He sounds like a pirate." She laughed then, adding, "He even looks like one."

Jonathan did not look at her now. "Originally Sinbad belonged to a sailor who had a vocabulary too salty for polite society, as you've already witnessed. He should be quiet for a time now." He scratched the macaw's head and Sinbad blinked affectionately.

"It seems you have had him for a long time," she remarked, wondering why she had not heard Sinbad's loud squawks before this. Surely the noise could be heard right through the door.

But Cathelen was delighted. The scarlet macaw was the most colorful bird she had ever seen, besides being the largest. The parrot's vocabulary was not new to her, not to a girl with a sea-roving brother who always came home with more salty phrases. For a moment Cathelen wondered what had become of Michal.

Jonathan moved away from Sinbad, but Cathelen continued to smile and study the bird. He was carrying a slice of tangerine to his mouth, and she laughed, finding the macaw very amusing and interesting to watch.

What she did not realize was that a pair of warm brown eyes sought the shell pink curve of her mouth. Then that gaze fixed on the delicate column of her neck before traveling down her slim figure to check every gentle line of her young body. He stirred. He was starved, for he had waited too long to take a woman.

"Cathy . . ."

Still smiling happily, Cathelen turned to face Jonathan Sauvage. The joy drained from her eyes and then her mouth, as if she were a lovely all-white statue melting in the sun.

"You called me Cathy again," she said. "Why?" Only one—no, two—other persons had called her that. Michal and, at times, Dany.

"Do you mind?" he countered her question.

"No. I suppose not."

"Why, Cathy, you're trembling." He looked down into her violet eyes that now ran to deep heliotrope. "Relax, I am not a hungry wolf that devours little doves." He smiled at what he had just inadvertently said about himself. He had lied a bit, too, for he was a very hungry man.

Suddenly the leaping flames left his eyes to be replaced by a dark opaque brown. "A woman who cusses like you did this evening, missy, must be learned in other baser talents usually reserved only for barmaids or waterfront trulls."

"T-trulls? What are they?" Her mind whirled at his harsh words, even as she wondered how she had angered him this time.

"Oh, come now." He laughed shortly. "You must know that a trull is a whore, not much classier than a barmaid." He winked wolfishly. "But much more of a pleasure when it comes right down to business."

"Monkey business," Cathelen dared to whisper. She looked down at his hands then, the moment saved as she remembered something of import. His hands, they were without the black gloves.

Quickly Jonathan noticed her perusal and strode at once to the desk. There, with his long, symmetrical back to her, he slipped on the gloves he had forgotten. When that was done he returned to her.

"Why do you wear them?" she asked, inclining her head.

"I have a—" He shrugged. "It doesn't matter. My hands are warmer this way at night."

Cathelen caught the glint of something in his eyes, an emotion unknown to her. "But you wore them—" She thought better of what she had been about to say and let it drop. Her own shrug said "Never mind."

He went quite still. Nervously Cathelen stared about the room, noting that the floor-length windows opened to the sea. From below, it was harder to see the water and the tall rocks. Night had arrived suddenly, following the glory of a red and purple sky. The moon had risen, and even from where she stood across from the window, Cathelen could see the waters were alive with specks of tropical phosphorescence that glowed like strings of pearls out there in the profound blue darkness.

"It is so beautiful out there," she murmured, almost to herself. "I love to walk outside on nights when the moon rides high, following the path that overlooks the rocks."

"Yes . . . beautiful," Jonathan agreed, his tone deep and cryptic.

Cathelen started as his words penetrated her consciousness and she realized his back was toward the windows. She was beginning to understand now, for she was not all that naive.

His restraint was drawing close to its limits. One glimpse at his bed and Jonathan began to perspire. What had begun as a plan for a gentle seduction was now changing as she continued to play the innocent. He could play her game a little longer . . . maybe . . . or trap her beneath the canopy of his huge bed where no one could hear her. . . .

Jonathan's leather-encased fingers moved to tilt her chin up. She felt the heat of him through the leather. It seared her tender flesh. What was he going to do now? Her face turned ashen, for she knew he wanted something of her. Yet, if he wanted his pleasure, she did not know the first thing to do. Besides, it was wrong. She had not been purchased for the man's sport. Rape was the only way he could ever have her, and then not totally.

"Cathy, would you . . . ?"

She licked her lips once, quickly. Her mind was busy, whirling, as she searched for something to say, words that would change his mind, peacefully. But she could not think of a single thing to say. Finally, she had to know—to get it over with.

"Yes . . . sir? What is it you wish?"

"Ah . . . would you?"

His retroussé nose flared as he tugged his upper lip with beautiful white teeth, teeth that flashed whenever he happened to smile.

"Would I what, Jonathan?"

He cleared his throat noisily. ". . . Clean this mess off the floor."

It was an order, not a plea.

Her slim shoulders sagged with relief, telling her that she had held them rigid in suspense. "Anything else?" she said without thinking.

Again the tension. He turned once while she stood waiting at the door, her eyes widened into enormous pools of deep lavender that made her small face seem even smaller. Breathless, she watched him raise an eyebrow.

Then Jonathan shook his head, slowly, reluctantly dragging his gaze from the slim face with the delicately high cheekbones.

"Yes, Cathy, I want something else. Bring me another dish of custard."

Chapter Thirteen

With agonizing slowness the days dragged by for Cathelen. Jonathan Sauvage had been away from the plantation longer than expected. The third week of his absence was beginning. Cathelen would never have believed it if someone had told her she would miss the man. But miss him she did.

She spent her mornings in the kitchen cooking and then cleaning up. But most of the food was consumed by Mattissa, Hondo, and Mairi. The old woman ate like a bear and hardly left her bed anymore except to tutor Cathelen in the preparation of Jonathan's favorite dishes.

Cathelen had learned, also from Mairi, that with the exception of crop time, the work on the plantation was unvaried and uninteresting.

Cane almost grew itself. If Jonathan were here, there would be little for him to do except to ride around his estate and supervise the discipline of his slaves. Deke Jameson saw to this task mostly, and to the digging of ditches and the weeding of the fields by planter's slaves and indentured Scottish servants. When crop time came, Mairi had informed Cathelen, there would be a wave of intense concentration in the heat of the mills. Cathelen could hardly wait to see the operation of extracting the juice from the stalks. That is, if Master Sauvage would allow her to go along and watch.

This morning Cathelen was standing out on the back veranda trying to cool herself with a palmetto fan after the intense heat of the kitchen. She could feel the northeast trade winds now, see them urge white-capped waves against the land. The day before, the trades had piled the sand high on the beach, bending trees inland and burning the coarse grass in the nearby fields with salt spray. Later she would go for a walk on the beach, maybe when the sky darkened.

She breathed deeply, her dreaming eyes taking in the delightful cascades of yellow cassia and golden logwood in the backyard. Her flesh again began to tingle with that unknown sensation, feelings she had only begun to experience. Her dreams were different, too. The faceless man who always turned from her had taken her in his arms and held her close, his warm lips brushing against her forehead. Still,

116

she had not been able to make out his countenance. But she had been awakened sharply, by little shocks running down her back when his lips had touched hers, and the sensation had made her feel as if he were right there with her. She had been lonely after that, wanting her dream to return. But it never did. Only when her mind least dwelled on him, during the day, did he come to her in the dream.

Cathelen smiled now, hoping Jonathan Sauvage would be proud of her, for she had learned how to clean fish and fowl, to fry plantains, roast breadfruit, and boil rice. The last skill she had had to work at, but finally, she had prepared the rice to fluffy perfection. When she'd accompanied Deke Jameson to town, she had also learned, with his assistance, how to buy and bargain at the market place.

Stepping into the back hall, Cathelen heard Mairi calling out for her. Taking a right Cathelen entered the old woman's gloomy domain. The curtains were again drawn closed, so it was hard to see after being out in the brightness.

"Mairi?" Cathelen said, searching the room with blinking eyes. "Oh, there you are."

"Did ye not hear the knocker, child?" Mairi asked from the depths of her saggy-cushioned chair next to the bed. "Hurry with you now—someone's near breakin' down the door!"

Cathelen paused, listening. "Yes, I hear it now. Mairi, I will return after seeing who it could be. Would you like some boiled rice and fruits then?''

"Och! Yes, yes! Get along with ye now, girl. Can't keep whoever it 'tis there waitin' all day!'' She grumbled on as Cathelen whirled and left the hall in haste. "Where the devil could those feather-brained maids be at this time of day? How many are there now? And that Mattissa, never around when she's needed. The slut, she'll sure 'sweet-up' when master Jonathan comes home!''

Alone in her room, Mairi's faded blue eyes narrowed as she thought of Master Jonathan. There was something different about the grown lad of late—that is, when he was around and not the absentee planter. He had been up to no good, Mairi's old bones told her, just like the younger pup, Adam. Adam's passing had been an unusual event. No one spoke of it much. Jonathan, coming and going all the time. Ahhh, Mairi thought as she stroked her chin where two white hairs stuck out of a brown mole, I think I be knowin' what that handsome lad is about. Who would be the next one to catch on to the lad's shenanigans? Mairi nodded her white head then, knowing the answer already.

Sweeping the door wide as soon as she reached it, Cathelen was not prepared for the sight that greeted her, the sharply handsome profile of a man who was just stepping from the veranda as he heard the door opening. Cathelen already had a strong impression of this man before he turned fully about to see her standing there. Delightful surprise was written on his

118

face—before his look changed to one Cathelen had never seen before. Perhaps, though, there had been a touch of this emotion on Master Jonathan's face the night she had been trapped in his room. But she could not be sure.

This man reminded Cathelen of a hawk. A black hawk, with dangerous talons.

"So. Who might you be, little dove?"

Her silence led Vance Moore to think she, whoever she might be, was possibly a deaf mute. Yet a very very lovely one. She must be a new housemaid. He stared rudely.

But Master Moore of Sugartree did not know why Cathelen stood there staring, staring as if she had never looked upon a man before. But Cathelen knew why. This man was by far the most wicked-looking human being she had ever laid eyes upon. He was handsome, yes, in a frightening sort of way. He had black hair and green eyes. Narrowed slits of green evil.

"Are you going to quit gaping and answer me?" Vance Moore whipped out with a lashing tongue. "Or can you not speak? If you are dumb, but can understand *me*, nod your pretty head."

Her dainty chin hoisted in the air, Cathelen said, as clear as a bell, "My name is Cathelen Elaine O'Ruark—and who might you be, *sir*?"

Moore stared as if this stirringly lovely young blonde had grown two beastly heads. Actually, he found himself suddenly in quite a rage at knowing the dunce Decatur had allowed this one to slip by his fingers. *The idiot!*

"I am Vance Moore—from over at Sugartree," he growled ominously, taking a pinch of snuff from a jeweled snuff box and bringing it to his aquiline nose. He sniffed loudly, causing Cathelen's eyes to widen.

"Sir," she said firmly, "if you are looking for master Jonathan, I am afraid he has not yet returned from a—" She paused, not really knowing where he had gone off to; then she tallied up. "He has been absent going on three weeks now."

"Has he seen you yet?"

"Why, what kind of question is that? Of course he has. Why do you ask?"

"Just curious." He snapped the lid on the little box shut and flashed her a green glare from his hot emerald eyes.

He was not very tall and Cathelen knew if she stood on tiptoe she could stare him straight in the eye. But for now she dropped her gaze to the whip coiled at his side, one he was stroking against his hip. When her eyes returned to his face, Cathelen caught the twisted sneer he was wiping from his lips.

"I'll not step in for refreshment at this time—perhaps tomorrow," he said in a sneering voice.

"I am not sure," Cathelen said shakily, "that Master Sauvage will have returned by then."

"So?" He lifted a black-winged eyebrow. "I shall still stop for a cool drink. At noon. Have it ready for me—uh—*Cathelen*," he said her name intimately.

Cathelen cringed from intense dislike as she

watched him go to his carriage. It was black, as were his horses and his attire, right down to his knee-high boots.

Shutting the door to block him from view, Cathelen pressed her back to the wood, believing she had just met the very devil himself.

Chapter Fourteen

Breasts, snowy little mounds that were tipped a shellrose, the same delicate tint as her lips, stood out firmly as Cathelen changed into the sprigged, pale yellow calico. She smiled warmly. Dear old Mairi had stitched the dress for her a week ago, and tonight, for some reason, she wanted to wear it.

Cathelen studied herself in the wavy piece of mirror, propped against the wall, on her dresser. Her face was strangely aglow. Haunting, violet-blue eyes stared back at her.

"What is wrong with you?" she asked the reflection in the mirror. "Why is this night so different that you should feel that familiar stirring?" She was *awake*, so how could this be? Only in her dreams had she experienced these bewildering, strange sensations that were rippling over her.

Shrugging and heaving a sigh, Cathelen turned from the mirror and stepped from her room.

Soft moonlight silvered the grounds out back and the path she walked along looked like gray velvet. Her soft, shining, clean, platinum blond hair stirred against her neck. She had let it hang loose to her hips.

She came to the big, wooden gate at the end of the path. From here she could hear the gently tossing surf and could make out the huge rocks standing in it. Dreamily she sighed, enjoying this delicious freedom. She would not think of tomorrow when that devil Vance Moore might come to visit. Tonight was hers.

With a grating squeak, the gate opened and closed beneath her hand. Slowly, wraithlike, she moved toward the wild, grassy ledge until she stood high above the rocky shore. From here she commanded a sweeping view of the coastline. She felt the constant breezes thread her silvery hair. It was wonderful. She could stand here forever, letting the wind caress her while she dreamed.

Lifting the mass of hair from her warm, moist neck and thrusting her chest high, she lifted her face to the stars and moon, the shining heavens. Cathelen closed her eyes in the ecstasy of the moment. She felt pure and golden. Then, a sound like footfalls swishing through the grass made her freeze.

Undulating waves of blond hair fell, brushing the gentle swell of her buttocks as Cathelen lowered her slim arms and turned about slowly.

Fear racing along her spine, Cathelen looked toward the tangle of dense, black brush. Suddenly she knew for certain she was not alone.

A shadow finally detached itself from the tall brush, and she saw a silent figure standing there. A scream collected in her throat but would not emerge. As in a nightmare, Cathelen found that her legs would not budge.

Transfixed, man and woman stared at each other. But the man gazed from one eye only, for the other was covered with a black patch.

Terror seized Cathelen. The man was a pirate. A *pirate*! She opened her mouth wider to scream, but he jumped forward to cover her cry of terror with a large hand.

She looked downward. He was wearing a loose white shirt with wide sleeves that billowed in the soft breeze. A basket-hilt sword, a most dangerous weapon once favored by pirates but outmoded for the last quarter of the century, dangled at his side. Her eyes leapt to his face and her fear grew tenfold when she took in the disfiguring scar that slashed one side of his face.

The fierce-looking buccaneer spoke. "Forgive me, fair lady. Seeing you standing there surprised the"—he chuckled then—"surprised me right out of my boots."

She dropped her horror-filled eyes to see, indeed, that he was carrying a pair of wide-topped boots of well-worn leather.

She could not utter a word. A strange sensation was coiling steadily through her limbs. Her skin was dewed all over with a faint film of sudden perspiration, and her eyes were luminous in the semidarkness.

"Aye, but you are a fair one." He gave her a long look. "I apologize once again." He began to lower his hand. "You will not scream?" He watched her now, his eyes unblinking. Then he chuckled low and smiled.

Her lashes nervously fluttered as Cathelen watched him transfer the boots he carried to his other hand. "Are you perhaps running from someone?" she asked, surprising herself with her unusual calmness.

"Aye," he drawled. "And are you afraid, milady?"

"If you are a pirate—yes."

"Buccaneer. There is a marked difference. You see, a pirate—" he broke off, looking thoughtful. "You . . . could say, milady, that I have turned 'pirate.' Aye, that you could, because of the—ah—Excuse me, but it is really a dark secret. It certainly would bore you."

"Are you a pirate captain?" she asked, stalling for the time when she could catch him off guard and make a dash for the house.

"I—" He shrugged. "If that were so I would be commanding my ship at the moment, don't you think?"

"I really do not know." She pointed to the boots. "Where were you going just now?"

"To meet my ship." He splayed a hand in the air. "Out there—somewhere."

"Barefoot?"

He grinned, his teeth contrasting with his sea-brown face. "My feet hurt."

"You were walking toward the house, Sir—Pirate. Do you know that you are on the Sauvage Plantation?"

"Ah. No, milady." He shook his head. "Is there someone I should be afeared of then?"

"There is. And he is not far away at the moment. In fact, he most likely has a barrel trained on you."

The pirate groaned. "Ah, no, a gun you say?" He shook his head. "Who might this dangerous fellow be, milady?"

"His name is Deke Jameson." She took a step backward. "I—I think you had better go now before he finds you speaking with me."

For a moment Cathelen thought the pirate looked about ready to take flight. But to her consternation, he began to stroke his chin as if debating with himself over a matter. Fear coursed through her then as the boots he held slipped to the ground and he stepped closer.

"Are you the lady of the house, if you do not mind my asking?" he inquired.

"No."

"What then?"

"I—I cook." She shrugged. "I . . . really don't see where it is any of your business, Sir Pirate."

"A mere servant?" He shook his head. "Incredible." His large hands opened and

126

closed rhythmically.

He tilted her quivering chin. "Aye, but you are a lovely morsel. Are you real? You are like an enchanting white phantom—or perhaps a shimmery mermaid risen from the sea." He stroked her cheek with a long finger she could not see in the velvet gray shadows her long hair created. "Could I have your name? Then I will let you go. I want to remember you—forever."

"C-Cathelen."

She waited with bated breath for him to step away from her. But he did not move a muscle. He just stared, with the one glittering eye. "You promised to release me," she said shakily, wondering at the liquid fire running through her limbs. What she did not realize at the moment was that he was not holding her against her will—she just felt he was.

"Did I?" His voice was a deep murmur.

"You said you would let me go if I gave my name. Will you, please?" she begged, afraid of what this lean marauder was doing to her emotions. "Oh, no," she breathed raggedly. That feeling, the one in her dreams, was coming over her. He could not be . . . *him*.

Cathelen tried to see the pirate better, but she could not make out his features clearly. His hair was dark, that she knew. He was well over six feet tall and a most remarkable sight, despite the disfiguring slash across one cheek. One thing was odd: This pirate wore no beard.

"I will give you a warning, fair lady."

"A warning? As to what?"

127

"That I am going to kiss you."

"How dare you?" Cathelen confronted him, at the same time stepping backward.

He laughed, following her, his eye gleaming.

"Why do you laugh?"

"Because you are so beautiful and vulnerable."

He came against her then, and Cathelen felt as though she were being thrust up against a rock. He muffled her cry with what was Cathelen's first kiss ever. Delicious shocks of pleasure seemed to be coming from his lips, and causing pulsating sensations in her breasts, her belly and, finally, between her thighs.

Like ripe little peaches, her breasts rose tautly against the firm, muscled wall of his chest. He snatched her even closer, pressing her to him, but her hard breasts remained unflattened, although they began to ache with a bittersweet torment. Now, unable to bear what he was doing to her inside and out, Cathelen wrenched her mouth away.

"Please—no more!"

But he was not about to release her just like that. "I want to lay down with you, sweet Cathelen."

Before she knew what he was doing, he had easily pressed her to the grass, his mouth returning at once to her tender pink lips. They were beginning to ache, too, and the inside of her mouth was being so plundered by his tongue that she feared she would soon cease to breathe.

"Oh," she began, "do not do this to me. I have never had a man before and"—she licked her lips nervously—"please do not rape me, Sir—" Her mouth was again covered, cutting off the rest of her frantic plea.

Then he lifted his well-shaped head. "I'll not rape you, puss. Promise . . ."

Even as he said this, he began to work at her tidy bodice. He smiled down at her winningly.

"Oh!" She beat at his chest with tight little fists. "Your promises are worthless, Sir Pirate!"

She brushed his hand aside, but effortlessly, his fingers were again on her flesh. Swiftly then, one hand miraculously cupped a bared dove, and he kissed its sensitive peak, which rose as his lips came away. Cathelen was pleasured by that one little thing, but then he shocked her when he began to pry her thighs apart with a knee.

"No! What do you think you are doing?" she demanded.

Nuzzling her neck, her cheek, her chin, then her ear, the pirate was all over her with his lips, his knee, his hands. Cathelen was beginning to think he had more appendages than an octopus. Also, his movements were executed with lightning speed. Before she knew it, the wickedly handsome pirate began a sensuous rhythm between her quaking thighs. Over her skirts, through the material, his swelled manhood ground against her golden triangle, and Cathelen could feel herself begin to bud and blossom.

She was mortified!

A deep, guttural sound emerged from him then, bringing Cathelen back to sanity. "Stop it! Stop it I say! You blasted pirate."

At once he lifted himself, as if by great effort. Cathelen felt his heat leave her and she almost wished him back. Humiliated beyond measure, she sat up, feeling all her bruised parts. But her worst injury was to her dignity. Actually, she was quite lucky to have come out of this without having been deflowered. She had a great desire now to call him every swearword Michal had unwittingly taught her.

She looked over to where he was lying, stretched full length on his back, looking up at the stars. He was breathing very hard and beads of perspiration dotted his upper lip. He was quite handsome, Cathelen reluctantly decided. He almost reminded her of—No, Jonathan's face was without a mark and his hair was shorter.

Suddenly the pirate whirled on her, grinding out a question, "Do you know what you have done to me?"

Without waiting for her to answer, he came to his feet in one swift movement.

Cathelen scrambled back, her elbows scraping against the ground where there was no grass. She peered up at him, afraid of this pirate's wrath.

"N-no!" she finally blurted. "I should ask you the same!"

He snatched up his boots, snarling down at

130

her, "I've yet to get you from my blood, fair lady."

"I did not know I was in it!" she dared retaliate.

"You are now. But, beware, Cathelen, of walking out alone from now on. Next time I will finish what began between us!"

Chapter Fifteen

Chin in hand, Cathelen sat staring out the kitchen window, slim ankles crossed beneath her skirts. She leaned forward and her heart was beating hard and fast.

In her castle in the air, Cathelen was reflecting on the previous night, on the pirate. . . .

"Cathelen, dearie."

Startled by the old woman, Cathelen stiffened her spine to whirl about and face Mairi. It was a moment before her violet eyes could erase the erotic moonlit scene and focus on this intruder.

"Mairi. I did not hear you come in. How are you? I hope you are feeling better today?"

Mairi stuck her witchlike chin forward. "Eh?

Ye already looked in on me this morn. What you in, lassie, a cloud?"

Cathelen rose to come around the table and smile at Mairi. "Is there something I can fix for you?"

Mairi, waggling a hand and shaking her head, said, "I am fine, child. I be fixin' meself a bite. It's the master who be wantin' you, not me."

Cathelen's eyes flew wide. "Jonathan? He is home?"

"I'm so happy ye think of the plantation as your home now, dearie. Sure, he's home again. But not for long, I'd wager. He's one among many of them absentee planters." She shook her head, peering round the kitchen for goodies.

"Is—is he angry?"

"Of course!" Mairi blasted out. "Why you think I be fetchin' ye?"

Brushing by a trancelike Cathelen, Mairi did as she had said she would. She piled an assortment of fruits in her huge apron, winked at Cathelen and made her way to her private domain.

Still, Cathelen had not moved from the spot. Her smile grew, stretching her mouth into delightful dimples that peeped out. Now that Jonathan had returned, so had Sinbad. Again she wondered why Jonathan had not left Sinbad behind. It would have been a great entertainment for her to have been able to look after the scarlet macaw.

"Finally!" Cathelen exclaimed, smacking her palms together as she set out to make Jonathan a perfect breakfast. She hummed as she worked. For some reason she could not explain even to herself, Cathelen had come to adore Jonathan Sauvage, even his roguish ways. She had missed him and he was in her thoughts each and every day.

Cathelen suddenly stopped her preparations. "Am I in love with Jonathan?" she whispered solemnly to herself. Could he ever come to care for her, even just a little? Oh, this was absurd! She was only a servant. Besides she did not want to become a wife, for then she would lose her virginity. Just as she almost had the night before when the pirate had intruded on her. Before he had come up on her, she had felt pure and golden. And she desired very much to remain that way. Her father had often said she should have become a nun. She might have, but she did not believe in the cloistered life. Besides, her mother had not been of the faith, nor had Cathelen wanted to be. She put her faith in only God, purely and simply, not in the ritual of religion as her pious neighbors had in Edinburgh. On their way to church, how they had stuck their noses up at her!

The coltish length of her legs moved quicker now under the soft lilac cotton skirt and white apron as Cathelen hurried to complete breakfast and serve her handsome planter lord.·

134

Cathelen pulled herself up short upon entering the dining room, the tray tilting precariously. That devil Vance Moore sat there, on his face a look of pure arrogance and a domineering sneer. But it was Jonathan Sauvage himself who took her by surprise, took her breath away too, and made her stare, awed. His face, lean beneath long sable brown hair that hung nearly to his shoulders, was baked by what she determined to be long exposure. He was a rich shade of burnished tigerwood. He was attired in tight-fitting breeches and an embroidered brown waistcoat. He wore a simple cravat of muslin at his dark throat.

Thick black lashes hovered over those brown eyes flecked with golden glints. "Cathelen"—he spoke deeply and melodiously—"come and serve us. We've company. Vance Moore from—"

"I know him," she said too speedily.

"You do?"

"Yes," Cathelen went on, feeling warm all over, "we met briefly, yesterday." She tried not to look at that one.

Jonathan scowled. "Is this true?" he asked Vance Moore.

"Of course, Jonathan." Vance shrugged. "Why would I have asked you about—uh—that matter. She answered the door yesterday. Very charming, I must say. So, what do you think? Will you accept my offer?"

Cathelen began to serve, but she kept her ears open to the conversation. As if knowing this,

Jonathan leaned closer to the black-haired Moore and spoke in low tones, his words inaudible to Cathelen.

Mostly, she was feeling anxious. Jonathan was decidedly different, colder, and she wondered why. Was it something she had done? Or had forgotten to do? He was not grinning and being playful with her as usual. Well, what did she expect. Jonathan Sauvage was for the most part a total stranger to her. For all she knew, he could be going off to plunder the Spanish Main. She laughed inwardly at the incongruous thought.

Later, following breakfast with Vance Moore, Jonathan stood at the front door. Cathelen had stepped into the alcove off the kitchen wall. Curiously, she felt their conversation concerned her. She shivered even in the heat, chiding herself for listening. But she felt she must.

"I will think on it, Moore, and send you my answer in two days. She is a good cook," Jonathan said with what sounded like a weary sigh, "but then so is Mattissa."

"Well, if you want to get rid of her as you said earlier, then let me know immediately. I'd hate to see her go to the Tandys. That man would make her with child before he took a second look at her. And, after all, she *was* at Sugartree first."

Cathelen pressed herself back against the wall. No! Jonathan could not be meaning to sell her back to that devil! She would do anything in order not to be sent there, for that would be like being sent to hell.

She had only two days in which to think of something that would convince Jonathan to keep her here. It was either that, or run away.

Chapter Sixteen

The sun drew life into the open, from the plantation's inner rooms to the shade of a breadfruit tree out in the yard. From the slaves' yards onto the edges of the road flanked by sugar cane, where women spread husked rice to dry.

Cathelen, proud of herself, prepared a vegetable meal at noon, seasoning it with cayenne pepper and saffron. Mairi had informed her that master Jonathan liked his dishes to be spicy.

Pausing in the heat of the kitchen, she poked her head out the window. Along the path branching off in different directions toward the cabins and the mill, she could see African women. The people intrigued her. Their features were coarse, their hair short and crinkly, their noses squashed back against cheeks, and their lips large and protuberant. On the other hand, having learned more about Mattissa from Mairi, she knew that the mixture of African and European blood produced a highly attractive female. Mairi had told her that a quadroon and a white produced a mustee, whereas the child of a mustee by a white man was called a mustee-fino.

"She is this," Mairi had added. "If Mattissa has children sired by a white man, they be free by law and rank as white persons to all intents and purposes, ye see."

Awed, Cathelen had stared at Mairi thoughtfully. "How do you know all this?" she asked.

Mairi shook her head making the snow-white bun she'd pinned carelessly in back wabble. "Heh-heh," Mairi chuckled. "Ye didn't know I was the plantation gossip, eh? Been flapping my tongue for more years than ye can shake a stick at, and it's the listenin' in between what really adds up to knowledge in yer brain, dearie, heed that well. Why, you should see us old maids get together when there's a to-do at one of the plantations."

"Parties?" Cathelen said, fascinated.

"Sure, there be parties. You never saw a party like these here plantation folk throw, dearie, dearie!"

"When was the last one?" Cathelen asked, breathlessly.

Mairi pushed her lips out. "Och! Not since Adam Sauvage went off and got himself done in. Been quite a while now."

139

Cathelen moved closer to the old woman. "Adam . . . Sauvage?"

"Ho, yes, Jonathan's brother, younger by . . ." Mairi puckered her brow, but then gave up trying to remember. She shrugged. "Not too many years now, though, since he's been gone. Two, I guess it was."

Mattissa had barged into Mairi's room just then, and Cathelen was sorely disappointed that she had not heard the whole story. Now, today, Cathelen moved away from the window, planning to go visit Mairi and hear out the rest of Adam Sauvage's story. She wanted desperately to know how he'd come to be killed. She was wondering why this was so important to her, when a sound broke her train of thought.

"Please, I will take that tray to Master Jonathan."

Hearing the sweet young voice, Cathelen turned to face its owner. The girl was very pretty, despite her scarecrow thinness. She had golden-brown hair and eyes to match, and Cathelen guessed she must be a few years younger then herself, sixteen perhaps. But Cathelen's fears that she would be replaced by another were staring her right in the face.

"Are you here to replace me?" Cathelen asked, holding her voice steady as she could. When the girl shook her head, not understanding, Cathelen tried, "Are you? . . . Please tell me your name." She laughed to loosen some of the tension they were both feeling.

"Jula." She looked down at her *café au lait*

140

hands in dejection.

"Here, what is it?" Cathelen said, stepping closer and feeling undue concern for the younger girl.

Tears glistened in Jula's large dark eyes. "They did not want me at Tandy Plantation. Samantha hated me! She does *su-su* on me all the time, and make me go away!"

"What is *su-su*?"

Jula made a play of whispering to an imaginary friend. Then she nodded. Cathelen got the message. This Samantha must have made up tales to get this pathetically lovely child in trouble. What sort of a woman could be so deceitful?

"So." Cathelen twisted her fingers. "You are here to serve?" Jula nodded "yes." "To cook, too?" Cathelen asked and Jula nodded "no" to this.

Cathelen smiled widely in relief and handed Jula the vegetable tray. Jula beamed happily, confiding in Cathelen, "I am quadroon. Do you still like me?"

The girl was asking Cathelen if she liked her despite her black blood? Jula had come from a mulatto parent and a white, making her a quadroon. Mattissa was more white than this charming child, but less likeable to be sure!

One hand planted on either side of Jula's bony shoulders, Cathelen said firmly, "Of course, I like you. We will be great friends, you and I. Later, you will come with me to meet Mairi. She is an old Scotswoman who is always

141

lonely and loves company"—Cathelen grinned—"but she can talk off an ear, so watch out!"

Happily smiling from ear to ear, Jula went out with the tray, thrilled to have found a friend at last. Cathelen watched her go, having completely forgotten her own troubles and that she might be sent away just as Jula had been. But Jula had been disliked by this Samantha. Why, Cathelen would probably never know. Suddenly Cathelen wanted to make Samantha as unhappy as she'd made Jula.

Tears misted Cathelen's eyes. What had she done to cause Jonathan Sauvage to act so bitterly toward her? Had he become disappointed with her because she was not more—what was the word—worldly? Yes, that's it, a worldly woman. God, had he really wanted her that way? Was that what the gleam in his eyes had been about? Cathelen shivered.

She spun about, leaving the hot kitchen confines. *Mairi*. Maybe she could find out something from the old woman. Besides, she wanted to know the entire story of Adam Sauvage, Jonathan's younger brother.

Unerringly, Mairi began the whole story of the brothers, the mean grandfather, and the lads' sweet mother. She was happy in the telling of it, for she loved to relate tales.

"The pair of lads were very bonnie, och, and they looked so much alike it was hard to tell them apart!" Mairi picked up her mending then, shaking her head sentimentally.

Cathelen's eyes lit on the wide-shouldered lawn shirt in Mairi's hands. It was white and looked soft and worn. Jonathan's? Cathelen wondered, her heart fluttering.

"You mean they both had the same coloring?" Cathelen asked, her eyes glued to the shirt, intrigued even more now. "Was there not some way you could tell them apart?"

"Ah, sure!" Mairi chuckled. "But they had to be standing side by side!"

"How was Adam killed?" Cathelen finally dropped the inevitable question.

Mairi crooked a bony finger in the air. "He was done away by a wicked pirate. Och." Mairi shook her grizzled head. "A doctor no less!"

Shaken, Cathelen inquired, "A pirate . . . *doctor*?"

"Aye! There are such." Mairi nodded sagely, growing weary for a nap.

"Why, though, Mairi—why did the pirate kill Adam? And how do you gain all your knowledge? Does Jonathan know all this?"

Mairi's old eyes sparkled. There was almost a wild, deranged cast to them as she stared beyond her. Cathelen reached out to gently shake her blue-veined hand.

"Mairi? Does Jonathan know?"

"No." Mairi appeared confused for a moment, then she stated matter-of-factly, "How could he?"

Now Mairi climbed wearily and slowly into her bed, made with freshly laundered sheets and covers, thanks to Cathelen. Soon the older woman was softly snoring, leaving the younger to stare at the bared floor in total bewilderment. Then the sun beckoned and Cathelen turned to go outside.

Now she had an even greater reason to stay here at Sauvage Plantation. In fact, she was determined to do so. For Cathelen was not one to let a mystery go unsolved. But she hoped she was not placing herself in grave danger, for she sensed that delving into Jonathan's and Adam's past was dangerous.

Later, Cathelen hugged the mansion closely as she took a stroll in the tropical night. Thousands of stars hung so close that she thought if she stood on tiptoe she could reach the largest one. Straining her eyes toward the velvet blue waters, she shivered, remembering.

From her talks with Mairi, Cathelen had learned that Adam Sauvage had been the unruly one. She would have to ask Mairi if Adam, like his brother's murderer, had been a pirate.

Without another glance toward the rocky shore, Cathelen went inside to her bedroom.

Chapter Seventeen

The image in the mirror was hard and handsome. It spoke.

"I will be going to Jamaica, Hondo," Jonathan tossed over his shoulder in a surly undertone before looking back to straighten his buff coat and the pearly shirt beneath.

"To the Coffee House in Cornhill, no doubt, eh, gov'ner?" Hondo knew this was the planters' club for the West Indies residents. "Think ya know enough to be goin' there so soon?"

With impervious brown eyes, Jonathan pivoted to face the little man who had oft sailed the seas with him. "Of course. Don't you know I've a solid footing in each of the two worlds by now?"

"Aye, and you have mighty large amounts

of capital."

"Hondo, you constantly amaze me."

"Well . . . ya could give up piracy, ya know."

Sauvage flipped a wrist daintily, as he said in a high mocking tone, "You could give up piracy, you know." A snort followed this remark.

Then Jonathan turned to go, snatching up a carpeted bag with a long-fingered hand. Looking at the mess the younger man had made, which Hondo himself had to clean up, the former mate wanted to know, "What ya want me to do with little Miss Cooky O'Ruark who's been snoopin' around up here?" Hondo watched Jonathan closely.

Jonathan made a dismissive wave with his hand. "Cathelen? She's been looking for Sinbad, that's all."

"Wasn't nice of ya to make her think ya was goin' to sell her."

"It wasn't nice of her to think so."

Hondo snorted. "Thought ya was hot in your breeches for that one . . ."

Bared teeth flashed. "How the blazes did you know that?" His hands were cocked at his narrow hips giving him the look of the lean Sea Wolf he actually was.

Chuckling merrily, Hondo gestured toward the younger man's area of greatest virility. "Whenever Cooky is around, gov'ner, no one can miss it." He shrugged to indicate that he had no part in any of this.

Hondo's gesture only served to aggravate

Jonathan's already hasty temper this fine tropical morning, and he went about the room cussing and gathering last-minute items for his infamous trade. Hondo, daring much, put another question to his boss.

"Ya should have brought Sinbad off the *Legend* with ya. Why didn't ya?"

"What? Why is that?" snapped the agitated man pulling his tall boots on.

"For the bonnie Cooky to play with."

"*Merde*. Can't you get Cathy O'Ruark off your mind for one minute, small man?" Jonathan grated out, his jawline hard.

"Are you really French? Is that why you swear in French all the time?" Hondo said, chuckling through his words.

"Spare me the questions. I know you're smarter than you make out to be, Mate."

Jonathan was ready to go.

"Bring the wacky parrot back with you?"

"Aww," Jonathan groaned. Then he said, "Do with Cathy O'Ruark what you will. Have Jameson deal with Vance Moore, will you? I've only just met the man though he doesn't know that, and he irritates me to my rope's end. Keep him out of my business—and out of my house—even if you have to camp on the doorstep, little man," he stated implicitly.

"Did he—uh—recognize you?" Hondo whispered. Jonathan stared as if waiting for more. "I mean, does he know who ya really are?"

"Why, whatever do you mean?" Jonathan said in his dandified manner making gestures with his muscle-corded hands. Then he, too, whispered, leaving his mate and manservant with this. "Please, friend, next time I come sneaking home, do make sure Cooky Puss is tucked safely away in her bed? The last time she came dangerously close to losing her precious maidenhood to me."

When Sauvage momentarily recalled the moonlit scene, it prompted an undesired physical response in him. On top of everything else he must deal with, he was now frustrated to boot.

"Next time, gov'ner?" Hondo grinned.

"Make damn sure there is not a next time."

"Aye, aye, Adam."

Instantly, Hondo cowered and pretended to gnaw his fingernails. With his head swinging to and fro, he gazed at the walls as if they had ears and eyes. He made quite a production, too, of saluting his captain.

A large booted foot swiftly left the floor, aimed at Hondo's fleeing backside. The boot was fleet and contacted the little man's britches. "Fancy that now, right in your skinny rump!"

"Oof!" Hondo gasped.

Jonathan tossed back his dark brown head and roared with laughter; then he snatched up his package which contained, among other things, the makeup for a wicked scar.

148

Chapter Eighteen

Michal O'Ruark awoke on the rolling deck of the *Sea Gypsy*. He opened his dark orchid eyes, eyes that were sore and bloodshot.

He squinted up at the sun, then swore at the pain this small movement caused him.

The preceding night whirled in eddies through his befuddled brain. Had he spent the night wallowing in unspeakable pleasures? Jamaica? Or St. Martin? He realized he could not even remember the name of the last dusky girl he had been with, nor if she had been pleasurable.

With disgust Michal saw that he had been sick sometime during the wee hours. The smelly stuff was even on the sleeve of his blue 'reef' jacket. Aye, it had been St. Kitts island. That was where they had caroused.

Michal eased himself over to sit with his back to the bulkhead, slapping his arm over a crate. Lord, what an existence, he thought, looking around at his crusty sleeping mates.

He wondered sadly just when he had begun to be this miserable human being. He had gambled. He had whored around. He had cheated, and now, dear God, now he had gone along with these stinking freebooters to plunder and rob every Spanish ship that heaved within their sight. The beautiful *señoritas*—how many had he made love to? If it could be called that. How many in the last five or six years? He could not even remember if they had all been willing.

And now—now he had murdered a man. Not today, not last night. But he had stayed drunk since them. So only God knew on what day or in what year he had committed that grave sin.

Loud snores enveloped him. He had not one soul to talk to. He was alone in his total and complete misery. *Dear God, when did I become this wretched hellish man? I am less than a man!* Michal realized.

With a deep choked sob, Michal thought of his little sister. The one beacon in his muckish existence. His eyes cleared just a little and his heavy heart lifted a bit. Yes, he would go and see Cathy as soon as he felt fit enough. She would be with Dany and her brother in Carolina by now.

"Michal O'Ruark!" Cathy would lovingly berate him. "Where have you been off to again for so long?"

Ah, Cathy was a fiery-tempered lass with a

haunting beauty that could steal all the fellows' hearts had she set her mind on winning suitors. And she was unique, always aiding the peasants. He groaned then, his sorely strained gaze roaming over the rough-planked decks. Pirates continually snored aloud, slumbering on without a care in the world. The only one alive was the man on lookout.

Cold shivers of drastic awakening again racked his frame. A pirate! How had he come to be this? He had begun as a ship's doctor. He had come upon this bunch years ago and had recognized them for pirates when he'd recovered from his drunken stupor. Too late. They bore the unmistakable stamp of sea robbers, the mark of their bloody trade in their heavy weapons and in the parakeetlike ensemble of garish colors. These were no simple seafaring men.

Now Michal O'Ruark had been reduced to one of them . . . and then the awful day had dawned. . . .

The pirates had roared. It had been the sort of sport they enjoyed. Oh, it was nothing to kill a man. "Will you fight fer her, Doc?" the captain, Jocko, had demanded, laughing, swilling, lusting, drooling through his long black beard.

But the blood of lust and desire had flowed, too, in Michal's veins. They had overtaken the Barbados-bound merchantman on which the girl, slender and graceful as a willow, was a passenger. Hair hung loosely about her shoulders, black as a raven's wing against the velvet snow of her face. Her black eyes smoldered, a fire in their liquid depths. Her blood red lips spat in flawless Castilian.

"Why did your men sink our ship?" she asked the only other Spaniard aboard, one of Jocko's own. "I am betrothed to this gentleman here." She lifted her chin to gaze at the tall dandy man beside her, and covered his long-fingered hand with both her own, hands like white birds. "Surely you must have heard the name of S——?"

The name of S—— What? It still evaded him. The name of who? *Who?* Who in God's name had he murdered on the order of a drunken, lustful captain? He had been this himself, but he remembered holding the bloodied blade in his hand, remembered having been told he had run *S* through. But how could this be, the man had been the Wolf. They told him he had made a mistake in thinking the man's name began with an *S*.

Of course, why had he not figured it out before. The *Sea* Wolf!

He sobbed like a lost boy. *My God!* Then they had all taken turns on the lovely, frail Spanish flower. He himself, Michal O'Ruark, had lusted after her, Cameo Salvador, his great hands shaking as he'd groped to free his pantaloons. And she had welcomed him, as she had welcomed the others with ivory white, opened thighs!

Was it his fault? he had wondered insanely over and over.

She had been worn out but ironically very

happy when the pirates had finished with her. Michal had not been able to believe she still had a tiny spark left in her. God, she had smiled as if she had enjoyed being ravished by so many randy men!

Michal had withdrawn into a deep, blue hell afterward. He had killed a man and raped an innocent all in one afternoon. All for sport. *Sport!*

Michal had seen his father hang in Edinburgh and less than a month had passed. How could he feel for Cathmor? The man had loved nothing and no one. Michal had tried, though. Oh yes, and he had run away from the High Sheriff's hanging and become a stinking coward. Add that to his ungodliness and piracy. But murder . . . that was the hardest to live with.

The name of Sea Wolf was known and feared the length and breadth of the Caribbean. No treasure galleon or any other craft was safe from his fast ship, *Legend*, and ruthless crew. In his wake, the Sea Wolf left deprivation and destruction. Now he was searching for Michal O'Ruark. At least, his ghost was.

His face whitened, his lips went even paler, his violet eyes sank into dismal pools of darkness. He did not even fear for himself any longer. He looked down at his surgeon's fingers. Shattered by his sins, Michal slumped to the deck.

Night darkened the ship again. They were

lying low in a cove off St. Kitts, the sky above dotted with cold, distant stars.

Maybe it was only the hangover. Maybe tomorrow would be brighter. But Michal wondered what new horror the day would hold.

He shook his dark golden head, and suddenly fear coursed through him. He was still alive then if he could fear. But was his fear ungrounded? It must certainly be, for he knew that ghosts could not pursue a man. Not in human form, anyway. He had killed this Sea Wolf, so why was he being cruelly haunted by one of the same countenance, on the same ship. Rumor had it that the Sea Wolf had risen from the watery grave to which Michal O'Ruark had sent him. But this time, it was said, he had a wicked scar slashed across one cheek.

Maybe Michal O'Ruark had given the lean marauder that scar?

"Cathy . . ." Michal cried in a hoarse sob. "Cathy . . . help me . . . dearest sister. Wherever you may be right now, pray for my soul. . . ."

Michal shook his grimy golden head, promising to atone for his sins and make up for all of dear sweet Cathy's loneliness. God, how lonely the little lass must have been with no one to love her in the world but Dany!

If only he could pick himself up out of this pirate's hell he had fallen into . . . and if he lived . . .

Chapter Nineteen

Deep summer. The wide undulations of the landscape were pervaded with the pale green of sugar cane. The time for mangoes and oranges had arrived, the "long days" when it was wise to plant beans and corn in the kitchen garden.

So far, Cathelen's back was holding out. She rose from her kneeling position and straightened her spine which had been curved a long time while planting seeds. Then she saw Mattissa coming. Cathelen stood rigid now and waited.

"You come in to cook now!" Mattissa called from the edge of the garden.

"You do the cooking!" Cathelen dared to shout back.

"Negroes coming up to finish garden. You

have to cook!"

"Oh, all right, all right," Cathelen grumbled. "I am coming!" she yelled.

Mattissa was still glaring hotly when Cathelen came in. She walked straight to the table and dropped the vegetables she had hastily gathered into her apron.

Mattissa's dusky red mouth dropped open and snapped shut all in one fluid motion.

"You gather vegetables in heat of day?" Mattissa almost gasped.

Beneath the table Cathelen's foot was tapping irritatingly. Mattissa's expression was mordant as she crossed slim arms over her high chest and flared her fine nostrils.

"Why you do tap-tap? You are not the boss!"

Because I have just about had it with you, Cathelen thought. As it had turned out, there had been no need for her to convince Jonathan Sauvage of her worthiness or for her to run away from the plantation. Jonathan had proved to be an absentee owner. And for some lucky reason, Vance Moore had not returned. But she must tread more carefully; Mattissa was still the boss of the house.

Cathelen gritted her teeth while she answered. "I am very busy, that is why, Mattissa. So why don't you just leave me alone so that I may prepare the meal?"

"I will send Jula in. She will help you. Soon I will be very hungry, and the old woman who eats like a pig will need her food."

With that Mattissa vacated the kitchen. It

156

seemed comfortably empty without her domineering presence. Certainly this was no milk and honey situation for this worn-out cook! Cathelen thought with a little self-pity.

But she took a deep revitalizing breath and decided she would have to figure out some way to break her indenture. Marriage, that was it! She had talked about this subject with Margaret, when she'd stopped her on the lane that led to the row of cabins.

The women were assured that when they found a husband they would be released from their engagement, and the men, Margaret went on, were promised a piece of land at the expiration of their service.

"Are there any men whose indentures are about to terminate?" Cathelen had asked Margaret.

Margaret shrugged. "No, I do not think so."

Now, in her kitchen, Cathelen blushed. To have to resort to such measures! Lord, I surely must be getting desperate to be searching for a husband and not considering whether he is fat or ugly, skinny or old! And there was always what must be consummated following the wedding. Cathelen was afraid of that. She had never been around couples who lived in connubial bliss. She did not even know if such a state existed.

A quickening shot through Cathelen then. She turned to the window just in time to see a colorful bird flit by. In a breath-stealing moment the image of her dream lover flashed before her mind's eye and then vanished just as quickly. If only, Cathelen thought, if only I could capture the way he looks. But he was as elusive as the last butterflies that flitted past her window at dusk.

Cathelen shivered, staring up at the dark orchid clouds over Barbados. Fireflies already lit up the trees and the countryside, and Cathelen hugged herself despite the warm evening. She could see the small house lizard creeping along the walls and devouring the insects that gathered around the light. Now and then it made a clicking noise.

Cathelen slowly returned to her dismal little bedroom. She would not care to be a planter's wife, she thought suddenly, because she would never see her husband. How could anyone raise a family that way? Making babies takes some time, they say.

She caught herself then. Family? What could she be thinking of? Jonathan would never consider her for a wife, not a mere indentured servant!

Cathelen stiffened and lifted her chin proudly in defiance of her miserable destiny.

I am a lady . . . so what am I doing here slaving in a hot kitchen all day?

How could she dare rank herself above the others? Her chin drooped lower. Papa, why did you have to go and kill the town commissioner? Why could you not have just had a little argument like most normal men and let it go at that?

Why did you always have to be a bit tougher and nastier than the rest of them? Damn you, Papa, anyway!

Seven years, all of that miserable, lonely time yawning before her. Her youth would have passed her by—all the good times. She was practically an old maid now, and in seven years, why, she would be twenty-five!

Cathelen peered closely at herself in the wavy mirror on her sturdy rough-hewn dresser.

"Well, Cathelen, this is what you wanted—to be a prim little virgin forever."

Shrugging a bit forlornly, she turned to her narrow bed beside the window. To be pure and golden. Untouched. The Golden Girl. Ridiculous? Absurd?

Cathelen shivered with an emotion akin to fear. But to be forever nunlike?

Undressing, Cathelen's eyes rounded in childlike wonder as she perceived even now how her senses had become awakened beneath that pirate's kiss, and she could not easily forget the feel of his strong body, the merest touch of his large expert hands. He must be quite a lover, she decided.

Shafts of moonbeams danced through her window, and she could hear the Negroes as they pounded out music on the taut stretched drum as they danced, the tafia warm in their veins. She listened until she, too, had become a pulse in that music's rhythm, a vehicle through which sensual forces moved.

When she finally fell into slumber, Cathelen

dreamed that she loved a pirate.

The next day, which was Friday, Cathelen went along with Deke Jameson and Hondo to Bridgetown. The men disappeared to attend to their own business while Cathelen made her way to bargain in the marketplace, her basket slung over her slim arm.

The air was gentle as she strolled the busy streets, the sea a sparkling aquamarine. On the way into town the countryside had been vivid with scarlet poinsettias and yellow allamanda flowers.

Her hair shimmered, reflecting the sun's rays, a thick, long white-yellow shock cascading in a coil to her hips.

Deke Jameson had filled her in on some very interesting facts that morning. Hogsheads of muscavado produced on the island were shipped to the English market through factors in Bristol and London, and produced so much wealth that the West Indian planter soon became a symbol of fabulous wealth. Sugar, said Jameson, had set Barbados and its planters on the road to seemingly everlasting prosperity. Jonathan Sauvage was one of these fortunates.

Cathelen found the harbor crowded with Dutch, English, and American ships. When she had asked Jameson about the social structure Jameson had told her it was desperately fluctuating and unconventional. Crowds of emigrants were being thrust into it to replace those who moved on to other islands or who took service with the buccaneers.

"Buccaneers?" Cathelen echoed, turning to Deke Jameson interestedly. "You mean pirates, don't you?"

Deke chuckled. "Pirates are a bit more nasty, missy. They take from everyone—just about."

Hondo cleared his throat, but Cathelen missed the conflicting exchange between the two men. Excited, she asked Jameson to tell her more.

"What do these pirates look like?" She could feel Hondo peering at her askance but she did not care.

"Here we are, missy. You do your marketing and we'll find you when we're done."

But, disappointed that the conversation had been cut short, on the return trip Cathelen pressed Jameson for the answer to her question. Pirates and Jonathan Sauvage had become her favorite topics of discussion. And she was learning much from the old woman Mairi.

Settled in the carriage once again, her overflowing market basket on the floor beside her feet, Cathelen watched the laboring backs of the dark chestnut horses that pulled them back to Sauvage Plantation.

"Well," Jameson began with a slow drawl, "some of the pirates wear golden earrings in their ears. Some have curly locks dangling in front of fierce eyes—"

161

Hondo guffawed, but Jameson went on. "—a cutlass in hand. Often a parrot on one shoulder."

"*Owww,*" Hondo moaned aloud.

Cathelen swung around to face the wiry little man. "Is there something bothering you? Or are you in some sort of pain?" She was becoming irritated with him. Just when she wanted to learn more about pirates, he seemed to be enjoying himself immensely, as he had one other time she could remember. "If you are not in pain, Hondo, will you please muffle your noises inside your jacket so that I can hear?"

"Sure, Cooky," Hondo muttered with a shrug.

"Buccaneers," Jameson continued, "raid mostly Spanish ships. They take jewels and gold and casks of money. *All* sailing vessels are tempting with their rich cargoes—especially to dishonest captains."

"Pirates."

Jameson nodded to Cathelen. "They attack ships on the high seas and rob them all of their spices and gold. There are many places in the Caribbean that serve as bases for these pirates."

"Sheesh!" Hondo expelled the comment like a sneeze.

Cathelen pursed her lips, then begged, "Go on please."

Jameson tipped his wide-brimmed hat to Cathelen O'Ruark, treating her like the lady she really was. Hondo slumped down further in back, groaning and mumbling inanely to himself.

"The bases—in Jamaica, in the Bay Islands off the coast of Honduras in Central America, in the northwestern part of Hispaniola, and Tortuga—"

"Excuse me, Deke," she said. He smiled and nodded for her to go on. "What is Tortuga like? The name captured my interest."

"Well, it has a vast waterfront market where everything from brass buttons to slaves is sold. Tortuga has always been like a pirate's second home, his ship the first. After 1639 Tortuga became a center for piracy and a stronghold for buccaneers. Driven from Hispaniola, the buccaneers found refuge and leadership in Tortuga. They weren't planters, and they were not interlopers who appeared in the Caribbean each year. They were a new element, an armed force permanently based on the rim of the Caribbean. They were seasoned to the climate and used to hardship, expert in living off the land, and bitter enemies of Spain."

Cathelen shivered. "Do these pirates take captives—female?"

"Of course. What other captives would be so delightful?" He heard a feminine chuckle and went on with a grin. "Usually they—pirate captains—will return all the Spanish females they capture. It's sad because the women are usually used goods by then."

"They cannot become brides, you mean?" Cathelen said with a shudder of compassion.

"Unless a man will take them, although they've been ravished."

Ravished. Shuddering now, Cathelen did fall

silent for the remainder of the ride back to the plantation.

When Cathelen walked into the house with her basket and began to head for the kitchen, Mattissa stepped in her path to tell her she had a visitor. Cathelen frowned and wondered who could be visiting her. Then she thought she knew as Mattissa quickly retreated, leaving her without an explanation.

Mattissa had gestured indifferently toward the door to the drawing room. As Cathelen stepped up to it, she peered through the opening where the wood had been left ajar, wanting to steel herself if the visitor was Vance Moore.

Blinking and blushing at what she had seen and hoping the woman had not caught her peeking through, Cathelen straightened. The lovely, raven-haired woman was a stranger to her. What could she want with me? Cathelen wondered as she tried to get up the courage to enter.

"Is someone out there? Oh, please do come in if you are Cathelen O'Ruark . . ."

The door swung wide beneath Cathelen's hand. Before her wide violet eyes sat the most gorgeous female she had ever seen. There was a wildness about her. It was in the set of the woman's eyes, in the careless twist of her lips, but her flippant gestures set this woman apart from any Cathelen had ever met before. Cathelen knew at once that this woman could only be related to Vance Moore.

Green eyes flashed merrily, and Cathelen

164

decided that this woman might look like her devil of a brother but she was not like him in nature.

"Oh, please, do come in," she said.

Cathelen slipped inside. Embarrassed she tryed to hide the basket behind her skirt. But the thing was too big, so she just set it down and sighed. "It—it is heavy," Cathelen told the gorgeous woman.

"Yes, I suppose it is." The black head canted. "I am sorry, my name is Raven Moore. You must certainly be Cathelen O'Ruark. My—ah—brother said that you were quite lovely, and he is put out that Decatur sold you to Sauvage."

Cathelen said nothing to that. She already knew that Vance Moore wanted her. "Are you here to try and buy me back?" Cathelen blurted, and was at once sorry.

"Heavens no!"

Raven Moore stood and Cathelen felt small by comparison. She was tall and gorgeous, all that Cathelen had ever wished she could be—outspoken too.

"Well, Cathelen, I confess I came by to see who the young woman could be that my older brother is so taken with." She giggled, displaying yet another side to her nature. "I love it. My *big* brother hot and panting over something—someone I mean—that he can't have. He's become a raving maniac. Vance is like a spoiled little boy who throws a temper tantrum when he doesn't get what he wants."

"He wants me that badly?" Cathelen was

aghast. There had only been one other who had come after her like a lovesick puppy, but Michal had thrown the huge, bumbling lad out on his ear. "Does he want me to work for him, as a maid or—or something else?" Cathelen had to ask.

"He wants you to—yes, he wants you for a mistress." Raven sighed. "To add to his collection. But the other ones are quadroons and musteefinos. You are the first blond woman he has desired. So that is why I find this so unusual. But now that I have seen you I can see why my brother desires you."

"I really do not see—" Cathelen looked down over her serviceable frock and blushed in embarrassment.

"Ah! He could dress you up—like a doll!"

Cathelen held her chin up stiffly. "I am afraid not, Miss Moore. I am not for sale—at any price."

"Oh . . . no." Raven slapped her forehead. "I did not mean for him to do just that, Cathelen. May I call you that?"

"Yes," Cathelen said, still miffed. "Just what did you mean then?"

"Please, sit down?" Raven took a spot on the sofa and patted the cushion beside her. She waited until the lovely, fragile blonde sat. "Now. Do you like it here, Cathelen? Are you happy?"

"I—I do not see why I should answer you, Miss Moore. I hardly know you to be discussing my affairs so familiarly."

"Oh, you think I am here for my brother. Well, I am not. I do confess that I was curious. But now that I've met you, I have decided to have you for a friend."

Decided! Cathelen said aloud, "You what?"

"I like you."

"You cannot have me for a friend. I am a servant, an indentured slave."

"Phooey! My maid is pure jet black, and she is my best friend. Are you any less than she? Besides, I know you are a lady and have been gentle born. It is written all over you. One would have to be a fool not to notice."

Cathelen laughed apologetically. "I like you too, Raven. It is hard not to."

"See, I am not prudish like my brother. I am a human being, unlike him," she laughed gaily. "He is all right, when he is absent, which is much of the time!"

"Yes, Jonathan Sauvage is always gone, too."

Raven shuddered and looked withdrawn of a sudden.

"What is it?"

"The Sauvages. They frighten me half to death, especially the younger one. Do you know, we've never met? Hard to believe yet it's true."

"He is dead."

Raven looked shocked. "Dead? Why has no one ever told me this before?"

"It is a deep dark secret around here, it seems. When Mairi speaks of it she almost whispers. There seems to be some danger in discussing the younger one—as if his ghost haunts this place."

"Indeed, I'll bet it does. He was a wild one. Even Jonathan gives me the creeps, with those dark, mysterious brown eyes. Admittedly, he is a handsome one. Why, I haven't seen that one for two years. Would you believe that some neighbors living side by side in Bridgetown have never laid eyes on one another for years? I've heard of folks like these finally introducing themselves to one another over the back fence."

Cathelen giggled. "I know just what you mean, it was this way even in Scotland."

"Is that where you come from?" Raven asked and received a nod. "You look more Scandinavian or Dutch to me."

"I am Dutch," Cathelen said, laughing gaily. "Not all though."

"No." Cathelen confessed.

Raven and Cathelen talked back and forth for another half an hour before Raven said that she must get back home. Paprika, her maid, would worry if she did not return soon. There was going to be a plantation party in the near future and there was much planning to be done for it.

"I'd love to have you come, Cathelen!" Raven said excitedly.

"Oh—I could not."

"Of course you can. I promise not to invite Jonathan Sauvage if you come."

"Not invite Jonathan?" Cathelen said, showing her disappointment when it was too late to conceal it.

"Aha," Raven said in a low breath while

Cathelen blushed brightly.

Suddenly Raven placed her hand to her forehead and swayed off to one side. Alarmed, Cathelen leaned forward.

"What is it? Are you ill?" She took Raven's cold hand.

"Pray for—pray for—" Raven kept saying, as if she were in some sort of trance.

"Pray for who? Tell me, Raven. . . ." Then Cathelen realized what was going on. She had known an old woman who had had the "sight." Raven was deep in a trance and was trying to reveal something important to Cathelen. "Raven," she said softly, "who do you see? Can you tell me?"

"He is feeling very bad, I can see. He—he has blond hair, like yours, Cathelen . . ."

"Michal!" Cathelen exclaimed softly. "What else, Raven? Do you see any more?"

"Yes, Michal wants you to pray for him. He is in some sort of trouble . . . *ahhh*. I can't tell you any more . . . now . . ."

"That is right, Raven. Relax and tell me no more. Please wake up, Raven."

Suddenly Raven was looking fresh and relaxed. After a deep sigh she opened her sparkling emerald eyes. Taking Cathelen's hand, she told her that having this "sight" became a problem at times. This was why Paprika did not like to have Raven away from home for too long.

"We will visit again, Cathelen. I have some dresses I would like to bring over. Don't look at me that way. It's not charity. The colors are all wrong for me. I had picked too hastily and they are just hanging in my closet. I'll have Paprika clean and press them for you. Is this all right with you? I don't want my new friend to be offended."

Cathelen lifted her head after staring down at her lap and her simple cotton dress. "If you like."

"I do."

Mattissa opened the door just then to see what was taking so long. "You have to cook," she said imperiously.

"Who are you?" Raven asked the other black-haired female.

"Mattissa. I am housekeeper here."

"Well, Mattissa. I am a visitor, and when I am done visiting I will let you know so that you may let me out."

Haughtily Mattissa turned, shutting the door none too gently. Cathelen sat gaping at the very idea of what Raven had dared with the dictatorial Mattissa. Smiling, Raven patted Cathelen's hand.

"Don't be afraid to let that fire in you surface, Cathy. It's there, I know it is. The other fire, too," she said cryptically. "Let it come and flood your being and it will draw the man of your destiny." Raven smiled then, thinking she already knew who that man could be. She sighed and twisted her rose red lips. "Perhaps you'll be more lucky than I have been."

With a beauty of movement Cathelen had

never witnessed in a woman before, Raven swept from the house as gracefully as a night wind borne on silken wings.

Later, when Cathelen returned to the homely cubicle that served as her bedroom, she had a sudden whimsical thought. She imagined Raven and Michal together, different as night and day, but what a beautiful pair the two would make!

Now, as she set about sweeping her room, having felt the need to clean it, Cathelen contemplated a life deprived of a man's love. She thought at once of Jonathan with his elegant, lazy charm, his twinkling brown glance. All those feelings she thought were dead and not for Cathelen O'Ruark were surfacing like fire on oil-slicked water.

To be a virgin forever no longer seemed such a good idea. Raven Moore had caused her to believe that to be a kind of death.

Chapter Twenty

In the mist of midnight the pirate sloop came stealing into the waters of Tortuga and lay low outside the port, hidden in a remote cove.

The Sea Wolf's *Legend* was a splendid predatory vessel: a two-master rigged with fore-and-aft sails, narrow and deep green of hull, seventy-five men strong, and bearing eight cannon and four swivel guns. A rapierlike bowsprit almost as long as her hull enabled her to mount a parade of canvas that made her even more nimble and quick than her sister and brother, the schooner or the brigantine. She could bear down on her prey and maneuver in the channels and sounds where brigands hid.

At her rail a man bathed in soft moonglow looked out over the small semicircle of quiet deep water to a white sandy beach that nestled at the foot of steep cliffs. The Wolf could almost imagine a fragile mermaid, fair of skin and hair, stretched out on a lonely strip of beach, waiting for . . . But there was no time for such wild imaginings in his life. Women came and went; that was the story of the Wolf's love life. There had been no one for him in quite some time now.

In the gentle breeze off the water, his great mane of dark brown hair swayed. He was relaxed now after a day of fruitless search. His mates had watched him, knowing he would rather be left alone this night, as on many nights before.

Wolf began to taste the hatred in his mouth, in his iron-hard body. It was becoming all-encompassing like a sexual craving, this terrible need for the Sea Wolf to capture his brother's murderer.

"I want him," he said aloud, tensing up again. He did not plan to kill the man, however. He was no cold-blooded murderer. Yet he wanted to see the man suffer, suffer as Jonathan must have right before he died. Wolf toyed with the fake, wax scar on his cheek. It was part of his disguise. No wonder Buckley had not recognized him as fitting the description of the Wolf.

"Captain." One of his mates called him from his vengeful musings.

If only, the Wolf wished, if only there were *some way* to take vengeance on behalf of Jonathan who now lay in his watery grave at the

173

bottom of the sea. An inhuman cry left the Wolf's throat, creating hairy fingers of apprehension along the buccaneers' spines.

Two weeks had passed since Cathelen had met Raven Moore. They were delightful, happy days filled with sunshine because Raven stopped by often to visit with Cathelen. Though fast friends now, Cathelen still felt somewhat guilty over all the pretty new dresses she owned. Raven was a very generous woman.

After her bath one evening, Cathelen stepped out onto the veranda where the moonflowers opened their white petals and wrapped her in a sensual perfumed spell.

She was wearing a white lawn nightgown with embroidered eyelet at the bodice, its fullness flowing softly, wraithlike to her bare feet. In the cracked mirror Cathelen had noticed that she looked more like her former self. Her skin had taken on a golden hue. She knew she appeared lovely—if anyone could see her, which was highly improbable—with her clean, snow-white hair cascading in satin ripples over her shoulders to her waist. Some wispy strands tickled her hips. These last wisps were pure white from her hot days in the sun.

Cathelen stepped from the veranda, then halted suddenly beside a garden trellis. She drew back to hide herself in the shadows, and peered through the trellis's diamonds. There, against the moon, was the silhouette of a tall man. She could hear him splashing in some water, see him bent over at the waist.

She made a fateful mistake then, by stepping from her cover to try to see the man better. The truth of the matter was, Cathelen hoped he was Jonathan.

"Jonathan?"

The man's shadowed form whirled to face the owner of that sweet voice. Cathy O'Ruark. "Damn," he muffled a curse into the towel with which he wiped his wet chin. "Go away."

"Is that you?"

Cathelen came closer yet. But the man kept his face averted.

"Go away, I said."

He took a step away, but then halted. Cathelen followed, daring much in the presence of this stranger.

"Who are you?" she asked. "What are you doing here?"

Then her eyes caught the tall boots on the ground next to the water bucket. Her face paled and she dragged her gaze slowly upward. "You," she said low. "Why do you dare come here again? There must be something you want here."

"Oh, there definitely is."

The next moment she was in his strong arms and Cathelen, half surprised and half frightened, heard a lonely starved sound escape from his throat. He savagely took her lips with kisses and tiny bites that thrilled rather than hurt. Then his tongue was thrusting into her mouth.

Barely able to breathe under the devastating onslaught of his kisses, his tight embrace, his flaming thighs pressed so hard to hers, Cathelen was still aware enough to be afraid. She was, however, overwhelméd by feelings unknown to her, not unpleasant, but rather startling and intensely passionate.

He broke away suddenly, leaving her shocked at her own behavior and stunned by his rejection.

"Damn you," he said shakily, "you have cast a spell on me . . . witch. . . ."

Cathelen, staring at the dark form that had begun to run toward the beach in long angry strides, touched two fingers to her lips, breathlessly murmuring, "My God . . ."

Cathelen was not herself when the sun tipped the rim of the sea while she gazed from her window. She was more spellbound than the first time the pirate had kissed her.

She dressed for the day and walked about the kichen in a dreamy daze, even cutting her finger while slicing some vegetables. She was soothing her finger between her lips when the door to the kitchen opened and there stood Jonathan Sauvage looking like the devil himself.

Cathelen could feel her cheeks flaming as she removed her finger from her mouth and then did not know what to do with it. Jonathan scowled. Then he stared at her pink. finger, tossing a hand in the air.

"I thought you were a grown woman," he snapped crossly, "but I see you have not yet reached adulthood." He stared about the kitchen.

"Can I help you?" Cathelen asked, with a little too much spirit. "Would you like a dish of vegetables?" She held up a carrot with its green top still intact, as if she threatened to toss it into his face.

"So," he began, stopping to lean against a cupboard with his arms crossed over his chest, one ankle crossed over the other, "what is bothering you?"

"You," she retorted too quickly.

"Is that so?"

"I—I did not mean it that way. I have not been myself this morning and—and you irritated me when you came into my kitchen like a bear."

"Have you ever seen a bear?"

Cathelen frowned. "No."

"Well then. How would you know I resembled a bear?" Letting it go at that, he turned to the cupboard and took down a pot of black India tea. "Make me some of this." He placed the tea none too gently on the table and turned to go.

Cathelen curtsied at the closing door, growling, "Yes, mastah, anything you says, mastah." She stuck out her tongue.

Jonathan strode along the hall and was just about to enter the study when a knock sounded at the front door. Mattissa seemed to materialize out of nowhere. "I'll get that," he said, dismissing her with a wave of his hand.

Frowning, Mattissa shook her head and went back to dusting and polishing the furnishings in the living room. But she peeked out from the door, curious to see if the Moore woman was visiting again. Sure enough, that was who it was.

"Well, what do we have here?" Jonathan said, his brown gaze warming as he looked the raven-haired beauty up and down.

Green eyes glittered as Raven sucked in her cheek on one side, then purred, "Jonathan Sauvage, don't you remember me? Your neighbor?"

Jonathan coughed to conceal a laugh. "I am sorry—" Then he caught her frowning and he looked himself up and down. "Is there something wrong?" He looked her straight in the eyes then. "I know, you think I look different, don't you."

"Why . . . yes, I do." Raven nibbled her lower lip. "I am Raven Moore, in case your memory takes too long in returning." She stepped in right past him. "Is Cathelen around? I do hope she's not out slaving in that garden again. Poor girl."

"Poor girl?" Jonathan said absentmindedly. "Oh yes, the cook."

Raven huffed through her slim aquiline nose. "Do you mind?" She indicated the drawing room with a wave of her long-fingered hand.

Sauvage followed in the wake of a bobbing scarlet skirt, shaking his head mildly over the cagelike contrivance and wondering what Raven Moore looked like without the hoops and stays.

178

She sat in a green velvet chair, clashing dramatically with her surroundings. She waited for Jonathan to offer her a drink, which she declined. And when he sat with a brandy in hand, one long leg crossed over the other, Raven opened her pretty mouth to speak—at the same time Sauvage did.

He laughed. "Go ahead, Miss Moore." He smiled. "I do hope it is *Miss*."

Raven was too drawing-room mannered to blush. "Miss Moore, yes. Now, are you coming to my party tonight, Mister Sauvage?"

"Have I been invited?"

"Of course. Didn't you see the invitation?"

"I'm afraid not. I only returned last evening."

"The absentee landowner," Raven remarked and Sauvage caught her meaning at once.

Just then Cathelen entered, her face lighting up when she saw Raven sitting there as pretty as a portrait in oils. But when Cathelen snatched a glimpse of Jonathan's profile as he was pouring himself another brandy, she could not help feeling a jolt of familiarity run along her spine. Raven watched Cathelen and wondered what was troubling the girl. It was as if she had recognized someone at last after a long separation.

The dream, Cathelen thought to herself.

Jonathan Sauvage turned just then, drink in hand, and saluted the women, his gaze coming to rest a little too long on Cathelen's mesmerized face. They both stared at each other. Raven watched the trance that seemed to envelop the two.

"Jonathan?" Raven broke the spell finally. "I wanted you to know that Cathelen has been invited to my party. Do you mind? We've become very good friends and I'll be terribly disappointed if she doesn't come."

"Fine." He tossed down the remainder of his drink.

"You don't mind?" Raven was incredulous and happy at the same time.

"Of course not."

With a deep breath and a sheepish smile, Jonathan excused himself. "Later, ladies, at the party." He stopped at the door before going out, addressing his demure cook. "Do you have a suitable gown to wear?"

Cathelen beamed with excitement, exclaiming aloud, "Yes, yes!" She laughed then. "I do!"

Raven watched Cathelen watch Jonathan exit from the room, and she wondered what the coming night would bring. As it was now, Jonathan already had a good start for partying.

Chapter Twenty-One

It was late afternoon when Cathelen returned to the Sauvage Plantation. Chiah had driven her in the wagon to Bridgetown, to the market.

Her basket had been laden with fruits and vegetables, to barter for salted beef and pork, and for the bright cotton and the ornaments with which the slaves loved to bedeck themselves.

"You are a 'sweet mout,' Miz Cathy," Chiah said, his black face shining in the sun. "You spoils the wimmenfolk."

Chiah was a tall, handsome African. At least, Cathelen thought, according to his kind he was, for the black women could not seem to tear their eyes from him. He was, she had to admit, the best-looking male Negro she'd ever seen since coming to Barbados.

"Oh, go on, you," Cathelen said. From her basket on the seat beside them she produced a kidney-shaped soursop. "It's hot out. Would you like some?" She held the fruit up.

His black eyes lit up. "Why sure, Miz Cathy."

From his wide belt he lifted a machete. "But you must cut it." He gestured with a grin.

Cathelen gulped, taken by surprise at the heavy knife. "Are you not afraid you will cut your leg off with that hanging at your side?"

But Cathelen took it from him as he proffered it, her grasp dainty as she gingerly plucked it from his hand.

"You knows what its for—" Chiah laughed with a deep chuckle at her studied carefulness. "It's used for cutting sugar cane."

"Oh—oh yes, of course." She grinned lop-sidedly. "But not a leg."

Very cautiously, she shaved off the small green prickles, then sliced the fruit and shared it with Chiah. Inside the fruit was white woolly pulp, sweetly acid, and Cathelen licked her lips clean of the strawberry flavor, her eyes dreamy.

"My favorite," she said. "This and the sweet-sop."

"Sweetsop. Sure is good eatin' that sweet custard, yessir!" Chiah readily agreed.

Cathelen smiled, enjoying the cool refreshment and even the wagon ride as they bumped along the rugged path up the back way to Sauvage. She recalled what Jameson had said to her about the slaves' English. In a compact

182

island like Barbados, which had a relatively large white group, many of the newly imported slaves soon learned English. There were so many white servants on the island, so many poor whites who worked in the fields, and so many Negroes who had become tradesmen, that there were thousands of slaves who spoke English. Chiah spoke good English and had a trade as well. He was the plantation's carpenter, even did some work for the neighboring planters for which Jonathan Sauvage allowed Chiah to be paid. Although this last had only come about of late.

Musing on the other planters, Cathelen was reminded of the plantation party she would attend later. She would have to enlist Jula's aid in her tasks, otherwise she would not get to the party on time. Who would be there? Other planters? Of course, silly, she chided herself. And their wives and eldest offspring, no doubt. Cathelen was so excited. Besides, Jonathan would attend too.

Jula, who turned out to be very talented with comb and brush, created an enchanting upsweep with Cathelen's white-blond hair. Her dress was pale orchid with a long-waisted, pointed bodice; a full bell skirt; a low, square neck; and a close-fitting sleeve with a violet-blue ruffle at the elbow.

Smiling with a little-girl-happy face, Cathelen stuck out a shoe just to admire it. A Saxony blue brocade slipper with French heels.

Jula brought the capuchin cloak to her. It was a gay scarlet color and Jula told Cathelen, in her simple language, that she looked just like a delicate bud opening its velvet-soft petals and blooming into a glorious flower.

Breathless, Cathelen said, "Do you really think so, Jula?"

"I know this, Miss Cathy. And Samantha Gable going to want to scratch out your pretty eyes"—Jula turned to the door just as Cathelen was patting her hair one last time—"you being just a—"

"Just a 'what'?"

"Oooh, Master Jonathan. You going to knock out all them folks's eyes!" Jula exclaimed, then grumbled to herself, "Shut my mouth!"

She scurried out the door, like a mouse the cat is chasing, merely brushing Jonathan as she went.

"If you are ready, I will accompany you to the waiting carriage . . ." He cleared his throat after she whirled to face him, and he spoke almost crisply and coldly after assessing her in the soft orchid creation. "Once at Sugartree, you are solely on your own, Cathelen O'Ruark."

Snatching up her cloak a bit irritably, Cathelen followed him out the door. He strode before her, a magnificent male animal in white and black, with a dove gray cravat at his brown throat. Cathelen let her eyes inch up and down the long length of his virile frame, stopping at the crisp brown hair tapering at the back of his

184

neck. His hair had become unusually long and she wondered only momentarily at this.

Cathelen's eyes were like lavender stars, rivaling the huge ones hanging in the sky as they stepped outside.

Hondo drove the closed carriage, but Cathelen almost wished Jonathan were on the box instead. The brandy fumes were quite potent, and she wondered if he had imbibed most of the day, or if he had quit and then resumed his nipping in the afternoon. Michal had once told her that when a man drank early in the day, he was beset by many troubles and tribulations. She feared that what had driven Michal himself to drink had much to do with Cathmor O'Ruark. So what was Jonathan's excuse? Did the man have that much trouble? Maybe women?, she thought.

Sauvage kept his dark, handsome face directed toward the window and the slowly passing countryside. It was growing dark already. He could still see the slave quarters set a quarter of a mile from the main mill. The cabins were arranged in regularly spaced rows about a large square garden. Simple, palm-thatched buildings, made of hand posts driven deep into the ground and then interlaced with plaster and with wattles.

Cathelen looked, too, since there was nothing else to keep her mind off her unsettling thoughts and emotions. The cabins, she saw, were a man's length long, and high enough to allow a tall man to walk erect. "What is that cabin?" she blurted suddenly, unable to contain her curiosity over the larger one she had just seen.

Jonathan saw what she was looking at. He could feel her soft breath as she was turned his way and looked past his shoulder out the window. He did not look at her as he answered, knowing she was leaning forward a bit tensely awaiting the answer.

"That is the cabin for a couple living together—in what passes for marriage," he said with a soft snort of what sounded to Cathelen like mild disapproval.

"Do any of the women live alone?" she wondered out loud, feeling a bit easier now that he had broken the tension and said something.

He sighed before going on. "The men outnumber the women by two to one. No woman lives alone," he said languidly.

Sauvage clenched his hands inside his soft leather gloves, staring back in time, recalling when, as a lad, he used to run in and out of the cabins—sometimes Jonathan would chase him with a long switch. His grandfather always used the whip. His gut churned now. He still had scars from his grandfather's tortures, from the burns he'd suffered when his grandfather, astride a half-wild horse, had chased him into an outside cookfire. He had fallen into the pit, splaying his hands on the fiery embers that were cooking meat. They'd become glued to him while he'd screamed out his bloody hatred, unable to move until Hondo pulled him free and prevented him from being scarred worse than he was. When he spread his hands, the ugly, thick scars layered between his fingers became visible. But the backs of his hands were only shiny and thinly scarred, his tan hiding many of the flaws in his skin. Otherwise his fingers were perfectly formed. His mother had said he possessed beautiful hands for a man—but that was not so anymore.

Out loud, he mused to Cathelen as he dragged his mind from the horrors of his childhood. "These couples have very little furniture."

"Do they have a bed?"

Their eyes met and locked. Cathelen was the first to tear hers away. Jonathan looked down at the slim, perfect, golden hands resting on her lap amid the soft orchid material of her dress. Then he continued.

"I should not have asked that question," she murmured.

"Why be embarrassed?"

Jonathan reached out to run a long gloved finger over the work-roughened hands that were visibly soft in spots here and there. "Your hands are lovely. They should not be doing—" He caught himself before he went further. "Their bedstead is a platform of boards, the bed covered with a soft blanket." He cleared his throat, keeping up the feathery strokes with his finger.

Cathelen stared down at his black-gloved hands, and wanted to get off the subject of beds, saying, "Do they have other furniture?"

"I should hope so. They have a table, and a

187

stool or two, with such pots and pans as their simple cookery demands. We have made sure there is wood in plenty for fires inside at night."

"Oh?" Cathelen was curious. "Tell me, why?"

He left off stroking her tingling hand. "Without a fire indoors at night the Negro cannot sleep in peace."

Cathelen fell silent, her troubling concerns for the poor slaves put to rest. They seemed to be well provided for. The life to which the slaves had been introduced was little harder than that which the peasants of Scotland and Ireland were enduring across the water, while the West Indies climate was infinitely preferable.

The carriage hummed up Sugartree lane, right up to the steps of the mansion's white facade. All of the main houses that Cathelen had seen on Barbados's plantations were white, with high pillars. Georgian style, she was told.

As Cathelen stepped down from the carriage, Jonathan reached over her to take her elbow, his long frame close behind her. "You could have waited and I would have gotten out first to help you alight," he told her rather crossly.

"What, and have you crawl over me?" she said over her shoulder daringly, then she flinched as his grip hardened.

"There is another door to the carriage, Cathelen."

She pulled away from his solicitous arm, "But, *Master*, you said once we arrived here I would be on my own."

"Cathelen," he warned. *"Shame Lady."*

She turned to face him. "What did you say?"

He smiled lopsidedly. "You fold up at the slightest touch."

Ash blond eyebrows drew together in a quizzical frown. "I still do not understand—"

"Never mind."

"Cathy O'Ruark!"

Raven swept out onto the porch to greet Cathelen and Jonathan Sauvage. After introducing Jonathan to another planter, the two men wandered off to find a drink and become better acquainted.

Sauvage looked back to where Cathelen stared after him, still lightly frowning. He winked over his shoulder and Cathelen drew back a little, startled by his rakish grin.

"Raven," Cathelen dragged her friend's attention from another group forming at the door, "what is a Shame Lady?"

"Oh—that's a very sensitive plant that folds up its leaves at the slightest touch. Another name for it is Dead-and-Wake."

"I see." Cathelen shook her head. Then she trailed after Raven, for she did not know the others present.

Cathelen learned much in the next two hours just by trailing after Raven. She would have wandered off to find her own company, who she could not say, but Raven kept pulling her along.

Raven endeavored to keep out of Sauvage's way, however, and Cathelen did not wonder

189

why. Raven had already stated she did not care much for the man. Maybe there was more to Jonathan Sauvage than met the eye, maybe like his brother he had deep dark, and possibly evil, secrets. Like his brother *had had*, she corrected herself.

What Cathelen learned from the ladies' gossip burned her delicate virgin ears. In the West Indies the white man was dominant, she came to know, and therefore, wealthy white men had privileges which they no longer enjoyed in England or in France. Concubinage and promiscuity were common. Words like adultery, bastard, and illegitimate ceased to have any real meaning, except where the inheritance of property was involved.

Mortified, Cathelen almost fled the room where many of the guests had gathered to watch a few couples waltz. She felt a strong urge to whirl about and slap the woman who was speaking in the face, but she quelled that urge, and tried not to listen. Still, it was impossible not to overhear; she was boxed in by gossips.

"He keeps more than two mistresses—and raises families on the side."

"How can you stand it?" an older woman's voice asked the younger.

"What do I care? As long as he keeps his hands to himself."

"But, Samantha. 'House children' and 'yard children' living in the same house—all together! Why don't you leave your brother-in-law's house?"

"Jessica, where *have* you been! That's nothing. This is the West Indies, honey. And white women are comparatively few here, so we do get good treatment. Mulatto girls are kept as mistresses by white men here of all ranks."

"But—marriage to a mulatto would be shocking!"

Samantha Gable sniffed importantly, even though she was divorced from her wealthy husband who had left her. "Heavens—who marries them! Jeremy just 'has' them. And to 'them,' mating with a white man holds the promise of greater benefits for their children."

Cathelen was reminded of Mattissa. So, pigmentation does determine prestige and power, she thought. And Mattissa understood that it was possible to "raise" her color, by very careful mating. How unusual and animal-like, Cathelen thought, like breeding animals. But the road to becoming white and therefore accepted must be a long one. Cathelen could understand Mattissa more and more. That woman wanted Jonathan Sauvage for reasons beyond passion.

"Some of these women are very exquisite, I'm told," Jessica put in, almost in a whisper.

"Where have you been?" Samantha asked the older woman emphatically, a haughty laugh in her voice.

"Here, in this godforsaken place—for one year."

"No wonder! But you are not totally blind. There are very few of the really beautiful Creoles

191

here. Still," Samantha sighed, "their beauty does not totally get rid of the loneliness of the planter's life."

Cathelen's brain snagged on the last one. Jonathan—a lonely man? Surely, the younger woman must be exaggerating. Cathelen's teeth clenched. This Samantha must be the very one who had dumped poor Jula out of the only home she'd ever known, cast her out without letting the girl speak her piece. Jula had told her a good deal about this Samantha Gable—but nothing good.

"Excuse me," Samantha said peering over Cathelen's shoulder, "but do I know you?" Samantha straightened as Cathelen turned to face her.

"I am afraid you do not." Cathelen stepped to the side of the gossipers, found an opening, and disappeared to mingle with the growing crowd circling the dancing couples.

"Care to dance?"

Cathelen turned as the man spoke. She and he were equally shocked, if for different reasons, to see each other. Cathelen experienced revulsion, Vance Moore utter delight.

"My, but aren't you the angel."

With that, Cathelen was very nearly swept off her protesting feet as the black-haired devil ungently escorted her to the middle of the dance floor. He did not even care that she would rather not dance with him!

With slightly blurring vision, Jonathan Sauvage turned in time to see his lovely servant go into the arms of the man he had already made up his mind to dislike intensely. His vision not only cleared, but he knew the renewal of quickening desire. He had to have Cathy O'Ruark, to get the lovely creature out of his system. Once he had taken her, it would be a simple task to forget she ever existed. Yet how could he have Cathy without her knowing he was her employer?

Impossible! Sauvage told himself. He sipped a bit more brandy, watching her, the ethereal vision of youthful womanhood, over the rim of his glass. He felt himself grow harder.

Ah, yes. Jonathan stroked his taut cheek and a twinkle appeared in his tawny eyes, sparking their golden flecks to fire. Why had he not thought of it sooner? He had already had the opportunity. He downed the last drop in his glass and left the noisy house.

A carriage moved away from the others and headed toward the man waiting on the steps—the man Hondo had recognized as Adam Sauvage.

Chapter Twenty-Two

The scent of white jasmine was wafted on the night air, and tree frogs and crickets made music. At the front door a woman, her complexion a rich, deep chocolate color set off by a bright bandanna that rose in butterflylike points above her forehead, very graciously handed Cathelen her cloak.

"Yo sho yo wants to leave so early, Miz Cathy?"

As the dark woman helped her on with her cloak Cathelen asked the friendly soul, "Do I know you?"

"I'm sho Miz Raven been talkin' to yo 'bout me . . ."

With a big black grin, the maid waited.

Cathelen smiled back at the pudgy, dark face.

"You must be Paprika. I should have known," she apologized.

Paprika acknowledged her statement with a hearty nod. "Thas me." She peered out the door then. "Yo want me to get yo a ride back home den? That Massa Jonathan done gone home already."

Cathelen sighed casually. "I suppose he has. But it is such a beautiful warm night that I think I will walk, Paprika."

The woman's eyes rounded into black saucers with white borders.

"Walk? Yo be footin' until the wee hours den, honey chile, if yo plans to do dat." She shivered visibly. "Oooh-weee, it's dark out dere, chile. Yo sho yo wants to walk? I kin wave dat driver over there and he kin drive yo on home."

Cathelen stepped out onto the porch, feeling the night air envelop her like a sultry caress.

"No thank you, Paprika." Cathelen breathed deeply, going off the porch.

"Uhmm-uhmm." Paprika shook her head, rolling black eyes to the night. "Sho is dark enough." Then she searched the shadows beyond, but saw no one there walking. "Wonder if dat honey chile told Raven she was goin' to foot it home." Of course, others had come on foot and gone home the same way—but usually by day not night. Paprika was suddenly sorry she had allowed the young woman to go on alone without telling Raven before she set out. Too late now, Paprika shrugged regretfully, planning to go upstairs and turn down beds for those spending the night.

Paprika hid an amused chuckle behind her hand when she noticed "Massa Moore" searching the rooms frantically. The maid knew it would not be long before that devil-man came asking Paprika what had happened to that sweet gal. Paprika set her countenance, prepared to answer Moore by telling him she did not know which way that honey chile went.

Outside Cathelen walked along the narrow dirt road, sugar cane flanking her on either side. There was sugar cane everywhere, the stalks grown taller than a man. She shot a glance off the road often. A person could hide in those fields.

She pulled her cloak tighter about her shoulders. This was exciting, though, walking in the night. She had done it in Scotland, where she had loved the night and the stars and the moon on the moors.

Soon Cathelen had to remove her shoes; her toes hurt. She set off again then, stepping carefully, gingerly, so the pebbles would not cut into her feet.

Rich fields of long, sword-sharp leaves surrounded her, the leaves sprouted from the joints of sugar stalks, sea green in color by day, now willow gray beneath the drifting moon. No other place, she had been instructed—no other in the world—depended on one crop of sugar as much as Barbados. Rich planters abounded, true, but the rest of the land was made up of peasant holdings. Still, great houses had taken place of the simpler structures of the previous century, and in England, the West Indian planters' extravagance had become a byword. She was grateful to have learned so much about Barbados life and history in such a short time, thanks to her tutor—Cathelen smiled—Deke Jameson.

Cathelen recognized the sound of a carriage before she saw the gray hulk bearing down on her. She stepped to the side of the road, saw the lanterns swinging, and blinked several times before she became accustomed to the increase in light. She knew the driver had seen her, for he was slowing down.

A muffled curse issued from somewhere aboard, and Cathelen felt the hair on her arms prickle as the carriage rolled slowly by without stopping completely. Suddenly a door swung open and a cloaked arm reached for her. Grasped around the waist, she was lifted free of the ground, and then the small cavern of the carriage swallowed her up.

Chapter Twenty-Three

"Do you know who I am?"

"Yes."

Indeed Cathelen knew. He had released his tight grip on her, but she had known all along on this night that the Pirate would come for her.

"Who?"

His deep smiling voice was beside her, and she was incredibly unafraid. "You are Adam Sauvage—the pirate," she said.

She heard his intake of breath. "You are he—and you are not dead," she added.

He seemed to be contemplating what she said, before he spoke. "So, if this is true, what are you going to do about it?" he mocked.

She reached out to finger his scarred face. "How did this happen?" She touched the scar and it felt awful. She drew away.

He did not answer that, but said, "I want you, Cathy, and I mean to have you."

"No!" Cathelen twisted away. "You, too, have been drinking, just like your brother!"

"A ghost that drinks?"

"You know very well what I mean!"

He seemed not to have heard her. "You are like a breath of fresh air, Cathy, after years of tainted winds. We are . . . more than ships that pass in the night, my wild sweet Cathy."

"Tell me, please, what happened to you and why are you here now?" she asked him, violence in her tone.

He took her hand as the carriage rumbled on to Cathelen knew not where, nor did she care. There was indeed a wildness in the air. She knew it was ridiculous, but this night meant more to her than anything that had gone before in her life.

Yet when the carriage halted before the wind-swept shore, Cathelen was beginning to have a change of heart. This man beside her, his breath a warm wind on her neck, this dangerous man was a pirate; one who, now that she had seen him in the lantern light, looked very much like Jonathan. Was Adam Sauvage really dead? And if so, who could this man be?

"Cathy," he began but she cut him short.

She turned to face his gold-cast countenance. "You called me Cathy again, just like your brother."

He laughed with a deep sound. "My brother?

199

Sweet Angel, I have none, and I usually give my 'women' a nickname, so that's nothing out of the ordinary."

Cathelen puffed up at that. "How many so-called 'women' do you keep, Sir Pirate?" She shook her head. Pirates could not "keep" women, they roved too much. "A woman in every port, hmm?"

"Jealous?"

"Well?" she insisted.

"Used to be that way," he said softly.

"And now?"

"Now I've only one thing occupying my time and thoughts." Wolf saw that she was waiting. "At least it did until you came along. And now—"

"Cap'n! We've gotta get the Hades outta here!"

Having been about to take Cathelen in his arms whether she liked it or not, Wolf twisted toward the driver's voice. "Damn it, don't screech so loud! What is it?"

Cathelen sat back, strangely unalarmed, to contemplate the sound of the driver's voice. He, too, sounded very familiar. She had accepted the familiarity of the Pirate's voice, believing him to be Jonathan's supposed-to-be dead brother.

"Who can it be?" Wolf called back up, keeping an eye on the woman beside him.

The reply floated down, muffled now though the words were audible. "That carriage coming around looks to be that—uh—that Moore fella

200

to me. What ya want me to do, Cap'n?"

Cathelen did not think it unusual that the driver called him captain. She gazed downward then, just as the carriage started up again. Frowning, she said, "Do *both* you and your brother wear black gloves?"

"I've already told you," he ground out, "I've no brother. Mine died several"—he cleared his throat—"a long time ago."

The moroseness of his tone reached her. "You hesitate?"

For an answer, the Wolf moved seductively in on her. One hand went about her tiny waist, while the fingers of the other wound about her neck to still any struggles she might try. "I've got to make you mine, sweet witch. Mine, tonight. Ever since you cast a— *Damn!*"

The carriage seemed to be under hot pursuit, for they were traveling much too fast. Cathelen swayed and bumped into the pirate, their lips mere breaths from each other. Dangerous excitement seemed to flow from every pore of this infamous man, igniting Cathelen's blood to fire too.

His lips brushed hers with the gentlest of kisses; then they fastened on her mouth as if he would never release her.

"Cathy, Cathy. My sweet witch," he said after he'd fairly bruised her soft lips.

"No—Pirate. I know what you desire. My answer is no—*a thousand times no*. Besides, you would kill me at this pace. Ouch!"

201

Cathelen's pert nose lifted and contacted his hard chin as they hit a rut and bumped together painfully.

"Not if you are used to—*love*."

His voice was a gentle sound.

"You are crude, Sir Pirate!" She felt her nose checking for blood.

"What did you expect?"

"Soon I'll be bleeding at this grueling pace!"

Wolf did not voice a comment at that. He kissed her cheek hotly, driven by the heat eating away at his loins.

"Unhand me!"

He tossed up his hands. "You are free, my sweet witch Cathy."

"I do not mean your hands and you know it. At the moment your legs are straddling mine!"

"Do you want to be tossed onto the floor?"

"Not by you!"

"Ah, Cathy. The time is so short between cradle and coffin. Come, let us enjoy life."

He pushed his hands, now ungloved, up her legs and Cathelen screamed softly, believing he still wore the gloves because of the leathery touch she felt. But Wolf had removed them only moments before, and he loved the feel of her satiny skin. "Hush, love, I won't hurt you."

"You devil pirate— Oh! Stop that, I say!"

"My. Tsk-tsk. Listen to the fancy lady swear." He chuckled then, and before she knew what was going on, he had one hand beneath her breast, the other kneading her thigh.

"You drunken spoiler! Rapparee! Picaroon!"

She yelled at his head, somewhat surprised herself by her salty language, but he only lowered his face as he freed a small, perfect dove. "How did you manage that?" she shrieked at him.

"Very easy, milady."

"Oh, so now it's milady again."

Cathelen thrust forward her hips to fight him off, for she could not go backward to escape him. A mistake, however, she realized too late.

"Ah, thank you for accommodating me." He slid her the rest of the way and pinned her between his steely legs.

"Let me up, you—you dark-haired Viking!"

Cathelen tried to kick his most vulnerable place, but she could not even raise her feet, much less her knees.

Now he began to make love to her, earnestly, bringing her untried passions alive, delving into her secret self. His hands were coarse, though at the same time gentle on her, his lips possessive yet pleasurable. Cathelen was soon afire and unable to extinguish the flames licking through her.

"Pirate," she murmured helplessly, "don't do this to me."

His head lifted at her begging tone, almost pitiful in its smallness. "But, Cathy sweet, I must have you. *Mon Dieu*, it is difficult on this cursed narrow cushion."

French? "That is your problem, Pirate," she dropped the "sir." Somehow, she slipped out from under him and rolled like a bear cub to the floor of the carriage.

He was, however, right down on top of her the next minute. "You are going to get your pretty dress all dirty." He chuckled into her shocked face.

"You—you are the one who is dirty, Pirate. You—you sea bastard!"

"Tsk, tsk, who's been teaching you, *sweet . . .* Cathy." He breathed against her silky throat.

The carriage trundled on and Cathelen began to scream at the top of her lungs. A hand clamped over her mouth, a voice rasped in her ear.

"What the hell! They'll think I'm killing you."

She hissed, "You are, damn you, what do you think? I'm enjoying this? You are insane, Pirate!"

"Go ahead and scream. Try. Do you think someone will hear you?" he mocked.

She did just that. Right in his ear.

He slapped her then. Cathelen felt her cheek sting hotly and tears began to gather on her lashes.

The Wolf buried his handsome though scarred face in her hair, now hanging loose like moonbeams, on the carriage floor.

"I do not want to hurt you, Cathy, I only want to make love to you."

Groaning from need and frustration, Wolf pressed himself against her thighs. Her skirts had ridden up and were now tangled about her waist. He hastily unbuttoned his fly, but she squirmed away to thwart him from gaining entry.

"No, you do not, Pirate!"

He tried to gentle her but she was like a wild kitten. "All right, love, let it be another time, another place, then." He began to draw away.

Just then the carriage began to careen and tip crazily, tossing the Wolf into Cathelen—and the deed was done.

Cathelen screamed, frightened of being crushed and of being sullied by this nasty pirate. His thrust burned like a brand of molten fire.

The Wolf, now that he was of a mind to complete the act and to love her fully, could not, nor could he lift his hips an inch. He was forced to grind himself into her, Cathelen crying out at the pain this caused her newly invaded secret self.

The carriage, meanwhile, had come to a halt on the slope of a ditch. Wolf was gratified only by the realization that she would not know the identity of this embarrassing fellow who had so unsuccessfully made love to her. He groaned. She must think him really a ghost now, he chuckled inwardly.

There were shouts, followed by a bawdy curse from the pirate. He lifted himself, arms quivering not only from the exertion but from his reluctance to leave her so undone. "I bid you *adieu*, milady."

The door opened. He lunged out. Then all was still except for the tree frogs and click beetles. Suddenly the silence was split by the sound of a thud and then a groan, followed by the patting off of dusty clothes.

"Who was that man?"

Finally, to Cathelen's profound relief, she was yanked upward, only it was not the Pirate who aided her but that devil, Vance Moore. Which was the lesser of the two evils? she wondered dazedly.

Hondo appeared beside Moore, looking a bit sheepish. "Someone must've stole my carriage."

"This . . . Sauvage's carriage?" she said, baffled.

"Aye."

Vance Moore noticed the dark stains on her thighs before she saw her mortifying position and violently jerked down her skirts.

"You're bleeding!" Moore gasped, his flickering green eyes making a crude assumption.

"Not only that, sir, but I am damn blasted angry!"

Chapter Twenty-Four

The black leather gloves stared up at Cathelen, almost with feeling.

"How many more of these does he have?" she wondered to herself.

And Jonathan—how about him? She picked up the pair, slapped them over her palm, and then tossed them onto a chair.

Cathelen was determined to be revenged on that raunchy pirate. Somehow, some way, dear God, she would discover a weakness, a hole in the man's steely facade—or make one in his rogue's heart!

She wandered into the living room which overlooked the fields. She could see the slaves hoeing, weeding, and preparing roads and wharfs and elementary machinery for crop time.

Jonathan was out there, for she had seen him earlier. He was becoming very dark—very handsome.

Jonathan came into view, and it was as if he'd known she was watching him. Swiping the plantation hat from his head, he drew a forearm across his forehead and looked up the hill. It was as if he could see her, and Cathelen drew back a little, hoping he had not caught her staring at him so openly. She was certain he could not see her, not even her face from this distance.

Cathelen's shoulders drooped. She had fancied herself in love with Jonathan, she knew that now. Had she also fancied herself in love with the pirate?

Perhaps it was only because the two men were so alike. Jonathan was much more the gentleman. The other the . . . the pirate—there was no other name for that one!

And he was no ghost, for the virgin blood on her thighs had proven that!

Remembering his painful thrust, Cathelen wondered sadly if it was always that way. If so, she wanted nothing more to do with making love. In Scotland she had once heard the screams of a neighbor who was bringing her babe into the world, and now she feared that both these things must be hard to bear. She certainly had never heard a woman cry out in ecstasy. That must all be put on for the man's benefit, she decided.

Then why did she feel so good all over just

looking at Jonathan Sauvage? Would it be different with him . . . maybe? Would he be gentle, not hurt her?

A cold chill ran over her. She felt faint. What if she should become with child? Would she ever see the pirate again? He would never marry her! He must have bastards strewn all over the country—the world!

"You are going to stand there all day?"

Mattissa came to stand beside Cathelen at the window and put forth another question. "Who are you watching, white woman?"

Cathelen would have groaned with frustration if she had not been too weary.

"White man," Cathelen answered, leaving the living room in a swirl of blue cotton.

Mattissa's eyes narrowed and then became very large as she saw out there the 'white man' Cathelen had been referring to. Murder was plainly written on the woman's face, and anyone watching would have shuddered to see her.

At noon work ceased, but many of the slaves, preferring to eat their main meal at night, just lay out in the shade to sleep during the two hours of heavy heat. During this period Jonathan headed for the house, Deke Jameson walking with him.

The men ate silently, out on the veranda. Shyly, Cathelen served them, never looking directly into Jonathan's dark, handsome face. She just couldn't, not after last night. Even though it was not Jonathan who had sullied her.

Quietly, Jonathan watched Cathelen move about; then he lounged in his chair after eating his fill. Deke closed his eyes, and laced his fingers over his stomach. But Jonathan's eyes were wide open. He sat back to admire the way Cathelen's blue cotton dress swept over her small hips, its thin material emphasizing her soft curves. The freshly dyed dress brought out the violet blue in her eyes. Her eyes changed color, that he had already noticed.

Jonathan was so engrossed in watching her dovelike hands move about the small table that he did not hear her.

"Well?" she said, unmoving.

"Did you ask something of me?"

"Do you want more? I asked."

"Yes," he said mesmerized by her haunting, ethereal beauty. He spied Deke then with one eye open, and coughed. "No, Cathelen." He rose. "We'll be going back out to the fields now."

Deke tipped his hat at her as she stood trance-like, but Cathelen only stared at Jonathan's tall frame moving with whipcord strength off the veranda.

During that week, Cathelen began to see a new Jonathan—a generous, warmhearted man, anxious to improve the condition of the slaves. Still, he recognized the dangers of the absentee system and she had overheard him arguing with Mattissa who had said that the other planters

210

accused him of spoiling his Negroes and spreading dissatisfaction. Cathelen could not understand Mattissa's ways at all. The woman had black blood yet she believed slaves should be whipped now and then. She said hotly that they accepted the blows that fell on them as they accepted the other details of their life. Torture held no mysteries for them. In Africa they had seen their fellows slaughtered, seen the sacrifice of the virgin; and they had eaten, in their religious feasts, the flesh of a young child.

"Enough, Mattissa!" Jonathan had shouted.

This only seemed to excite Mattissa and she went on. "Your neighbor, his man uses chains and the iron collar. What has happened to you, Jonathan? Deke has been soft on them. It is because of the little white woman, no?"

"What do you mean our neighbor?"

"The overseer at Sugartree, Theodore Decatur. Have you died and come back to life as a merciful saint, Jonathan Sauvage?" she hissed at him, staring at his gloved fingers.

With that he had stormed out of the house, Mattissa's laughter following him. "He has even become soft on the woman here." She shook her turbaned head. "All womans."

In spite of his genuine affection for his slaves, Jonathan had no illusions about them. There were several thousand workers on his estate, and according to the estate account books that Jonathan had kept, he was now one of the richest plantation owners in Barbados.

In the tropics most plantation work was done

in the first cool green hours. Shortly before sunrise a conch shell would be blown. The slaves would gather for roll call and then go out with the overseer. While the men and the stronger women worked in the fields, the Negro cooks would prepare breakfast. It was a savory but strange-looking hash composed of plantains, yams, eddoes, calalu, and okra—seasoned with salt and cayenne pepper.

On chill and foggy mornings there would usually be a number of absentees. Deke Jameson had to take care of the delinquents, but his whip was not as cruel and biting as Decatur's over at Sugartree.

The slaves expected to be beaten—just as Mattissa had said—when they arrived late at roll call, when they were lazy in the fields, or when they made blunders in their work. And should they become aggressive and unruly, be rebellious toward Sauvage or Jameson or, worse still, escape into the hills they expected to receive heavy punishment.

Indeed heavy punishments were then served out to them, especially at Sugartree. Jonathan had heard of Theodore Decatur's brutal and licentious punishments. He thought the man must have no better employment for his imagination than devising refined tortures for refractory slaves. Jameson had told Jonathan of the short chains cunningly set into an iron collar fixed around the neck. These were attached to the ankle and they prevented a slave from walking. They made it possible only to hobble on numb and agonized legs.

On learning of this punishment, Jonathan's eyes had glittered angrily. "Have you ever done any of this? Has my"—he looked around the field and saw that they were alone in the immediate area—"has my brother?"

"He—we—buried a slave up to the neck in the earth and covered his face with sugar so that the flies and mosquitoes slowly stung him to a frenzy." Noticing Sauvage's tightly drawn lips, he held up his hand. "Once. At Sugartree they do it—ah—better. They coat the naked slave with sugar and pour over the man scoop after scoop of living ants."

"Is that all?" Sauvage asked, his contempt for Moore and his man evident.

"There is the iron cage studded with spikes that fits close to the neck and feet, so that the pain in one limb could be relieved only by shifting it to the other." Jameson sighed as if weary of the telling. "Some slaves over at Sugartree hate their master so much that to do damage to him they take their own lives. They know that their deaths will mean a loss of money. Not long ago, over at Tandy's, the slaves revolted and set upon the overseer. They tore him to pieces, not caring for the punishment that waited them. Jeremy Skelton hung the overseer's murderers in a cage and left them to die of rage and hunger."

"'Putting a man out to dry?'"

"That's it," Deke returned, "you got it."

Sauvage looked up. Refreshed by rest and

213

food, their muscles already loosened by the sun, the slaves returned to work almost heartily amid the cane, the sound of their song accompanying the crack of the machete.

Sauvage smiled as he looked around the fields. "This cane sure is greedy, exhausting the soil almost before we get the manure down."

"Yep." Jameson smiled back.

"Well? Are you ready to go shovel some dung?"

"Sure am."

Sauvage, after working with Deke and the slaves all afternoon, relaxed with a cool lime drink and a slim cheroot.

Across from the hard-driving man he was coming to respect exceedingly, Deke reflected on the excellent French he had heard Sauvage speak earlier.

"What were you saying, Boss, when you saw Cathy O'Ruark riding off in that smart carriage with gorgeous Raven Moore this afternoon?"

"Haven't you ever heard a man curse violently in French before?"

With that Sauvage shut his eyes. But Jameson, not finished with the conversation, had another topic he wanted to bring up.

"Moore was over when you were away last week. The aristocrats serve in the cavalry. Aren't you going to?"

"What?" Sauvage opened one eye. "And put on one of those peacocklike uniforms and strut around in a white-plumed helmet?" He snorted in a derogatory fashion.

"The artisans and the shopkeepers serve in the infantry."

"Let them. It appears that the infantry is little more than servants for the cavalry."

"Oh?"

"Not a very formidable force for Barbados in a time of crises."

Deke lifted blond eyebrows. "Five thousand men, not enough? Under arms at that?"

"A great number of the infantry, my friend, are bondmen and Irishmen shipped out against their will for perhaps five to seven years. Under harsh masters who at the expiration of their sentence usually find some excuse for prolonging their durance."

Deke wondered who was teaching who here. He shook his head. Sauvage shut both eyes again but Jameson once more intruded on the man's slumber. However, this time the subject was of great interest to Sauvage.

"Do you know that Cathy O'Ruark was forced into indenture?"

Both eyes, chocolate brown now, opened wide. "What did you say?" He sat up and brought his arms down from behind his head.

"She was tricked, I should say. We've talked, you know, on the way to Bridgetown."

"What did she have to say?"

Jameson saw the glint of interest in Sauvage's eyes. "The slimy captain of the *Windward Lady* pressed her into bondage. Her father was hung for murder."

Sauvage whistled softly. "That is bad."

"Yep. She's gentle born. Of course any fool can see that. She's meant to be a lady, used to the finer things in life." Jameson shook his blond head. "She sure took to being a servant without any trouble. Most highborn ladies would complain until your ears burned from their whining."

Sauvage held up a hand, and Jameson leaned forward.

"What is it?" he asked, wondering at his boss's thoughtful expression.

"Does any one else know she was tricked?"

Deke shook his head. "Don't think so. Even if she were able to go back to Scotland, all that's left is a brother who, she says, is hardly ever home, and he was probably tossed into prison for trying to save his father's neck."

Sauvage put a finger to his lips. "If she were set free, where do you think she would go? If, for instance, Raven Moore were to lend her money?"

"Back to Scotland, of course, to find her brother. She misses him terribly, thinks he's in some sort of trouble if he's not in jail." Jameson tried to read the dark eyes. "Why, what are you thinking of doing?"

"Making her my mistress. Keeping her here."

"What!"

Not thinking she had heard Mattissa right, Cathelen whirled to face her spite-filled countenance. The woman nodded, pursing her lips together so hard that they wrinkled.

"He wants you for his mistress. Deke Jameson has told me this."

Cathelen thought Mattissa appeared deflated, worn out all of a sudden. But still Mattissa kept her chin tilted at a proud angle.

"That is right. You sit down," Mattissa said sarcastically as Cathelen dropped onto a kitchen chair. "You will not work hard after this day. You will move into the room adjoining the master's." Mattissa closed and opened her eyes slowly as if it caused her great pain to relate this.

Cathelen shot up from the chair like a wooden soldier. "I have some say in this. I will not be—be—subjected to such humiliation. I—I am not a common trull!"

Mattissa snorted disdainfully. "Again I do not understand your language. But you must mean whore, do you not?"

"Indeed! And I am not this!"

Bored, Mattissa sighed. "You will be anything Jonathan wishes you to be. Unless," her eyes darkened to black onyx, "unless you wish to be whipped?"

"No one could wish that, Mattissa," Cathelen said to the woman as if she were daft. She sat down, more heavily this time. "What would you do, Mattissa?" Cathelen asked, slyly.

"For long I have wanted Jonathan Sauvage. I would run and jump into his bed if he asked."

"Because you want his baby," Cathelen said.

"Yes. You are very clever, white woman."

Cathelen sighed. "But not clever enough to get out of this predicament. I do not want to be a

217

whore, I want to be a wife," she said sadly. "All my life I have yearned for love. My own father did not want me, and I cannot even remember my mother any longer."

For just a moment Mattissa's eyes softened, but then her face hardened again. "You must bathe and make yourself ready for Master Jonathan. He has been hard for a long time."

"What?" Cathelen looked up, puzzled. "He has been hard? Where?"

At Mattissa's smirk Cathelen realized the meaning of Mattissa's last statement, and she blushed with hot embarrassment. How could a woman know this? she wondered shakily.

At the door, Mattissa taunted Cathelen one last time. "He will, I think, kill you." She gave the slight figure a once-over of pure disgust. "Jonathan Sauvage is a big man."

After the woman had gone about her tasks, leaving Cathelen to collect what she would for the move upstairs to the room adjoining Jonathan's, Cathelen stared at the floor in abject confusion and despair. She had already been ravished by the pirate and had her virginity taken. There was only one thing to do, she decided, and that was to lie still and take what Jonathan did to her body. She did not want to, but what else could she do?

Cathelen perked up. Lie still? Of course. She had a pretty good idea that trulls did not give a man pleasure by just lying there like a dead log. They must do something to make men want them over and over, even pay for it. If she were to lie still, then maybe Jonathan would tire of her and want a more lively piece. Maybe, if God in heaven heard her prayers, Jonathan would not even hurt her as the pirate had. Was that the way of it? she wondered.

Cathelen nipped the knuckles on the back of her hand, trying to choke down her fear of the coming night. She bit them too hard and drew a speck of blood. That damned pirate! He'd sullied her and made her not even want to be Jonathan's wife any longer.

She caught herself. Jonathan's wife? When had this wish come about?

Oh, she was so confused. Both Jonathan and the Pirate had made her feel things she had not wanted to be aware of. She would have to ask God to forgive her her sinful desires, then maybe, just maybe all men would let her be!

Part II

Cast Love's Spell

Chapter Twenty-Five

The black gloves had disappeared. Cathelen had searched high and low in her dreary cubicle of a bedroom but had not come up with the pair.

Set into motion again, Cathelen crossed to the other side of the hall. "Mairi?" She merely peeped in.

"Come in." Mairi nodded as she bade the girl to enter.

"I am missing something. Maybe you could help me. I am moving upstairs"—she pouted upward, her fine nostrils flaring—"to the room next to Master Jonathan's." She pronounced title and name exaggeratedly. Then Cathelen stared hard, not blinking, and could not credit what she saw. A moment ago the old woman had been wide awake, now she was asleep—snoring!

Tiredly the young woman turned to quit the room. She did not see the old woman peer at her from one squinted eye.

Cathelen made her way upstairs with the tiny bundle that contained all of her possessions. She was not surprised to see Mattissa waiting for her when she reached the top. The handsome woman stood stiff as an army general, her clenched hands the only sign of resentment Cathelen could see.

But inside Mattissa fairly seethed. She wanted to strangle this fair woman, toss the body out the window, and turn her back on Cathelen O'Ruark. Wickedly she imagined doing these things as she led the way to the room adjoining Master Sauvage's.

Cathelen held her breath after stepping into the room, and Mattissa watched her closely as she walked to the window which occupied most of the wall space. The bedroom looked onto the sea and was a small replica of Jonathan's, Cathelen could see.

"Have you nothing to say?"

"It is beautiful. But I still cannot believe that I am to occupy this room, Mattissa," said Cathelen, trying to be civil to the woman.

"Tah! You should be grateful. Your lover is a highborn Frenchman. His mother I do not know if she was French—this does not matter. As long as you do not refuse Master Jonathan his pleasure, you are very fortunate, white woman."

In the folds of her skirts, Cathelen clenched her hands into tight tiny fists. She was afraid if she relaxed them she would be impelled to slap Mattissa's haughty face.

Cathelen sighed. "How long before I am to be ravished?" She made the question sound like a statement of doom.

"Jonathan is eager for a woman and will not be put off. On this night he will await you in his bed. You must bathe and be ready by after dark."

Tonight! Of course, Mattissa had said as much earlier. To be in a man's crushing embrace once again, to feel that steely shaft enter and hurt her. Dear God, give me strength, Cathelen prayed.

"I will be ready," she said, by now resigned to her terrible fate.

Mattissa smiled crookedly at the girl's obvious distress. She thrust the dagger deeper. "You are a virgin, I know, and you will suffer greatly." Cathelen already knew that, but Mattissa's next words caused the color to drain from her face. "He will ride between your thighs over and over, and after your first blood has been shed more will come, until you are drained. You will scream in agony after an hour. Remember, I said Jonathan is a big man." Her voice became a hiss. "He will tear you apart, little one."

Cathelen stumbled back against the bed, clutching her throat with one hand. "I would

225

rather die," she muttered, her eyes dazed.

Mattissa laughed at the dead-white girl. "I think maybe you will have to kill yourself. Jonathan will be sorry to hear that his whore took her own life."

But anger began to gnaw away at Cathelen's fear, reviving her spirit. She straightened with renewed courage.

"I value my life, Mattissa, too much to ever throw it away for a moment of fear. Maybe you do not know I am a Scot, which makes me most courageous and strong willed."

"Pah! You are a skinny wench and you will not live the year out."

Cathelen fought down the urge to attack Mattissa—to smash her small hard fist into the woman's red mouth. That would silence the black witch!

"Get out of my room!" Cathelen suddenly blasted.

Mattissa was taken aback, but she recovered quickly. "Ah, so you think you are wise."

"I am. I have just realized my position is above yours now," Cathelen said, smiling at her own words.

"You slut!"

"Not yet," Cathelen tossed back.

"You will be. Master Jonathan will have you and then toss you to the pirate pigs, white woman."

"Jonathan will have me and love it!"

With a gasp, Mattissa fell back and grasped the door frame. She worked her mouth to retort but no words would emerge, so she shot around the door and into the hall.

Cathelen smiled to herself and dusted off her small hands. There was one victory. Now to work toward another. She must carefully think out the plan that had formed while Mattissa was cruelly taunting her.

Prepare herself though she might, Cathelen did not expect herself to tremble so when she stepped from the perfumed bath Mattissa had ordered Jula to prepare.

Steely resolve, that was what she needed, so Cathelen squared her shoulders like a fledgling lad going into battle. She said a prayer, knowing that was a comfort in times like this.

"Where did that come from?"

Cathelen pointed to the filmy nightgown spread over her new four-poster bed, and Jula appeared a bit sheepish as she spoke.

"Mattissa say she wash to make fresh and hang many hours to make wrinkles come out."

Jula brushed dark fingers over the slippery silk. "It is very pretty, no?"

Cathelen sighed. "Yes. It is lavender, one of my favorite colors. But Jula, you did not answer me. Who does it belong to? Mattissa?"

"Oh no," Jula shook her head. "Mattissa much too big for this pretty. I not to say, Missy Cathelen."

"You are right." Cathelen laid a gentle hand on Jula's shoulder. "I would not want you to get

227

in trouble over my curiosity."

"You very nice to Jula." The girl's eyes sparkled darkly.

"And I am very happy to have you for a friend."

Cathelen turned back to the lovely nightie. "When do I have to put that thing on?"

Striding up the well-beaten path, Jonathan headed toward Mattissa who was standing on the front porch looking for all the world like a stiff Spanish duenna.

Mattissa eyed him covertly, not liking what she saw in the man's eyes. There was heat in them. Desire. They burned past Mattissa, into the house, up the stairs.

"Mattissa." He stepped onto the porch, long legs pulling and stretching, reminding Mattissa of a magnificent muscled cat. "Has all been taken care of?" he asked in French.

"Oui."

"Merci."

That was it. Mattissa watched this princely man go out of her life; she would never conceive that baby now. She had wanted to make a baby with a Sauvage, especially with this brother. Now even the other was gone. This one would make strong sons between her thighs— but no more. The white woman will bewitch him with her snowy soft flesh. But he may grow tired of her, soon, Mattissa thought, for he could never love such a pale thing as she. And Jonathan had known many women in the past. Not many knew this, but Mattissa had seen much. She was puzzled of late, though, for Jonathan seemed to be leading a celibate life. Still, what did she know of his doings during his long absences.

Upstairs Cathelen merely nibbled at the tray of food Jula had brought. Her stomach was too full of nervous butterflies.

Shoving the tray aside, she slid off the downy bed and went to gaze at herself in the mirror. Then she shook her snowy head. "This cannot be me."

Jula had poured perfumed oil into her bath, and so Cathelen's skin glistened, appearing even more golden from her days in the garden. Her hair, tied up in back with a white ribbon, fell in a snowy blond mass of shining waves to her waist. This was also the result of Jula's handiwork.

A smile broke out as she recalled the scene that had occurred when Jonathan had opened the door for their very pretty neighbor. Pretty— Cathelen huffed—until she had been angered by Jonathan's reluctance to let Jula go back to Tandy Plantation.

Lean hands on hips, Jonathan had said, "I don't believe I remember you, madam? I am sorry."

"Why, Jonathan Sauvage!" Samantha Gable had bristled. "How can you say such a thing!"

From the hall Cathelen had seen Samantha step up to Jonathan and say something low, meant for the man's ears only.

"Hmm, really?" Jonathan said as if this was an interesting secret. "I am afraid I don't recall the particulars, madam. Would you like to refresh my memory?"

"Jonathan Sauvage, you stop calling me *madam!*" Samantha's voice had stayed on an even keel—high-pitched and shrewish.

Angry at herself for eavesdropping, Cathelen had already started to step away from the front door when Samantha's next words drew her back.

"Two nights a week? At the old mill? Does that do something to you, darling?" Samantha purred provocatively as Sauvage coughed. "Come now, Jonathan darling, how could you forget that you laid—"

"Ho!" he chuckled, cutting her off. "Now I remember something. How remiss of me."

"Should we walk, Jonathan?"

Impelled to step closer to the door as Samantha looped her shapely arm into Jonathan's, Cathelen gawked as the couple strolled toward the gardens.

Mesmerized, Cathelen watched them until Jonathan came to a sudden halt at the corner of the house, Samantha stomping her foot and letting go of his arm.

"I think I see why you won't let me have Jula back!" Samantha's voice—almost a shriek—carried. "No wonder you have quit our clandestine meetings—you are bedding the Negro!"

Jonathan, with a pitiless smile, only shook

230

his dark head. "Jula is not a Negro, Miss Gable. Or is it madam? I truly don't know at this time."

"I—I am divorced from my husband and well you know it, Jonathan! And Jula *is* a Negro, she has black blood. Damn it, Jonathan, I don't care about the bitch's color or even her happiness. She's a good hairdresser among other things, and good at pressing the wrinkles out of my pretty dresses, so *I want her back.* My hair has been a mess since she's been gone."

"You should have thought about that before you so cruelly cast the girl aside. Have you no care for the girl's feelings?"

Cathelen had stepped out onto the porch, as if the voices had hypnotically drawn her there. Jonathan, just then, had looked up and seen her. He'd frowned at her dazed look, bringing Cathelen out of her trance.

"Cathelen," Jonathan had called up, "Have you prepared my lunch? I am famished."

"What?" She had remembered blinking. "Oh, yes. It is ready, and—" Truly it had been her intent to search for Jonathan and tell him lunch was ready.

"Ah!" Samantha cocked her head, hands on her hips. "Your other whore, the white one. Do you take them both at the same time, Jonathan?" she taunted.

Hands clenched, he said tersely, "You may leave my place now, *Madam Gable*, for I remember you and your husband very well now. I've always felt sorry for George since you made a cuckold of him."

"Oh?" She tossed her golden blond head in a challenge.

Cathelen was frowning hard now, but her feet would not move.

"If you recall, madam, it was I who came upon your first scene of adultery at that old mill. Only I was not alone, your husband stood at the other door. We just happened at the same moment to catch you in a, shall we say, rather heated embrace?"

Samantha's mouth dropped open, then she stammered, "B-but that was Adam, not you. Adam Sauvage."

Cathelen had seen a bit of color drain from Jonathan's handsome face and she wondered at the cause. Had he also been there with his younger brother and did he not want Samantha Gable to know that? He must have made a slip due to his anger.

"But you did not know that three were present, dear Samantha?" Jonathan said smoothly.

As she looked into the mirror, Cathelen saw, in her mind's eye, Samantha Gable stalking off in a great huff. The memory was gone with her and Cathelen regarded her own lovely countenance.

"I do look nice, if I say so myself, like a bride on her wedding night."

Mildly shocked, Cathelen glanced over at the darkened window panes. She must have stood here reflecting for a very long time. Shaking the dust off her feet, Cathelen approached the bed,

232

yawning. She had slept little lately.

Climbing into the downy nest and settling down, she was soon fast asleep. Two men walked toward her, one was Jonathan, the other Adam, both striding through a mist to claim her heart.

Chapter Twenty-Six

The sight that greeted Jonathan caused him to catch his breath.

Not wanting this lovely vision to dissolve, he moved quietly toward the bed and stood looking down at Cathelen O'Ruark. *Cathy.* Obviously she must have changed her position as she slept, for had she known how sweetly sensuous she appeared to him now, he did not doubt that she would have tugged down the nightgown to shield her shapely willow legs from his hungry gaze.

He placed the lamp he carried onto the bed-table, and it was then that his countenance hardened to a murderous aspect.

The nightgown!

Cathelen awoke, afraid she was being attacked and shaken to pieces by a foaming-mouthed beast.

"You!" the animal was growling. "You are a thief. You took those dresses from the locked room—"

"Wait a minute! Locked room?" Cathelen bravely questioned her shadowy attacker.

"Supposed-to-be locked then."

His fingers bit deeper into her shoulders. "But what in blazes are you doing in Elizabeth's gown?"

When the meaning of what he was saying dawned, Cathelen lowered her bewildered eyes to the nightgown she was wearing. Mattissa, she thought.

Cathelen winced as his fingers painfully slipped over the soft flesh of her arms. She lifted moist eyes to his. They were full of raging fires.

"Elizabeth?" was all she could manage to get out.

"That is what I said. Exactly."

His teeth clenched as he dragged her to her knees.

"Take it off!"

"I will not!" Cathelen puffed up with righteous indignation. "Not until I've another to cover me!"

Surprise registered on his face.

"I don't believe I heard you correctly."

"Oh, you did. Exactly!" she fired.

235

Cathelen scooted to place her back to the headboard, putting herself at what she thought was a safer distance from this angry man. But she was wrong.

His long arm snaked out to wrap around her slim neck and pull her to him. She was mere quivering inches from his face, so near she could pick out those golden flecks in his eyes. Only they were not flecks now but flames of passionate golden fire.

This fire troubled her, for it was not only anger she saw there, but something else she could not name.

Oh, yes. Something else was bothering her. But Cathelen decided swiftly that she would not let him see this. She needed more time to discover whether or not she was right about what she had seen. Besides, she was growing angrier by the minute.

"Then, Miss O'Ruark," he said mockingly, "I will just have to remove the nightgown myself. It'll be a pleasure."

Cathelen stiffened. *This was going too far!* "All right, *Master Sauvage*, I shall remove your precious Elizabeth's nightie myself. I really do not care for the color anyway," she lied.

It took all of her willpower not to look into those brown mysterious eyes as she crawled from the high bed, his eyes tracking her every movement.

"If Mattissa had not had Jula bring me the nightgown, I probably would never have known

236

it existed. You can take this back to your beloved Elizabeth and, and—"

Jonathan laughed.

"What are you laughing about?"

Cathelen came back from out of the shadows, clutching the nightgown she had worn the day before. He was laughing softly and shaking his head. His burnished hair shone in the mellow circle of light and Cathelen's heart skipped a beat at his handsomeness. Strange, flaming emotions spread over her and gathered below her waist, making even her breath seem fiery.

Deliberately she collected her wits, mentally stepping from the burning circle of her emotions. "What is so funny, I ask you again?"

He stopped and looked over to where she stood, only her pale face illumined by the weakest finger of light. He took in the curious red splotches dotting her cheekbones. Her eyes were feverish. His heart began to thunder in his wide chest. The lavender bodice of the gown was oval and gaped deliciously close to a shell pink nipple. Only the barest hint of rose could be seen.

She does not realize her effect on me, thought the man, a flood of overwhelming desire spreading from his face to his loins, his anger being washed before it.

When he stood suddenly, Cathelen gasped at the great manly bulge thrown into high relief by the bedside lamp. Even as she watched, mesmerized, the strength of his lust increased to frightening proportions.

He seemed to be cast into a spell. Cathelen smiled, a woman's secret smile.

It was then, while he was caught unaware, that Cathelen noted his hands. Large hands, the light showed where the scar tissue was worst.

Now Cathelen knew why Jonathan Sauvage hid his hands in black gloves. How cruel fate had been to him, she thought with momentary pity.

But before Cathelen could dwell on this further, Jonathan was crossing the room to come and stand before her.

"Elizabeth said you would come," he said, feeling in his voice.

Cathelen, awed by his manly presence and height, shook her head.

"Please tell me, who is Elizabeth?"

Staring in breathless wonder, Jonathan murmured, "Elizabeth Sauvage."

Staring back at him, up into his eyes, her own were very big, luminous pools of deep violet.

"I do not understand why your wife would want me to come." She shrugged. "I did not even know you were married."

Cathelen began to turn away, but the hard fingers she now knew were badly scarred spun her about.

Rivers of intense delight washed over her this time, such great pleasure coming from those scarred appendages. "Cathy . . ." he murmured.

She let the old nightgown slip to the floor.

Desire, greater than any she'd experienced before this moment, took Cathelen by surprise as Jonathan encircled her in his arms and began to kiss her gently, then thoroughly. Before her earth-shaking reaction could sweep her further into dangerous ground, Cathelen twisted away from him.

"No!" she gasped. She whirled, turning her slim back to him, curving it as if expecting to receive a painful blow. "I did not know you had a wife. . . ." She shook her head, could not go on.

"Cathy!"

He gripped her shoulders, but did not force her to face him this time. His slowly heaving chest moved closer to her back. "Why did you turn cold when you were so warm?"

"You are married!"

"I am not! *Mon Dieu*, what made you think that?"

He came back to earth then. "Oh God, the nightgown." He made her face him now. "Cathy, Cathy, Elizabeth was my mother." He found her hand. "Don't look so sad. It's true."

She could feel one of his hands clutching hers gently, the other stroking her throbbing temple. Shocking herself, Cathelen captured his scarred hand, and with her soft velvet cheek she caressed its scarred fingers.

He snatched his hand from her as if she had heaped more fire onto him.

"Dieu, don't do that!"

Instant tears appeared on her lashes. She quivered from head to foot. Bells rang in her head. Her heart soared with the birds of paradise.

"Jonathan—" She picked up his hand to kiss the fingers—hard and scarred and shiny pink in between—one by one she kissed them and ran her tongue from base to tip. Her eyes captured his. "I think I am in love with you, Jonathan."

Again he briskly pulled his hand away.

He stared down at her, his brown eyes brittle and cold. "My mother must have been crazy."

He moved backward, his booted heels meeting the circle of plush, tapestry carpet surrounding the bed.

"I must be crazy."

Cathelen stared as he stormed from the room as if a tumultuous wind had gathered him up and away.

She bit her lower lip. *What a ninny!* Why did she have to go and get all emotional?

She would never be able to look him in the face again.

A smile, wicked yet sweet, broke out on her small, oval face. It transformed her into a pixie. It was mischievous. Victory, as she knew it now, was drawing her to the fulfillment of her innermost secret dreams.

Well after the stroke of midnight, Cathelen

was again most rudely awakened.

"Hmmmm?" No flesh touched hers. There were no hard welcoming hands. No masculine voice beckoned her to wake. The room was dark.

Someone large stood at her bedside, however; she could feel his presence as if he had truly touched her.

"Jonathan." Soft as a low rustle of silk. She knew his aura. "Why are you back?" she asked . . . but her heart already knew the answer.

"Marry me, Cathelen O'Ruark."

Her heart beat so hard and violently that Cathelen thought it might jump from her chest and right into Jonathan's scarred hands. Where it belonged. She acknowledged that now, forever.

When she had hesitated too long, he said, a bit sadly, "Is it my hands—the scars—that bother you?"

This time she would not make the same mistake.

"Jonathan"—her voice was soft as night air—*"now I know I love you."*

He fell down to his knees beside the bed, tucking her nervously cold hand into his. He could not believe he was actually doing this. But his hands were again covered by the soft black gloves.

"Please . . . take them off?"

He hesitated, then did as she asked.

"Are you sure you love me?"

"Sure I love you? Oh, yes!"

"Then be my bride!" he said in a deep breathless voice. "I adore you. You are my breath, Cathy."

"*Yes*, I will." Her curiously moist gaze fell to his hands; she hesitated. Then she smiled secretively and finished with, "Yes, *Jonathan*."

Chapter Twenty-Seven

It was just too wonderful to be real.

Cathelen could not believe she was standing here in a bridal gown, before the new floor-length mirror her husband-to-be had purchased for her personal use. These belonged to her, everything, even the gown. They were hers, forever—to keep.

"Jula," Cathelen breathed, "pinch me! Is today really my—our"—she blushed—"*our* wedding day?"

"I pinch, Missy Cathy, if you not be still so Jula can finish your hair!"

Sighing and dreaming of a future as the mistress of Sauvage Plantation, a life secure in Jonathan's arms, having his children, Cathelen was unaware that a third person had joined them in her bedroom.

"I am sorry to disturb."

A chill, not a very comfortable one at that, ran along Cathelen's spine like a centipede.

Mattissa spoke again. "But I think you should know that Mitchell, the minister is here." Cathelen turned in her full bridal raiment.

Humbly, Mattissa's eyes fell, but her shoulders bristled.

"You are the beautiful woman *this* day, Cathelen O'Ruark."

Cathelen caught her emphasis, but she was determined not to let anything spoil her wedding day.

"You will soon be a Sauvage," Mattissa went on, "and you are lucky to be this. If you need for anything"—Mattissa shrugged lightly—"*madam*, you have only to ask Mattissa and I will do any task you wish."

I know that, Mattissa. Cathelen wanted to shout. But her countenance softened. "Thank you, Mattissa." Still, she could find nothing more to say to the woman. Mattissa had tricked her with Elizabeth's nightgown. Cathelen smiled. To my advantage, she thought. What Mattissa did not know was that the unkind gesture had only served to bring Jonathan and herself closer. He had seen something in her that night. It was as if the lavender bit of cloth had drawn Jonathan to her magically. Whatever it was, she had felt a powerfully sweet spell spread over them both.

Cathelen's brow puckered slightly in a frown. Still, if it had been a spell that night, why had it not yet broken? She asked herself this over and over, even wondering if she had been asleep all this while? Was this really love? Did Jonathan truly love her as she loved him? It was too wonderful if true. She did not know if she could stand to have Jonathan say the words outright. She would just have to wait and see.

Jonathan, although absent for two weeks in both December and January, had returned in the same frame of mind on both occasions. Always he squeezed her hand gently and tenderly and delved deeply into her eyes, her soul, with his beautiful brown eyes.

It was wonderfully true, that Jonathan still wanted her as his wife. To have and to hold . . .

"The folks's here," Jula cried, beaming, her long tan fingers crossed in uncontainable excitement over her lips. Her bare feet did a rapid dance on the carpet. "I be so happy I gonna pee right here, Missy— Oh! *Madam*, if you's please!"

Jula curtsied in a coarse fashion before the bride, then gave Cathelen a little shove toward the stairs while Mattissa hovered nearby, her eyes dark and unreadable.

"Here she comes!"
"Oh! Here comes the bride!"
As all eyes turned up the staircase, the young master of Sauvage Plantation squared his

strong shoulders, taut in a fine new suit. He swallowed hard when his bride came into view and he saw her standing there, ethereal, beautiful. Then, his eyes curiously misting, he watched Deke Jameson, his best man, take her arm.

Hondo and his Olivia, the witnesses from the plantation, followed close behind the bride and the best man. Master Sauvage was the first to reach the makeshift altar set up in the festooned living room. Garlands of paradise blossoms—pink, white, carnellian, sun yellow, magenta—perfumed the air and decorated tables and windows and archways. Food odors wafted deliciously throughout the halls as cooks busied themselves in kitchen and bakehouse, only pausing momentarily to catch a bit of the ceremony before going back to preparing the feast.

Raven canted her head dreamily as the groom turned to await his beloved. He crossed his hands in front of him as Cathelen drifted toward him, riding a cloud up the aisle, while folks from all over Barbados and from some of the neighboring islands like St. Martin, St. Kitts, Antigua, and Jamaica, lined up for the ceremony. Even the governor, who represented the Crown, had made the wedding with his wife.

Reverend Mitchell, before pronouncing them man and wife, read from the Song of Solomon—Jonathan Sauvage had requested this selection beforehand—while the enamored pair stared deeply in each other's eyes:

"'My beloved *is* mine, and I *am* his.'" With that the couple sealed their union with a slow and tender kiss. He lifted his virile head to catch her serious look, for her ears only asking, "Regrets?"

Cathelen gazed into his brown eyes, losing her very soul in their leaping flames of gold.

"Never, love," she told him in a whisper from her heart.

"You are not afraid?"

It was more like a statement than a question.

"No." Cathelen lied a little and lingered at the dresser, brushing out her pale honey locks.

"Come here then, my captivating bride."

He patted the huge purple and black spread on the bed that occupied a goodly space in his vast bedchamber.

"Weave your spell about me again, my wild sweet Cathy."

Blond hair undulating and swaying down to her hips, Cathelen made her way to the bed where her ardent husband awaited her.

In gestures old as time itself Cathelen, eyes aglow with the mystery of womanhood, lifted her abundant hair from her neck while allowing her oval-necked gown to slip down over one shoulder in a provocative fashion.

Lips moist and parted she, this siren, this newly made bride, pressed a knee to the bed. And then squealed with surprised delight as her

247

husband tugged on a shapely thigh.

"Enough. Come hither, wife, you've bewitched me enough this day," he growled impatiently. "I will have you—Hmmm, you smell like English roses. Velvet sweet and sensuous."

"Jonathan, flowers are not sensuous!" she giggled.

"But this flower is. . . ."

He tossed her onto her back and, in one swift motion, ripped the expensive gown clear down to her waist. Then he stared at the shell pink-tipped beauties he'd exposed and began to lower his head.

"Jonathan, you—you wolf! You ruined my nightgown!"

"I'll buy you a thousand more. But this one will remind you always of the spell you cast on your own poor husband this night, sweet witch."

She laughed, happy, joyously in love, as he nuzzled aside the remains of her trousseau gown.

"Wolf, am I?" He snarled and growled and nipped playfully at an earlobe. Then suddenly stopping his play, he looked down at her. "That I be, sweet Cathy, how did you know?"

"Are you really a wolf?" She shoved at his muscled chest, giggling delightedly.

"Aye."

Then their play ceased as both turned serious eyes on each other's face. Eyes glinted and lips parted moistly, as of their own accord. Jonathan lowered his lips to begin the play of love. Cathelen's head fell back, her throat exposed swan-like as his kisses burned fiery trails down that white column, then across her chest and her nipples. She shivered expectantly when he went lower, lower.

Her legs were gently parted and she clung to him, her fingers tangled claws of passion in his thick burnished hair.

"Jonathan . . ." she gasped, her throat lifting from the pillow in a sharp arch of ecstasy. "Oh God, what are you . . . doing? . . ." Her words were expelled in a breathless rush.

He at once came to his knees. Gathering himself between her thighs, he lifted her rear in one large hand, cupping her feminine cheeks. His fingers touched her carefully, unfolding that first tiny covering, and then his swollen manhood replaced his testing hand.

"My sweet Cathy—keeper of my heart—"

His eyes locked with her staring, waiting, ones.

Then, with one great plunge, he joined himself with his quivering, wanting, bride. She greeted him with one full cry of ecstasy, receiving the whole of his manful thrust.

Body in body, soul in soul, they loved and climbed and soared. Entering the unearthly wonderland where only those who really love go, this newly made man and wife finally knew the meaning of true bliss. Their deep passion tossed them hither and yon, to the stars where they exploded in the farthest reaches of the heavens, only to return later to earth. Then again, and again . . .

While Cathy slept like a young tree felled and
tumbled down a hillside, Jonathan stared up at
the ceiling, sleepless. He sighed and smiled,
sated for the very first time in his life, awed at the
heights of passion he'd reached with this one
tiny woman. He'd truly drunk of paradise this
night.

His handsome face was suddenly marred by a
frown. How was he going to tell his wife she had
not married Jonathan but *Adam Sauvage*.

He rolled to his side, securing a quivering,
love-labored arm at her tiny waist. He would
tell her when the honeymoon was over. He had
let Cathy decide where they would go for their
honeymoon. He grinned now as he recalled
what she'd said. "Right here, silly. I have finally
come home and *I never want to leave*."

Chapter Twenty-Eight

Cathelen discovered that her husband made frequent trips to handle plantation business, worked and sweated beside his slaves, and was tied up most the day in his office-study.

At times she grew bored with her own new idleness. Her husband did not allow her in the kitchen—to work, that is. Besides, the fat cook, a new one, was very guarded about her province.

With a book in hand, Cathelen watched from the library as Jonathan passed the door with his new bookkeeper, blew her a kiss, and then went on to his business. Busy, busy, Cathelen thought. Then she yawned and gazed out the window in a languid fashion.

For their major requirements planters, like Sauvage, were dependent to a very high degree on outside markets and outside sources of supply. They were obliged to buy slaves to keep up the strength of their labor force, to buy fish with which to feed them, timber for housing. For most of these necessities they were dependent upon the colonies on the American mainland. But some were imported from Ireland, as were manufactured goods from Britain. And the prosperity of the plantation depended upon the price sugar brought in England.

Raven had informed Cathelen just the other day that the planters circumstances shaped them.

"They tend to be insensitive to things of the spirit and mind; they become materialists who grumble at the bad times." Raven had sighed helplessly. "Yet they blatantly enjoy the good times."

Cathelen had thought Raven's description suited Vance Moore. He was one of a small group that was composed of the self-centered planters. But Jonathan was younger, less dandyish than the other planters she had met at Moore's party and her wedding. Heaven help her if he ever turned out like the others. Cathelen was determined that her husband would never become such a hypocrite, nor would he ever be in need of intimate feminine companionships elsewhere.

Cathelen recalled more of Raven's gossip. She had said Jamaica and Barbados were reproducing the atmosphere of ancient Babylon. In Jamaica most of the unmarried planters had native housekeepers who spoke of them as their husbands, but these were not established relationships. In St. Dominique, on the other hand, dusky mistresses were as accepted a feature of Creole as of Parisian life. And the children from these unions had a status in the French islands that they did not have in the British.

In Barbados mulatto girls were kept as mistresses by white men of all ranks, and the exotic conditions of the tropics bred a "special" type of woman: pale and languid, with small hands and feet, and luminous long-lashed eyes; with indolent and graceful movements and slow singsong voices that had been acquired from colored nurses.

Cathelen had sat on the veranda at Sugartree, trying not to gape openly at all of Vance's mistresses who roamed free as birds about the place. They were lily white, appearing almost sickly, Cathelen noticed. She had only heard one speak, in a voice soft and spiritless. And that woman's every step betrayed languor and lassitude. Cathelen decided that these women had grown too lazy and sorely lacked exercise. Like the planters' wives, their countenances lacked a healthy glow. Cathelen promised herself there and then, before she grew lax like those other women, that she would find some form of exercise very soon and would keep it up until she grew so bone-creaky that the rocking chair need be the only exercise she took.

*　　*　　*

253

With the merest suggestion of a bustle in back, a heart-shaped neckline, and full sleeves embroidered with green sprigs, the orchid-and-white dress was stunning.

Cathelen liked it because of its simple style and design. Bows, laces, and rosettes simply did not appeal to her down-to-earth nature.

Mairi had outdone herself in making this dress. To show her appreciation Cathelen went to sit with the old woman over a pot of green tea, of course knowing that Mairi had a penchant for any form of gossip: mild, wicked, or otherwise.

She noticed that Mairi seemed troubled over something, however, and she tried to get her to talk about it.

"Lord ha' mercy!" Mairi lifted her admiring gaze from the richly woven Oriental carpet, a recent gift from Jonathan.

Only Mairi knew that Jonathan was not Jonathan but Adam Sauvage. It had not taken too much figuring for Mairi to realize what the naughty boy was doing. Mostly, what bothered her was how she was going to tell this blissfully happy child sipping tea that her young husband was a scalawag who had tricked and deceived her from day one.

Whereas before Mairi had had her suspicions, she now acknowledged the truth of why "Jonathan" wore those black gloves all the time. Worse yet, how long would it be before an enemy of Sauvage's found him out? That Vance Moore—Mairi did not like the looks of that one.

254

She had spied on him and Cathy to make certain there was no funny business when that one came to the door. She would have fetched Deke Jameson if that devil had laid one finger on the girl.

Now Mairi heaved a deep sigh, one that Cathelen almost felt inside her own soul.

"Please," Cathelen pleaded sweetly, "do not be so troubled, Mairi. If you tell me what is upsetting you, maybe then I can bring some comfort to you." She shrugged. "I feel so helpless, though, knowing of your unhappiness and not knowing what to do about it."

"'Tis not for this old woman to say, child."

"What is not?"

As she looked down at her blue-veined hands, Mairi reminded Cathelen very much of Dany. Tears gathered in Cathelen's eyes and her heart wrenched painfully at the memory of her beloved Dany. Someday, Cathelen knew, she would again be with Dany, in paradise, for she had no doubts that Dany's spirit had gone to heaven.

"Mairi? Will you not confide in me?" One tear glistened on an amber lash.

"You will know soon enough," Mairi stated. "Och, that is, I pray ye will!"

The natural glow of a happy bride returned to Cathelen—and she brightened threefold. Mairi's head came up as she sensed the change in atmosphere.

And when old eyes met young, both women knew that they indeed shared a secret.

The only sad part of it was that the revelation of it, to Cathelen, was so long in coming. They both knew this too.

"Mairi." Cathelen went to whisper in the old woman's ear. "What is my pirate's name?"

Mairi glanced up into the young bride's haunting violet-blue orbs, then away.

"Och."

Her voice was low when it finally rasped in Cathelen's waiting ear.

"That would be the Sea Wolf, child, and well ye know who *he* is."

"Aye . . ." Cathelen drawled throatily.

Chapter Twenty=Nine

Cathelen sat across the table from her husband. They were having a fruit-and-cake dessert and Jonathan's compliments went to the cook.

"I will tell him," Jula happily said, picking up some dirty plates on her way out. "Georges will be happy to hear."

"Vance would never allow a servant to speak so freely." Raven sighed. "Jula seems so happy here."

Sauvage leaned back in his chair. "Seems?" he asked Raven Moore. "Jula is happy. She loves Sauvage Plantation, and it loves her back." He reached over to meaningfully squeeze his wife's hand.

Cathelen cringed as she glanced at his soft

black gloves, and when she lifted her eyes, she chided him silently for donning them. He shrugged firm-muscled shoulders, but in his brown eyes burned a golden promise of joys of the flesh and heart later.

Her heart tumbled in anticipation of what was to come. Though she had no other to compare him with, Cathelen knew beyond a doubt he was an expert lover. There had been no pain on their wedding night, although her fear of it had been far overweighed by the desire and love she had felt. Just thinking of that night caused her body to swirl with desire.

Now that he was going away on one of his mysterious trips, she was in a fever to have him make love to her long and strong before he departed.

All the while Cathelen had been musing, Raven had been chattering away. Jonathan had listened but his mind had been filled with thoughts of Cathy. Now his trained gaze fell on her lovely little breasts, and he smiled warmly to himself when the nipples hardened visibly beneath the taut cloth of her bodice. The cloth of his own breeches grew taut also as his bold desire strained against its confines. It excited him to realize that she wanted him fiercely.

Cathelen looked at him just then, her cheeks flushed hotly beneath his ardent gaze, and Jonathan knew he could not wait much longer. He had to have Cathy now!

". . . and so wouldn't you know it, with Vance's luck of late—"

"Oh! My gown!"

Cathelen, smiling inwardly at her slyness, shot to her feet after dropping a whole dish of syrupy strawberries into her lap.

Jonathan was around the table immediately, dabbing futilely at her soiled gown. Raven also joined in the effort, dipping her napkin into her water glass and working at the red stain. Their lovely dark-haired neighbor missed the first eye contact between the married lovers, but when Sauvage looked up again saying he would have to take his wife upstairs and help her out of the gown, Raven realized what was going on. The couple wanted to steal away and be alone.

Raven decided to play it cool. She said nonchalantly, "As I was saying, with Vance's luck, wouldn't you know his interisland sloop was taken by that scourge, *Sea Gypsy*. Why yes, you two go right ahead. . . ."

Instantly, without thinking of the outcome, Jonathan slapped the soiled napkin onto the table and whirled to grasp a stunned Raven by the shoulders. Cathelen looked on, her curiosity tinged with fear, as her husband forgot all about her and fiercely began to interrogate Raven.

"Where?" he thundered. *"Where is she now?"*

Cathelen watched Raven's red mouth work and her emerald eyes become a paler green.

"I—I have no idea, Jo-Jonathan. What is wrong? Have your sloops been plundered, too, perhaps?" She massaged her shoulders as if they hurt when he finally released her.

When her agitated husband finally turned,

Cathelen caught her breath at the feral look in his eyes. Passion's golden fires had altered frighteningly. Now Cathelen felt she was staring into the glowing red eyes of a savage wolf.

No wonder, she thought with a quiver, no longer curious as to how this stranger in him had gained his name.

He did not even realize at the moment that she existed, and Cathelen watched with great sadness as he took himself to his room. Not much later he left the house.

Quiet, swift, and deadly, like the wolf he was named after. Cathelen sat staring at her hands, feeling helplessness wash over her.

"Cathelen? Can I help in some way?"

With a faraway look in her eyes, Cathelen turned to her best friend. "There is a thing driving him and I only wish I could help. If only I were stronger, bigger, more . . ."

Her throat constricted as a wild notion struck Cathelen. Excitement raced along her spine like a huge centipede.

"What is it?" Raven demanded as she regarded the younger woman's hot then cool eyes. She watched, curious, while Cathelen rolled nonchalant eyes to the ceiling.

"Oh, nothing."

Chapter Thirty

As Cathelen reached the fringes of Bridgetown, the strong wind was abating. For a moment the island was aglow with the molten copper rays of the evening sun. In a sense of adventurous excitement Cathelen cried out impulsively, momentarily thinking the suddenly plum-colored sky above was going to swoop down like some magic carpet and fly her off to the Wolf's exotic haunts.

The purple velvet curtain of night was steadily falling by the time Cathelen appeared in Bridgetown. Those who gave her a fleeting glance thought her a lad, perhaps a cabin boy or merely a poor white.

The population in Barbados fell into three outstanding groups: Merchants and planters, poor whites, and slaves. Scotchmen and Welsh-men were esteemed the best servants. The Irish the worst. The islands had been plagued with too many broken traders, miserable debtors, penniless spendthrifts, discontented persons, traveling heads, and scatterbrains. This mélange made the Indies a kind of bedlam, so the Barba-dians paid them little attention.

And so, the dainty lad walked on, musing on one of Deke Jameson's history lessons.

In its early days, Barbados had seemed to be a combination of a mining camp and a penal settlement. There were Royalist prisoners of war seething with bitterness, Negro slaves, Irish rapparees spared in the massacre of Drogheda and then shipped to Barbados, and indentured white servants.

Briefly Cathelen wondered if she were still under indenture. She laughed at herself then. How could that be? She had married the *master*. Where was he now?

She watched a little boy, cinnamon brown in color and handsome, come toward her. He led a cute little donkey with a straw saddlebag hanging from its back. Cathelen smiled at the gray-and-yellow bird perched on the boy's shoulder. Riding in a relaxed fashion, the pretty bird apparently enjoyed his trip. The boy returned her smile, thinking Cathelen a lad. When he went by, she suddenly felt alone.

In some places, Cathelen could pick out the dim figures of men and women sitting silently before their doors. Now and then she saw the glow of a pipe. But finally only the splendid harbor of Bridgetown stretched before her.

Cathelen was grateful for the warm, encompassing clothing she wore because the evening had become quite cool. She stood, staring out over the black waters to where towering masts rose skeletal, against the night sky that was slashed with the last traces of vermillion and fiery orange.

A ruddy face suddenly loomed in her vision and she cried out softly, would have screamed aloud if a small, strong hand had not been clamped over her mouth.

"Mistress Sauvage, what be ya doin' out here alone in the night?"

He released her after he'd spoken. Cathelen breathed a sigh of intense relief and blinked at Hondo who was at eye level with her.

She gulped and said, "How did you recognize me?"

"Well," he began, scratching under his cap, "I was surprised meself. Ya see, I'm out here guardin' the *Wind Sound*. Been some riffraff hanging 'round her like they was maybe goin' to try and spirit her away. Then when I saw you I thought maybe you was one of them."

Cathelen gritted her teeth in exasperation. "Well? Will you not ask me what I am doing dressed up like a boy? Is that not your next question?"

"Well . . . I was sorta curious." He grinned. "Maybe ya was wantin' to take a ride on—oh— Jonathan's *Wind Sound* and you didn't want anyone to know you was a lady? Because it's dangerous out here and you kinda wanted to play it safe?"

"No."

Cathelen began to walk.

"Huh?"

Hondo hurried after her surprisingly long strides.

She whirled and the little man almost crashed smack into her chest. He was afraid of that look on her face—the look a woman wore occasionally. It spelled trouble. In this case, though, he would learn that quite a trial lay before him.

Violet eyes glittered with hard determination.

Hondo gulped, waiting for the boom to fall.

"Yes, I want to take her out."

Hondo was ready to cry. "The *Wind Sound*?" Hondo squeaked. He could never resist a beautiful woman; and this one was even more gorgeous and intelligent looking than the Greek Diana. "B-But, the cap'n will kill me. The *Wind Sound* mostly bears dispatches from plantation to plantation." He peered at her closely. "You can't be thinkin' what I'm thinkin' you're thinkin'? Can you?"

Cathelen pointed straight to the sloop. "She bears eight cannon, medium in size but just as deadly in force."

Hondo's voice rose in a long drawn out wail, "*Ohhhh.*"

The *Wind Sound* turned into the prevailing

wind and soon slanted over on a seaward tack. Cathelen's blood sang with the twitter of taut rigging and the rustle of stern wake.

If this was where Adam Sauvage, the Sea Wolf, her husband, yearned to be, then she wanted to be with him, alongside him, searching for whomever he sought—she breathed deeply, pungently, of the salt sea air—until his vengeance had been won.

Her baggy trousers flapped in the trade winds, her long blond hair sailed to the sky.

The Sea Wolf was out for blood. Alert and tense he strode the deck of the *Legend*.

Her decks were still warm from the sun, and her crew, aristocrats of the trade of pillage, moved more quickly now in the stark sunlight, their destination dead ahead—a splash of emerald, an island.

In tight black pantaloons, white billowing shirt, and boots with high red heels, the Sea Wolf frowned, his imagination conjuring up Cathelen as he had seen her last. He regretted that he had left her in such haste. What would she be thinking?

Her beautiful eyes had been tear bright and filled with haunting sweetness. He could see her . . . as if she stood here in the flesh, so near to him he could almost feel her presence and gaze at the clean innocent features of her face, her hair with sunlight spun into its strands.

Damn, only angels straight out of heaven had

such hair, too beautiful to touch. "Cathy, my sweet love," he whispered to the encroaching night wind. Did she miss him?

Wolf damned the swollen ache in his loins as his scarred, brown fingers moved softly, fanwise, over the barrels of the pistols that bulged beneath his red sash.

Argghh, he groaned as his mood changed suddenly. Cathy was far from his reach, and with the work to be done this night, he needed all his wits about him. It would not do for him to pine for his lady, for that would only get him killed.

Like a low, white-winged bird, the *Legend* pushed the sea before her dark green prow. In the past she had concentrated her attention on Spanish galleons that carried gold and silver. The Wolf and his Legend were known and feared throughout the Caribbean and men—all men, including the English—spoke of the fury of Wolf's attack. Now he spared no ships, except those of the Royal Navy, for he had become a ruthless hunter stalking his prey.

Early evening passed, and under cover of night, the pirate sloop swooped into the waters of St. Kitts, her canvas a fluttering gown descending in the velvety darkness, her black corsair flag whipping.

"Why so glum, Captain?" Ted came up to the Wolf. "There's not an armed vessel left in the whole saltgone Caribbean sea who can hope to match the *Legend* in open flight."

Sea Wolf, with his keen night eyes, studied

the waters straight ahead. A wisp of ribald song floated in the tropic air and he could make out the shape of the pirate vessel wallowing before them, the red shimmers of her torchlight reflected in the inkiness.

The laughter was growing more ribald and loud.

"Not this one, for sure." Wolf grinned, flashing his white teeth. "Sink me, Ted, I do believe that the Gypsy's crew've all congregated around a barrel of dark rum!"

"Aye."

"It'll be 'pie,' Ted!"

"Aye, that it will."

Michal O'Ruark felt remarkably awake and unfatigued. Something was about to happen, he could feel it. Danger lurked very near the *Sea Gypsy*. What form it took had yet to be made known to her drunken crew, and to himself.

But Michal had the advantage of being, for once, a degree more sober than his shipmates—the worst crew of villains in the entire Caribbean.

He listened with half an ear to the raucous voices of the pirates interspersed with the low laughter of Cameo Salvador. Hah, he'd once thought that jet-haired beauty to be an innocent. She had never been that. And now the spitting, volcanic woman was nothing but a pirate's trull. She had spread her white legs for many since she had developed that talent. Yet, she was love starved, voluptuous, a tempting siren who lured men with the sultry promise of a night below deck. Michal had succumbed a few times, but no more.

Cameo Salvador had become infamous. She had won the hearts of a thousand pirates and had conquered as many merchants as buccaneers. But she had confessed to losing her own heart only to one man. She could not have him now. The Sea Wolf was rumored to be dead.

It seemed that Cameo had read Michal's thoughts when she gazed at him and tossed back her wild, flowing black mane. She had learned to speak English and used it, along with her own flawless Castilian.

"My lean marauder rides the seas. But where? Is he alive or dead?"

"You know the answer to that, Cameo."

A glaze entered her eyes. "If he would only have called me *mi amor. Madre de Dios!* So he is a ghost?" She shrugged ivory white shoulders. "*Diablo*, what is that?"

Hair swirled like black fire as Cameo turned her face toward the sound, her countenance suddenly bathed in torchlight. Jocko came into view, tilting a bottle to his red lips and weaving slightly. He turned a smiling leer on the young Spanish woman.

"It's the cat ye heard, me lovely wench." He pawed her taut round breast and she allowed this without responding at all. But the captain was more interested in his bottle and soon let her alone. "The only exercise Puss can get on shipboard is in catching an occasional mouse or beetle." He snorted as the ship's doc came into view, no bottle in his hand this time.

Michal was carrying Puss, patting the golden cat. Puss's fur was riffled by the stiff January breeze, and he was not purring as he usually did when the handsome blond man caressed him. Michal's dark violet eyes contacted the creature's green ones. As if in a small mirror, he saw himself in those feline orbs.

"What is it, Puss?" Michal's deep, masculine voice snagged Cameo's attention.

"Ho, join me in a drink, Doc?" Jocko slurred the question.

Michal's fair hair glinted like a red-gold lion's mane in the torchlight. His lips stirred, he licked them eagerly, and it was a moment before he could control the muscles in his mouth to speak.

"No," he said firmly. "I think I have had enough." *For forever*, Michal thought angrily to himself. He had to straighten his life out, search for Cathelen. Something told him she was not in Scotland, nor was she in Carolina.

"Fah!" came the pirate captain's snorted reply. He took a stride toward the voluptuous Cameo; then he shook his empty bottle and changed his course. "Got to get me some more where this come from."

Captain Jocko headed for the hatch, thinking to get a bite of Chips' cooking, too. Chips, big and burly, could knock four heads together in a fight and never feel the blows during the course of a good battle. It had been a long time between fights and Chips, who often growled out his frustration and struck the bulkheads, was spoiling for a good one.

Michal found himself alone with Cameo. But he was not looking at her with lust in his heart as she sprawled against a tall coil of ropes, to attract and entice. Instead he stared up at the sky, at millions of bright silver stars. He felt close to something important, felt that finally there was meaning to his life. There had been a woman in his dream early that morning. Her loveliness had not only stirred him into hardness, but he had loved her delightful laughter and her clear shining eyes.

Michal looked down, meeting Puss's green eyes. The woman in his dream had eyes this color. He looked over to Cameo's narrowed black eyes, thinking they appeared evil, even reptilian.

"What has your thoughts, golden one?"

Michal flinched at her crude pronunciation of English. *Not you*, he thought. He stared back up at the sky, black as a raven's wing, and at the myriad twinkling stars. Some of them appeared green—but they were the farthest away. The hardest to reach.

Cameo tossed her inky hair and laughed aloud provocatively. Michal paused in his study of the stars, wondering which one could be hanging over the house of his dream love. "You laugh," Michal said, but he added, "And I don't wonder why." He shrugged his wide virile shoulders. "I do not even care, you see."

"Ha, you should, *Miguel*. I laugh because your Puss has run away."

Michal looked down to see that Cameo was right. Again, he shrugged. The stars were waiting for him up above, one coming closer all the time.

High feminine laughter floated across the water. It reached the longboats stealthily nearing the torch-illumined bulk of the *Gypsy*. The scarred captain grinned at Ted and winked at their luck. A happy woman aboard meant that this crew was not only tipsy but sated from coupling with the trull. The Wolf shook his head, thinking of what this woman must look like.

After a quick jerk of his head in the direction of the *Gypsy*'s rigging, Wolf waited while the mate glanced it over. The man's nod indicated that nobody seemed to be in the rigging, no lookout. Her gun ports were shut—which was comforting.

Was it going to be as easy as he thought? He hoped so. He was eager for only one thing—to discover his brother's murderer.

Chapter Thirty-One

Slowly and stealthfully Wolf and his men crept up on the *Gypsy*'s drunk-dumb crew.

"Up the side now, men." Wolf gestured to his men who were ever so quietly bringing the longboats alongside the hull of the *Gypsy*.

Climbing like monkeys, their weapons clamped in their teeth, mere ghostly shadows in the tropical night, Wolf and his men began their attack. They paused to look swiftly around before flinging themselves over the rail.

Puss's green eyes watched them peer over the rail. The orange hair on his back bristled, and his sharp little teeth were bared in a gaping feline hiss of warning.

No one was paying any attention to Puss, however, as he glared at the strangers along the rail. Here, there, everywhere, the tops of kerchiefed heads appeared, then eyes that spied all about, and finally impish grinning faces with teeth bared like Puss's own.

The attack was imposed swiftly. Groans and moans and startled shouts ensued. This sight being overburdensome to the cat, he scurried off, having exercised the usual good judgment of a feline.

The obnoxious smells aboard the *Gypsy* struck the nostrils of the boarding party, the slovenly condition of that vessel being a direct contrast to the gleaming decks and polished bulkheads of their own.

As this was a free-for-all, Cameo, not a stranger to this scene, joined in the fight. But she soon discovered that this was no mere foray.

"Captain!" Cameo shouted over the bloody din, a saber held aloft in one dainty hand. She stepped gingerly over a coil of rope. The captain of their attackers, Cameo had noticed, was searching for someone in particular. She was curious; he appeared familiar somehow.

Wolf was going about his usual routine. He had been told how to recognize the man he sought—told by a pirate who had sailed with Jocko. It was sung and said that Wolf's murderer had golden hair and eyes the deepest shade of bluish purple. Of late Wolf had also learned that the man was a ship's doctor.

Wolf clenched his teeth in frustration, annoyed by this game of hide-and-seek. During his long search many had given him clues while others had chosen to remain silent. What made him angriest was that most seamen thought him a mere shadow of the Wolf. He was no ghost. And at home he was weary of hiding behind Jonathan's facade. He wanted to be himself, Adam Sauvage.

Home? Wolf brought himself up short. When had he begun to think of the plantation as home? Impossible to answer that now. Was someone calling him? Was it the wind? A trick?

Wolf whirled, his cutlass at the ready. "Come forth and show your worth!" Was it a woman's voice?

But yes. The voice was feminine, with a low husky purr in it.

"Captain," again.

Wolf found himself staring curiously at this woman. She was very beautiful. If one liked dark women. Her black hair tumbled about her bared shoulders in gypsyish disarray, ending in a blue-black puff down her back. Her eyes matched her hair, and Wolf, as he stared, thought perhaps her soul too.

"Madre de Dios," she breathed. "Jonathan?" Her eyes became round and full of hunger. Sea Wolf, alive?

She reached out boldly to see if he was real. Not knowing why, for she was desirably beautiful, Wolf drew back as if her intent had been to burn him with her long, fiery nails. His voice emerged, hoarse now.

"How do you come by that name? Where have you heard it before, and why do you call me—"

She interrupted him, her voice very low. "You are Jonathan Sauvage, no?" She shook her head. "Ah, you have fool me. You are the Wolf and cannot ever die. Why must I be guilty for this?"

Cameo shrugged, the gesture causing her white blouse to slide down even further. "Hmmm," she purred. "You like?" She sidled closer. "I think the Wolf more than like what he sees?"

Cameo gasped with surprise and some measure of pain as steely fingers closed around her shoulders. He shook her, and Cameo looked up at the tall captain with wounded affection.

"Oooh, Cameo is sorry. Will you forgive?"

Wolf spoke in a hiss through clenched teeth. "What the devil are you blubbering about, woman?"

He gripped her harder. She threw her head back, but he snapped her upright once again. "Tell me, or this will be the first time I use this sword on a woman!"

She shook her majestic cloud of hair about her neck and shoulders. Some of it even covered part of her face. Her look was now sly and wary as she peeped up at him through the black wisps.

"For loving you!" she spat, then rolled off an epithet in pure Castilian.

He shoved her away from him. "You *are* crazy!"

Cameo gaped as the virile captain tossed her aside and whirled precisely to fend off an attacker. His movements were agile, his muscles evident in them, and Cameo felt a sudden heart-stopping thrill just watching this apparition of a pirate captain. Her face was aglow, her cheeks flushed and her high bosom panting. She was oblivious to the butchery going on around her. She saw only the Sea Wolf.

But Cameo turned as a roar came from the *Gypsy's* crew. It was followed by a violent jostling surge to escape in the longboats.

"I'll not have all me men killed in this nasty romp!"

Cameo blinked up into the livid face of the *Gypsy's* captain. "What do you mean?" she spat at Jocko. "There is nothing I can do!"

Jocko pushed her from him. She was panting with anger, flushed and distraught. The captain glanced up just then and saw dark clouds scudding eerily in the sky. "You," Jocko said, pointing an accusing finger at Cameo. "You have bring bad luck to Jocko and his ship. It was you who— Eh?"

This time, when Jocko looked up he saw stars. But they did not last long, for he was out by the time he slumped to the deck.

The cook groaned when he looked at the man he had knocked out. His dumb face gaped. His own captain!

"Argghh!" Chips growled like a mad dog and came after Ted.

Ted hotfooted it, fast.

After heaving a man overboard by the seat of his pants, Wolf whirled but found no one

attacking him. Instead his breath hung suspended as he stared into a pair of deep orchid
eyes that belonged to a handsome young man.
This was the fairest, yet strongest-featured male
face he had ever looked upon. Something clean
and bright was struggling to surface in the painful murk of those odd-colored eyes. Strange eyes
for a man.

"You have been looking for me. . . ."

Wolf could not believe this was happening.
The lad was giving himself up without a fight.
Wolf was certain this was the ship's doctor; he
could see the long, slim surgeon's fingers.

Now Michal ran those fingers through his
golden hair, uttering as if in pain, "When will
you kill me?"

The Wolf's eyes glittered strangely at the
young man. "Ah, I see we understand each
other." But his voice had plummeted to a low
hiss. He began again. "I will now have to do
away with you much more slowly, coward. You
have made me more angry, for you deny me the
pleasure of a fight. You stand here mocking me
with your fair countenance—your—" His gaze
dropped as the young man held up those long,
beautiful hands. Wolf stared, mesmerized by
their perfection. His own would appear beastly
beside these.

"I am a doctor, not a murderer or a fighter
of—" Michal was unable to finish, he was so
choked up by emotion.

"You dare lie to me!" The Wolf slapped
Michal's smooth face—hard—one cheek and

277

then the other, with his gloved hands.

As he turned his face up to the night sky, Michal saw distinctly against its throbbing blackness a slim golden form outlined. This image—Michal knew it must be Cathelen. His memories of her seemed to be slowly losing themselves in blurred mists that came and went like a slow sea.

"Mon Dieu," Wolf snarled. "Why won't you fight . . ."

His slaps became jabbing punches, but still Michal would not move a muscle to defend himself. This young man had robbed him of more than his brother, Wolf was thinking. He looked at the blood streaming from his victim's eyes and nose, from the young man's cut lips.

"Please," Michal whispered, "just kill me, please."

"Eh?" Wolf was startled at so unusual a request. He stared down at the boyishly handsome face, now bruised and bloodied. Perhaps he was seeing things. Yet this lad appeared familiar, somehow.

"I—I'm weary—afraid of seeing that dead man in my dreams"—Michal choked—"of you, the Wolf, coming after me. I—I never meant to kill him. You are no ghost; I know that now." He looked up to the sky, searching for Cathy. She'd seemed so near a moment before. His bloodied, young face contorted from pain and loneliness.

"Who was he?" Michal choked out, knowing *this* man was real. He had felt him, his flesh, his strength.

Behind him Wolf heard shots. They sounded as if they came from the bow of the vessel. Then silence. There was a clamor as if companionways and hatches were being flung open and searched. His men, of course, would be searching the ship for goods to be taken aboard the *Legend*.

Dark and almost silent figures scurried about the decks, doing their jobs, handing stuff over from one man to another.

Michal gasped as a hand reached down, searched between his legs, then removed itself. He looked up, in shock, staring into hard golden brown eyes.

"I had begun to doubt your masculinity, *pup*," Wolf casually declared. "So. You want to know who you murdered? Like the coward you are?"

Wolf glanced around and saw that all was in readiness for the return to his ship. He stuck his face close to Michal's. "Before you die then, I'll tell you. But first, you are going to suffer. I'll make a man out of you before you die. Too bad you will not live to enjoy being that man." Brown eyes stared into blue-violet.

Now Wolf cocked an arm at his hip, his black pantaloons stretching taut over the lean hardness of his legs. "Now I will have your name, lad. I've longed to hear it and I'll not tolerate more frustration. You see," he said, bending closer, "I've waited a long time to know your name. Speak."

Michal looked over to where Cameo was being hauled down into the longboat. Ever the spitfire, she hissed and clawed at the Wolf's men. But she looked very tiny in contrast to the burly pirates. Michal decided then and there that he would not give his true identity to this pirate, who lusted for his blood. This man, this Sea Wolf, must be a twin to the man he'd murdered while—while drunk. He had to think of a lie fast.

"You will answer me now!"

"Ned . . ." Michal said quietly.

Just then a dying man reached up a hand toward him. "Michal . . . Doc . . ."

"Michal?" Wolf's brown eyes narrowed and bored into the young doctor's.

"Ned Mitchell."

"Well, Ned," Wolf snapped softly. "See to the man there. Then you must come with me."

Michal stared at the tall, dark pirate, realizing he would never again know a moment's peace—at least not until this merciless man sent him to his grave.

Chapter Thirty-Two

The *Wind Sound* hissed slowly through the warm darkness. Neither shout nor stir came from her decks.

Cathelen's long week at sea had ripened her fair complexion to a tawny gold and made her body firmly resilient.

She turned her face, a polished golden apple, toward the hot morning sun and then shook her gleaming hair free. She was unsure of what she was doing. It had struck her earlier. What would *mon Sauvage*—she had taken to calling him that one night while abed early in their marriage—what would he do when she crept up on him aboard his ship?

She laughed at the idea. Had the trulls and taverns of the islands lured him ashore? Had he been true to her all these times he'd left her to go gallivanting at sea?

Cathelen's face grew hot, her hands became moist, and her heart beat faster, as she pictured her husband with another woman. She gnawed her lower lip.

If he had been unfaithful to her she would never speak to him again!

In fact, through tiny gritted teeth, she said aloud, "I will kill him—and her!"

That was it. She smacked a fist into her palm. He had been roving all this time because there was another woman. One he could not erase from his blood! Oh! If he was so hot for the bitch, why did he not bring her home with him? To marry, or keep as a mistress? The first option was out, for he already had a wife. But Cathelen groaned. Happy husbands did not rove.

"Maybe he has *more* than one. He cannot march them all to the plantation. There would be no room—at least not in the same house, not with me. Not over my dead body even, would he!" Cathelen was almost shouting, so angry was she over her husband's many infidelities.

"Who might ya be talkin' to, and why are ya lookin' so fired up?"

"Huh?"

Cathelen turned to see who had come up beside her at the rail, then she looked back to the iridescent green sea, wishing Hondo would leave her alone so she could go back to her mental anguish. *How could Jonathan do this to her!* Next she worried about why her husband

282

did not love her enough to leave other women alone. Was she not good for him? Perhaps she was too—too inexperienced. That must be the way of it.

Cathelen's soft, shining, platinum blond hair stirred against her neck as she stared dreamily across the shimmery turquoise waves. They were nearing a cove where the captain had said she might be able to catch up with Jonathan.

"But why would he be there, of all places?" she had asked, eyeing him with suspicion.

"He—ah—he told me I could catch up with him here—ah—in case I needed him for an emergency."

"Why would there be an emergency?" she pressed Foxwood.

The captain almost broke out in tears. "Ah, Mistress Sauvage, why couldn't you just forget the whole thing and return, like a nice little lady, to the plantation?"

"I am not a nice little lady. I am a very determined lady, and right now I want to find my husband." She placed her hands akimbo.

"Mister Jonathan's sure going to be dark with wrath when he sees you all the way out here. And God knows I brought you through the Indies to follow him."

Captain Foxwood scratched beneath his blue cap as was his habit when perplexed. And he had been perplexed a good deal of late. "Why *do* you want to catch up with him?" He looked her over closely. "Oh geez, you ain't in the family way, are you, mistress?"

"I—" Cathelen faltered, then she brightened to rose pink. "Why, yes. That is the very reason I am seeking my husband. You see—uhmm—I am in the family way, as you guessed, but I am having a—uh—little problem. . . ."

"Problem?" Foxwood gulped. If anything should happen to the missus, there would be hell to pay, especially if he did not get her to Sauvage in time. Adam—*Jonathan*! he thought to keep himself in line and not make a mistake—the man he worked for had made it very clear that should there be any "problem" back at Sauvage, he was to come search for the *Legend* immediately. Foxwood knew all about the *Legend* and the Wolf. Now he did, anyway. But for months he had never realized he was working under such an infamous man. Was it a year now? He, Foxwood, had learned his boss's temper could be an ugly, rearing beast at times.

He sighed. "I'll be taking you to him," he said without further argument. Foxwood had learned long ago that it was useless to argue with a woman.

"Look there, missy," Hondo called out. "Mark those two."

Hondo pointed to a brig and a schooner. "They're dangerous villains."

"Oh. Aye, sir," Cathelen said as gruffly as she could.

Now Hondo frowned uneasily as he made a visual search of the harbor, checking the masts and hulls of ships already at anchor. The *Legend* should have been there, her banner disguised, but he saw no sign of her. At anchor, however, were two bitter foes of the Sea Wolf: Captain Casey's sixteen-gun brigantine *Sultana* and the smaller but hardly less menacing *Sea Biscuit* of Captain Bob Blythe.

Cathelen felt a sudden heart-stopping thrill as the canvas billowed above her like a great white Scottish cliffside.

"Where are we?" she asked.

Her eyes were wide with violet wonder as the ship sailed up a winding inlet. The shore on both sides was breathtakingly beautiful.

Hondo laughed at her joy and innocence, but only briefly. "Somewhere right near St. Kitts, I'm sure. Yup, in another half a league you'll see the water turn sky-blue. Then it widens into a lagoon as blue as angel eyes."

Cathelen laughed. "How do you know angel eyes are blue?" She turned smilingly to face the little, wiry man, her side vision catching glimpses of the vivid green vegetation on either bank.

"Hear that?"

Hondo squinted one eye and assumed a listening expression.

"That strange sound?" she asked, and he nodded. "Do you know what it is yourself?" She lifted a tawny eyebrow.

"Yup. It's the whoop of howler monkeys."

"Oh. I hear parrots now." She peered into the trees, toward the direction of the sounds, trying to catch some sign of movement.

"Smell that breeze?" Hondo sniffed with

noisy enjoyment.

Cathelen tossed her head at the hot morning sky. "Trade wind," she guessed correctly.

"Blows the galleons and they come up by Jamaica way through the Windward Passage to stealthily creep for the open sea."

The trades made it smooth sailing for a ship that entered the Caribbean from the east. But due to them it became difficult to leave except by well-established routes between the northern islands. The trades laid down the pattern for sailing in the Caribbean. Their importance was recognized, especially by Spaniards, who referred to the whole group of the Lesser Antilles as the Windward Islands because they lay in the teeth of the trades.

"Yup. They always try to steal away."

"Why?" She knew this wise little man was baiting her.

"Away from the likes of those lean marauders!"

He grinned, waiting.

"Pirates," she said.

A hundred years of conflict with Spain had made violence endemic in the Caribbean and had put the power of life and death into the hands of desperate men. The "sweet trade" of piracy had its own conventions and codes of morals, and there were communities who lived by these, raiding and plundering. That year of 1717 was a nasty one for pirates of the Caribbees, because a determined effort was being made by the European nations to crush freebooting. Only England was failing in her effort.

Great merchants had grown wary, and ships containing valuable goods were sent out only under convoy and only when heavily armed. Piracy was indeed falling upon bad days.

But captains of sailing ships out of Europe soon learned to fall in with the trades. The ruling factor in Caribbean warfare was the trade wind that blew steadily from the northeast. A well-found sailing ship might cover the eight hundred fifty miles from Antigua to Jamaica in seven or eight days, yet take three times as long to return, beating against the wind. With the wind behind them, though, ships entered the Caribbean through the eastern channels: Spanish treasure fleets, French and English smugglers, the navies of Britain and France; it was one-way traffic. Shops departing the eastern Caribbean sailed north, making for the prevailing westerly winds, known as the Westerlies. These blew in latitudes north of the semicircle of the islands, and ships bound for Europe must fall in with the Westerlies.

Cathelen gazed straight ahead and gripped the fife rail. In the sun the wood was hot against her soft hands. The wind tossed her hair and rubbed her flesh to a rosy gold. She stared at the ship that had been her home for over a week. The *Wind Sound* was a beautiful craft, immaculate, and Hondo had informed her that the sloop had been built to operate as a privateer.

Hondo saluted her and went off to some task at the other end of the sloop.

The scented tropical breeze somehow made Cathelen yearn for the misted crags of her home, Scotland. Leaning forward a bit, as if she herself served as a figurehead, Cathelen sighted thick coconut palms growing along white-sand beaches. Squinting her eyes beneath the sun that shimmered down, she made out spider crabs and blue crabs scurrying and squiggling in the water. Mango trees were alive with blushing fruit and palmetto and coco trees provided shade.

Soon they were anchoring below Bluff Point. Only Hondo, Cathelen, and the captain rowed ashore, riding the crests of the warm shallow waves. Then they made their way by foot up Monkey Hill road.

The two men had wanted to leave her aboard the sloop while they went to ask whether Jonathan had dropped anchor around the cove bend. But Cathelen would have none of that! She had a great desire to see all these places her husband had haunted.

As the three approached the Red Hawk Inn Cathelen wondered if Jonathan might be there since Hondo had said this was the only good inn left on St. Kitts, the others having been destroyed in the recent conflict with the French.

The main dining hall was a wide chamber, handsome and of French design. Cathelen's violet eyes were bright with excitement as she entered it and glimpsed its mahogany cornices and panels. She was glad she had worn her simple blue-green calico gown.

The staff of the Red Hawk Inn handled the crowds of buccaneers and what-have-yous expertly. The host, who answered to the name of Crockett, presided in back of a long, oak counter. He passed mugs, tankards, and glasses to a shapely young woman and to her sons, striplings of fifteen and seventeen. Their already roughened hands showed these lads were no strangers to hard work.

Cathelen smiled winsomely at one of these lads. Straight and fair as a live oak, he would be the seventeen year old. His yellow hair was drawn back into a pigtail, and his cotton shirt was buttoned right to his neck. Though well worn his breeches and woolen stockings showed that the lad took some pride in his personal appearance. Cathelen noticed that at every opportunity he bent an ear to the talk of strange places and yet stranger people.

Cathelen's heart gave a lonesome tug when the lad looked up to see her watching him. He blushed. His smile touched Cathelen. She could have sworn she'd gone back several years to when Michal looked this same way. Michal had been her protector and he had brought some sunshine into her dull life. But now she did not know if she would ever see Michal again. She had mentioned Michal to her husband, told him that she would love to see her brother again, and Jonathan had been surprised to learn that she thought he was still living.

Now Hondo, Foxwood, and Cathelen shared a tray laden with turtle broth, grilled flying fish, and cheese pie; every course but the broth served on palmetto leaves instead of dishes.

Childishly, Cathelen licked her pink fingers clean of the white pieces of fish she had enjoyed. She had already drunk two goblets of wine which was unusual for her.

"For a little lady ya sure can gobble up a tub o' food."

"I'll say." The captain agreed readily with Hondo. "Uh-oh. I think we might have some trouble here. It just walked in. Over there, Hondo."

Cathelen was somewhat startled by the reaction of the others in the room. Chin down, she peered over her shoulder to see who was creating this disturbance. A tall, thin, handsome man had entered. His confident grin flashed whitely.

"Ah, he's a fancy saber man."

Hondo placed his hands on his thighs under the table, closer to his weapons should he be needing them.

"He's sure of his own skill as he has every right to be," Foxwood commented, rubbing his bristly beard with two long fingers. But the captain noticed drunkeness betraying itself in the lazing, half-closed eyes of the saber man.

A man rose to greet the saber man, but it was not a friendly greeting, Cathelen realized. Were these two going to fight? Right here?

The pirate called Buttons was shorter than the saber man, and Cathelen shivered, thinking this smaller one with the tiny sprouts of hair atop his head was no match for the taller,

290

mightier one.

It was as if they were watching the start of a play. Crockett had not moved a muscle to stop what would inevitably lead to a bit of swordplay, maybe even to death. Cathelen's eyes matched the round ones of the two lads. But theirs revealed a strange mixture of fear and excitement. The lads must be used to this sort of thing, Cathelen thought, but I am not.

"What will happen now?" Cathelen asked Foxwood, unable to tear her gaze from the saber man.

Before Foxwood could reply the two men began to circle. Round and round each other they went. Then they slashed and parried. Saber man's chest was soon heaving and sweating, the slash in his blouse revealing his glistening black hair. He began to sob with drunken frustration at each stamp of his feet.

"Oh, how awful." Cathelen covered her eyes and her shoulders slumped forward.

Within moments the saber man, wine-befuddled, overreached his stroke, and the pirate Buttons had killed him. Blood oozed from the saber man's rapier wound.

When Cathelen dared look again, the man's tall body was being hauled out the door. She did not ask what would be done with it.

Buttons's small teeth were bared. He had taken a few gashing cuts, and he was panting quite heavily. But he was the victor.

A young pirate in the corner of the smoke-dimmed room had been smiling quite content-

291

edly at the amusement provided by the fight. Now he frowned darkly as a young woman at one of the front tables turned his way. She did not make out his shadowed countenance, but he saw her. All too clearly.

"Sacre bleu," Wolf hissed through white clenched teeth.

Ominously he rose from his table.

Cathelen's hands were still quivering as she reached for a goblet of wine. This would be her fourth glass although usually a few sips sufficed her since she was not all that fond of inebriants.

Cathelen took a healthy swallow, then set her glass down. She did not see Wolf approach her table. "I needed that," she said, licking her lips.

"Enough!" a male voice hissed, too low for anyone to hear.

Wolf's men were roaring with glee at the incident they had just witnessed.

Cathelen hiccuped, then covered her mouth daintily.

Hondo's head came about to face his pirate fellows. Instead he was greeted by a masked face. Hondo could not see Wolf's expression, but he knew the mouth was drawn into a hard line, for the brown eyes had turned to black ice.

The knuckles of Wolf's hands tightened in his black gloves until the leather almost popped from the strain.

Noticing Hondo's shocked expression, Cathelen's head came up and she stared at the masked man in breath-gone fascination. Her eyes widened until they resembled enormous blueberries, making her small face even smaller by comparison. Her mouth worked but her voice box would not comply.

Hondo gulped. "Hello, boss. Ah—" He thought better of his greeting. "Ah—gov'-ner . . ." He could hear the echo of Wolf's muted rage rumbling in his throat.

What does the masked man want? Cathelen wondered, her terror barely held in check. Turning, the masked pirate barked commands at his now-quiet crew. The words he spoke were all in French. "Away!" he roared in that language. "Get your rears to work, else I'll see how a bit of the cat-o'-nine can speed you!"

Cathelen watched as, like sullen lads deprived of their fun, crewmen slunk away, some glancing greedily at the fair woman denied them. But now Cathelen saw none of them. Her misted violet gaze was fixed upon black-gloved fingers so lean and familiarly shaped. Reluctantly her curiously damp eyes drifted back up to the golden mask.

"Could I be of assistance to you, *mademoiselle?*" He inclined his head. "I am at the service of one so fair and winsome."

If the voice had been terrifying to her at its lionlike roar, now in its soft, deceptive gentleness it was even more so. It rose from the depths of that golden disguise and plummeted to the innermost recesses of her soul. Its eerie, imprisoned sound already evoked nightmares to come. Yet the depth of her fear rested in the man's possessive manner. She could sense in

293

every nerve end that he was going to take her away. But why did she want him to, even though he terrified her?

"No!" she heard herself shouting the next moment as the black-gloved fingers snaked out to grip her wrist and yank her upward. "Help! Hondo! Captain Fox . . ." She never finished.

They had vanished, as if by black magic, from the Red Hawk Inn.

Chapter Thirty-Three

"Come along quietly."

Cathelen faced her captor squarely. "And if I do not?" she said in a brave little voice.

"You just might find yourself in a very ungracious position, milady."

With a sweep of his gloved hand he gallantly gestured toward the planked floor as if it were a fluffy bed.

A shivering hiss escaped Cathelen's mouth before he led her from the Red Hawk Inn. His grip had been merciless, as were his slitted eyes. And she knew he had seen the look of pure helpless terror in her eyes, brief though it had been.

His touch burned clear through the gloves, creating tingles up and down her arm, and to her shocked horror, her nipples were growing hard. What disturbed Cathelen even more was that she was a happily married woman. But this did not seem to be of much importance at the moment. Was she going crazy or something? This fearsome pirate was awakening desire in her. Even his long stride beside her daintier one caused flaming darts to flicker up her thighs.

"Who are you? What are you doing here on this island?" He rasped out the question in a low voice.

At his ominous tone, a tiny frown appeared between her amber brows and she drew them together. Why is it, she mused, that this dangerous man moves me deeply?

He halted on the verdant green path and she was impelled to turn and look at him. Her breath became suspended in her throat.

"Well?" He awaited her answers.

Cathelen tried to still the tumultuous throbbing in her blood. She had glimpsed his breeches of chamois leather. Swiftly her eyes returned to his golden mask. She had seen that he wanted her. His lust was great. He must not have had a woman in a long time now. She moaned inwardly, *Why her, a married woman?*

She yanked herself free and cocked her slim arms akimbo on calico-covered hips. Daring much, Cathelen glared up at the emotionless mask.

"Would it perversely pleasure you, *masked man*, to know that you have abducted a married woman?"

Cathelen smiled to herself as she watched him

stiffen. She would have gone on but just then something about his deep chuckle strummed a familiar chord in her. "Just who are you?" she asked in a low hiss. "Why do you hide yourself behind a pretty mask? Are you so hideous to look upon that even the strongest man would cringe and cower at the sight of you?"

"Yes," he answered.

As he grabbed her wrist again and pulled her after his tall frame, Cathelen peered into the face of her worst imaginable vision, her eyes naked violet blobs of terror.

What lay beneath that unfeeling mask? A hideous beast? A dragon that would soon consume her tender flesh.

"No!" Cathelen cried.

The masked man merely turned to stare at her, and Cathelen wanted very much to bolt. Her heart was over taxed and thumped madly in her breast. She tried hard to think. What would he do to her now? And where was he taking her?

"Sacre bleu!"

Cathelen stared as his mouth—somewhere beneath that mask—expelled the expletive. But all she could see was the slight rustling of the heavy golden material.

Cathelen thought fast; but the pirate was faster.

"Oh!"

He knocked away her hand as she tried to snatch the disguise from his head. Then he became deadly still. Cathelen felt as if her life would end here with this dangerous and dis-

297

gusting pirate. Would she never see Jonathan again? she wondered. She felt very sorry for herself suddenly.

"Don't ever try that again," he said, using a deceptively gentle tone.

Before her lower lip could tremble and display what a coward she was, Cathelen caught it between her teeth. He stared at the pink flesh of her lip as if mesmerized.

Cathelen had a terrible impression that he was thinking of kissing her. She blinked and her teeth slid away from her lip. Was that naked, animal desire she saw in his eyes? Surely it was not human!

Slowly he reached out, and Cathelen in a reflex movement jumped back. Kiss her? No! Never! Not this beast she had conjured up in her mind!

Again the hollow, confined voice rose from the depths of Cathelen's terror. Yet, fascinated by a thing she could not give a name to, she listened.

"There is a house not far from here. You will stay there with me."

"F-For how long?"

He stared narrowly at her gold-spun face and hair.

"Until I have done with you what I want."

Cathelen gulped and bit down on her lip, this time tasting the saltiness of blood on her tongue. She was afraid she might gnaw her flesh so badly that only hanging shreds would remain when they reached their destination.

As they walked, seeming to climb always upward, Cathelen darted glances right and left, trying to penetrate the island's mist. Night, she realized would come on swift feet this day.

With each passing moment, the path rose higher, their surroundings became greener. But it was a gradual incline, Cathelen noticed. A ray of slanting sunlight stole through the palm fronds and fell on her hair so that it blazed brightly. Wolf noticed this, through the eye slits of his mask. He also saw that her face was oddly pensive and sad at the moment. She seemed to be strangely elegiac. That was not what he strove for in this game. Actually, if the truth be known, he wanted to throttle her. He would see her terrified out of her wits before this day was over. He would teach her the danger of intruding where women should not go.

Cathelen stumbled once on a jutting stone.

"Come, *ma petite* . . . come."

Though he had spoken softly, the underlying menace in his voice was unmistakable to Cathelen.

She blanched. Then warily she contemplated the silver pistol that was partly hidden under the lawn folds of his shirt and sash. She noted the superb sword riding at his hip.

With hooded eyes Wolf watched her, feeling near tenderness, watched her as a hawk might have gazed at a crumpled bird caught in his talons!

Before they moved along again, Cathelen stared into eyes that looked tigerlike. Then she shivered and followed along meekly.

In the shadier light that filtered through the overhanging tropical greenery, Cathelen saw a creature in the path by her foot. It scurried and she stepped back, emitting an unchecked gurgle of fear. The insect—or whatever it was— appeared to be two feet long and was wide as a velvet ribbon.

"Oh . . . dear God." Cathelen stared balefully at the creepy creature while she threw herself against the hard male frame.

"What in God's name is it?" she asked, her voice muffled in the folds of his blousy shirt.

"Santapee," he said casually, taking her with him as he backed up. He grinned to himself at this provident chance to play the gallant protecting his lady. Still, there was real danger here.

When his flesh kindled at her nearness—and Cathelen could easily tell it had—she moved away from him carefully. But not too far. The ugly creature still had not left the path.

Again Wolf smiled behind his mask. "If the mood strikes, the santapee will fling itself from a tree onto you, and within an instant its twenty poisoned claws will hook into your flesh. It will cling while it pulsates poison through its horned jaws." He breathed deeply, measuring her beauty from head to foot. "The santapee is one of the most dreaded insects in all the islands."

With a shriek and a whirl of her skirts Cathelen threw herself at him in a movement as unpremeditated as a blink of the eye. The santa-pee had moved a fraction of an inch. Or had she only imagined it? Cathelen wondered, feeling safer. But not for long.

"Ah . . ." he sighed. "I will save you."

But Cathelen frowned at finding herself in worse danger than the *santapee* had threatened.

"Of course!" she hissed up at him.

He only laughed softly. There was no advantage to be gained this night by treating her in a surly fashion, although at first, he had wanted to take her out to the *Legend* and drop her overboard!

Wolf's nostrils twitched. She was so close that her feminine softness scorched the turgid flesh of his loins. His nostrils were like those of a stag during rut, and he sensed her awakening desire. She was a married woman. But could she be feeling desire when she thought him to be another? Or had she seen through his disguise? he wondered briefly.

Cathelen flushed profusely as she felt the movement of his manhood. She shoved away from him once again.

"I am—ah—somewhat recovered. Thank you." She moved in a wide arc from the santa-pee's tree.

Wolf gritted his teeth in utter frustration as he wrenched his glance from her disheveled blue-green skirt to the relative safety of her shining mane. He found no help there, either, for the wanting still racked him when he beheld her tresses, white as moonbeams, dusted with warm yellow sunshine. Her secret place matched perfectly with—*Mon Dieu*, how he desired her! He could almost taste his passion.

Cathelen's eyes caught the row of white-trunked palms before she saw the great red mansion they flanked. It had a picture-book charm, but it was in poor repair.

Wolf groaned, bent down, and swept her in his arms to carry her the remainder of the way.

Suddenly lethargic, Cathelen did not struggle. She could feel his big body trembling through both their clothes. Now a sweet lassitude stole through her limbs. And Wolf, he could feel Cathy's heart beating beneath her small perfect breasts. Her heart was pounding swiftly as was his own.

Cathelen could scarcely breathe when, with one booted foot, he kicked open the door and entered the cool gloom of the big house.

"Wh-Where are you taking me?"

He stared at her vacantly, not sure he had heard her correctly. The sweet meter of her voice shook him. "To the bedroom . . . naturally," he said.

Mutely, Cathelen allowed this. Without a struggle, to her own surprise.

He shouldered open a second door, then paused for a moment at the foot of a large bed canopied with white netting to deter pesky insects.

"No," she whispered, peering at the frightening eyeslits in his mask. She made out two bright points of passion, even though the room was closed to any outside light.

Unbudging, as if he had not heard her small, imploring voice, Wolf very gently laid her down upon the bed. He looked down at her for a space. *My love, my heart, my bride!*

"Not yet, please . . ." Cathelen could not capture her own breath so her throat could open and close normally.

Yet, inwardly Cathelen cried out to this dangerous stranger: *Do what you will. I am ready!*

As if he had indeed heard her cry of quickening desire, Wolf bent down. His lean, iron-thewed fingers trembled on the fastenings of her dress.

All at once Cathelen caught at his wrists. She turned the great blaze of her violet-eyes from his gloved fingers to slant them up into his masked face. He was hard with passion. His face was almost contorted with it. Wolf could feel it, but she could not see it. Cathelen could only sense this.

Now he changed. Cathelen sensed that his manner was gravely watchful. What did he see? *An unfaithful wife?* She felt he was devouring every nuance of her expressions and movements.

"Why did you stare at my hands like that?"

She shuddered at the eerie sound of his voice. "They are gloved," she said simply.

Hiding behind her disturbed emotions, Cathelen assumed a cool front.

"So they are," he said sardonically.

He moved away from the bed. Her wide, misty

eyes followed his tall, lean frame. So . . . *familiar*.

Before he stepped out, he set the solid wooden bolt on the other side. His masked face turned to her once more, and then he was through the door, securing it with the bolt.

Cathelen nodded slowly to herself. Suddenly she was no longer afraid. How could she be?

Mmmmm, Cathelen purred and fell back and stretched her graceful limbs luxuriously like a very contented cat.

Chapter Thirty-Four

All at once Cathelen sprang up from sleep, her dainty fingers gripping the flesh of her fair throat.

Fool! Why had she not noticed him before? She would have saved herself much terror-filled grief. Yet, the very discovery made her almost sick with joy.

But now, now she was really afraid. He frightened her more than the stranger in the golden mask had.

Her loins grated with deep sentient emotion. She turned her head to the flung-open veranda doors to gaze through the white netting.

Beneath the green Caribbean stars, the garden's yellow lysaunder trees were lighted by thousands of fluttering candleflies and the smell of tropical flowers and plants filled her nostrils with their sweet perfume. Her heart picked up, and there was a quickening in her. She had never been so affected by her surroundings.

Would he come to her soon? As the masked pirate, or—Her heart stopped. The bolt was being lifted. Now the thought came to her: Why had he seen fit to lock her in? She had sorely needed some sleep, but how could he know that? Had he been off somewhere? To what? She gritted her small teeth. Worse yet, to *whom*?"

Now she really was angry. Barbs of jealousy stung her again. How dare he come fresh from another woman to her bedside? And . . . how dare he conceal his identity from her for this long a time! If a man could not trust his own wife, then who could he trust? Aha! A whore, no doubt! Several of them, in fact. No wonder he wore so many disguises. Did he perchance make love to each one in a different guise?

Cathelen punched the bed at her sides. *Ohhh*!

The door opened fully as she did so, and the masked man presented himself once again. She seethed inwardly. Then she began to wonder what game he was playing with her.

"Good evening." The deep eerily masked voice was sibilant.

"Huh!" *What is so good about it*!

"I have brought you fresh fruit," he said generously.

Wonderful!

She knew it! She just knew he would still be masked.

Cathelen scurried to her knees on the bed, holding her hands up like tiny barriers. "Stay away"—she made herself taller, but the bed was making her sway—"stay away, or I will—I will—"

"Or what?" He came closer to the trembling bed, taking deep, measured strides.

Cathelen reached behind her and snatched up a dusty pillow. "I will—I will—ah—I—ah—ah—*achoo!*"

Wolf chuckled deeply as she sneezed several more times and then sat staring dumbfounded at the pillow.

She muttered to herself in low tones, "Strange—I did not sneeze when my head rested on it. . . ."

"But then," he began, "you were not raising dust, either."

Hell, you mean.

Again Cathelen positioned herself on knees that were shaking mildly. Up the pillow came, as a barricade this time.

"I—if you come any closer . . ."

"So. You would like to play games, eh?"

"I warn you, I have more weapons available at my bedside."

But a hasty glimpse at her immediate surroundings showed Cathelen only a lamp—that would be too messy, bloody—and a leather-bound volume. Aha! That should do very nicely.

"What is that behind you?" she said slyly.

Wolf smiled to himself, knowing this game. But he decided to play along. He turned. He shrugged and faced her again.

"Now, Mister Pirate . . ."

As he came even closer Cathelen swung in a wide arc that started behind her. The dusty pillow missed his swollen manhood by a mere inch, but he looked up in surprise as the heavy book crashed over his skull. Wolf had not been expecting her to have another trick up her sleeve so soon after the pillow assault.

"Quick work." He complimented, her, massaging the sore spot on his head, thankful she had used the book on his head and not in her initial lunge. He might need his wits about him this night, but he would need the other much more.

Gingerly he stepped back, and Cathelen gasped aloud as he drew his wicked blade from his red sash. The blade slashed in a downward stroke, to pierce the pillow point-deep and raise a puff of smoky dust. Cathelen frowned at this odd play. As he withdrew the blade Cathelen, with a birdlike flicker of her eye, gauged the distance between the bed and the door.

Her eyes swung back. His breeches clung tight as snakeskin, black and reflecting the lamplight. With a tense, tremulous sigh, she mustered up the courage to lift her warm gaze to those eye slits. Mysterious, but how well she knew those eyes.

"Ah, so you like my blade?" he said.

She gasped softly. "Wh-What do you mean?" *He could not mean . . . no, of course not.*

Still he had not moved an inch. He stood like a statue of bronze, with a mask of buffed gold, a blade of dove gray steel; a statue that looked down on her with complete impassivity. Her breath tightened in her throat and became a long deep burn.

A low whistle escaped his lips and the blade was cast aside. As Cathelen looked on, wide-eyed and wondering, he methodically began to undo the red sash at his lean waist. Captivated by the swift and sure movements of those gloved fingers, she could only stare, hypnotized, like a poor snake watching the charmer.

But pools of passion formed in her eyes, making them deep purple. Her shell pink tips hardened, and the secret place between her thighs blossomed like a dewy rose, its center beginning to flutter while awaiting the nectar of life—and love, oh yes, love!

This is my husband, this is my husband, she repeated silently.

He blew out the lamp, and came to her, a frown she could not see between his brown sculpted eyebrows.

He was angry with her willingness to receive him. For a moment silence reigned. All Cathelen wanted, cried out for, was her husband's love.

"Come to me, *petite*. . . ."

309

He growled deep in his throat as her arms, like soft sweet camellia petals, opened for his approach. "Oh, darling, darling," she breathed out, "I am ready."

At first he was forceful, then gentle, then savage. It was as if he wanted to punish her. In the hot pulsating darkness, Cathelen learned more about the male drive than she would have guessed it possible to know. Why had he held back before?

Cathelen moaned as he captured a shell pink tip and whirled it in his mouth, his ungloved hand bold and hot between her thighs. He startled her, astonished her—was pure animal in his approach. He was taking her to a brink where she would have expected to be left with only the sensations of shame and fear.

Oh, my love, Cathelen's heart cried, for she was caught up, carried away by his lovemaking.

His mouth left her secret place quivering as he lifted his tall frame to mount himself above her. He parted her legs and, with a cry of pleasure entered her. She could feel his fingers digging into her sensitive backsides—those fingers that were smooth of flesh yet ridged with terrible scars. Beginning to move in and out, he surprised Cathelen when he spoke.

"Do you really love your husband that much . . . then?"

He continued to move inside her, stroking with his silken shaft.

"It—it really is none of your—oh!—your business," she panted, "Sir Pirate."

He pulled out, to linger on the smallest fold. Her cheeks flushed hotly, and she felt a great trembling need for his return.

He bent to kiss her neck, her small breasts. She writhed and whimpered, wanting him back inside.

"Tell me," he murmured.

Yes, I love my husband . . . you are he!

"Tell!"

"No." She could not say the words out loud. Even if he must leave her quivering and unrelieved. She herself had started something and must see it through to the end!

"Bitch . . ."

You may think so now, my love, but later you shall eat that word!

"If you want it so bad then, *wench*, open up."

Angrily and like a savage lover, he lifted her willowy legs to wind them about his waist. Smiling cunningly to herself, Cathelen clung and clutched him, breathlessly waiting for the wild ride to ecstasy's shores.

His well-endowed manhood plunged deeply, yet carefully so as not to abuse her gentleness, for he was every inch a big man.

Thoroughly Cathelen received every hard throbbing inch of him. He led the way up the steepest, brightest path to passion's sun, guiding gently, then savagely coaxing; now they raced together to the summit of bliss and ecstasy.

Golden fluids of love merged and melded them. Cathelen's lips were mute but her wildly beating heart cried out:

Adam!

Chapter Thirty-Five

Abruptly the gentle green Caribbean dawn came. One minute it had been royal blue velvet outside the windows; then the dark seemed to spin and twinkle into the first pale green of morning.

The half-dressed man slowly paced before the window, glancing now and then at the wall that separated him from Cathelen. Wolf had a problem—indeed many of them if the truth be told.

He paused at the window, seeing himself reflected in predawn light. He sighed, replete with love.

In the distance Wolf heard a tumultuous roar—the outbursts of thousands of frogs waking to greet the sultry St. Kitts day. His gaze flicked downward.

"Hondo!" he hissed down to the lower veranda where the wiry little man sat with a sodden cloth over what seemed to be a headache. "Get your rear up here. I'd like to have a word with you."

Hondo twisted his head and looked up as if pained by the turning movement.

"Talk?" Hondo echoed lamely.

"Aye, talk."

The older man rose as quickly as his aching head would allow. He was relieved to see, as Wolf beckoned him up to the balcony, that the big lad was not so angry after all. That must have something to do with the cries of passion Hondo had heard; he smiled as he had during the night when, cradling his jug of wine, he'd remembered that Wolf himself had made a good share of that racket.

"Hondo, good man"—Wolf was all business now—"the *Sea Gypsy* needs a bit of swabbing and careening."

"Oh?" Hondo scratched his head, then came alive. "Aye, sir!"

"Ted and yourself will pick some of my best lads. Blackie can take the *Gypsy* and see her made sound. He can follow me up to Tortuga. I'll want you with me this time."

Hondo could scarcely credit what Adam had just said to him. He shook his head in confusion then. "How about? . . ." Hondo jerked his thumb in the direction of the connecting bedroom.

"She's away with us," Wolf said tersely.

Hondo thought about the young doctor Wolf had taken from the *Gypsy*'s crew. Yesterday he had learned that they'd overtaken the *Gypsy*, and he had regretted that he had not been along. But just why Wolf had taken the fair lad captive was a puzzle to him. The rest of Jocko's crew had been set into longboats. But why not the young doctor? he wondered.

"The doc?" Hondo finally got up the courage to ask. "He stays with the *Gypsy* after she's done?"

Wolf frowned darkly. "No, he'll go with us too." He gazed down past his shoulder, then up after a moment's thought. "Just make damn certain he stays far away from my wife."

Hondo blinked. "Why's that, gov'ner?"

Handsome nostrils flared. "I don't trust him," he said simply. Then, "Do you know exactly who I have in my power, Hondo?"

"Eh?"

Hondo looked down at the leather-encased fingers powerfully gripping him by the shoulders. He was given a shake or two and then released. Wolf turned on his booted heel and strode back inside. Just then Hondo's brain cleared and he saw before him Jonathan's cold-blooded murderer.

Hondo came down off the balcony, muttering to himself, "Aye, I'll be sure to keep that one away from Wolf's woman." He chuckled ironically, thinking she might be the more likely one to stir up trouble, not the fair-haired doctor! He should be warned to watch out for *her*!

Lordy, they all should, Hondo corrected himself. He made the sign of the cross as he went to find Blackie, Wolf's lieutenant.

The young pirate captain went inside and paused at the bedside of his sleeping wife. One hand, so dainty but golden from long days in the sun, was flung up above her head in the position of a ballet dancer and lay half buried in the soft, honey cloud of her hair. That luxuriant mass tumbled over the edge of the bed and spilled onto the floor like shining moonbeams.

Wolf stood there a long time. Only once he spoke. "My God, she's beautiful. Is she really mine?" He gritted his teeth as his crisp lips formed an expletive. Damn, she'd better be! Only time would tell.

He watched her sleep, studying her, and as he did he could see her facial expressions change. Possibly it was a dream. Her lips softened imperceptibly, then grew pink and moist, parted just a little until he could make out a show of pearl between them. First she'd breathed out slowly, but he heard the rustle of a deep sigh. The pulse at the base of her throat could be seen to beat swiftly, as if she were excited by her dream.

Wolf, angry beyond reasoning, wanted to throttle her. But how well he remembered her arms, like liquid gold fire around him; her thighs, cold then hot brands, and her honeyed secret places so warm and inviting he wanted to tear into her now.

Angry as he was, he would hurt her. He

wanted to hurt her, by God. She'd been unfaithful by giving in. She had yielded, damn her. He had wanted to frighten her, scare the silly fool out of her wits. And what had she done? Yielded. Given herself like a whore to an utter stranger in a golden mask!

Not wanting to look upon her irksome loveliness any longer, Wolf took himself from the sun-bathed room and went to his ship.

Let Hondo take her out, he'd seen to her before. Wolf would be damned if he would cater to the unfaithful vixen. He spat into the sand, vowing to make her pay for all the trouble she was causing him.

"Scottish wench." he hurled curses into the crisp morning air. "Bondservant. Slave. Simple cook . . ." He shook his head as if to clear her beautiful image from his mind. "Wife? Hah! Never again."

Cathelen turned her head against the pillow and opened her eyes. She had been awakened by the tumultuous throbbing of her own heart.

Now Cathelen stared curiously down at her thighs. She gasped. They were bruised!

A blush spread over her cheeks as she remembered their wild unfettered lovemaking. She tingled from head to foot, wanting him again. Even her sore place cried out for more. Bold had their passion been, the power of their love consuming them both.

"Oh no . . ." Cathelen groaned aloud. Her

hands flew to her hot cheeks. "What must he be thinking of me now—in broad daylight—after I gave myself last night with such . . . such abandonment?"

Michal's eyes followed the virile pirate captain about the deck. He was obviously a man of great daring, reckless and spectacular. Wolf, now for some reason sporting a golden mask, was to Michal the sort of man who could fight with gun or cutlass, and the devil take the loser, poor soul, for it would not be the Sea Wolf.

How long before Michal would fall beneath that black-gloved hand? He looked down at his chained ankles, felt the ropes burning and cutting his wrists. He had been humiliated beyond feeling one whit of pride for himself. Indeed, he could no longer even think about Cathy. Wolf would make him suffer, ever so slowly. He would die degradingly and shamefully, and he would never see his sister again, share precious moments with her.

When Michal's hands clenched, the rope burned. How could the man still be alive? He had killed *him*, shot *Wolf*. . . . Had there really been a shot? Who had tossed the body overboard? Michal groaned softly, hurting inside and out.

Standing alone at the rail, chained to it like a mad dog, Michal let his deep violet eyes stray over the waters. Then, abruptly, his gaze came to a halt. For in the longboat a young woman

318

had swept off her scarf and shaken her shining head. Michal could see from here that she was uncommonly lovely, with blond hair so light that it was almost the color of sunshine and eyes as— Michal blinked, wishing he could rub his own. Eyes the same hue as his? Could he be sure from this distance?

Yet, as the longboat neared, Michal grew increasingly excited and began to strain at his bonds. Tears, hot and scalding, blurred his vision and he cried out hoarsely for he could not see her clearly now. He was utterly helpless with his hands bound behind his back.

"Cathy—lass," he choked out, unhuman sobs and sounds coming from deep within wracked his wretched frame.

Wolf whirled about to stare at his prisoner, his dark eyes narrowing in his golden face. "What's this?"

Michal felt the captain's eyes stab him as he would physical blows. *Dear God, I have made a mistake*, Michal cried inwardly. The Wolf must not learn Cathelen was his sister. he would punish and kill her along with him.

Fear cleared his eyes and Michal could see the pirate captain look Cathelen's way again. She already stood in the longboat, as if she were eager to mount the rope ladder to board.

In his bonds, Michal furiously clenched his surgeon's hands. If the pirate dog had touched her, Michal vowed he would find a way to murder the animal.

Wrenching himself aside, Michal averted his

face as she came aboard. *Dear God, why is she here? Do not let her see me like this!*

"Good morning, *Captain*," she said, mocking laughter in her voice. "I trust you slept well?"

She glanced over to Hondo who had just come to stand beside the fair-haired man. Hondo, too, had his hands tied behind his back.

"I see, Captain, you have your prisoners bound up tightly. Even my friend Hondo, eh?"

Listen to her! She sounds like a pirate wench herself. Michal could feel the tenseness in the air, feel the sparks the two ignited. The Wolf growled an inaudible reply, to which she laughed throatily, mocking him even further. *Why was she being so familiar with the dog?* Michal wondered angrily. *She must have gotten to know him—intimately. He must have—* Michal inadvertently cried out, in a helpless rage for his sibling.

"Who is that?" Cathelen whirled about to face the prisoners again. This time she saw a pair of strong muscled shoulders that heaved against a blue shirt, perspiration stains dotting it all over. It was as if the young man strained painfully not to cry out again.

"Why is he in such agony?" Cathelen spun to face the captain.

"Don't meddle where you are not concerned, wench," he rasped down to her, his tone suddenly eerie and grating to her nerves.

"Am I also a prisoner, Captain?" she snapped irately.

"Aye."

She offered her wrists to him then. "Bind me, too, Captain."

Cathelen stood, waiting, because he had not moved a muscle to do so. "Well?"

He bound her wrists, but not with rope. Leather-encased fingers clamped her slim arms and began to drag her toward his cabin. She strained and twisted to be free.

"Noooo!"

The captain halted his stride and, still clutching Cathelen, turned slowly about to face the man who had dared to cry out in a shivering wail of inhuman rage.

"No?" Wolf said, letting go of Cathelen's wrists.

Long strides of black rage consumed the distance between the captain and the lad whose gaze was lifted to the sun, glistening with sweat and tears.

Now Wolf glowered down into the young man's face.

Cathelen came out from behind the captain's tall frame and saw the young man clearly for the first time.

"Dear God in Heaven—*Michal*!"

She brushed the captain aside and went to her brother. Cathelen would know him anywhere. No matter how dirty he was or that his unwashed body stank, that his face was burned lobster-red or that his hair was bleached nearly as light as her own.

"Michal—Michal—" she sobbed, her tears

sliding from her chin as she clung to his still firmly muscled shoulders. She cupped his beloved face in her slim fingers.

He said, "Cathy," very softly.

Wolf stared at the blond heads pressed together, the man his brother's murderer, the woman his wife. His eyes darkened visibly, until no trace of gold remained at all. Anyone who looked closely would have seen the pain in them. He was torn asunder by the sight and sound of so much grieving love.

"Cathelen," he said hoarsely, "come away from him."

Upon hearing the order, Cathelen's heart lightened, but she also experienced a great desire for revenge. Such an emotion was new to her, and for the moment it gave her a perverse pleasure.

"I will not," she said protectively, not once looking up into that golden mask. Why does he not just take the mask off? Why does he continue to wear the thing? she wondered. If he could not see by now that she had found him out long ago, then he was surely a complete idiot. Blind as a bat. What was it that obstructed his heart's vision? Jealousy? Anger? And now what?

Cathelen decided he had had his fun long enough—deceiving her! She would be a fool to let him learn Michal's real identity. She bent close to Michal's ear, begging him not to give any clue as to their kinship. "Please, Michal, beloved brother, this is very important to me. Do not ask me why, just trust me?"

He looked at her, baffled for a moment, then he nodded almost imperceptibly. Cathelen whimpered. "You are so weak, my brother. Whatever has happened to you, do not tell me now, darling, there is not time and this not the place." She hugged him close, then stood, smoothing her blue calico skirt. He understood; at least, Cathelen hoped he would.

Everyone, except Wolf, missed the deadly expression in the dark violet eyes aimed at the pirate captain. But Wolf merely stared back at the young doctor, anxious to get him well enough so that he could make him pay for his sin.

Wolf turned on his heel to stride across the deck, feigning indifference to her after ordering her to be led to a small cabin. Cathelen looked back once at Michal. He was staring as if he could not believe his eyes. So was another, from the deck above, and a distressed sense of loss leaped from the eyes that peered through the golden slits.

Chapter Thirty-Six

Sharp as a low-swooping seabird, the pirate sloop set out on the soft blue sea below Monkey Hill.

Cathelen, watching at the rail, bit into a ripe yellow mango that sprouted its sweet juice into the morning air. She attacked the fruit with relish, almost with a vengeance. Cathelen had decided that her nasty captain had done all he could to humiliate Michal and herself. Indeed, he was unconscionable!

She smiled shrewdly. Maybe she would *never* tell him that Michal was her brother. Let him suffer and wonder!

Cathelen had tied back her snowy blond hair with a ribbon fashioned from a length of eyelet she'd torn from an inconspicuous spot beneath her skirt. Her cheeks were pinkened as if by the wind in her beloved Scottish mountains.

Despite himself Adam found her lovely as he approached. His voice coming from behind her jarred Cathelen.

"What're you doing up here? I thought I told you to stay in your cabin. I think you should have listened," Wolf said, his voice grating.

Cathelen ignored him, but she soon found this to be a grave mistake. The entire Caribbean sky seemed to reel over her head when she was gripped hard and turned to face the captain. She glared up at him, defiant and aware that he was glowering at her too.

"You would match swords with me, eh?"

Her eyes brightened to lavender. "Och, indeed I would, Captain," she said, her fine Highland burr surfacing and surprising the man.

She waited, chin uptilted.

"I'll give you something to do then." He turned from her, shouting, "Ted! Come over here."

Cathelen took the time to study this man, Sea Wolf: his masked profile, the lean virile length of him. Unleashed anger and bitterness boiled from every pore of him. What did he have in mind for her? Whatever, Cathelen thought, she was prepared for it.

"So you want to go to sea?"

The deep voice so close to her cheek made her jump from her reverie. Mate Ted was standing just a little behind his captain, off to one side.

"Aye," Cathelen finally answered.

Some of the pirates on deck turned from scanning the blue Caribbean to regard Cathelen with silent curiosity. Most of them had seen her only briefly when they were on St. Kitts.

There was no wind. Yet the motion of the sloop created a movement of air that was like warm human breath. She stared up at the golden mask; even what little tenderness he had shown her had disappeared.

She had said "Aye," not giving herself an opportunity to consider the wisdom of her reply. A hundred pairs of eyes fixed their gazes upon her. Men with brown faces, brutal faces. A few with handsome young faces. The sunlit tops of the tall masts and the vast sails shimmered above her, and it seemed that from every crosstree a face peered at her.

Suddenly she was lifted off the deck as the captain swooped her up and bore her to the rail. "What are you doing!"

"You said you wanted to go to sea. I shall make your wish possible, that's all."

"Put me down, you horrible monster!"

"You, mademoiselle, are going overboard."

"No!"

At the rail, while Wolf held her high above the churning waters, Cathelen stared into those eyes, only those eyes. "Go ahead, then, if that is what you want. To drown me."

Cathelen closed her eyes, waiting for the toss into the air that would end her life. She did not know what sea creatures would be waiting for her tender flesh. "Just get it over with, damn you!"

Just then the foremost lookout let out a tense cry. "Ship ahoy!"

At once Wolf deposited Cathelen upon the deck. But before he could turn away, she lifted a knee and drove it into him where it would hurt the most. Wolf hollered in pain and dropped to his knees. *"Merde,"* he swore, trying to right himself but staggering as he made the effort. "My glass!" he roared through the fog of pain surrounding him.

Ted, looking distastefully at the young woman who had very nearly disabled his captain, rushed over to hand Wolf the telescope. "Man-o'-war!" the captain shouted after peering through his glass.

The pirate sloop bustled into action as Wolf called out his orders.

"Ya going to fight her, Cap'n?"

"Of course we're going to fight. I don't care what the hell she's got. Get ye mateys, to heat the roundshot in the galley!"

The men ran to the tasks they knew best. Cathelen stared all about her in horrible fascination. For the second time, she was swooped up by Wolf's strong arm, about her midsection this time, and deposited in the hatch.

She peered out as soon as she was left alone. "We-we are going to fight," she mumbled lamely, unable to keep herself from watching.

The better marksmen were grabbing the longest muskets. Behind each scrambled a shipmate bearing cartridges, wads, and ramming pins.

The *Seaflower* was altering course toward them, as could be seen by her topsails. She was a British ship of the line based at Barbados and ordered to seek out and destroy the Sea Wolf. But if there was a ghost . . .

"There's time for ya to turn tail before the wind and beat it, gov'ner, with a fair chance of escaping her."

Wolf pulled Hondo out of sight, saying, "Run like a coward?" He snorted. "Never!"

He then bellowed an order to veer away. But not to flee, simply to gain a few more preciously needed minutes. The *Legend* was never unready for action. But she could not hope to be as prepared to fight as a frigate of the King's Navy.

Cathelen watched covertly, admiring the agility of the young pirates who swarmed about the sloop's farthest reaches. How can they be so cheerful and excited at the possibility of facing death? She just could not understand it.

Wolf seemed to be planning something other than a head-on action with the King's warship. He had halted the rush to begin knotting the long, high screens of canvas cloth that would shelter all on deck from direct view of the enemy's cannoneers.

"Cap'n, she's leaving us!"

"*What?*" He gripped the telescope hard.

"It's your mask, sir. They always get spooked

by it. Remember last time?"

"Aye. That I do."

Theirs was the first pirate ship ever to frighten off a British man-of-war. Through a telescope the mask must be a terrible thing to behold. Perhaps those who saw him that way thought him a leper. A golden mask might hide the face of living death from all men. Besides, it was rumored that the *Legend*'s captain was a ghost.

Wolf strode over to where Cathelen was waiting for the commotion to end. "I thought I told you to stay in your cabin," he hissed.

"You said no such thing!" she replied, but she did make her way there, glad it was at the other end of the ship from the captain's cabin.

Wolf shrugged, tore off his golden mask, and stared at the spot where she had stood moments before. The impression of a slender, soft-curved woman remained. Damn. He tossed aside the mask—for now. *Damn!*

Cathelen spent as much time with Michal as she could, sneaking off to see him whenever she knew the captain was at the helm. He did not speak much, only stared off into space—what there was of it in the stinking cubbyhole where he was kept. There was no need to keep the door locked for he was chained and bound.

"Michal," Cathelen hissed into the dark, opening the door and whirling around to shut it. "Michal!" again.

329

He sat in a corner, overcome with self-pity. If only their father had not gotten into that argument with the town commissioner and killed him, for that was the start—the cause—of all this. Indeed, it had become a nightmare getting involved with this man called Wolf who was her husband. Jonathan. Adam. What name should she call him by? Cathelen wondered.

"Oh, Michal." Cathelen sat down near him. "Please talk to me, darling," she said, renewing her soft Scottish burr. She had never forgotten the guttural pronunciation. It was a natural part of her, but she had gotten used to trying to speak without it, like normal English folk did. Now she did not know if they were all that normal or not.

"Do you know"—he finally spoke, his beautiful colored eyes sad—"that Sea Wolf is in love with you?"

Cathelen stared in mild shock at her brother. "H-he said that?"

"No. I could tell. The man's in love." How Michal wished he could find someone to love like that.

But not with me, Cathelen thought.

She did not rush Michal into conversation. But took it slowly, trying to bring Michal up from his deep depression.

"There is good in everybody, lass, if one digs deep enough. There is good in the pirate captain, too."

Michal stared down at his hands, fine hands, long-fingered and smooth.

"It would not be wise," she began, staring at the ropes that imprisoned him, "if I were to cut you loose, Michal."

"Of course, love, I understand." He cupped her hands as best he could. "Where would I go, anyway? Over the side?" He smiled wanly.

On that score she was right, she knew. "I am so happy to see you smile," she said tearfully, trying hard to be strong for the both of them. "Even if it is a teensy smile, it is a start. More will come."

"'Tis a weak man I am, lass."

"Do not, Michal, do not ever say that again!" She sighed. "Are you ready to hear a story, Michal, *a true story?*"

"Aye, lass. I've one to tell you, too. 'Twill be up to you to say it's true or no."

"You have one, too?"

"Are you afraid of ghosts, pet?"

"I—" She paused, then said determinedly, "No!"

"Good."

To enter Tortuga's closely held pirate strong-hold, it was necessary for the Sea Wolf to signal his own identity. He had been reluctant to do so, however, being aware of the keen interest his arrival would arouse.

Wolf frowned uneasily as he scanned the masts and hulls already at anchor in Cayona. His own anchor chains were rattling out, and the *Legend*'s square-rigged sails were being methodically folded.

"Locked in again!" Cathelen groaned as the sloop entered what Hondo had informed her was the toughest, most blood-stained port in the world. Tortuga also had a harbor frequented by the worst thieves—the least of her worries! "What do I own to steal?" she snickered, then sucked in her breath. The captain himself had warned her that the lot in Tortuga would lay a woman on the spot as readily as look at her!

By afternoon, as Cathelen had known it would, the sloop was deserted by all but herself, Michal, and the five men who stood guard. Hondo had sneaked down to tell her.

As Tortuga's sunset flamed briefly across the livid sky, the various ships at anchor began to blur into lantern-specked silhouettes.

Later, after Cathelen had napped, the sloop was hissing slowly through the warm darkness. She overheard her husband, in the companion-way, speak in hushed tones a name that would live in her mind forever, one that would come between them. The name was Cameo Salvador.

Now—Cathelen glared into the dark over her bunk—now she had the name of his mistress. The woman he loved!

The next morning Cathelen awoke to hear a voice nearby. It was Hondo, poking his head through the crack in the door.

"Gonna warn ya. Cap'n's letting you off here into a longboat—I mean us. You and me and the doc."

"What?" she asked, sleepily. "Oh!"

She scrambled up from the bunk to toss her shawl on.

"Where are we?" She blinked the sleep from her eyes.

"Near *home*," he whispered back.

Hondo was about to close the door, when Cathelen took hold of it with both hands. "Little man . . ."

"Huh?" He blinked, puzzled by her sly expression. "What is it?"

"I know," she smiled, catching her breath, "I know who your cap'n is."

Hondo shook his head and jerked it once. "Always knew ya was a smart lass. Does the boss know that you know? Well"—he shrugged—"ya know?"

"Ya know what?" She aped him.

"Huh?"

"Ya better keep ya mouth shut!"

She slammed the door in his gaping face. Hondo stared at the all but splintered wood. What a wench! He shook his head, thinking better of that one. *What a woman!*

Chapter Thirty-Seven

The fields of Sauvage were busy. Men, bare to the waist, sweated under the sun as they cut the tough stalks of sugar cane. When they were through, the fields would resemble tangled thickets.

In a pink cotton dress, embroidered at the bodice and sleeves, Cathelen lazed on the veranda, enjoying the windless warmth and the sun.

The month of the sugar crop was supposed to be a happy time. It was compared to the harvest time in the vineyards of Bordeaux and Burgundy.

Cathelen had gone out to watch some of the procedure with the "boatswain of the mill," a handsome Creole lad from Jamaica. She had stood on the sidelines as the tough, yellowing stalks were cut as close as possible to the ground, for the root—the boatswain said in his rich patois—the root was the part richest in sugar.

"If it is left in the ground, mistress, the stalk shall continue to ratoon for many years."

"But will not the quality of the cane fall off, Jaime?"

"*Oui*, mistress, I was coming to that," he chuckled, his large mouth gleaming. "But you beat me to it."

She laughed for the first time in several weeks. What she did not know was that not far away someone had paused in his labor to keenly watch her—just as he did when she went to visit Michal at the old mill where he was kept prisoner.

"Now sugar cane must be made into sugar, mistress." Jaime grinned. "Rum too."

Shielding her forehead from the mellow sun (for she was feeling a little queasy and faint) Cathelen watched several wagons set into motion. They would carry the cane from the field to the mill. There, she was told, the rollers would extract the sweet juice, which still had to be clarified, heated, and filtered to make raw sugar, *muscovado*. That, in turn, had to be further clarified and boiled.

"Molasses or treacle is the product from which rum is made, mistress," Jaime sagely informed her.

"Tell me some history, Jaime." She turned to him, smiling brightly. "Oh, I am sorry. But do you have time?" She placed a fair hand softly on his dark arm, the contrast starkly startling.

"Of course. *Oui*." She liked hearing Jaime speak French, so he often did this to delight her. "I am very knowledgeable," Jaime said; then he began to explain. "It was not always sugar here. . . ."

Early in the 1640s, he told her, Barbados had its first flush of prosperity with the tobacco trade. But that market had been lost to Virginia, which produced more and better tobacco. The Barbadians took the advice of Dutch traders who encouraged them to take interest in sugar, and to learn the methods of planting and the techniques of production used in Brazil. The Portuguese were making fortunes there by cultivating sugar on a large scale, using African slave labor.

Planters who could find the capital bought out the small landholders, and the sugar plantation replaced the tobacco patch. African slaves were imported in large numbers to labor on the estates.

So sugar set Barbados on the road to what seemed to be everlasting prosperity, Cathelen thought to herself after Jaime finished.

"You may come to the mill with me now, mistress, if you like," Jaime said, the timbre of his voice deep.

Cathelen noticed for the first time, as the sun slanted over Jaime's cheekbones, that he was scarred. From what she would never know. But

336

this, she decided, did not detract from Jaime's handsomeness.

"I do not think Jonathan wants me there," she said softly.

With large hands on slim hips, Jaime tried to explain. "It is not my business, mistress, but the master has said you may go with me to the mill, as it is your wish to watch the operation."

"But he said just two days ago, when he arrived, that I was to stay out of his way while he is working in the fields and at the mill."

Hondo, Michal, and herself were "freed." Wolf had also said that. Yet, in her mind she asked herself why her husband had noticed none of the similarity in Michal's coloring. Had he no idea that she and Michal were blood-related? All she'd seen was his insane jealousy! He believed Michal was her lover, no doubt! Now Cathelen wondered if he would ever believe otherwise.

Did he think her a blind fool not to notice the two burly men who had arrived not long afterward? These two had been tracking them all the way from Bridgetown, and had taken charge of Michal's imprisonment as soon as they'd arrived. He must think her a real idiot. She would show him, the unfaithful wretch. Indeed she would!

Jonathan had returned two weeks after she and Hondo had settled back into their old way of life. Poor Michal was still confined.

Cathelen clenched her hands hard at her

sides. "He will not continue to treat Michal like a dangerous criminal!" she hissed under her breath.

"Did you say something, mistress?" Jaime asked her as they stepped from the path at the mill.

"No, Jaime, it was nothing."

"Nothing, mistress?" He shook his dark head sadly. "Sure wish there was something I could do to help you."

"Thank you, Jaime."

As Cathelen was gently placing her hand on Jaime's brown arm, a momentary gesture of gratitude and friendliness, Jonathan entered the mill. He saw them standing close together in what appeared to be an intimate scene.

"Oh . . ." Cathelen breathed, as she always did when he was near. But he never heard the sound; it was so soft.

He swept by, like the great master of the plantation he'd become. He did not look her way after that first glance, but went to stand where the juice was being extracted by grinding stalks between rollers operated by a mule and a horse outside. The apparatus was clumsy but did its job well enough.

Jaime gestured here and there while Cathelen watched, every so often her eyes straying to the silent figure of her husband.

Cathelen set her teeth, and a small muscle worked in her cheek. How she would love to confront him with all of the questions that whirled like eddies in her brain. Primarily she wanted to know why he had avoided her ever since his return. He did not even share the same bedroom with her any longer. He was the fool, not her!

Jaime continued to explain the procedure in his rich patois, gesturing all the while. He showed her the open coppers where the boiling was carried on. The resulting syrupy mass was allowed to granulate. Then after draining, which removed much of the molasses, the raw, or muscovado, sugar was packed in hogsheads for shipment to overseas refineries, Jaime explained.

"Rum is distilled from the scum that rises during boiling, and also from the molasses." He pointed with a long brown finger. "It is run into the puncheons for transportation to market. . . ."

Deke Jameson interrupted, "Rumbullion, alias Kill Divil, made of sugar canes that are distilled." He shivered visibly. "It's a hot, hellish, and terrible liquor! Hate it myself."

Jonathan turned once to glower at Jameson for his treachery then he immediately went back to watching the operation.

"But that is not the only product, I hope," Cathelen put in, hoping in the future to halt the making of this fiery, dangerous brew. She hated strong liquor; the stuff ruined thousands of lives as she had already learned in her short life.

Jaime chuckled. "It is a magic potion. For the West Indian planter it can cure all griefs and heighten every happiness."

Deke snorted, unable to credit that. At least, Cathelen thought with a little snicker, there was one man on her side. Jaime was young and had not experienced many of life's trials, but he would learn, being a man, the danger of believing such nonsense.

Cathelen turned to go back to the house, not aware that a pair of gold-flecked brown eyes followed her.

Even the most scrawny of the Negroes looked healthier once the mills were set into action, so constantly could the slaves indulge in the green tops of the cane and the skimmings from the boiling house. Even pigs and poultry were fattened upon the refuse. Though everyone was working hard, everyone was happy. An atmosphere of health, plenty, and busy cheerfulness prevailed throughout the whole plantation. This atmosphere was equally enjoyed by the master. He could forget his ill humor, his impatience, his loneliness, his nostalgia for the earlier days of his marriage as he stood by the mills, watching the cane squeezed and pressed between the new rollers Chiah had fashioned until the last drop of juice was wrung from it. Brown eyes aglow, he watched the juice run down the lead-lined gutter to the boiling house, to the great copper clarifiers in which it seethed under the heat of a fire only a degree or two short of boiling point. There the white scum rose in blisters to the surface. And at this stage the pure, almost transparent liquid was drawn into the grand copper.

For hours he stood in the heated room, watching the liquor boil, while Negroes swept the rising foam with scummers till the seething residue took on the fine rich color of Madeira. When the froth rose in large clean bubbles he smiled to himself, knowing that the brew was good. He watched the Negroes test the liquid, to decide when it was fit for striking. With their thumbs they took up a small portion of the hot liquid, drawing it, as the heat diminished, into a thread with their forefingers. When the thread snapped and shrank from the thumb to the suspended finger, they would judge by its length whether the order to strike could be bawled out.

The master also spent time in the curing house, watching avidly as the thick molasses dripped slowly through the spongy plantain stalk into the tank below. When this golden drained juice had fermented and mellowed, he arranged to have hogsheads of sugar and the casks of rum carted to the coast. He would again become the absentee owner.

Chapter Thirty-Eight

"Dear God, Michal, are you entirely certain?"

The young doctor hunkered down beside his sister, took her slim hand in his long-fingered one, and shook his blond head, flinging strands out of his eyes. He squeezed her fine hands, then released them.

"Damn, I—" He looked up at her in anguish. "Sorry, Cathy, I should not have cursed." He shook his chains miserably.

"Michal, forget that. I have heard you swear often enough." *You have even taught me a few choice words unwittingly*, she thought. "Tell me"—She bit into the knuckle of her forefinger—"do you remember anything else at all about this man called Sauvage, the one you were supposed to have killed. I do not believe that

342

you did, Michal, even though you were, as you say . . . inebriated.''

"Drunk, Cathy, I was always in the bag." *And in the sack with one trull or another, like Cameo.*

"Michal"—Cathelen gazed at him, deep in thought—"back at the ship you said that this Cameo Salvador was aboard at the time the *Gypsy* was attacked? Michal, do you realize that it was *Jonathan* Sauvage that you ran through and not—"

"I—I thought he was shot." Michal looked into Cathy's pale violet eyes, wondering what ailed her.

"You are not sure, are you, Michal?"

He shook his head. "Now I really am not sure."

"Whether he was shot or run through . . . or not sure you killed him?"

"Cathy, why do you go over and over this without ceasing?" He held up his bound wrists. No one could untie those ropes; they were wet down, soaked three times a day. When he was released—if that day ever came—these ropes would have to be cut very carefully with a knife. He watched her eyes rise again to his face. "Why?" he asked again.

"Because, I told you, I do not believe you killed Jonathan Sauvage!" She came to her feet abruptly and paced the confines of the dark, stone building that was the old mill. The smell was almost unbearable in here during the warmer hours of day. There was only one small

343

window for ventilation and that was open only a short time each day. Cobwebs were everywhere and creatures lurked in the dark corners. Cathelen shivered. "This is no place for a man—especially not my brother, my own flesh and blood." She whirled to face Michal. "I am going to open the door. I do not care who sees. You need the air."

After she had set the door ajar, she whirled to face Michal. "Darling, I am going to get you out of here. I do not care if there are a hundred guards standing by." She rushed to kneel before him, taking his graceful but manly hands into her own. "I will, I swear to God!"

"Is that so?" a voice drawled nearby.

His voice. Cathelen whirled to face the door which had moss growing in the lower corners.

"Yes!" she dared to the tall, dark outline framed like a titan in the doorway.

"Come to the house," he said with a snicker, "away from your lover, Cathy."

"You are supposed to be gone," she snapped, rising swiftly to her feet and swaying just a little, her fingers sliding away from Michal's.

"Cathy"—it was Michal, wondering out loud—"if you are a bondservant, why does Master Sauvage want you in the house? 'Tis puzzling to me."

"Michal, remember the story I told you? On the ship? Well, all that was true. . . ."

"Enough!" came the thundering voice. Jonathan stared at the clinging contact of their hands; both fair-skinned, similar somehow; one miniature, the other large and long fingered. He flicked his staring eyes back to her face and noticed how flushed she was. Because she had been with her lover, naturally. He wondered if they had made love yet. That would be quite difficult, he thought, even though he had made love to Samantha here. He grimaced at the four walls. But she was a different breed of woman from Cathelen. Or was she? He was beginning to wonder. A damp, dark cavern for two locked in a lusty, straining embrace. Too bad, Mitchell, he thought to himself, full of male pride, I had her first. Now you, young pup, must take the leavings. . . .

"No!" Suddenly, quite unconsciously he had cried out, surprising even himself. He lurched forward to snatch Cathelen's arm. "I said, 'Come with me.' Do I have to drag you?"

Cathelen, standing her ground, angrily shook off Jonathan's arm. "I can walk myself, thank you. There is no need for you to drag me!"

Haughty and impetuous, Cathelen moved past her husband and out the door. She heard the door shut behind them, then another sound made her halt and whirl around, alarmed and fearful.

"Wait a minute!" She walked up to the tall man clad in the white, blousy shirt, and black shiny breeches. Did he not realize that dressed thus he was the image of the Sea Wolf? Did he not think she could recognize him? Was she the only one who could do this? He must really think her a dunderhead!

"Why are you bolting the door?" she finally asked.

He turned so abruptly that Cathelen gasped softly when those intense brown eyes contacted hers. She seemed to swim in their depths, could feel them overpower her, seek out her most hidden thoughts, dreams, and desires. Desires . . . oh yes. How she wanted him. Her woman's body was crying out with desire. Was there any love left, though? Could there be, seeing how he had deceived her and was continuing to do so? When would he tell her he was truly Adam Sauvage? It had to be soon. She was weakening, and would give in as soon as he snapped those long, brown fingers for her to come to his bed. That was puzzling in itself. He had not made love to her in over three weeks, nor had he even shown any inclination to do so.

Cathelen swayed suddenly, and the only thing she could find to hold onto was his strong arm. She clutched him as if her very life depended on it, crying out as she did.

"Jonathan, I—I feel faint!"

He caught her, easing her slim frame down to his thigh while he bent on one knee. He watched her lashes flutter, her forehead break out in beads of sweat. "Are you with child?" he rapped out tersely.

Sleepily she blinked up at him. "W-with child?" Suddenly she came quite awake. Of course. That would explain the reason for her nausea in the mornings and the utter weakness she had felt the last month. A month gone? Or

346

more! "Yes," she said shyly. "I believe I am, Jonathan."

"Well, you might as well go in and tell your lover the news. I'm sure he'll be excited to learn he is going to be a father." He pulled her to her wobbly legs and shifting feet.

She righted herself and slapped him smartly, her small hand exerting more force than he expected and leaving a vivid imprint on his face. Going right past him, she began to tear into the bolted door. She hit it with small, bunched fists and lifted her soft boots to kick at the wood and at the large heavy bar that fastened the door. She could not move it.

"Cathy!!" Michal hollered in alarm from inside. "What is wrong?"

"I am angry because I cannot get back in to see you!"

"Are you all right?" He sounded concerned.

She looked askance, then glowered hotly at the smirking countenance behind her, noticing the red handprint she had left on his cheek.

"It is all right, Michal, I will get you out of here." She turned from the door, brushing her hands together in an angry gesture. "Somehow." She jounced on past a narrow-eyed Jonathan. *"So help me God!"*

Upstairs in her bedroom, Cathelen flung herself upon the bed with its colorful Matisse-like print. Lifting her fine chin, tears streaking her flushed cheeks, Cathelen pounded her pillow wishing it was Jonathan's handsome face. He was ugly as a bullfrog! And just as lazy when it came to the happiness of their marriage!

Cathelen sat up, taking the damp pillow with her to the center of the bed. A frustrated sound came from her throat as she raised her wet face to the palm-thatch fan, still now that the cooler months were here. She wished she could set it into motion, but she did not know how it worked.

A knock sounded on her door just then. "If it is Mattissa or Jula, you can go away!" Under her breath she muttered, "If it is Jonathan—or whatever your name is—you can go to the nether region."

"Cathy. It is Raven. Can I see you? It's important—very."

"I told you not to disturb the mistress. Master Jonathan says she not be feeling well, Miss Raven!"

"I am feeling as well as possible under the circumstances, Mattissa. Let Raven in, and that will be all."

"Yes, mistress."

Raven rushed in as soon as Mattissa opened the door for her. But Mattissa lingered in the opened portal even after Raven had begun to speak to Cathelen. "I have had a vision again, Cathelen. Paprika was with me when it happened and she told me everything I revealed in my sight."

"Mattissa," Cathelen began crisply, "that will be all. Raven and I wish to talk—alone!"

Humbly Mattissa inclined her head, but stood ramrod straight as soon as the gesture was completed. "Yes, mistress." Her eyes glowed and flickered as she shut the door ever so quietly.

Preoccupied, Cathelen did not really hear what Raven was telling her immediately. Mattissa had caused her to feel tingles of premonition along her spine. This had been the case ever since her return. What it meant she could not begin to fathom. She had caught Mattissa staring at her strangely, as if the *musteefino* knew something she was not telling Cathelen.

"I've had the sight again, Cathy." Raven eased her graceful backside onto the edge of the bed. "Only this time the blond-haired man who wanted your prayers before came to me. He—"

"Michal," Cathelen breathed.

"I don't remember if you told me before what he means to you. Who is he, Cathy?"

"He is—" Could she trust Raven not to spill the beans if she told her Michal was her brother? What if Raven spoke of him as such while having the sight? She just could not take that chance, not yet anyway. "He is—a friend." Cathelen shrugged. "That is all."

Raven peered at her friend suspiciously. "I've a feeling you're not telling me everything. Am I correct?"

"Hmm?" Cathelen shifted uneasily under the emerald green eyes. "Tell me, Raven, what did Paprika say about the vision? Was Michal in trouble again?" *Indeed he is!*

349

Raven stared around at the impressive furnishings of the house. They were much richer than those at Sugartree which was a smaller plantation. But both houses were larger and better built than those in the town. The good taste of the planters was as remarkable as their riches. There was so much silverware that it rivaled the priceless items carried by the galleons of the Spanish treasure fleets. Downstairs Raven had often gazed in wonderment at the large collection of books in the English tongue, although most of the library was in French because of the Sauvage lineage.

"Ship ahoy! Ship ahoy! Ahhhh . . . blow me down! Blow me down!! *Awwwwkkk*!"

A long-fingered hand flew to Raven's breast as she breathed in astonishment, "What in God's name was that?"

"Sinbad!"

Raven watched as her flushed and excited friend flew to the door and rounded it, leaving it open, to go racing along the hall. In a swish of chemise and with skirts awhirl, Cathelen was gone, leaving her guest to stare at the gaping portal. Finally Raven mustered up enough courage to go see what all the commotion was about, and she found her friend talking to a colorful bird.

"This is Sinbad?" Raven said, craning the white column of her neck, but stepping no closer to the dangerously curved beak. The room was very warm, so Raven allowed her roquelaure cloak to slip down and drape over her elbows. "Cathelen, are you forgetting you've company?"

"Oh, I am sorry." She turned back to the bird at once after acknowledging her friend's presence. "I have not seen Sinbad in such a long time that I was excited upon hearing him talk."

"Talk!" Raven said incredulously. "It sounded more like a ship of fools—or at least one being taken over by pirates."

"Yes . . . pirates," Cathelen murmured. Her face glowed slyly as she finally realized the connection between her husband and this noisy bird. Birds of a feather flock together, pirates one and all. "Even Sinbad," she clucked at him and repeated several words.

"How about a bit o' loving, me girl? Ahhhh . . . blow me down!"

Raven flushed at the lusty language. "He's a bit bold and colorful, isn't he?"

Cathelen finally faced her friend and acknowledged her fully. "Oh, Raven, let's be away. This is Jonathan's room, and I do not relish the thought of him finding me snooping in here."

For the second time Raven stared, astonished, after her friend's vanishing figure. She shook her head, muttering, "Why can't she be in her own husband's room?" Raven had known something was going on between these two but she'd never realized it was that bad. To not want to be found in your own husband's room!

As soon as Raven entered, Cathelen asked her to stay for dinner. "What are you having?"

Raven asked, familiar enough with Cathelen to be so bold.

"Black crab pepper-pot."

"Ugh. I think I'll eat at home. We're having flying fish and I simply love it!"

"I asked," Cathelen said, not really wishing to discuss Michal or Raven's "sight" too deeply. "Uh—was it serious, I mean what you saw having to do with Michal? I already know he is in trouble." *Oh, shut my mouth!*

"He is also the man I'm supposed to be married to in the near future."

Cathelen whirled from the closet where she had been taking down a tight-sleeved gown with undersleeves of linen. She halted, frozen in a semblance of motion even though she had gone quite still. "Michal?"

Raven laughed, thinking Cathelen's incredulous expression rather humorous. "Yes. Michal. Is there something wrong? Perhaps he's not the same Michal after all."

Oh yes, she thought, he is the same man all right. Then she grew excited. How wonderful!

Cathelen tilted her chin thoughtfully. Now all she had to do was to get them acquainted without seeming obvious. And, she mused, if that was to be the case then Michal would be freed in the near future. Her face fell just as swiftly. What if Raven's vision proved to be wrong?

"Raven," Cathelen began, "how many times have your visions come true? Are there any times when they have not?"

"They've always come true," Raven said rather proudly, her fine chin aristocratically high. She smiled and lowered her chin. "At least Paprika says they do, one hundred percent."

Rubbing her damp palms together, Cathelen asked Raven, "How would you like to go for a walk with me and meet Michal?"

"What?"

"Oh, drat, 'tis secured too good for us to get in!"

Raven shook her head as Cathelen's Scottish burr surfaced. It had done so lately when her friend was emotional over something. In fact, she thought, Cathelen had been acting most unusual the past few days.

"Cathelen—" Raven began but was rudely interrupted.

"Cathy!"

Clutching her breast, Raven whispered as if she did not want the occupant of the mill to hear her. "You were serious, weren't you. There really is someone in there?"

"Michal?" Cathelen said close to the door.

"Aye, lass. Have you brought me some good news? 'Twill be a relief to be out of here finally. Cathy?" he continued when she did not answer.

"Michal, I have brought someone I want you to meet. A woman."

Michal chuckled deeply. "Is that so? Sorry, ladies, that I cannot ask you in for tea and crumpets. And pray, Cathy love, how do we

353

shake hands, the lady and myself?''

"Well . . .'' Cathelen looked from the door through which Michal's voice emerged to Raven's astonished face. "You can start getting acquainted by saying 'Hello, 'tis nice to meet you.'''

"Hello, 'tis nice to meet you,'' Michal began, feeling like a pure idiot. "What do you look like? Are you blond like Cathy? Brunette? Raven-haired?''

Raven laughed at that. "Raven. That's my name. Hello, Michal, I am also happy to meet you''—she laughed—"even though I, too, wonder what you look like.''

"I am fair haired and handsome, lass. Are you comely yourself?'' Michal chuckled at the fun he was having. Then he suddenly became quite still. A few moments passed before he spoke again. "Raven?'' he said, his voice low and intimate.

"Yes?''

"Do you have green eyes, lass? Like the color of rich emeralds?''

Turning to Cathelen, Raven said with a small laugh, "Do I, Cathy?'' She blinked and enlarged her glorious eyes.

Cathelen turned back to the crack in the door. "Aye, Michal, as green as the Highlands of our beloved Scotland!''

Michal went utterly silent. Asking no more questions, he slumped back to his bed of prickly hay and hung his blond head. "Go away!'' he shouted; then he wrenched a bloodcurdling cry of helplessness and rage from his throat.

Raven stared at the wood through which the soul-shattering sound had come. Had that really been the cry of a human being?

"Come away for now, Raven," Cathelen said gently. "Michal wants to be alone."

Chapter Thirty=Nine

Cathelen hurried to half-run through her bedroom and peer down from her balcony. Hearing a noise she stepped back, wondering whether Jonathan was nearby and if he might see her. But it was only the gardner, Jack.

She fled back into her room and paused briefly to pour herself a glass of soothing water. It was fresh and delicious. Mattissa must have brought it in on her rounds and left it while Cathelen was outside.

Cathelen sighed, letting the refreshing cool water slide down her dry, nervous throat. The water was stored in the ground between the coral and the older rocks. Deep wells tapped these springs and brought up some of the best-tasting water in the West Indies.

Now! Cathelen sprang from her bedroom to the storeroom at the back of the long hall. Inside, she paused and peered about, waiting for her eyes to adjust to the frail light filtering in from the tiny window. She knew where her cache was, but caution precluded haste. If she tripped and made a racket, the others in the house would hear and come to investigate.

Thank God, Jula had helped her in this wild plan of hers. The woman who usually brought Michal his food had been persuaded—by a gift of some pretty madras handkerchiefs—to stay away from the old mill today. Jula had informed the woman she would take the white man his meals on this day.

When Cathelen was finished dressing, she gazed at the gaudy half-caste she made in the cracked mirror. Her face and neck she had rubbed with a potion. Heavy gold earrings hung from her ears and from her neck a coral necklace. Knotted in her hair was a gay madras handkerchief and she wore a fine linen blouse, low cut and trimmed with fluffy lace upon her bosom.

"My arms . . ." Cathelen gasped as she looked in the mirror. "I almost forgot!" Again she took up the heartwood and the roots she had mixed with dirt to make a dye that turned dark brown in color when rubbed on the skin. Raven's maid Paprika had taught her this bit of West Indian magic.

Now to get out of the house without someone seeing her!

Her bare feet almost flew over the floor and

down the stairs. Cathelen felt like a wraith as she went out the back door. She raced across the yard, heading in the direction of the back gate. It opened beneath her nervous hand and she headed toward the shore.

But Cathelen never made it to where she had stored her second cache, the tools she needed to break Michal out of his prison.

Out of breath from running so fast and trying at the same time to keep the full red skirt bunched and gathered high above her knees, she fell against a tree panting like a poor fox fleeing from the hounds. She had veered off her path.

Cathelen could not recognize her surroundings. Had she run so blindly in her frantic haste? "What is happening? . . . Cathelen asked herself, her heart beating frantically. She peered up at the sun coruscating through the trees, and pressed the back of her hand against her forehead. "Why do I . . . feel . . . so . . . sleepy? . . ."

The island spun madly. Cathelen entered the whirling, dizzying merry-go-round, slumping to the ground in a gaudy heap.

"Mistress coming to!" Jula hollered and jumped from one foot to the other. "She gonna be all right! Mastah! Mastah!"

From an unknown, distant land Cathelen heard the pounding of hooves thundering and echoing in her brain. They came to a halt before her, for Cathelen could feel the wind of their coming that ended abruptly where she lay.

Cathelen moaned. Were those several pairs of beast-eyes peering down at her? She tried to see them more clearly, but her eyes would not open all the way no matter how hard she tried.

"Oooh," Jula crooned mournfully. "But the mistress is swelling up bad!"

"Jula"—it was Master Sauvage—"have you found Mattissa? She will know what to do." Running his fingers through his mussed dark brown hair, he stared aghast at his red-faced, swelling wife, not knowing what to do for her in this case.

"I am here."

The two at the bed turned collectively to see Mattissa, a regal portrait of womanhood and *musteefino*. She came to stand before the bed of the woman she hated.

"*Manchineel,*" Mattissa muttered, at once rolling up her dress sleeves. "There will be more bad swelling and her flesh will be irritated until she is like a crazy woman."

"*Manchineel,*" Jonathan murmured. Why had he not remembered? He'd heard horrifying tales of shipwrecked sailors and pirates, unaware of the danger, falling asleep under the shade of this tree and dying, through inhaling the poison that the tree gives out. Contact with the milky sap caused severe swelling and irritation. What a close call! She was indeed lucky to be alive. *Mon Dieu, he* was lucky she had been spared.

"God, He is gracious," Jula echoed her master's thoughts aloud.

Mattissa, who had left, now returned with a sticky preparation, a bowl, and washcloth. She began her ministrations at once while Master Sauvage looked on, staring as if he were in a thick fog.

The master had been about to pull out with a load of hogsheads bound for the coast. Stark fear had burned in his brown eyes when the urgent message had been brought to him that his wife had been found unconscious down by the shoreline. He had dropped everything, and his heart thundering in his breast, he had made his way to the house.

"Lord," he had breathed upon seeing her swelling body. Great fear for a loved one, which is a kind of death itself, had coursed through his system and made it difficult to catch his breath. "What is she wearing, for God's sake? Jula, what is this stuff all over her?"

He had asked a million questions but Jula had made a half shrug, muttering, "I am not sure, Mastah. But it looks like a dye that is prepared from a tree growing here and"—she pretended to look closer at the inert blond woman with streaks of the stuff yet at her hairline—"dirt."

Needless to say, Master Sauvage was baffled to the point of madness. The whole household knew this. Mairi had even labored up the stairs to throw in her bit of advice on the healing—and Mattissa used that, too.

"The mistress is lucky to not have breathed in the poison," Mattissa said gruffly, her face revealing a trace of anguish and disappointment.

Master Sauvage stayed with his wife that night while the weary women went to seek some sorely needed rest. He lounged, fully dressed, beside the bed in a tall-backed chair he'd pulled there, his long legs stretched lengthwise on the bed and his handsome face close to the severely swollen and red-blotched woman who was his wife.

When Cathelen became semiconscious and thrashed about in her attempts to scratch the irritating spots, Sauvage tied her wrists together and applied more of the sticky salve until she became still again.

But in the wee hours of morning, Cathelen began to cry and moan, calling out a name which made Sauvage quake with jealousy and to suffer from disheartening feelings and disappointment.

Finally, he could take it no longer.

"Cathy— Love, stop it!"

He stood and bent to grip her by the shoulders. "I can't stand it. *Enough!*"

"Michal . . . Michal . . ." She sobbed and thrashed, trying to get at the burning welts that itched and drove her to the brink of insanity.

"Cathy," he gritted out, "what were you doing out there? Why were you dressed like a half-caste? Trying to leave Sauvage without being seen with your lover? You did not think I would discover the cache you planned to use to break out your boyish lover?" He shook her. "Damn

361

it, say something!"

"Michal . . . help him . . . get away from here!" She screamed then because her flesh itched crazily from the poisonous bite of the manchineel.

"Bring the clothes to him"—she panted—"dress him. Get Michal away . . . Michal . . . before Wolf kills you. Oh, *Adam* will kill you! Yes, yes, Adam Sauvage!"

The stricken man standing beside the bed now went quite still. *Mon Dieu,* she knows! he thought.

Adam whirled away from her. What a fool he'd been. Any blind idiot could figure it out—especially after being made love to by one's own husband. Why had he deceived her this long? He had been afraid? Was that it? Afraid to lose her?

His cheekbones tensed. All this time she had been playing the game too. But when had she actually discovered he was not Jonathan but Adam Sauvage? In the yard when he had been sneaking home after the *Legend*'s crew had set him ashore? Had she known even then that he, Adam Sauvage—the Wolf—was the man who so desired her? Did she also know he was the same man who had taken her first on that wild carriage ride?

"Damn." Adam swore softly.

"Michal . . . go away! Hurry, love, hurry!"

Adam, eyes glowing and teeth bared like the wolf he was named after, whirled back to face the wretched girl who was a red splash of suffer-

362

ing flesh, vivid against the white sheets. He must win her back from that young greenhorn pup Michal.

"All right, damn it," he whispered to the suddenly sleeping girl. "You win. I shall release your Michal, but only for the game. So, my lovely slut of a wife, it is your turn to be cast under love's spell. You will truly learn what love is all about, I promise, and know a winner when you see one."

Chapter Forty

Cathelen's new dress, expertly stitched by Mairi, was a pale almond color with sea-grape embroidery adorning its tight sleeves and hem. The bodice was white lawn, a cooler material to lie against her breasts now that spring was in the making. She laughed gaily as she turned to the attentive companion seated on the veranda with her.

"Michal, you are looking simply marvelous. 'Tis your tailor I must compliment, so when shall I meet him?"

"Tailor?" Michal said, picking a bit of lint from his dark-blue trousers. He could not quite believe that the master of Sauvage had given them to him. Couldn't Cathelen see how kind the man was becoming?

"They belonged to a . . . friend." The deep masculine voice came from the doorway.

After Cathelen's surprised "Oh," the blond pair on the veranda grew silent as Master Sauvage came out and chose a great wicker chair to accommodate his huge frame. "I see you have healed quite well, my love. Maybe we can talk now. Are you up to it?"

The blond man began to rise, intending to absent himself, but Sauvage would have none of that and waved him back down. "Stay. This is for your benefit also, Michal. So, my young friend—how do you like your new position?"

"I like it well enough, sir. 'Tis not much different, however, tending to the ailments of slaves or to those of Scottish peasants or"—he was about to say pirates, but decided against doing so—"sailors."

"Ah, yes. The sailors." Sauvage emphasized the word.

Michal, as usual feeling slightly embarrassed in the presence of this unpredictable man who seemed to be everywhere at once, fell silent. He had come a long way in one week, but he just could not understand it. One day he was a prisoner, the next he was treated like a guest— and then the topper: He was given a job as plantation doctor. Would he ever understand Sauvage? And it was even more odd that he had been given a room next to Cathelen's after he had healed the ailments of several slaves. That had only been a matter of putting them on a proper diet because they had been eating the wrong things. What he wondered most about now was why his dear sister was called mistress here. Was she indeed Sauvage's mistress—his prisoner? Yet, Cathelen seemed quite at home here . . . as if . . . No, Michal told himself abruptly. That could not be possible. But the notion stuck with him.

"We all seem to be keeping secrets from each other." Sauvage suddenly broke the silence. "I believe it is time for some truth, don't you agree, love?" His eyes caught and held Cathelen's wary ones, and he smiled winningly.

What is he up to? Cathelen wondered. He seemed to be bent on some strange cajolery. Her cheeks flushed to the color of a damask, as her husband continued to study her in what seemed a gallant, come-hither manner. A recklessly daring mood came over her, as it had often in the past, and she returned his look.

Sauvage smiled, capturing his Cathelen's heart at once. "I see this will be quite easy," he said, but beneath his breath this time. His heart beat expectantly at the thought of having her beside him again, as when they were first wed.

"Did you say something, Jona—"

"Cathelen," he said firmly.

"What?" His voice affected her deeply by its very tone.

He stood up now, tall and towering. "Allow me to introduce myself," he said carelessly, a mocking smile tugging at his crisp lips.

Both Cathelen and Michal exchanged glances of surprise. The big master of the plantation caught this at once, but he did not seem to be too agitated by their comradeship.

Breathlessly Cathelen and Michal waited, she having known he would do this someday. Still, Cathelen had not thought the revelation would come from him so suddenly, without any notice whatsoever.

She folded her nervous hands to still them, but her feet moved restlessly beneath her silver-threaded petticoats. New additions to her wardrobe—thanks to her generous husband and, of course, to Mairi, for her talent at sewing.

"Adam Roland Sauvage."

The boom fell. He bowed swiftly and Cathelen caught the hint of mockery leaping toward her from his brown, glimmering eyes.

Quick as a flash, Cathelen stood to her feet. "You contemptible cad! You *knew!*" she hissed, wanting badly to scratch his lean handsome cheek.

"Knew *what*, madame? Whatever are you babbling about?" A questioning eyebrow shot up.

"When did you find out?" She was upon him in one seething stride, ready to attack. "Ah! When I lay almost unconscious no doubt I spoke the words aloud."

"You are very perceptive, madame. Discerning."

"And you, Monsieur Sauvage, are very deceitful!"

"Now, now, my dear sweet Cathelen. I shall reveal to you why I ruthlessly overtook not only

367

Spanish vessels but anything in my spyglass while I captained the *Legend*."

"Ah, yes." She cocked a slim arm at her hip. "So now the Wolf doth speak."

Again, that stiff mocking half bow. "Might I now explain, *my love*?"

"Explain away, m'lord, all you want." But you will never tell about your Spanish mistress, she thought.

Michal hung his blond head, and his deep moan drew the eyes of the arguing couple to him. "'Tis all my bloody fault. I am a drunk and a murderer. I see it now, the way 'twas," he said forlornly, looking at the tall man he'd come to respect during the last week. "It 'twas your brother Jonathan, was it not?"

"Indeed it was," Adam told him curtly. "And you will still pay for it, young man. The price for any murder is very high."

"But only for God to judge. No man, sir!" Cathelen blustered at her surprised husband.

"God?" he drawled. "What do you know of Him?"

"Plenty, Master Adam, and I fear no man."

"Not even me, *ma chérie*?"

"'Twas not premeditated murder." She changed her tack. "Michal has had some trouble with inebriants but he is a God-fearing man!"

"And I am not?" He did not allow her time to think this over. "Sticking up for your young lover again, I see." Unable to squash his rising ire and his jealousy of the handsome blond man with the smooth fleshed hands, Adam wondered briefly how well they had known each other in Scotland. Perhaps they had even grown up together!

Cathelen, feeling her temper rise, looked away from those leather-encased fingers. And she used to love him, not out of pity but because every last inch of him was a man—oh, indeed, even those badly scarred fingers.

"Why, you hypocrite!" Cathelen saw that Adam's eyes were condemning her brother. His look tried Michal and meted out a dreadful sentence. "Are you any better than your fellow pirates? You too murdered at the mere drop of a hat while under attack."

"Cathelen," Adam said quietly, "you just said it yourself, 'while under attack.' It is a way of living, and always has been since piracy began. Lord, I could've been a soldier fighting in a war, where it is kill or be killed."

"But piracy"—she gasped—"is a nasty business! Cruel! Ah—ah—immoral!"

"Aye!"

Cathelen was caught between the two as they collectively affirmed her statement. Hands akimbo, Cathelen stared: first at her brother, who was smiling a bit sheepishly, and then at her husband, who looked directly at her. "I see you both need church," she said, prim and pious, her fine upturned nose in the air.

"Now, my dear wife," Adam said, emphasizing the last word, "I think you'd better come upstairs with me like a good girl. The doctor, too. Because I would like him to check you to

369

confirm your *pregnancy*."

Shooting from his chair, Michal gaped at the pair, sputtering, "W-wife? P-pregnant!"

"Indeed," Adam drawled with maddening nonchalance, "my *wife* is *pregnant*."

Michal's examination proved Sauvage's boldly spoken disclosure to be the truth. "Your wife is indeed with child. But she is sorely in need of rest, sir." Michal addressed his employer respectfully despite his urge to strike out at this big man who was so possessive about his sister. But Michal began to relax when he observed the handsome planter rounding Cathelen's bed and taking her pale hand in his to gallantly bring it to his sensuous lips. Michal began to think there was something more causing Jona— *Adam*—Sauvage's bitter attitude toward him. Then Michal suddenly understood. The man was jealous, insanely so, and thought that he, Michal O'Ruark was her lover. Hah!

"Cathy, I'll be going down now. You take what I prescribed and rest the day out. You'll be needing plenty of it, lass."

"Michal," she called out as he reached the door. "Thank you. You're a love."

"Why didn't you kiss him to settle the matter?"

Cathelen whirled in the bed to face Adam. "Oh, do be quiet!" she snarled like a lion cub.

Coming to tower over the bed, Adam said, "I'll allow you to rest now. . . ."

"Oh, thank you kindly, sir." She affected a simpering tone.

"Don't interrupt when I am speaking, Cathelen. Later I shall expect you to join me in my private quarters."

As he was going briskly out the door, Adam heard her laughing reply, "Aye, sir!"

Their argument was loud and clear should anyone have cared to eavesdrop in the hall.

"That was my intention anyway!" the deep male voice was shouting.

"To bring Michal here and keep him prisoner so you could take malicious pleasure in his torment?" Cathelen shouted at his abject countenance.

"Of course, damn it. He killed my only living kin!"

"Was Jonathan really what you made him out to be when you were acting for my benefit? Or was he actually a rogue like yourself?"

"Not for your benefit, dear Cathy," he answered, "but to delude those who were hot on my tail. There was, and possibly still is—though I've cooled my activities—a price on the Sea Wolf's head. I've had to make it appear that he'd been killed, Sea Wolf."

"But you pursued Jonathan's murderer as the Sea Wolf, did you not?"

"I did, Cathy. But many thought they were seeing a ghost."

"Why did they all—including Michal—mistake Jonathan for the Sea Wolf? Were you so much alike then?" she asked, gazing at his tall frame.

"Jonathan was a few years older, but unless you saw us standing side by side, you could mistake one of us for the other. Yes, we looked very much alike. How do you think I've come back to the island safely all these times? A quick change of clothes and no one could tell me from the other planters. The Wolf was nowhere to be found once I'd changed my garb in Bridgetown."

"Where?" she wondered, though it was not really all that important.

"In a building," he said with a tight grin, shrugging his wide shoulders.

Cathelen lingered at the door, her snow-white hair flowing wildly behind her to her hips, the gauzy material of her nightgown clinging to her softly curved shape.

"No more of that, love. Come to bed. You'll catch a chill standing there in only your nightgown."

"B-but 'tis spring. . . ."

Cathelen dropped her eyes from the burning intensity of his. Again he called to her softly, the deep voice of Jonathan and Wolf and Adam combined beckoning her. She had to go to him.

She slipped naked between the sheets, wanting to forget his mistress existed for now. She would win his love back! Totally this time. No mere trull was going to steal her husband away from her if she had anything to do about it!

His gaze hungrily roved the perfection of her body, and he murmured hoarsely when she was finally in the circle of his arms.

"Cathy, dear sweet Cathy. *Ma petite amour.*" He fondled her gentle womanly curves tenderly.

"Did you say *l-love*?"

"Damn it, woman," he said, his eyes burning coals. "Don't you believe me?"

"Believe—" Cathelen echoed. "Yes." In a smaller voice. "Yes, I—I do." She threw back her head as he nuzzled the slim ivory column of her throat.

Then the hollow there, pulsing with life. Next her breasts. And all the while Cathelen shivered as his stiffening shaft grew ever bolder against her thighs. He cupped her small, taut buttocks to press her firmly against him. His mouth moved along her ribcage, nipping gently. She undulated next to him, her womanly heat increasing.

"Please . . . now, take me now, Adam," she cried, her arms reaching for the small of his back. "I want you, love, as I have never wanted you before—or any man." She felt him stiffen at her last words.

But Cathelen paid his twinge of anger no mind. Oh God, how she ached for him!

His lips twitched as he hovered above her. "Do you realize you are begging me, *chérie*?"

Beneath him, Cathelen blushed. "I—" She caught her breath at the feral look of him. His eyes seemed to be getting angrier, darker. "Wh-what is it?" she asked, afraid of this newer, more threatening version of her husband.

Then, quite suddenly, his anger faded completely. "It is time to end this torture between us, hmm?"

Shyly she peered up into brown, blazing eyes, thicketed by midnight black lashes. Her feline body arched, yes, like a cat's; and she was just as shameless as a lionness in heat, her passion primitive and demanding. It was a wild thing this wanting him.

A shadow crossed Adam's eyes, and then it was gone.

"Yes, Adam . . . yes!"

As he kissed her passionately, her hand touched the hard steel of him, her small fingers closing but barely meeting around his thickened shaft. She wriggled beneath him, and he ground into her without entering but rotating and grinding his pelvis. Breathlessly she again invited, "Now, oh now . . ."

His face contorted with pain and desire, his emotions and hungers began to mount for the ride that would take them both to a pure paradise of sensation.

"Damn you, Adam Sauvage . . . please take me. I want all of you"—she ended on a sighing breath—"every last bit."

With one swift movement, he placed her legs at his waist and gathered himself between her parted thighs. She was indeed prepared to receive him, he noticed at once. He entered her in one stab of bittersweet motion, and Cathelen indeed took all of him—all at once.

She raked and pulled at his hair. "Ooooh, Adam, yes, yes!"

He loved her until she was breathless and panting with her first sweet release of the night, and then he loved her into another and another, their lovemaking a thing of wild naked beauty.

"Cathy, *damn you,*" he hissed when his ebullition was strongest.

But Cathelen, driven by her own needs, did not even seem to have heard his cry of utter frustration. Adam knew she had not. But he did not care. How he wanted to choke the life out of that bastard Michal! But now was not the moment for insane jealousy. He might as well enjoy what his slut of a wife had just given him. He too could pretend as well as she.

They slept then, entwined lovers pressed close. Cathy's slim arm was draped wearily over Adam's taut waistline, one tapered finger wrapped in a black curl on his stomach. They looked like handsome children who had tired themselves out at last.

In the wee hours of morning, Cathelen began to thrash about in a nightmare. She woke Adam unknowingly. He turned to face her contorted little face and immediately grabbed hold of her restlessly moving shoulders.

"Cathy. Wake up!"

"Michal . . . don't leave me, darlin'!"

His solicitous gaze hardened into one of cruelty and displeasure. Adam lifted the slender form and carried her through the hall to her own bedchamber. There he laid her in the center of the cold lonely bed, his eyes glowing coals in the dark as he covered her and strode back to his bedchamber to jerk his clothes on with quick, angry tugs.

"Women!" he said darkly. "A fickle lot, all of them!"

Adam Sauvage left the room where they had so recently made love, without looking back at the mussed sheets.

Chapter Forty-One

"Docca! Docca!"

Smiling down upon the little black girl with the badly infected toe—bandaged now—Michal was just about to pick her up and place her into her mother's arms when Chiah came running up the lane, raising dust as his flapping sandals hit the dirt.

"Docca, Miss Raven has been bad hurt!"

Michal turned away from the frightened man to place the wary child in the pleased mother's arms; the woman was oblivious to Chiah's distress because of her own concern over her child's toe. She had feared the girl would lose it. But now the good doctor had made her Selmah better. As she turned away, cradling her babe, Michal gave his full attention to the black man who was almost hopping up and down.

"What is it, Chiah? Did you say someone has been hurt?" He rinsed his already tanning hands off briskly; then he ran his fingers through his sunstreaked hair to smooth back the waves that had fallen over his forehead.

"Show me then." Michal was ready to go.

As he trotted off down the lane after the easily loping black, he caught a flash of soft rose color in his peripheral vision.

Cathy was shading her violet eyes from the glare of the sun with one hand while resting the other on the railing of the veranda. Seeing Michal, she waved but immediately returned her hand to her forehead to protect her eyes. Curious, she watched him head out to the road with Chiah. She could barely make out the shape of a carriage. Why, she thought to herself, a little bit alarmed now, that looks like Raven's cabriolet.

"Damn," she exclaimed, placing a hand over her gently rising tummy. What a time to get a cramp, just when she wanted to go see what the commotion was all about. She shrugged, hoping maybe it was only Vance Moore, after all he did borrow Raven's cabriolet on occasion.

"Something amiss?"

Adam joined his wife out on the veranda although it was not much cooler than the inside of the house on this humid, early summer day. He peered down at the gentle bulge of her tummy a bit resentfully. "Having a cramp again so soon?"

"How can you tell?" she asked, not looking his way.

"You always tense up. I told you not to consume so many sweets. They aren't good for you in your condition."

"I crave them." She snapped at him peevishly. They had not gotten along since the night of their wonderful, compelling lovemaking. Hah! But that seemed ages ago, and she had given up wondering what she could have done to create this rift between them.

The love had been so good, but for them it never lasted. That night had, indeed, been months ago. She stared down at her growing belly. Now she understood. She had lost her trim waistline. That must be the reason for his bitter disregard of her.

"Give them up," Adam was saying, "or I warn you as your—as the doctor has that you will keep right on feeling ill and suffering from those terrible cramps. Who the hell brings you all those imported chocolates anyway?"

"You needn't swear, Adam."

"Who?" he pressed angrily.

"Raven!"

"Tell her to bring you something else"—he waved his hand—"like fruit."

"Ugh, I am sick of bananas, limes, mangoes, and the like!"

"Well then my shrewish wife, go to . . ." Frustrated, he waved his hand as she waited for him to swear again. "Never mind!"

"Och!" Cathelen seethed. She stomped her

foot and was rewarded by another cramp that nearly doubled her over. "Damn him, damn him, *damn him!*"

Dejectedly Cathelen slowly went to plop herself down into a red wicker lounge. She was about to snatch up her palmetto fan when Michal's voice, deep and forceful, rang out from down the lane.

"Michal?"

Cathelen shot up to resume her former position at the railing, again shading her delicate eyes as an alarm sounded in her. There had been an accident!

Cathelen caught sight of Raven's green dress, one of her favorites which she often wore to visit. "Oh dear God, not Raven!" she cried.

Adam! she wanted to shout. She needed him, but she had to call him by that name she had come to detest: Jonathan. It seemed that Adam's brother reached bony fingers from his watery grave to haunt them. She believed he had hated Adam. She had also decided not too long ago that Jonathan had not been much of a gentleman. Raven had told her this at private "teas," after she had learned more about Jonathan from Samantha Gable. What a little slut! Yet Jonathan had had a roving eye and had lifted the skirt of many a lass: black, white, or of mixed blood.

"Oh . . . *Jonathan!*" she called back into the house. "Oh God," she choked out at seeing Michal carrying Raven's slender, limp form in his sinewy arms. "Raven . . . has been hurt!"

380

Adam appeared on the veranda in a flash. He had heard his wife's cry of alarm and now looked her over thoroughly to make certain it was not she who had been harmed or who was ill. This done he turned his concerned gaze on the lovely, black-haired Raven.

"Move it out further," Michal ordered as he headed for the long wicker lounge, but Adam changed the doctor's course by directing him up the stairs to Cathelen's bedchamber.

"What in God's name happened?" Adam questioned Cathelen, studying her closely and unaware that he was clutching her pale trembling hand in his large, brown one.

Her misted violet eyes were larger than ever. "I am not sure, Adam, but I think it is just the sudden heat that overwhelmed her, I pray it is anyway. Raven should not have ventured outdoors on such a hot day just to come over here!"

Looking down, Adam released Cathelen's hand abruptly. She too had not been aware of his grasp until he broke it off, leaving her feeling cold and bereft. He was glowering down at her again. Cathelen could barely stand the looks he gave her. They were cold and despising.

"What is wrong with you?" she finally blurted.

He leaned over her, scrutinizing her face. "Perhaps Raven was seeking the company of her dear friend. Did you ever stop to think of that?"

He left the question dangling in the air and Cathelen turned her neck to watch him go.

Twiddling her fingers nervously, she ambled closer to the bed where Raven lay so white and still. Michal had ordered Jula to bring water and a washcloth.

He was just loosening the laces of Raven's taut bodice and slipping a cool hand inside her camisole to lay aside the unbuttoned material. A momentary shiver of desire passed through Michal, but he quelled the emotion and became the concerned doctor again.

"Jula, give the cloth to me."

Michal glanced over his broad shoulder to see if the girl had dipped the cloth in cool water and wrung it out as he had asked. "Thank you," he said, then turning back to Raven, he found her beautiful emerald eyes resting on him curiously.

Michal's large hand paused in mid air.

Raven's breath caught in her throat.

"Michal," she finally murmured, her eyes growing wide with mild shock. "You—again . . ."

Cathelen moved closer. "Now I know what happened to her."

Michal rolled his luminous eyes, never letting Raven out of his peripheral vision.

"She had the 'sight,' Michal. Remember the old woman in Scotland who used to see visions when she entered a trance?"

"Aye. I remember, Cathy." He faced the black-haired beauty again. "You've had visions of me, lass?"

"Y-yes," Raven confessed, shy for the first time in her life because of this handsome, compelling doctor. If she did not know better, Raven would have thought this was love at first sight. *Sight!* She had envisioned this very same man often enough to feel that she had known Michal most her life.

And Michal, he was utterly smitten, like a schoolboy still green behind the ears. Raven was his Star, the shining emerald Star he had searched for so longingly in the night sky. Her large eyes, luminous and magnificent, caused his heart to hammer madly. He just gazed at them and lost himself in their liquid depths.

"Raven?" Cathelen tried to interrupt the gazers, hoping her dear friend was better now.

"Can't you see that they wish to be alone?"

She turned slowly about to see Adam scrutinizing her closely, so she followed him out into the hall at once, having realized from his expression that he had something important on his mind.

What could it be? she wondered as she shuffled down the hall.

Chapter Forty-Two

"I am leaving you, Cathelen."

A trembling hand went slowly to her breast and Cathelen stared at Adam as if he had pronounced a death sentence. But how could she not believe her own ears? When she spoke her voice emerged as a low and tiny croak.

"L-leaving me? Whatever for, Adam?"

"Don't you realize anything lately?" He shook his head, causing a restless brown lock to fall over his forehead. "I see that you genuinely do not."

Adam turned away from her astonished features, so childlike and helpless now that they had lost their shrewishness. He almost whirled back to take her in his arms in spite of himself.

Cathelen hurried after Adam when it struck her that he was indeed walking away without so much as an explanation. She tugged at his arm finally, and Adam halted to glower down into her small, upturned face.

"What is it?" He smirked. "Why, Cathelen, don't tell me you can't handle this little matter all by yourself." He plucked her straining fingers from his sleeves, thrusting them away. "You were digging into me," he remarked as if getting her to release him was most important.

"What is the matter?" She stomped her little foot when he began to stride along the hall once again, arrogantly and indifferently heading toward his own room.

"Tsk, tsk, Cathy." He looked over his shoulder as if she were a mere pest he wanted to be rid of. "Too bad you've suddenly found yourself saddled with stiff competition." He shook his dark head before entering his bedroom.

As the door shut firmly in her face, Cathelen stared at it transfixed. She clenched a fist, ready to pound on the door, but thought better of it. She had never seen him so cold and casual about what he was doing.

A whirling blur of soft rose cotton, she raced back to her bedchamber to find Raven seated on the edge of the bed, Michal's strong arm slung about her slim shoulders to steady her as she tried to stand.

But Cathelen halted before she could fully enter the room, because Raven and Michal were having a very private moment. Michal was lifting Raven's chin so that he could gaze into the green stars he loved so much. To Cathelen, however, their behavior appeared to be a case of love at first sight.

She chuckled, forgetting all about her own very serious problems and delighted that these lonesome people had at last found each other.

"I am sorry," Cathelen said, turning to leave when they noticed her presence.

"Nonsense!" Raven said. "This is your room, Cathy. I—I was just getting acquainted with your—ah—charming brother." Raven pursed a corner of her red lips. "Shame on you, Cathy, for withholding the truth from me all this time."

Cathelen shrugged. "It *used* to be a secret. At least I still want to fool Adam after all the deceitful games he has played on me. He has used me cruelly, and I shall never forgive him for this p-pain!"

"Adam?" Raven was too shocked to notice Cathelen's distress. "Did I hear you right?"

Michal took Raven by the elbow and led her back to be seated again. Smiling as if this were going to be another long session of explanations and revelations, Cathelen sighed as she settled into a nearby chair. She rolled her back on the seat, for she was feeling some discomfort.

"Go ahead, Michal. Raven might as well hear the whole story."

Cathelen folded her hands demurely in her

lap, below the tiny bulge of baby.

"Well!" exclaimed Raven after the tale ended. "I do feel sorry for all of you—*Adam* Sauvage included." She turned to her best friend. "Cathy, what are you going to do now? Tell Adam the truth—that Michal is your brother? It certainly would help matters." She peered down at Cathelen's growing belly. "In fact, I think you really need your husband here now more than ever!"

"No!" Cathelen shot to her feet, clearly agitated. "Not on my life! He will have to see the light himself. I saw it when he f-fooled me the second time around."

Fury and agony stormed Cathelen's heart as she paced to remove the kinks from her sore back.

"Yes, but you were *asking* for his wrath." Raven pressed on. "You followed where no woman should go—ever!" Then she studied Cathelen very closely. "Oh, I think there is more to it." She turned to Michal, surprised that he had been studying her profile so intently. She blushed before she went on. "Has Cathelen always kept secrets like this, Michal?"

"Aye." His violet-blue eyes delved into her emerald ones. "Cathy was a secretive little lass, always. But I think I know why," he said sadly, his sober expression making Raven feel for the both of them.

"I'm curious," Raven piped up. "Don't leave

387

me hanging this way!"

"Do you mind?" Michal asked Cathelen, who was in a pensive mood now that her anger had cooled. He smiled as she shook her head, No, she did not mind. "Good," Michal said. "You see"—he turned to Raven—"Cathelen was a lonely child. Our father was not much of a—a loving parent to his children if the truth be told. He hated and mistrusted everyone who came along, even his wee bairns. Especially, you see, he did not want a girl cluttering up his selfish life. And I"—Michal shook his blond head—"I was away far too much."

"Oh," Raven said softly, reading the anguish in Michal's bleary eyes. "How sad."

Cathelen sat back down again after pacing fretfully back and forth. She gnawed on her lower lip and a thoughtful frown rode her fine brow line. She did not even notice when the pair—different in coloring as night and day—slipped on silent feet from the room. As the door closed, however, Cathelen glanced up but was still partially ensconced in a trance.

Much as she wanted to, Cathelen could not bring herself to tell her husband the truth about Michal and herself. Adam had been very adept at telling lies. Cathelen reined up at that thought: Had Adam ever actually lied directly to her? Not actually, she told herself now. But it was his perfidy which bothered and tormented her most. Damn! he should have trusted her, even a wee bit!

"Oh, dear Lord, I am so miserable." She

sighed forlornly. "What am I to do?" Cathelen wailed softly mourning her dilemma. Perhaps, she prayed, the answer will come soon. There had to be trust in their marriage—mutual trust. Cathelen sighed once again. But Adam was leaving and her heart was breaking in two!

Chapter Forty-Three

Caaa . . . caaaa—awwwk!

"Cease that rattle!" Adam whirled from the window to shake his fist at Sinbad. If he did not know better, he would have thought Sinbad was turning into a bloody blackbird.

A muscle worked in his smoothly shaven cheek as Adam stared moodily out the window, overwhelmed by a never-before-experienced gloom.

"Damnable women!"

His arms crossed below his bulging pectorals, he glared out over the wild shore facing north, realizing that soon he could look for the *Wind Sound* to approach and take him from this God-forsaken place.

Caaaa-keee!

"Shut up, damn you!" Adam grabbed the first thing he could find among the items laid out on his bed and tossed it at the noisy parrot who had driven him crazy with a new word he was trying to learn. He would have to scold Mattissa or Jula for teaching Sinbad new words; the blasted bird talked his head off already!

Sinbad let his wings sail out as the object struck his perch, but he hung on nevertheless, still taunting his master with squawks and shrill screeches, and continually trying out his new word.

Violently Adam whirled to face the bird. But more than the bird caught his eye. In his bitter mood, he eyed the belongings laid neatly on the bed in preparation for his departure, those and the garments he would take with him to Jamaica. Suddenly, in an unleashed surge of rage, he lifted the bedcovers and swept them up, sweeping the neatly piled items and carefully laid clothes onto the floor. Some of the items, like his heavy brush, landed with noisy thuds. Then, going one step farther, he tore the black gloves from his hands and hurled these onto the pile on the floor at the other side of the bed.

A rather tentative knock sounded. "Come!" he shouted, but before Mattissa could see what the matter could be, Adam was tearing past her in a flurry of violent movement. She splayed herself against the jamb, even feeling the great wind of his wrathful passage.

"Lord!" she huffed out, clutching her bodice in a tight grip.

Mattissa halted just inside the room and shook her head at the great mess strewn all about on the floor. But before she could galvanize herself into acting, the master had returned, flames in his sherry-brown eyes.

"J-Jonathan?" she questioned, feeling a bit nervous. "There is something? . . ."

He thrust out his hands and said in a low hiss, "Mattissa, I am Adam," he groaned, *"Adam Roland Sauvage! Do you hear?"*

"Uh-huh."

Mattissa stared with shivering apprehension at those long, scarred fingers, and then realization dawned even though his harsh words had borne testimony of his true identity. *"Adam. Dear God."* She caught her breath, realizing that it was Jonathan who had passed to his watery grave. Here stood Adam Sauvage, the infamous Sea Wolf alive and well—in the flesh!

"You may relay the message to the household, Mattissa," Adam said, noticing her glazed eyes and dazed expression.

"Wh-where you going now?" she got out despite his dark look, as his long, lean back moved indifferently through the door. He did not wait to reply but the answer came to her of her own accord in the next moment. She shook her elegantly coiffed head.

How bad it must have been for this handsome young lad to hide himself all these years, Mattissa thought while bending to pick up a pile of the clean clothing that he had dumped so carelessly to the floor. She shuddered. And those scarred fingers. Mattissa puckered her crimson lips here, though. That sure did not take away from Adam's rugged handsomeness. No sir, not one bit.

Mattissa just wondered how Adam Sauvage was going to live with it now that he was baring not only his true identity, but also his black soul.

"The poor wee mistress," Mattissa said, pitying the young woman who was this infamous rogue's wife and able to do so since no one would hear. She would not want to give anyone the impression that she cared about that silly little white Mistress Sauvage, Mattissa thought as she set about straightening up the rest of the mess, a frown marring the perfection of her lily-white brow. She halted once, hearing that noisy old bird Sinbad trying to say the new word. She chuckled. The name she had been trying to teach him! He would say it someday, he would.

"What is all the excitement about?" Cathelen asked Jameson as she came down off the veranda, her skirts held high in one hand. "Is that Ad—I mean Jonathan? . . . Oh, I—Forget it! I shall go see for myself, thank you!"

Deke Jameson shook his head over the mistress's peevishness. Of late she was like a young tigress, spitting at everyone who crossed her path the wrong way. He hadn't even said "boo"

393

and she had become vexed. Must be because she's in the family way. Jameson chuckled. Just the other day he had heard the mistress give that haughty Mattissa a real good shaking out—like a rowdy pup with a big juicy bone. Mattissa had cowered and turned tail!

"She sure has undergone a change since she come here," Jameson remarked to no one but himself, thinking that Sauvage Plantation was not the same either since the little blonde had arrived.

"Might as well mosey down there myself and see what's going on." Deke followed in the mistress's stormy wake.

Chiah, Jaime, Doc Michal (as he was now known), Mattissa, and Jula, had all gathered near the overseer's cabin to listen to the master's announcement; Mattissa already knew about it, but had come down from the house just the same, to be with the others.

"I am Adam Sauvage," the master wasted no time but came right to the point of this hastily called meeting.

Cathelen showed up just in time to hear his announcement, and she stood alone at the fringe of the blacks who had gathered. They leaned this way and that, some smiling and some not because they feared what this meeting entailed.

"Jonathan," Adam said loudly and clearly, "my brother, is the one who is dead." His voice dropped an octave. "I am alive." He paused to look over Doc Michal in a head to foot glance. "You see—" Adam held up his scarred hands, and those who had been on the plantation prior to Jonathan's untimely death nodded to one another that yes, this was the truth. The younger brother now stood here in the flesh. Some shook their heads in pity, that he so boldly exposed himself like this, but most thought it took a lot of guts to be so truthful and caring. Yes, he cared for his plantation folk. He had even seen to it that most of the blacks had learned a smattering of English and were every day getting better at explaining themselves.

When the meeting ended everyone left except the master and his dewy-eyed wife. Cathelen went to Adam and tugged on his arm, but he ignored her heartlessly. "We are strangers, dear Cathelen. Go away. Don't you see?"

Cathelen looked over her surroundings, the plantation she had come to love so much—and all her friends. Blacks. Whites. Racially mixed people. All were dear to her. Suddenly she was bitter and angry, knowing Adam was the cause of their estrangement.

"That is just it! We are strangers, Adam, and for all I know—" She almost broke off here but emboldened she went on. "You could possibly have another woman stashed somewhere—a m-mistress." Having blurted this out she was shocked at herself. Yet, Cathelen grew angry at his response—a maddening chuckle. "What about your long trips? I do not know where you go—not always—nor what you might be doing. When you leave, I wonder if I will ever see you again. You are my husband, Adam." Her eyes beseeching him for help.

"My business is quite finished, Cathy. You know why I left so often, who I was searching for."

Cathelen's nerve strings tightened. He was finished? Did that mean he was also through with her and Sauvage Plantation now that he had caught Michal, Jonathan's murderer? Had it all been a pretense, pretending he was Jonathan in order to— Oh, that did not make much sense. And why hadn't Michal been punished more? One ray of hope, she thought. Perhaps Adam thought Michal's suffering was completed. Dear God, if only that was the case.

"Now you are free to love as you wish, Cathelen."

"What?"

"Just that. Whomever, whenever."

"You are not being honest with me, Adam."

"There's no need anymore. . . ." his voice trailed off.

"Love should be honest and—" Oh, drat! Cathelen blushed furiously at her stupid outburst.

"Cathelen!" He turned to grit his teeth into her frightened little face. "Don't be so stupid. You are free. Don't you hear, don't you understand?"

"Wh-what do you mean . . . free?"

Cathelen's heart beat so dangerously fast that she thought the poor organ would burst from her chest. She stared up into his mockingly cruel yet handsome face, the face of a stranger.

"There'll be no need to dissolve our marriage, Cathelen, for you see . . . it is not valid."

Her heart plummeted.

"What are you saying?" she asked.

Adam prepared to pierce her heart with his swift, cruel blade.

"We are not man and wife, my dear," he said.

"N-not man and wife?" Her whole countenance sagged. What did he mean?

"Oui," he reverted to French. "Your husband is quite dead, madame."

Long minutes had passed before Cathelen shook herself and realized she stood alone in the dusty path leading to the house. Sunlight coruscated through leafy branches as she finally came out of her daze. She reviewed what had happened in the past five minutes now that she could think a bit more clearly.

After he had thrown that shocking declaration into her face, Cathelen had stared after Adam's tall frame as he strode away from her, mesmerized. Chills raced up and down her spine and bile rose to her throat.

"Oh, no." Holding her slim hand over her quivering mouth, she choked and swallowed hard to keep from vomiting.

It was true. She shuddered as her knees grew weak. "Oh God, why can't you spare me this?" she sobbed.

He had never married her at all. As far as everyone knew, the marriage was legal. Yet it had been nothing—a farce! *Adam Sauvage was not her legal husband.*

Chapter Forty-Four

Little Adam was born when the first showers fell and the plants and shrubs exploded into intense green foliage. So far, the babe promised to look just like his father.

Holding little Adam in her lap while he nursed at a swollen breast, Cathelen looked over to where the wall was boarded up. The hurricane had destroyed a whole section of the house. She thanked God that Adam John, now two weeks old, had not been sleeping in his crib at the time of the storm.

The hurricane had come on suddenly, blowing at a speed Jameson had determined to be twelve hundred furlongs an hour. Most of the West Indies islands were visited by them. Barbados had been hit just three weeks ago. The hurricane had inflicted great damage, destroying houses and uprooting trees.

Jameson had told Cathelen, quite regretfully and kicking himself in the backside all the while during the telling, that it was the custom every year when the hurricane season approached for the prudent family to ensure that their shutters and locks were all firm, and that there was a store of food and blankets available in case of trouble.

But they had not been prepared. Jameson had informed the mistress too late.

They were not a family, Cathelen had bitterly realized. If only Adam had been . . . here, she thought sadly. But wishes did not come true for Cathelen O'Ruark any longer.

Now she rose quietly and took sleeping Adam John to the crib Chiah had made for the babe after the section of the house that contained the nursery adjoining Cathelen's room had collapsed during the hurricane.

Cathelen stared at Adam senior's bedchamber. She had been forced to move into his rooms, a bedroom with a study attached and a small bath. Adam John occupied the study.

She sighed pensively and moved toward the window so she could look out and dream that someday he might return to Sauvage. He had been gone for five months. She pressed her cheek against the cool pane. Or was it six months? She could not even count the days any longer, nor did she care to.

"Is he sleeping now?" The query was soft-spoken.

"Yes, Mattissa."

Cathelen joined the woman who gazed tenderly in the direction of the mahogany crib. "Is there something you wished?" Cathelen asked her.

"Yes," Mattissa replied crisply. "There is a strange woman downstairs who wishes to see you. She says she must see you now. She would not go away when I told her the mistress must not be disturbed."

"What did she say or do then, Mattissa?"

"She persisted and stepped right inside. I would have called Jaime to throw the woman outside, but—" Now Mattissa's expression altered to a wary look. "This woman says she must see you, yes, but . . ."

"What is it, Mattissa?" Cathelen took hold of the woman by the arm and surprisingly Mattissa did not cringe as she would have done in the past. "Is it about . . . Adam?" Cathelen asked, hope springing to her eyes.

"She asked for Master Jonathan first."

Now Cathelen did frown, so hard that a line of wrinkles appeared above her puckered brows. "Did you tell her that Jonathan Sauvage has passed on?"

"Yes." But Mattissa stiffened.

"Well—what did she say?"

"I—she says she saw the Wolf not too long ago and has learned that this is his residence.

401

She has reason to believe"—here Mattissa's eyes glinted like black ice—"that he is alive."

"That *who* is alive? H-how would *she* know?" Cathelen stared down at the floor with an intensely thoughtful expression. Then she again took hold of Mattissa's arm, this time making the housekeeper flinch. "I am sorry, Mattissa." She loosened her grip. "But—did she give her name?"

"Yes, madame."

Cathelen's eyes opened wide. "Well, for damnation's sake—what is it?"

"Cameo Salvador."

That was all Cathelen needed to hear. She flew along the hall and sped down the stairs. Once, she almost tripped, but she regained her foothold. At last! Cathelen's heart pounded and raced. She would finally have a look at Adam's mistress. Cathelen pulled up short in the hall, just before the door. But what was his mistress doing here?

Gowned in flashy red silk, Cameo Salvador sashayed about the room that served as the sitting room, now that the original one had been destroyed by the high waters during the hurricane and needing much work to restore it. She sniffed, recalling the skinny little girl, barefoot and dark, who had peeped in and tried to strike up a conversation with her when there was only one person she wanted to see on this plantation. Not a silly little serving girl!

"What is keeping the woman?" Cameo asked herself in her heavily accented voice.

Jonathan Sauvage's wife, eh? Cameo had done some investigating of her own to learn that. Even going so far as to take up residence in a small house in Bridgetown. It had been easy as pie. Cameo smiled at her reflection in the highly polished table. Yes, easy, when a woman had many lovers to keep her life one of ease and luxury.

Cameo was still bent over the table when the door behind her opened very slowly. She was picking at the stray black curls surrounding her white-complected face to make herself a bit more presentable when a husky sweet voice invaded the room.

Cameo whirled about, startled out of her wits.

"Can I help you?"

The dark-haired woman gaped at the slim back of the younger woman who was closing the door. *Madre de Dios!* Cameo thought she had stepped into a mythical forest where only princesses and little elves dwelled, so lovely was the slim form before her.

"Can I help you?" Cathelen repeated, coming farther into the room. Her lavender skirt swayed with a gentle motion and her full breasts moved sensuously as she came closer to Cameo and finally halted before the dark, suspicious-eyed female.

A blond goddess, no less, Cameo thought to herself. She prayed to her Saints that this woman was not Mistress Sauvage. But Cameo knew that she was. Barbs of envy and jealousy stabbed her. She is like a graceful statue come to

403

life. Cameo straightened to make herself taller than the other woman.

But Cathelen, though she was a head shorter and by far the daintier, obviously possessed great strength of character and fortitude, both of which Cameo sorely lacked. But Cameo lived by sex, nothing more. Cathelen, now older and more mature than when she had come to Barbados, read this in the other at once.

"Would you care for a glass of lemon-lime?"

Cathelen's dress, as crisp as a flower petal, rustled when she brushed past the molten-eyed woman. As she poured, Cathelen glanced over her shoulder—and just in time. All she saw was the flash of something flying toward her back.

As the raging Cameo came at her, Cathelen whirled away from the dagger that would have sliced her back and pierced her heart.

Cameo swore in Spanish at her bad luck; then she spoke to the dainty blond in her own language. All the while she was backing Cathelen toward the door. They had come full circle in this insane dance of death.

"You are the wife of the man I love, the man *I* want! But you must die first. Then Jonathan will want me. He desired me once long ago," she hissed at the pale face before her.

Cathelen stared down at the glittering blade, keeping her gaze ever trained on the weapon. "Your man died long ago, Cameo. On that ship it was indeed Jonathan Sauvage who was—accidentally murdered." Cathelen realized now it had been nothing more than that. If only Adam,

404

too, realized that Michal did not stab Jonathan in the back.

"So," Cameo tossed her black mane, "why is it you are married to the man then?" She spat. "Can you tell me that?"

"Have you seen Jonathan, alive, lately, Miss Salvador?" Cathelen slyly asked.

"I have. It was two weeks ago. Before he, with his ship, overtook the *Sea Gypsy* on which I was living."

Hope sprang in Cathelen's breast. "Y-you mean you have not been living with Jonathan? He has not been *with* you these past months?"

Suspicious now, Cameo said, "He is a hard man to find. Wolf does not let me find him; he finds me when he wants me," she lied.

"How long has that been, Miss Salvador?" Cathelen inched closer to the door, switching her gaze often to the gleaming blade.

"Uh? Oh—it has been a long time. You see, we had a fight on that ship we were on together. I do not know how many years ago. I—the ship's doctor killed him. But you see, Wolf did not die. It is true he was thrown over the side. Still, he did not drown as we thought. I"—she choked—"I did try to find him!" Her eyes glazed over with bitter regret. "He does not believe me." She tossed her head then, realizing she had been rambling to the lovely woman standing warily across from her. "He was going to bring me here—as his mistress. I did not want to be Jonathan's whore. I wanted to be his wife," she hissed her *s*'s while staring into the face that was

405

not so pale any longer. "Why do you look so happy? You should be sad your husband wanted to bring a mistress here!"

A smile spread over Cathelen's glorious face. "We were not married then, Cameo." She made free use of the other woman's first name. "You see, I am not married to *Jonathan* Sauvage. Adam—" She caught herself just as she was about to say Adam was her husband. But he was not! Still, Cameo did not know this.

"Ah! This is good," Cameo said. "You are his mistress, no?"

"Ah—yes. Yes, he is not *really* my husband." *Wasn't that the truth?*

"I will go now." Cameo whirled, at the same time dropping her dagger into her reticule, and headed for the door.

"Wait a minute." Cathelen came around the chair she had been using as a shield, just in case the passionate woman attacked all over again. "You tried to kill me."

"No," Cameo lied. "I only try to scare you."

"But why?" Cathelen looked the woman up and down in incredulous wonder.

Leaning forward from the waist, Cameo hissed, "Because you are his whore and I hate you!"

Her mouth slack, Cathelen watched the fiery-tempered woman leave the house. Then alone in the hall, she clapped her hands over her mouth and chin and executed a happy little leap off the floor before she raced upstairs to gather Adam John in her arms for a great big bear hug,

406

never mind if he was sleeping or not.

Mattissa emerged from the shadows where she had been concealing her person. She watched the mistress run upstairs and then she turned her attention back to the door the Spanish slut had left open. As Mattissa went back to the kitchen a fold of her black skirt opened as she walked, revealing the long kitchen knife she had been hiding there.

Chapter Forty=Five

Cathelen stood at the foot of the veranda and rewarded herself with a breath of the cool night air. Adam John was sleeping soundly, so she had some time for herself before turning in.

She looked at her surroundings, the plantation she had come to love. An imponderable wave of emotion swept over her.

Cathelen had been taking a walk and had found herself among the white-framed structures behind the main house. Chiah had been busily following Adam's plans for the new buildings. She had strolled there most of the morning: the slave huts, the slave hospital where Doc Michal had been so busy that all she received was a curt nod; and the overseer's quarters, the sugar works, the thrash house—all these stood at a discreet, though convenient, distance from the great house. The shell had been blown as a signal to stop work, and the excited chatter of the slaves going to rest had followed. Cathelen had returned their greetings while returning to the house.

It was then that she had seen Adam. A strange quiet had hovered in the air as their eyes met. But when she had begun to walk over to greet him after his long absence, wondering whether he was here to stay or not, he had pivoted on his heel and walked busily over to speak with the carpenter.

Cathelen, her eyes smarting, picked up her pink and white skirts and walked slowly to the house, her back only slightly hunched in dejection. Then she drew herself up and reclaimed her earlier carefree stride—the one she had left the house with earlier in the day.

Adam watched her go. He had seen the streak of anxious worry that crossed her delicate features. He jammed his hands into his pockets and made his way to the slave hospital.

Upon entering it, he found Raven and Michal in a most compromising position—a rather amorous embrace to be exact—and he was momentarily taken aback.

"Oh," Raven gasped, breaking away from Michal. She flushed scarlet, for the conspicuous arousal she had noticed Adam had also seen. Michal only jammed his hands into his blousy shirt pockets when he caught Adam Sauvage looking him over and releasing a chuckle that resembled a snort.

"All right, you two, aren't you afraid Cathelen will catch you in that clinch and become jealous? I mean you, Michal. Sorry Raven."

"What?" Raven gaped at this incredulous question.

Michal heaved a deep sigh, then turned to Raven and said, "I think 'tis about time we tell him. Do you agree, love?"

"Indeed I do!"

Removing her camisole, Cathelen walked over to the window and allowed the slightly cooler night air to bathe her pendulous, swollen breasts. She glanced downward, proud of their new weight and praying when Adam John weaned she would retain some of the melonlike fullness.

Looking up at the huge orange moon, she sighed a bit forlornly. Mattissa had informed her that Adam had visited her son while she was out for her walk. Cathelen had flooded the silent housekeeper with questions, but Mattissa would not say whether Adam liked his son or not.

"He said the baby has dark eyes," Mattissa began, "and he said, 'So do I.'"

"That is all, Mattissa?"

"Nothing more." With that Mattissa had gone about her tasks.

"Adam," Cathelen breathed the name like a caress, splaying her hands on her chest above her rising curves, making her fingertips meet in her cleavage. She was standing before her floor-length oval mirror, dreamy and lost.

A slight scraping behind her made Cathelen jump and ask who was there. Briskly she fumbled for her robe and tossed it on. No answer came to ease her jitters.

Again the sound. This time from the baby's room. Her heart pounded with relief and joy. Adam had come for a second look at his son, and then she thought happily, anything could happen afterward. She was certain that her husband had seen himself in Adam John's brown eyes; their color was exactly the same right down to the gold flecks leaping from their depths.

"Adam?"

Cathelen entered the nursery, slowly walking around the door to become bathed in moonbeams filtering through the small gap in the parted curtains. Something glinted near Adam John's crib, an ominous thing that galvanized Cathelen into action.

"No!" she screamed, reaching out for the dagger that gleamed in the frail light.

She caught hold of the feminine flesh, soft and reeking of perfume and liquor. Too frightened for her baby's life, Cathelen could not even scream loudly enough to summon others to her aid. This was a bad nightmare, one in which she found herself almost paralyzed by fear.

Dear God, if only she were dreaming—nothing more. But the blade began to change its course and come around the crib toward her. All

411

Cathelen could make out was a shadowy form, a silhouette that came at her. It was inhuman, an apparition with wildly streaming hair and a black silk cape that rustled and billowed as if a great wind were lifting it.

She had to get to Adam John. That was her only thought. But what could she use to ward off this stranger—this *murderer*? Who would want to kill her baby? Surely not Mattissa? If this were so, then why had Mattissa waited so long, and why would she do it now when Adam had returned? What exactly was this demented person after? she wondered frantically, praying that her child would not be imperiled—only herself.

The blade came down, cleaving a section of the door, but Cathelen would not flee from the room. She had to save her baby . . . somehow.

"Damn you, stay away from me and my baby. Leave this house before you are found here," Cathelen warned her tormentor, speaking in a raspy whispering voice. She had never been so weary or out of breath, and her heart pounded as if it would leave her body. "What do you want? Money? Jewels? I have jewels, you can have them all. Just come out of this room and away from my baby!" she cried, her heart breaking. "Please, come out!"

As the witchlike apparition flew past her to comply, Cathelen splayed her quivering body against the wall, her eyes following the black form out the door as if she herself were becoming quite insane.

412

"Oh, thank God." Cathelen breathed shakily as she inched her way out the door, closing it firmly behind her. If only she could call for help, but that might only serve to bring the attacker back. Then too, who knew where the crazy one was hiding now?

She peered out from her niche, searching the shadows, but all Cathelen could make out were the familiar walls, and the few pieces of furniture decorating the halls. Now and then she heard a board creaking in the far reaches of the house.

Dear God, where had everyone gone? Why had no one heard what had happened in the nursery?

Cathelen slumped wearily against the wall, her jittery nerves leaping, her eyes darting here and there. Then she saw it, the billowing cape and the apparition slipping like a night bird into her room. Her hand went over her mouth. Would the crazy one discover that the door from her room led into the nursery? Oh God, that evil maniac was right by her babe again!

"No, no," Cathelen sobbed softly as she slipped into her own room to find the candle on the bedside table doused. Eerie shadows greeted her. "Are you there?" Cathelen whispered the question. She came into the room a few steps more. "Where are you?"

"Arrgghh!" The low growl came from behind Cathelen's armoire. It was followed by a body leaping grotesquely into the air.

Cathelen was suddenly pinned in the alcove

that led onto the balcony, the breath knocked from her heaving chest, her arm nicked by a downward slash of the dagger. Warm blood trickled down her arm and onto the floor, making Cathelen feel faint at the thought that the blood could have been Adam John's instead of hers. Moments passed and then Cathelen heard the voice hissing close to her ear.

"You have him; you have his *bébé*! You will die for this, I swear!"

Cameo Salvador!

"Out, get out of the room!"

"What? I do not understand," Cathelen said, trying to stem the flow of blood by clutching her arm with her hand.

Cameo prodded her with the tip of the dagger, and then Cathelen understood. She moved like one in a death march, out to the balcony where she had a good idea Cameo would end her life. But if that happened, who would be there to protect Adam John? She was not going to give up all that easily, not when her baby's life was at stake!

Cawww! Catty! Catty! Awwwkkk!

Whirling, her blade on the alert, Cameo hissed, "What was that? Did you hear it?" However, she kept the blade trained on Cathelen and on the open door leading to the balcony.

They stood near the white railing now, Cameo clutching Cathelen by one arm, holding the dagger on her with the other. The taller woman glared downward, into dewy eyes that were smiling, and rosy pink lips that were breaking out into a grateful grin.

"Why do you smile? What is that terrible screeching?" Cameo insisted that she be told where the noise came from.

"I—I really do not know," Cathelen lied, knowing that Sinbad, beloved Sinbad, was sounding the alarm. To save her!

Cameo glowered now. "That is a parrot. I am no pirate's woman if I do not know this!"

"You must be many a pirate's woman, Cameo Salvador." Cathelen could not help but taunt her now that she knew help was on its way.

"He is telling the others that you are in trouble." Cameo made a mistake, and placed a hand on her hip in a cocky fashion. "How does he know this?" she demanded imperiously.

"He is—very wise."

"And very *ruidoso*!" Cameo hissed, then cried out as Cathelen's white leg emerged from the slit in the robe and flew up at the unguarded weapon.

For a moment Cameo's grip loosened on the blade, but not long enough. While Cathelen moved swiftly to keep herself out of harm's way, Cameo whirled the downward slashing blade in sweeping circles. But she could not keep up with the smaller, daintier woman, just as before when they struggled in the nursery.

But Cathelen, too, made a mistake. She headed for the nursery door. Cameo was there before her, holding her blade high while one hand rested on the knob. "I am quick, too, you see. I have fought with pirates, lived with them, ate with them. I am *pirata*," she finally said.

"A pirate's whore!" Cathelen spat into the face that turned into a gaping grimace. "No less!"

"How dare? . . ." Cameo spun about as the door to the hall flew open and a very white-skinned woman stepped in. "What is this?" Cameo stared at the long machete the glittering-eyed woman held very expertly, as if she were quite used to using it for cutting the cane.

"I know you. You are bad, woman. You have been here before." The dangerously soft voice came from the door. "Now you must go, or you will die!"

"Mattissa!" Cathelen cried. "No. She will kill *you*! She is insane."

"She will not harm you, or the babe, mistress," Mattissa vowed solemnly.

The two hot-blooded women rounded on each other, blades glittering, each life-threatening when one knew how to use it. It was clear to Cathelen that both women were experienced in fighting with a blade. Now Cathelen knew where Mattissa had received the tiny scars that marked her arms here and there. Mattissa must have grown up where such brawling was common—among the slaves. She also realized that Mattissa was fending for her life and Adam John's.

Muffled sobs flowed from her parted lips as Cathelen tore from the room to get help. Before she could reach the stairs, however, she raced back to the nursery to grab a startled Adam John from his sleeping place and carry him to the relative safety of Mairi's room.

"Och! What is going on?" Mairi shouted, surprised into growing a few more white hairs as the bundle was thrust into her arms.

"Guard him with your life, Mairi." She ran for the door. "There is a crazy woman in the house!"

Mairi cried out in a loud-pitched screech, just once, as if she'd been surprised by a sharp nettle in the rear, then she leaped from her sagging bed with the whimpering babe wrapped securely in her bony and veiny arms.

"We'll be hiding ye, *bairn*," she crooned, taking the babe outdoors with her, never realizing the havoc she would unintentionally create.

Looking this way and that as she paused on the front veranda, Cathelen tried to decide in what direction she should go. "Oh, dear God, where have they all gone?" she cried out in dismay. Then she headed for the overseer's new cabin just completed that day.

Ribald singing that would burn a lady's ears reached Cathelen first. They were all drunk! But their bawdy tunes did not bother Cathelen at all this night; she had a single-minded task to perform.

Adam saw her first when the door burst open and thudded against the cabin wall. He grinned stupidly, introducing her, "My wife, gen'l'men. And guess what," he snorted, going round to relate the latest, "we're goin' to get us-selves married again." He burped loudly. "Pardon me, madame." He leered at her. "Where's my gorgeous son?"

"His life is being threatened at this very minute!"

It was not the pitch of her voice that was alarming but the wild look on her white face. Adam took this in and sduddenly turned stone cold sober. "What the hell do you mean, woman?" He stood, steadying himself quite well considering. He bent to peer down at her then. "Is this some woman's trick, to get me into your bed?"

"Stop it, Adam! Your son is in trouble!" She wrung her hands together and sobbed, "Mattissa is trying to fight her off! They are crazy, both of them! Hurry!"

"Who—" Adam swallowed and paled. "Who is this other woman?"

"Cameo Salvador."

Michal rose from his chair and tipped it over. "'Tis her!" he cried. *She is the murderer!*

Adam turned, glowering. "Jonathan's murderer? Is this what you're saying, lad?"

The three of them took off out the door then, with Cathelen following as close as she could. She huffed and puffed trying to keep up with their long strides. Words of explanation tumbled like hot lava from Michal's lips. He was talking so fast that Cathelen only caught snatches of his words.

"Aha!" Michal was exclaiming. "She wanted Jonathan and could not have him. Even when his sloop had been taken by pirates, she still wanted your brother, he who had saved her from the first attack on the Spanish galleon. She had been traveling to meet her future husband in Jamaica. But Jonathan had caught her eye, I know it. He was a very wealthy plantation lord, Cameo knew. I remember her saying that she would not go to a man who could turn out to be a fat pig when Sauvage had rescued her and they could be married at once." Michal panted from trying to keep a furious pace and talk at the same time.

"She said Jonathan had been the first man to have her. 'Tis what made him her first love, she said, for her maidenhood was his, and she was bound to him forever. She was outraged when he offered her a 'position' at his plantation, not as his wife but his mistress.

"But Cameo was too proud to become Jonathan's whore. When the second attack at sea came, she spat in Jonathan's face and said she would show him how really desirable she was to other men. When the pirates had pressed on them in a circle, Cameo leaned over to Jonathan and whispered that she could 'handle' them if he would only take her home, but as his wife not his slut."

Adam grabbed Michal's arm as they began to trot. "How do you know all this? Did you hear her?" he ground out.

"Yes, it was all coming back to me as we sat in that cabin. Incredible as it may sound, but I was about to rise from my chair and have a word with you when Cathelen burst in the door."

"I see. Tell me more if you can," Adam called back over his shoulder to Michal, who was shouting to make himself heard as they pounded up the lane to the dark house.

"Someone must have doused all the lights!"

"Cameo!" Michal yelled.

As they ran to the house Michal breathlessly related the rest of the tale. Jonathan had rebuffed Cameo though the woman implored him. Jonathan had not wanted a wife. He was not afraid of the pirates, so she could not strike a deal with him—his life in return for her becoming mistress of Sauvage.

Pirates would not kill a fellow pirate, Jonathan had thought although he had "disguised" himself as a dandy. The Wolf often dressed himself that way. He had intended to claim he was the Wolf. But Jonathan had made a deadly mistake. Though the Sea Wolf was known and respected, he was at the same time widely envied and hated for his prowess on the sea as a buccaneer. It seemed that all the women in the West Indies were in love with the lean marauder.

"So Cameo Salvador believes we are one and the same."

"Ah, 'twould seem that way, sir," Michal tossed over his shoulder, having gone ahead onto the veranda.

Adam halted suddenly. "Where is Cathelen?" He turned to see if she was coming, but there was no sign of her. At the door he said, "I'll go up first. Damn, it might be too late!" he cried as the sound of a strangled gurgle floated down.

420

He was just entering the door when a body fell from above and thudded on the ground below them. It was a woman, sprawled like a broken puppet, her neck twisted and a red stain growing on her chest.

"Mon Dieu," Adam said.

What Adam and Michal did not know was that Cathelen had gone to Mairi's room to fetch her son, but she would never reach Mairi's room at all.

Chapter Forty-Six

"Mattissa, it is her, not the other!"

"That means the demented witch is yet in the house," Adam rapped out. He turned from the broken body to scan the area for a sign of Cathelen. "She might have tripped in trying to keep up. Go check it out, Michal! I'll take care of the other!"

Their eyes locked, and brotherly love tinged with commiseration shone in them. They would be friends bound by unspoken promises forever.

"Michal," Adam called out as the other hurried away. "I always knew there was a man inside you just hollering to get out."

Michal said nothing as he continued to search for his sister. He ran the half distance to the cabins, then realized she must have taken another route to the house. Dear God, she could be in grave danger by now. . . .

Cathelen, meanwhile, was searching high and low for Adam John, not even thinking that the crazy one could be lying in wait for her.

"Mairi? Oh, where did you go?" Cathelen held a flickering candle as she walked the halls in search of the old woman and her babe.

She had heard nothing to indicate that the women were still at it when she had entered the back door and slipped quickly into Mairi's bedroom, only to discover that the room was empty. Coming down the back stairs, Cathelen decided Mairi must have gone outside. Where else could she be if not there?

Cathelen whirled at the creak of a floorboard. "Who is there?" She held the shaking candle before her, tipping it to light another and then another in the long corridor. Then she saw a door swing open. The root cellar—they must have gone there.

It was dark as Cathelen slipped down between the close walls—down the many steps. Below her was a void, pitch-black. A pit straight out of hell. The hair on her arms rose, as did the hackles on her neck.

She could have sworn the hair on her head was standing on end, too, for the sight that rose in front of her petrified her blood and enervated her body.

"Oh dear God . . . no . . ." Cathelen swayed against the last bit of wall that would protect her from the hideous apparition before her.

It was Cameo Salvador, was it not? At least what appeared to be the remains of her once-voluptuous countenance. Her face had been hacked beyond recognition; her lackluster hair was streaked and matted with blood. There were several stab wounds in her chest and her arms were sliced into ribbons of hanging flesh. Cameo sagged against the vegetable baskets, still clutching her bloodied blade in her nerveless fingers.

My God, Mattissa did this to the woman? All because she had been trying to save Adam John and herself. The woman had no argument with Mattissa. The housekeeper would have remained safe—if only she had stayed out of the way. But Cathelen had no idea what shape Mattissa was in.

"The machete is not only for cutting the sugar cane, eh?" Cameo said weakly, while bitter tears streaked down her cheeks to mingle with the blood at the corners of her sagging mouth.

"Cameo, I must tell you something." Cathelen came only an inch closer, in order to be heard. "You see, I tried to tell you before. Jonathan is not my husband." The woman looked up and moaned, a terrible sound. Cathelen went on. "Adam Sauvage and Jonathan are two separate people. It was Jonathan—"

"That I killed," Cameo confessed. "Ah, yes.

You look at me surprised, no?" She cackled insanely, then coughed to spit out blood. "I killed him—because the *bastardo* did not love me! He wanted me to be his whore . . . and I, Cameo Salvador do not want to be that. But I have become that now. It does not matter, you see, for Jonathan is gone . . ."

"Yes, it is true, Cameo." Cathelen shivered. "But one thing does matter. You need help— and I would like to know where my son is. We can do both. You tell me where he is and I will get you a doctor."

A scream of pure madness rent the musty air as Cameo flew at her nemesis. But the sight was pitiful, for Cameo could only stab futilely at the stone in front of her. Just then she looked up, to see a tall form descend the stairs.

"Cathelen! Are you all right?" Adam asked, his eyes sweeping her from head to foot. She nodded, her head now against his chest. Adam grimaced at the hideous sight that greeted him at the bottom of the stairs.

"Oh Adam, take the dagger from her—right away!" Cathelen reached up to grip his wide shoulders and try to make him understand.

He moved down one step and reached toward the bloody hand still clutching the blade. "Cameo, give me the dagger," he coaxed softly, his voice deep and soothing. "You won't be needing that any longer." He stepped closer.

Another mad scream rent the air and Cameo flew at Adam with renewed strength and vigor. Her blade flashed and came down into Adam's chest, but it pierced only a half inch before he thrust her arm into the air. She stared in horrible fascination at the spreading bloodstain on his white shirt and reached out a hand that dripped her own blood to try to mingle it with his own. One last try to be one with this man whom she thought was Jonathan—even more so in her dazed state.

"I am Adam Sauvage," he told her just before Cameo's eyes closed and she nodded, saying something in her native language.

She died in his strong arms, his handsome face swimming in her vision like an angel come to claim her, for the pits of hell, or heights of heaven, Cameo would never know. She only knew on her last dying breath that the man she loved was holding her close.

"She loves you," Cathelen breathed, her eyes sad over the pathetic sight. "How awful . . ." Cathelen shook her head and closed her eyes, tears squeezing through them.

Adam, with his free hand, shook her, murmuring gently, "She loves *Jonathan*." His eyes freely worshiped this small woman beside him who now had shared life and death with him. "Only next time I'll be there when our child is born."

Cathelen looked up. "What?"

Adam gently closed Cameo's eyes that saw no more and he lowered her bloody body to the cold earth. He shook his head, as Cathelen had moments before.

"Cathelen O'Ruark, will you marry me?" He

reached out to tenderly squeeze her cold hand. "I love you."

She gave the body one more glance before she said, "Oh Adam, let us please get out of here. This is no place for a proposal of marriage!"

Mairi and Adam John were found outside, fast asleep in the kitchen garden, between the beans and the okra. Cathelen slumped in Adam's arms, so relieved was she to find her babe and her dear friend alive and well. They turned away as, in the dawn's frail light, the bodies of Mattissa and Cameo were taken away for burial in the slaves graveyard.

"Mattissa will want to be there anyway, among her friends."

Cathelen sobbed softly against Adam's wide chest, finding comfort in his manly strength. "Oh, Adam, she saved my life—and Adam's. She truly did love us, and I always thought—"

"It does not matter now, my sweet. What matters is us, the living."

"Mairi . . ." Cathelen called to the bone-weary woman who was taking the child back to his crib in the great plantation house.

"Not now, love. Let them go," Adam begged in a gentlemanly fashion. "I need a few more minutes to find out if you will have me for your husband. Ah—Adam John sorely needs a father."

Dewy-eyed, Cathelen peered up at Adam. "We were always married, Adam, to me we were. We said the words and I took your name.

Sauvage. Only the first name was different."

"But, love, you must marry me again, to take my whole name." He gazed down from his towering height. "I love you so much I want to make everything right between us. I want to have a hundred children."

"You shall have to get another wife then so that each of us may raise fifty."

"Never!" he shouted to the sky as the sun's rays burst across it. He laughed ironically at that word.

"Good," Cathelen laughed, hugging him around the waist, her cheek pressed against his shirt. "I agree," she said, knowing her dream had at last come true.

RAPTUROUS ROMANCE BY CONSTANCE O'BANYON

SAVAGE AUTUMN (1457, $3.50)

The white woman Joanna gave a cry of terror when the tall young leader of the Blackfoot tribe carried her away from all she held dear. But when he took her in his arms in his tepee, her soft moans were as rapturous and her kisses as urgent as his own. He knew the heights of passion awaited them in the . . . SAVAGE AUTUMN.

ENCHANTED ECSTASY (1386, $3.75)

Fearless and independent, the Indian princess Maleaha was the most sought-after woman in the New Mexico territory. No man had ever claimed her supple body, but Major Benedict knew she couldn't refuse him, and then he couldn't let her go!

SAVAGE SPLENDOR (1292, $3.50)

Married to the mighty King of the Lagonda tribe, beautiful Mara was respected and admired, but was she truly happy? By day she quesioned whether to remain in her husband's world or with her people. But by night, crushed in the muscular arms of the King, taken to the peaks of rapture, she knew she could never live without him, never let him go . . .

ECSTASY'S PROMISE (978, $3.50)

At seventeen, beautiful Victoria burned the family plantation to keep Sherman's Yankee troops from having it. Fleeing to Texas, meeting handsome, wealthy ranch owner, Edward Hanover, Victoria's passion burst into a raging blaze as his fingers brushed her silky skin. But Hanover had fought for the Union—was an enemy—and the only man she would ever love!

Available wherever paperbacks are sold, or order direct from the Publisher. Send cover price plus 50¢ per copy for mailing and handling to Zebra Books, 475 Park Avenue South, New York, N.Y. 10016. DO NOT SEND CASH.